THE COMPLETE WORKS OF
MICHAEL DRAYTON

VOLUME I

POLYOLBION

Elibron Classics
www.elibron.com

Elibron Classics series.

© 2005 Adamant Media Corporation.

ISBN 1-4021-6561-7 (paperback)
ISBN 1-4021-2783-9 (hardcover)

This Elibron Classics Replica Edition is an unabridged facsimile
of the edition published in 1876 by John Russell Smith,
London.

EFFIGIES MICHAELIS DRAYTON ARMIGERI, POETÆ CLARISS. ÆTAT. SVÆ L. A. CHR cIↄ.DC.XIII

Lux Hareshulla tibi (Warwici villa, tenebris,
Ante tuas Cunas, obsita) Prima fuit.
Arma, Viros, Veneres, Patriam modulamine dixti;
Te Patriæ resonant Arma, Viri, Veneres.

THE COMPLETE WORKS OF

MICHAEL DRAYTON,

NOW FIRST COLLECTED.

WITH INTRODUCTIONS AND NOTES BY

THE REV. RICHARD HOOPER, M.A.

VICAR OF UPTON AND ASTON UPTHORPE, BERKS,

AND EDITOR OF CHAPMAN'S HOMER, SANDYS' POETICAL WORKS, ETC.

VOLUME I.—POLYOLBION.

LONDON:

JOHN RUSSELL SMITH,

SOHO SQUARE.

1876.

To

HIS ROYAL HIGHNESS,

ALBERT EDWARD,

PRINCE OF WALES, K.G.

SIR,

By your gracious permission, I dedicate to you the present edition of the Complete Works of MICHAEL DRAYTON, now first collected.

DRAYTON was not only a great Poet, but great in many styles of Poetry; and one work of his may be pronounced unique. His POLY-OLBION is a wonderful description of that *Happy Island*, over which (at some distant day, we trust) you will, in the course of Divine Providence, be called upon to exercise your sway.

The Author felt the greatness of his subject, and esteeming it, as it justly is, a work worthy to be laid at the feet of a Prince, dedicated it to two of your illustrious predecessors in your noblest title, the PRINCES HENRY and CHARLES of WALES.

The Poet, however, little thought that the day would arrive when another PRINCE of WALES, in the person of YOUR ROYAL HIGHNESS, would graciously accept his work; nor could he have dreamed that the realms which you may be called upon to rule far exceed the wildest visions of poet's brain.

SIR, when you have visited that glorious empire to which you are now setting forth, may you return to the home of your birth to find that amid all the vast possessions of the BRITISH CROWN there is no spot where you are more loyally loved and revered than the HAPPY ISLAND which MICHAEL DRAYTON has so faithfully depicted.

Your Royal Highness's

Most faithful and devoted servant,

RICHARD HOOPER.

UPTON, BERKS,
September, 1875.

ADVERTISEMENT.

THE Editor feels that an apology is due, not only to the public, but to the publisher and printer, for the delay in the production of this work. He trusts, however, that the present three volumes will prove with what care and accuracy the Edition is being prepared.

UPTON, BERKS,
September, 1875.

INTRODUCTION.

GOLDSMITH, in his "Citizen of the World," makes the Chinese Philosopher visit Westminster Abbey. "As we walked along to a particular part of the temple, 'there,' says the gentleman (his guide) pointing with his finger, 'that is the Poets' Corner; there you see the monuments of Shakespeare, and Milton, and Prior, and DRAYTON.' 'DRAYTON,' I replied, 'I never heard of him before, but I have been told of one Pope, is he there?'"

. A recent eminent writer † has inferred from this that the fame of Drayton had sunk so low that he was comparatively unknown, or at least that he was unknown to Goldsmith. But Goldsmith, though a charming writer, was very ignorant of our older literature. In fact, in Goldsmith's time, the star of Pope was in the ascendant, and that alone was considered poetry which had the ring and epigrammatic smoothness of the school of the writers of the Augustan age, as the days of Queen Anne have been styled. The elder Disraeli has observed ‡

* Citizen of the World, vol. i. p. 44, ed. 1762 (the 1st).
† Dean Stanley.   ‡ Amenities of Literature.

that " Dr. Johnson and the critics of his day were wholly unacquainted with the Fathers of our poetry;" and no better proof can be given of Johnson's vitiated taste than that he preferred the miserable (and now deservedly neglected) translation of Tasso by Hoole ("a gentleman long-known and long-esteemed in the India House," as he calls him) to that by Edward Fairfax, which is confessedly one of the finest versions in the English language. Nor was the ignorance of Drayton's merits confined to Goldsmith and his contemporaries.

The writer of the article 'Drayton' in Aikin's General Biography (which Mr. Gifford styles " a worthless compilation") mentions that the poet's works were reprinted in folio and 4 vols. 8vo. in 1748—53, and expresses his opinion that they were not worth republication. That edition, it is true, fell still-born from the press, but probably from its incompleteness and inaccuracy. Yet Mr. Disraeli, no mean authority, says " Drayton is worthy of a complete edition of his works."* His merit, too, is now generally acknowledged, and he takes a conspicuous stand amongst that "race of giants" who clustered round the towering figure of Shakespeare. It is probable that much of the neglect of his works may be attributed to their great extent, and that had he written less he would have been better known; and again, as many of his poems are historical, they are likely to be of less interest to the general reader. It

* Amenities of Literature.

cannot be denied also that his diction is somewhat in-
volved, and his works require attention and study. But
the same may be said of many of his contemporaries.
Some of his lighter efforts are exquisite, and he has
written in so many styles that the possessor of his works
has a continual source of enjoyment. "The merits of
Drayton as a poet are very great. His historical poems
have about them a heavy magnificence, the most gor-
geous images and the boldest descriptions follow in
stately array, clothed in well-turned and appropriate
verse, but unfortunately the obscurity of diction renders
them unattractive. * * * * Drayton has left one
work which, in its way, has never been surpassed—a
short fairy poem called, 'Nymphidia.' A more elfin
work than this could not be penned : the author
has contrived to throw himself into the feelings of
the diminutive beings whom he represents. His description of helmets made of beetles, ear-wigs being
used as chargers, and other oddities of a like nature, display the very highest powers of fancy : a Lilliputian air
breathes through the whole performance. Had Drayton
written nothing but 'Nymphidia,' he would deserve immortality." *

It may be thought that I savour too much of the advocate in pleading the cause of the author whose
works I am anxious to re-introduce to the reader, if I
express my opinion that Drayton is undoubtedly one of

* English Cyclopædia, Art. "Drayton."

the greatest poets of the Elizabethan or any period, but I shall fortify my opinion by that of two writers whose knowledge of early English literature is entitled to our highest respect.

Mr. Payne Collier, in a very beautiful edition of some of Drayton's earlier poems, printed for the Roxburghe Club in 1856, puts Shakespeare entirely out of the question, in considering the rank that the poets of Elizabethan times are entitled to hold with reference to each other. The same pre-eminence, he thinks, is due to Spenser, though on different grounds; and Ben Jonson's claims to admiration for strength of thought, vigour of expression, and learning, can hardly be disputed. With these exceptions, Mr. Collier enquires what place Michael Drayton occupies among the secondary poets when he lived. "At the head of these," he says, "he has unquestionably the right to stand. He is inferior to Daniel in smoothness of versification, and, perhaps, in grace of expression, but he much exceeds him in originality of conception, and in force and variety of style. Drayton has written ill in no species of poetical composition, and he has written well in most. He tried many, and he excelled, more or less, in all he tried."

I think this a fair estimate of our poet's merits, though I am inclined to question his inferiority, as a *poet*, to Ben Jonson.

The late Rev. Joseph Hunter, whose inestimable MS. Collections on our Poets are now in the British Museum

(Addit. MSS. 24,493), says:—"I see not why Drayton should not now be placed, as he was by his contemporaries, in the *first* class of English Poets : not *primus inter pares,* but he who produced such beautiful Lyric and Pastoral and Heroic poems, ought not to be placed only in the *second* rank. One proof of his claim to this high distinction is, that while so many of his contemporaries are forgotten, and their works known only to the few antiquaries who cultivate this field of literature, the name of Drayton is still, like Shakespeare and Milton, a household word ; his memory is kept alive by the popular voice, and few are they who have not been more or less delighted with his verse." I am afraid that the last sentence is a little overstrained. The "popular voice" is unfortunately, in many cases, *vox et præterea nihil.* People are unwilling to betray their ignorance, and therefore use Drayton's name, as many do Spenser's and Milton's, without much familiarity with his works. They are not, perhaps, quite so ignorant as Goldsmith's Chinese philosopher, as to say, "Drayton! I never heard of him before," but I really believe that the grand domain of Michael Drayton is a *terra incognita* to multitudes who have heard his name.

But there are many reasons for this. Drayton's works in their original editions are scarce and expensive, and the only pretended complete edition (that of the middle of the last century), besides its inaccuracy and uninviting form, is now only to be purchased at a great price. They are to be found, it is true, in the large collections of Chalmers and others, but such voluminous works are not in every one's library. Nor is the text in these collections to be trusted. No poet ever altered his works so frequently as Drayton. Each succeeding edition (with but few exceptions) differed materially from its precursor. Nor were his second thoughts always the wisest. A thorough edition of Michael Drayton's works, then, requires much painstaking collation, and indication of the poet's change of mind. And such, if I am spared, will be the form in which the present Complete Edition will appear. Of each of the works, however, which comprise the present volumes, there was published in the author's lifetime but one edition, so there were no variations to be noted. It was thought expedient to print the "Polyolbion" first, as the greatest, and best-known, of Drayton's works, and the "Harmony of the Church" has been added as the *first* production of his pen, at least as far as is known. Of this latter little work the history is curious. According to Mr. Payne Collier (Roxburghe Club, 1856), on February 1st, 1591, the printer, Richard Jones, entered it at Stationers' Hall :—

"Primo Februarii [1590-1]

Richard Jones. Entred for his Copie &c The Triumphes of the Churche, conteyning the spirituall songes and holie himnes of godlie men, Patriarkes and Prophettes - - - vj^d."

It is more than probable, says Mr. Collier, that at this date the work had passed through the press, but perhaps the title-page had not been worked off, or finally agreed on, for when it came out it was called "The Harmonie, &c." In the books of the same Company there is another memorandum of still more importance, dated in the same year, which proves that, for some reason or other not assigned, all the copies of the book had been seized by public order; that Bishop, the stationer, had bought them, with other works in the same predicament; but that the Archbishop of Canterbury had issued his warrant for forty copies to be delivered to him, and that they remained at Lambeth under the care of Dr. Cosen. The note in the original register runs thus :—

[1591]

" Whereas all the seized Bookes mentioned in the last accompte before this, were sould this yere to Mr. Byshop, Be it remembered that fortye of them, being Harmonies of the Churche, rated at ij*s* le peece, were had from him by warrante of my lordes grace of Canterburie, and remayne at Lambithe with Mr. Doctor Cosen : and for some other of the said bookes, the said Mr. Bishop hath paid iiij*li* as appeareth in the charge of this accompte, and the residue remayne in the Hall to th' use of Yarrette James."

" The books seized," adds Mr. Collier, " during the year were sold, doubtless, to Bishop on the undertaking that he should destroy them; but as what is above called "the last accompte before this" is not extant, it is impossible to ascertain the character of the books seized with Drayton's. It will be seen that the Archbishop had forty copies—the rest probably were destroyed by Bishop and Yarrette James."

Why it was destroyed does not appear, and what became of the Archbishop's copies, is equally unknown, with the exception of *one*, which is in George III.'s Library in the British Museum, and had belonged to Archbishop Whitgift. From that unique copy Mr. Dyce printed his edition for the Percy Society, and Mr. Collier his for the Roxburghe Club. Drayton never reprinted it himself, either from the somewhat unintelligible suppression just noticed, or that he did not deem it worthy of the later efforts of his muse. Nor is there—which is remarkable—any allusion in his subsequent works to this strangling in the birth, as it were, of his earliest production. He is ready enough to complain of ill-usage, especially in his advances to King James I., as may be seen in his Epistle to his friend George Sandys, the poet; but nowhere do we find any reference to the suppression of the "Harmony of the Church." As I shall discuss this question more at large in my biography of the poet, I may merely mention that the existence of the book was probably unknown till discovered by modern research, and its first re-publication is due to the exertions of my late dear friend, the Reverend Alexander Dyce. The veteran

Elizabethan scholar, Mr. Payne Collier, whose friendship I equally prize, followed in his steps, and the present text is a careful collation of their labours with the unique copy in the British Museum, the orthography only being modernized. It is the first time that the work has been published in a collected edition of Drayton's Poems.

On the "Poly-olbion" a volume might be written. "This extraordinary poem," says Mr. Disraeli,* "remains without a parallel in the poetical annals of any people; and it may excite our curiosity to learn its origin. The genealogy of poetry is often suspicious; but I think we may derive the birth of the 'Poly-olbion' from LELAND'S magnificent view of his designed work on 'Britain,' and that hint expanded by the 'Britannia' of CAMDEN, who inherited the mighty industry without the poetical spirit of LELAND: DRAYTON embraced both. The 'Poly-olbion,' which is a stupendous work, is a chorographical description of England and Wales; an amalgamation of antiquarianism, of topography, and of history; materials not the most ductile for the creations of poetry. This poem is said to have the accuracy of a road-book; and the poet has contributed some notices which add to the topographic stores of Camden; for this has our poet extorted an alms of commendation from such a niggardly antiquary as Bishop Nicholson, who confesses that this work affords 'a much truer account

* Amenities of Literature.

of this kingdom than could be well expected from the pen of a poet.'

"The grand theme of this poet was his fatherland! The muse of Drayton passes by every town and tower; each tells some tale of ancient glory, or of some 'worthy' who must never die. The local associations of legends and customs are animated by the personifications of mountains and rivers; and often, in some favourite scenery, he breaks forth with all the emotion of a true poet. The imaginative critic has described the excursions of our muse with responsive sympathy. 'He has not,' says Lamb, 'left a rivulet so narrow that it may be stepped over, without honourable mention, and has associated hills and streams with life and passion beyond the dreams of old mythology.'

"But the journey is long, and the conveyance may be tedious; the reader, accustomed to the decasyllable or heroic verse, soon finds himself breathless among the protracted and monotonous Alexandrines, unless he should relieve his ear from the incumbrance by resting on the cæsura, and thus divide those extended lines by the alternate grace of a ballad-stanza."*

Ellis, in his "Specimens of the Early English Poets" (vol. ii. p. 301, ed. 1801) says, "His Poly-olbion is certainly a wonderful work, exhibiting at once the learning of an historian, an antiquary, a naturalist, and a geo-

---

* From Drayton's punctuation, preserved in the present edition, it will be seen that this was his design.

grapher, and embellished by the imagination of a poet."

In the "Historical Essay," prefixed to the four-volume edition of Drayton's Works in 1753, which is generally supposed to have been superintended by the antiquary William Oldys, it is observed:—"It is not easy to conceive a harder task than that which our author imposed upon himself when he set about this undertaking; and yet it would be full as great a difficulty to imagine a thing of this kind brought to a higher degree of perfection. This will appear still more wonderful to the critical and learned reader, when he considers the time in which it was written, and how few helps the author had towards completing so vast a design, in comparison of what he might have had if he had lived in later times. The true way of judging of the merit of this book, is to compare it with Camden's celebrated work in prose, from whence it will appear how little Mr. Drayton borrowed from others, and what infinite variety of curious facts he inserted from our old manuscript History, and how judiciously they are applied. We need not, therefore, be surprised that not only writers next in point of time, such as Weaver and Fuller, borrow from him so largely, but the later antiquaries, such as Musgrave, Kennet, Wood, and Hearne, cite him as a most authentic author."

It would be impossible now to trace the sources of Drayton's vast information. That he was a mere copyist of printed books we can hardly suppose, as the illustrious Selden would scarcely have deigned to illustrate the first eighteen songs with his learned notes had the subject-matter appeared before. There is something specially nasty in Bishop Nicholson's sneer, "The first eighteen of these songs had the honour to be published with Mr. Selden's Notes, the other twelve being hardly capable of such a respect." Why Selden should not have continued his illustrations, one cannot say. Possibly the author was so dissatisfied with the slow sale of the First Part, that he did not ask his friend to contribute more of his learned time to a work which had been so singularly neglected; but the last twelve songs are fully equal in historical research and poetic beauty to their predecessors.

Drayton had hoped, and very justly, that the nobles and gentlemen of England would have (to quote Mr. Disraeli) "felt a filial interest in the tale of their fathers, commemorated in these poetic annals, and an honourable pride in their domains here so graphically pictured. But no voice, save those of a few melodious brothers, cheered the lonely lyrist, who had sung on every mountain, and whose verse had flowed with every river." That the work was greatly neglected, and that the author felt its neglect severely, may be seen by his Preface to the Second Part; but had Drayton lived some half century later, he would have seen that his lot was shared by one whose fame he might himself envy. But there were consolations for the neglected poet. In Professor Masson's late charming volume, "Drummond of Hawthornden," will be found a glowing description of the friendship of Drayton and his Scottish friend. In p. 80, amongst Drummond's "Characters of Several Authors," we find:—"Drayton's Poly-olbion is one of the smoothest pieces I have seen in English, poetical and well-prosecuted; there are some pieces in him I dare compare with the best Transmarine Poems. The 7th song pleaseth me much; the 12th is excellent; the 13th also (the discourse of hunting passeth with any poet); and the 18th, which is the last in this edition of 1614." Drummond's friendship with Drayton will fall more properly within the province of our biographical notice, but we may allude to one or two of his letters. "I long," says he, "to see the rest of your Poly-olbion come forth, which is the only epic poem England, in my judgment, hath to be proud of; to be the author of which I had rather have the praise than, as Aquinas said of one of the Fathers' commentaries, to have the seignory of Paris." It would appear that Drayton was seeking an Edinburgh publisher for his Second Part, and he complains of the ill-usage he had received at the hands of the London booksellers. "How would I be overjoyed," says Drummond, "to see our North once honoured with your Works as before it was with Sidney's.* Though it be barren of excellency

* The third edition of Sidney's *Arcadia* was published at Edinburgh in 1599.

in itself, it can both love and admire the excellency of others."

On the 14th of April, 1619, Drayton writes to Drummond :—" I thank you, my dear sweet Drummond, for your good opinion of *Poly-olbion*. I have done twelve books more ; that is, from the 18th Book (which was Kent, if you note it) all the East parts, and North to the River Tweed ; but it lieth by me, for the booksellers and I are in terms. They are a company of base knaves, whom I both scorn and kick at." However, he had at length succeeded in getting a London publisher, and the concluding Twelve Songs appeared in 1622, as the reader may see by the facsimile title to the Second Part in these volumes.

Little more need be said of this truly great work, or, as its author styles it, " Herculean toil." The title may puzzle some readers. The Greek words *poly-olbion* mean *very happy*, and the allusion is to *Albion*, which is supposed by some writers, (but erroneously) to be derived from *Olbion, happy*. Drayton, however, probably meant it as a punning allusion to Albion.

The indefatigable Mr. Hunter found a passage in Xenophon's Cyropædia (Lib. i. cap. v.) which he thinks might have suggested the idea to Drayton, but this is questionable, though Drayton was undoubtedly a man of learning. The passage is as follows :—"'Αλλὰ νομί- ζοντες καὶ οὗτοι τὰ πολεμικὰ ἀγαθὰ γενόμενοι, ΠΟΛΥΝ

MEN OΛBON, πολλὴν δὲ εὐδαιμονίαν, μεγάλας δὲ τι-
μὰς καὶ αὐτοῖς καὶ τῇ πόλει περιάψειν."

. The text of the present volumes is a most careful
collation of the original folio of two parts. The orthography has been modernized, but not in the case of
proper names, or in that of rare and antiquated words.
The original punctuation of Drayton has been adhered
to, at the suggestion of one of the most eminent scholars
of the day. Selden's laborious and learned notes have
been most carefully revised, and are now probably for
the first time presented to the reader in a correct form
They were most carelessly reprinted in Wilkins's Edition of Selden's works. To annotate Drayton's Poly-
olbion would be a work of immense labour, and would
swell the volumes into an unwieldy form, even if it
were possible (which may be well doubted) to do the
work at all satisfactorily. Such notes would embrace
every subject—history, topography, antiquities, and ob-
jects of natural history—which the author has written
upon—and many volumes would be required even fo
the notes alone. It has, therefore, been considered ex
pedient to present the reader with the work as Drayton
left it, *i.e.*, with Selden's notes only attached to it. The
obsolete words in Drayton are comparatively few, and
the Editor proposes, on the completion of the Edition,
to give a glossarial Index to the whole works.

The future volumes will each be complete in itself,
with a separate Introduction, and a thoroughly new

biography will accompany the last volume, and thus, if the Editor be spared, will be given for the first time a complete edition (as Disraeli said he deserved) of the entire Works of Michael Drayton, Esquire.

* Drayton was very proud of his title of Esquire. He was an Esquire to his friend Sir Walter Aston at the installation of the latter as a Knight of the Bath, on the Coronation of King James 1st, July 25th, 1603.

POLY-OLBION

GREAT BRITAINE

By
Michaell Drayton.
Esqr.

London printed for { M. Lownes. I. Browne. Cum priuil
{ I. Helme. I. Busbie. } by W. Hole

W.I. Alais, re fecit.

POLY-OLBION.

UPON THE FRONTISPIECE.

 HROUGH a *Triumphant Arch*, see *Albion* plac'd,
    In *Happy* site, in *Neptune's* arms embrac'd,
    In *Power* and *Plenty*, on her *Cleeuy* Throne
    Circled with *Nature's Garlands*, being alone
    Styl'd *th' Ocean's** Island.* On the Columns been
(As Trophies rais'd) what Princes Time hath seen
Ambitious of her. In her younger years,
Vast Earth-bred *Giants* woo'd her : but, who bears
In†goiden field the Lion passant red,
Æneas' Nephew (*Brute*) them conqueréd.
Next, Laureate *Cæsar*, as a Philtre, brings,
On's *shield*, his Grandame‡ *Venus :* Him her Kings
Withstood. At length, the *Roman*, by long suit,
Gain'd her (most part) from th' ancient race of *Brute.*
Divorc'd from Him, the *Saxon*§ *sable Horse*,
Borne by stern *Hengist*, wins her : but, through force
Guarding the ‖*Norman Leopards bath'd in gules,*
She chang'd her love to Him, whose line yet rules.

   * *Insula Cæruli.*
   † So *Havillan* and *Upton* anciently delivered. I justify it not ; yet, as well as others can his other attributed Arms, I might.
   ‡ Object not, that it should be the *Eagle*, because it is now borne by the Emperors ; and that some Heralds ignorantly publish it, as *J. Cæsar's* Coat, *double headed.* They move me not ; for plainly the *Eagle* was single at that time (unless you call it Οιωνῶν Βασιλῆα δίδυμον, as *Pindar* doth *Jove's* Eagle) and but newly used among the *Romans* (first by *Marius*) as their *Standard*, not otherwise, until afterwards *Constantine* made it respect the two Empires : and since, it hath been borne on a Shield. I took *Venus* proper to him, for that the stamp of her face (she being his ancestor *Æneas* his mother) in his coins is frequent ; and can so maintain it here fitter than many of those invented Coats (without colour of reason) attributed to the old Heroes. As for matter of Armory, *Venus* being a Goddess, may be as good Bearing, if not better than *Atalanta*, which, by express authority of *Euripides*, was borne in the *Theban* war by *Parthenopæus.*
   § *Hengist* hath other Arms in some traditions, which are to be respected as old wives fictions. His name expresses a *Horse*, and the Dukes of *Saxony* are said to have borne it anciently, before their Christianity, *Sable* : therefore, if you give him any, with most reason let him have this.
   ‖ The common Blazon of the *Norman* Arms justifies it. And, if you please, see for it to the XI. Canto.

A

CHOROGRAPHICALL

DESCRIPTION OF ALL

THE TRACTS, RIVERS,

MOVNTAINS, FORESTS,

and other Parts of this Renowned
Ifle of GREAT BRITAIN,

With intermixture of the moft Remarkeable
Stories, Antiquities, Wonders, Rarities, Pleafures,
and Commodities *of the fame.*

Diuided into two Bookes; the latter containing
twelue Songs, neuer before Imprinted.

Digefted into a Poem
By
MICHAEL DRAYTON, *Efquire.*

With a Table added, for direction to those Occurrences
of *Story* and *Antiquitie,* whereunto the Course of the
Volume easily leades not.

LONDON,
Printed for *Iohn Marriott, Iohn Grifmand,*
and *Thomas Dewe.* 1622.

TO THE HIGH AND MIGHTY

HENRY,

PRINCE OF WALES.

HIS First Part of my intended Poem I consecrate to your Highness: in whom (beside my particular zeal) there is a natural interest in my Work, as the hopeful Heir of the Kingdoms of this Great *Britain*, whose Delicacies, Chorographical Description, and History be my subject.

My soul, which hath seen the extremity of time and fortune, cannot yet despair. The influence of so glorious and fortunate a Star may also reflect upon me: which hath power to give me new life, or leave me to die more willingly and contented.

My Poem is genuine, and first in this kind. It cannot want envy; for, even in the birth, it already finds that. Your gracious acceptance, mighty Prince, will lessen it. May I breathe to arrive at the *Orcades* (whither in this kind I intend my course, if the Muse fail me not) I shall leave your whole British Empire, as in this First and Southern part, delineated.

To your Highness,

The most humbly devoted,

MICHAEL DRAYTON.

BRITAIN, *behold here portray'd to thy sight*
Henry, *thy best hope, and the world's delight;*
Ordain'd to make thy eight Great Henries *nine :*
Who, by that virtue of the treble Trine,
To his own goodness (in his being) brings
These several Glories* of th' eight English Kings:
[1]Deep knowledge, [2]Greatness, [3]Long life, [4]Policy,
[5]Courage, [6]Zeal, [7]Fortune, [8]Awful Majesty.
He like great Neptune *on three* †*Seas shall rove,*
And rule three Realms, with triple power, like Jove.
Thus in soft peace, thus in tempestuous wars,
Till from his foot his fame shall strike the stars.

* The several happinesses of the eight *Henries.*
† The West, North, and East Ocean.

TO THE GENERAL READER.

IN publishing this Essay of my Poem, there is this great disadvantage against me; that it cometh out at this time, when Verses are wholly deduced to chambers, and nothing esteemed in this lunatic Age but what is kept in cabinets, and must only pass by transcription. In such a season, when the idle humorous world must hear of nothing that either savours of antiquity, or may awake it to seek after more than dull and slothful ignorance may easily reach unto, these, I say, make much against me; and especially in a Poem, from any example, either of Ancient or Modern, that have proved in this kind, whose unusual tract may perhaps seem difficult to the female sex; yea, and, I fear, to some that think themselves not meanly learned, being not rightly inspired by the Muses: such I mean, as had rather read the fantasies of foreign inventions, than to see the Rarities and History of their own Country delivered by a true native Muse. Then, whosoever thou be, possest with such stupidity and dulness, that, rather than thou wilt take pains to search into ancient and noble things, choosest to remain in the thick fogs and mists of ignorance, as near the common lay-stall of a city, refusing to walk forth into the *Tempe* and fields of the Muses, where through most delightful groves the angelic harmony of birds shall steal thee to the top of an easy hill, where, in artificial caves, cut out of the most natural rock, thou shalt see the ancient people of this Isle deliver thee in their lively images : from whose height thou mayest behold both the old and later times, as in thy prospect, lying far under thee ; then conveying thee down by a soul-pleasing descent through delicate embrodered Meadows, often veined with gentle gliding Brooks ; in which thou mayest fully view the dainty Nymphs in their simple naked beauties, bathing them in crystalline streams ; which shall lead thee to most pleasant Downs, where harmless Shepherds are, some exercising their pipes, some singing roundelays to their gazing flocks.   If, as I say, thou hadst rather (because it asks thy labour) remain where thou wert, than strain thyself to walk forth with the Muses, the fault proceeds from thy idleness, not from any want in my industry.   And to any that shall demand wherefore having promised this Poem of the general Island so many years, I now publish only this part of it ; I plainly answer that many times I had determined with myself to have left it off, and have neglected my papers sometimes two years together, finding the times since his Majesty's happy coming-in to fall so heavily upon my distressed fortunes, after my zealous soul had laboured so long in that which, with the general happiness of the kingdom, seemed not then impossible somewhat also to have advanced me.   But I instantly saw all my long-nourished hopes even buried alive before my face : so uncertain (in this world) be the ends of our clearest endeavours. And whatever is herein that tastes of a free spirit, I thankfully confess it to proceed from the continual bounty of my truly noble friend Sir *Walter Aston ;* which hath given me the best of those hours, whose leisure hath effected this which I now publish.   Sundry other Songs I have also, though yet not so perfect that I dare commit them to public censure; and the rest I determine to go forward with, God enabling me, may I find means to assist my endeavour. Now, Reader, for the further understanding of my Poem, thou hast three especial helps: First, the Argument to direct thee still where thou art, and through what Shires the Muse makes her journey, and what she chiefly handles in the Song thereto belonging. Next, the Map, lively delineating to thee every Mountain, Forest, River, and Valley; expressing, in their sundry postures, their loves, delights, and natural situations. Then hast thou the Illustration of this learned Gentleman, my friend, to explain every hard matter of history, that, lying far from the way of common reading, may (without question) seem difficult unto thee. Thus wishing thee thy heart's desire, and committing my Poem to thy charitable censure, I take my leave.

Thine, as thou art mine,

MICHAEL DRAYTON.

TO MY FRIENDS,

THE CAMBRO-BRITANS.

*T*O have you without difficulty understand, how in this my intended progress through these united kingdoms of Great Britain I have placed your and (I must confess) my loved Wales, you shall perceive, that after the Three first Songs, beginning with our French Islands, Jernsey and Jersey, with the rest, and perfecting in those first Three the survey of these six our most Western Countries, Cornwall, Devon, Dorset, Hamp, Wilt, and Summerset, I then make over Severne into Wales, not far from the midst of her Broadside that lieth against England. I term it her Broadside, because it lieth from Shrewsbury still along with Severne, till she lastly turn sea. And to explain two lines of mine (which you shall find in the Fourth Song of my Poem, but it is the First of Wales) which are these,*

And ere Seven Books have end, I'll strike so high a string,
Thy Bards shall stand amaz'd with wonder whilst I sing.

Speaking of Seven Books, you shall understand that I continue Wales through so many; beginning in the Fourth Song (where the Nymphs of England and Wales contend for the Isle of Lundy) and ending in the Tenth; striving, as my much-loved (the learned) Humfrey Floyd, in his description of Cambria to

Abraham Ortelius, *to uphold her ancient bounds,* Severne, and Dee, *and therefore have included the parts of those three English Shires of* Gloster, Worster, *and* Sallop, *that lie on the West of* Severne, *within their ancient mother* Wales. *In which if I have not done her right, the want is in my abililty, not in my love.   And beside my natural inclination to love antiquities (which* Wales *may highly boast of) I confess the free and gentle company of that true lover of his Country (as of all ancient and noble things)* Mr. John Williams, *his Majesty's Goldsmith, my dear and worthy friend, hath made me the more seek into the antiquities of your Country.   Thus wishing your favourable construction of these my faithful endeavours, I bid you farewell.*

MICHAEL DRAYTON.

From the AUTHOR of the ILLUSTRATIONS.

PERMIT me thus much of these Notes to my Friend. What the Verse oft with allusion as supposing a full-knowing Reader, lets slip; or in winding steps of personating fictions (as sometimes) so enfolds, that sudden conceit cannot abstract a form of the clothed truth; I have, as I might, *illustrated.* *Brevity* and *plainness* (as the one endured the other) I have joined; purposely avoiding frequent commixture of different language, and whensoever it happens either the page or margin (specially for *Gentlewomen's* sake) summarily interprets it, except where interpretation aids not. Being not very prodigal of my Historical faith, after *explanation,* I oft adventure on *examination,* and *censure.* The Author, in passages of *first inhabitants, name, state,* and *monarchic succession* in this Isle, follows *Geffrey* **ap** *Arthur, Polychronicon, Matthew* of *Westminster,* and such more. Of their Traditions, for that one so much controverted, and by *Cambro-Britons* still maintained, touching the *Trojan Brute,* I have (but as an advocate for the Muse) argued; disclaiming in it, if alleged for my own opinion. In most of the rest, upon weighing the Reporters' credit, comparison with more persuading authority, and *synchronism* (the best touch-stone in this kind of trial) I leave note of suspicion, or add conjectural amendment: as, for particular examples among other, in

Brennus mistook by all writers of later time, following *Justin's* Epitome of *Trogus*, ill-conceived ; in *Robert* of *Swapham's* Story of K. *Wulpher's* murdering his children, in *Rollo* first D. of *Normandy* his time ; none of them yet rectified (although the first hath been adventured on) by any that I have seen ; and such more. And indeed my jealousy hath oft vexed me with particular inquisition of whatsoever occurs bearing not a mark of most apparent truth, ever since I found so intolerable antichronisms, incredible reports, and *Bardish* impostures, as well from ignorance as assumed liberty of invention in some of our Ancients ; and read also such palpable fauxeties of our Nation, thrust into the world by later time; as (to give a taste) that of *Randall Higden* affirming the beginning of *Wards* in 6 *Hen.* III ; *Polydore's* assertion (upon mistaking of the Statute of 1 *Hen.* VII.) that *it was death by the* English *laws for any man to wear a vizard*, with many like errors in his History, of our *Trials* by 12 *Shrives, Coat* of the Kingdom, *Parliaments,* and other like ; *Bartol's* delivering the custom in this Isle to be *quod Primogenitus succedit in omnibus bonis.** The Greek *Chalcondylas* his slanderous description of our usual form of kind entertainment to begin with the wives' courteous admission to that most affected pleasure of lascivious fancy (he was deceived by misunderstanding the reports of our *Kissing Salutations,*† given and accepted amongst us with more freedom than in any part of the Southern world, erroneously thinking, perhaps, that every Kiss must be

* *Ad C. de summ. Trinit., lib.* 1, *num.* 42.

† *Unum blandientis, ad pulsum linguæ longè mellitum.* Apuleius *De Aur. Asin.* 6. And you may remember (as like enough he did) that in Plautus *Curcul. Qui vult cubare pangit saltèm suavium ;* and such more in other wanton poets ; with the opinion of *Baldus,* that a kiss in those Southern Nations is sufficient consent to imperfect espousals, nothing of that kind, but copulation, with us and our neighbouring *Dutch* being so.

thought seconded with that addition to the seven promised
by *Mercury* in name of *Venus* to him that should find
Psyche; or as wanton as *Aristophanes* his μανδαλωτόν); and
many untruths of like nature in others.   Concerning
the Arcadian deduction of our *British* Monarchy; within
that time, from *Brute,* supposed about 2850 of the world
(*Samuel* then Judge of *Israel*) unto some 54 before *Christ,*
(about when *Julius Cæsar* visited the Island) no relation
was extant which is now left to our use.   How then are
they which pretend chronologies of that age without any
fragment of authors before *Gildas, Taliessin,* and *Nennius,*
(the eldest of which was since 500 of *Christ,*) to be credited ?
For my part, I believe as much in them as I do the finding
of *Hiero's* shipmast in our mountains,* which is collected
upon a corrupted place in *Athenæus* cited out of *Moschion ;*
or that *Ptolemy Philadelph* sent to *Reutha* King of *Scots*
some 1900 years since, for discovery of this Country,
which *Claude Ptolemy* afterward put in his Geography ; or,
that *Julius Cæsar* built *Arthur's Hoffen* in *Stirling* sheriff-
dom ; or, that *Britons* were at the Rape of *Hesione* with
Hercules, as our excellent wit *Joseph* of *Excester* (published
falsely under name of *Cornelius Nepos*) singeth : which are
even equally warrantable as *Ariosto's* narrations of persons
and places in his *Rowlands ; Spenser's* Elfin Story ; or *Rablais*
his strange discoveries.   Yet the capricious faction will (I
know) never quit their belief of wrong ; although some
Elias or *Delian* diver should make open what is so inquired
after.   Briefly, until *Polybius,* who wrote near 1800 since
(for *Aristotle* περὶ Κόσμε is clearly counterfeited in title) no
Greek mentions the Isle; until *Lucretius* (some 100 years later)
no *Roman* hath expressed a thought of us ; until *Cæsar's*

---

* Ἐν τοῖς ὄρεσι τῆς Βρέτανίας, ἀντὶ τε Βρέττιανῆς, quæ nempè verior
videtur lectio.

Commentaries, no piece of its description was known that
is now left to posterity. For time therefore preceding
Cæsar, I dare trust none; but with others adhere to *conjecture*. In ancient matter since, I rely on *Tacitus* and *Dio*
especially, *Vopiscus, Capitolin, Spartian* (for so much as they
have, and the rest of the *Augustan* story) afterward *Gildas,
Nennius* (but little is left of them, and that of the last very
imperfect), *Bede, Asserio, Cthelwerd* (near of blood to King
Alfred), *William* of *Malmesbury, Marian, Florence* of *Worcester*
(that published under name of *Florence* hath the very syllables of most part of *Marian* the *Scot's* Story, fraught with
English Antiquities; which will show you how easily to
answer *Buchanan's* objection against our historians about
Athelstan's being King of all *Albion*, being deceived when
he imagined that there was no other of *Marian* but the
common printed Chronicle, which is indeed but an epitome
or defloration made by *Robert* of *Lorraine*, Bishop of *Hereford* under *Hen.* I.) and the numerous rest of our Monkish
and succeeding chronographers. In all, I believe him
most, which, freest from *affection* and *hate* (causes of corruption) might best know, and hath with most likely assertion delivered his report. Yet so that, to explain the
Author, carrying himself in this part an *Historical*, as in
the other a *Chorographical* Poet, I insert oft, out of the
British Story, what I importune you not to credit. Of that
kind are those *Prophecies* out of *Merlin* sometime inter-
woven; I discharge myself, nor impute you to me any
serious respect of them. Inviting, not wresting in, occasion, I add sometime what is different from my task, but
such as I guess would anywhere please an understanding
reader. To aid you in course of Times, I have in a fit
place drawn *Chronologies*, upon credit of the Ancients; and,
for matter of that kind, have admonished (to the Fourth

Canto) what as yet I never saw by any observed, for wary consideration of the *Dionysian* Cycle, and misinterpreted root of his Dominical year. Those *old Rhymes*, which (some number) you often meet with, are offered the willinger, both for *variety* of your mother tongue, as also, because the Author of them, *Robert* of *Gloster*, never yet appeared in common light. He was, in time, an age before, but in learning and wit, as most others, much behind our worthy *Chaucer* : whose name by the way occurring, and my work here being but to add plain song after Muses' descanting, I cannot but digress to admonition of abuse which this learned allusion in his *Troilus* by ignorance hath endured :

𝕴 𝖆𝖒 𝖙𝖎𝖑𝖑 𝕲𝖔𝖉 𝖒𝖊𝖊 𝖇𝖊𝖙𝖙𝖊𝖗 𝖒𝖎𝖓𝖉 𝖘𝖊𝖓𝖉
𝕬𝖙 Dulcarnon 𝖗𝖎𝖌𝖍𝖙 𝖆𝖙 𝖒𝖞 𝖇𝖎𝖙𝖘 𝖊𝖓𝖉.*

It's not *Necham*, or any else, that can make me entertain the least thought of the signification of *Dulcarnon* to be *Pythagoras's* sacrifice after his geometrical theorem in finding the squares of an orthogonal triangle's sides, or that it is a word of *Latin* deduction ; but indeed by easier pronunciation it was made of *Dzu-l-karnaïn*, i.e., *Two-horned :* which the *Mahometan Arabians* use for a root in calculation, meaning *Alexander*, as that great Dictator of knowledge *Joseph Scaliger* (with some ancients) wills, but, by warranted opinion of my learned friend Mr. *Lydyat* in his *Emendatio Temporum*,† it began in *Seleucus Nicanor*, 12 years after *Alexander's* death. The name was applied, either because after time that *Alexander* had persuaded himself to be *Jupiter Hammon's* son, whose statue was with *rams'* horns, both his own and his successors' coins were stamped with horned images : or else in respect of his 11 pillars erected in the

---

* *Chaucer* explained.　　　　† Epocha Seleucidarum.

East, as a *Nihil ultra** of his Conquest, and some say because he had in power the *Eastern* and *Western* world, signified in the two Horns. But, howsoever, it well fits the passage, either, as if he had personated *Creseide* at the entrance of two ways, not knowing which to take ; in like sense as that of *Prodicus* his *Hercules, Pythagoras* his Y, or the Logicians' *Dilemma* express ; or else, which is the truth of his conceit, that she was at a *nonplus,* as the interpretation in his next staff makes plain. How many of noble *Chaucer's* readers never so much as suspect this his short essay of knowledge, transcending the common road? and by his Treatise of the *Astrolabe* (which, I dare swear, was chiefly learned out of *Messahalah*) it is plain he was much acquainted with the Mathematics, and amongst their authors had it. But, I return to myself. From vain loading my margin with *Books, Chapters, Folios,* or *Names* of our *Historians,* I abstain : course of Time as readily directs to them. But, where the place might not so easily occur (chiefly in matter of *philology*) there only (for view of them which shall examine me) I have added assisting references. For most of what I use of *chorography* join with me in thanks to that most learned Nourice of Antiquity

——————————— τόν τις καὶ τηλόθι νάιων

Τιμᾶ ἀνὴρ ἀγαθός,†———————————

* *Christman,* Comment. in Alfragan, cap. 11. *Lysimachi* Cornum apud *Cœl. Rhodigin. Antiq.* lect. 20, cap. 12, hic genuina interpretatio.

† *Of whom even every ingenious stranger makes honourable mention.* Comitem verò illum Palatinum *R. Vitum Basingstochium.* (cuius Historiæ magnam partem quasi Βεργαιζοντος, chorographica substructio pleráque ad antiquitatis amussim, ab eruditissimo hoc suo populari accepta, ne dicam suppilata, est) adeò inhumanum fuisse miror, ut benè merentem non tam libentèr agnoscat, quàm Clariss.

my instructing friend Mr. *Camden, Clarenceulx.* From him
and *Girald* of *Cambria* also comes most of my *British.* And
then may *Mercury* and all the Muses deadly hate me, when,
in permitting occasion, I profess not by whom I learn!
Let them vent judgment on me which understand : I justify all by the self authors cited, crediting no *transcribers*
but when of necessity I must. My thirst compelled me always to seek the *fountains,* and by that, if means grant it,
judge the *rivers'* nature. Nor can any conversant in letters be ignorant what error is ofttimes fallen into by trusting authorities at second hand, and rash collecting (as it
were) from visual beams refracted through another's eye.
In performance of this charge (undertaken at request of
my kind friend the Author) brevity of *time* (which was
but little more than since the Poem first went to the
press) and that daily discontinued, both by my other most
different *studies* seriously attended, and interrupting *busi-
ness,* as enough can witness, might excuse great faults, especially of *omission.* But, I take not thence advantage to
desire more than *common courtesy in censure.* Nor of this,
nor of what else I heretofore have published, touching
*Historical deduction of our Ancient Laws,** wherein I escape
not without tax,

> *Sunt quibus in verbis videórque obscurior, hoc est*
> Evandri *cum Matre loqui,* Faunisque, Numâque,
> *Nec secùs ac si auctor* Saliaris *Carminis essem.*

I have read in *Cicero, Agellius, Lucian's Lexiphanes,* and
others, much against that form. But withal, this later

Viri syllabis et inventis codicem suum sæpiùs perquam ingratè suf-
farcinet. Atque id ferè genus Plagiarios, rudes omninò, et ἀμούσους
et Vernaculos nimirùm Nostrates jam nunc imponere sarcinam video
indignantér et ringor.

* Janus Anglorum.

age (wherein so industrious a search is among admired
ruins of old monuments) hath, in our greatest Latin critics *Hans Douz, P. Merula, Lipsius,* and such more, so received that *Saturnian* language, that, to students in *philology,* it is now grown familiar; and (as he saith*) *Verba à
vetustate repetita non solum magnos assertores habent, sed etiam
afferunt orationi majestatem aliquam, non sine delectatione.* Yet
for antique terms, to the Learned, I will not justify it
without exception (disliking not that of *Phavorin, Vive
moribus præteritis, loquere verbis præsentibus;* and, as coin,
so words, of a public and known stamp, are to be used),
although so much as that way I offend is warranted by
example of such, of whom to endeavour imitation allows
me more than the bare title of *Blameless.* The purblind
ignorant I salute with the English of that monitory epigram

$$\text{————————} \text{'Eι δέ γε πάμπαν}$$
$$\text{Νῆις ἔφυς Μουσέων, ῥίψον ἃ μὴ νοέεις.†}$$

Reprehension of them, whose language and best learning
is purchased from such volumes as *Rablais* reckons in *S.
Victor's* Library, or barbarous glosses,

Quàm nihil ad genium, Papiniane, *tuum !*

or, which are furnished in our old story, only out of the
common *Polychronicon, Caxton, Fabian, Stow, Grafton, Lan-
quet, Cooper, Holingshed* (perhaps with gift of understanding)
Polydore, and the rest of our later compilers; or, of any
adventurous *Thersites* daring find fault even with the very
Graces, in a strain

Cornua quod vincatque, tubas————

---

* Quintilian.
† *If thou hast no taste in learning, meddle no more with what thou
understandest not.*

I regard as metamorphized *Lucius* his looking out at window; I slight, scorn, and laugh at it. By *paragraphs* (§) in the Verses you know what I meddle with in the *Illustrations;* but so that, with latitude, the direction admonishes sometimes as well for explaining a following or preceding passage, as its own. Ingenuous Readers, to you I wish your best desires. Grant me too, I pray, this one, that you read me not, without comparing the *Faults escaped.* * I have collected them for you. Compelled *absence,* endeavoured *dispatch,* and want of *revises* soon bred them. To the Author, I wish (as an old Cosmographical Poet did long since to himself)

——————— ’Αλλά μοι ὕμνων
’Αυτῶν ἐκ μακάρων ἀντάξιος εἴη ἀμοιβή.†

To *Gentlewomen* and their *Loves* is consecrated all the *Wooing Language, Allusions* to *Love-Passions,* and sweet *Embracements* feigned by the Muse amongst *Hills* and *Rivers.* Whatsoever tastes of *Description, Battle, Story,* abstruse *Antiquity,* and (which my particular study caused me sometime remember) *Law* of the Kingdom, to the more *Severe Reader.* To the one, be contenting *enjoyments* of their *auspicious desires ;* to the other, happy *attendance* of their chosen *Muses.*

From the *Inner Temple,* May 9, 1612.

---

* These have been amended in the present edition.
† *That the godlike sort of men may worthily guerdon his labours.*
                                        Dion. Perieg. 1185.

A TABLE
TO THE CHIEFEST PASSAGES
IN THE *ILLUSTRATIONS*.

Which, worthiest of observation, or inserted by digression, are not directed unto by the course of the volume.

[In the present edition the references are to the lines of the Songs in the Illustrations.]

d

POLY-OLBION.

THE FIRST SONG.

THE ARGUMENT.

The sprightly Muse her wing displays,
And the French Islands first surveys;
Bears up with Neptune, *and in glory*
Transcends proud Cornwall's *Promontory;*
There crowns Mount-Michael, *and descries*
How all those Riverets fall and rise;
Then takes in Tamer, *as she bounds*
The Cornish *and* Devonian *grounds.*
And whilst the Devonshire-*Nymphs relate*
Their loves, their fortunes, and estate,
Dert *undertaketh to revive*
Our Brute, *and sings his first arrive:*
Then Northward to the verge she bends,
And her first Song at Ax *she ends.*

F *Albion's* glorious Isle the wonders whilst I write,
The sundry varying soils, the pleasures infinite,
(Where heat kills not the cold, nor cold expells
    the heat,
The calms too mildly small, nor winds too roughly great,
Nor night doth hinder day, nor day the night doth wrong, ₅
The summer not too short, the winter not too long)

What help shall I invoke to aid my Muse the while?
  Thou *Genius* of the place (this most renownéd Isle)
Which livedst long before the all-earth-drowning Flood,
Whilst yet the world did swarm with her Giganticbrood, 10
Go thou before me still thy circling shores about,
And in this wand'ring maze help to conduct me out:
Direct my course so right, as with thy hand to show
Which way thy Forests range, which way thy Rivers flow;
Wise *Genius*, by thy help that so I may descry   15
How thy fair Mountains stand, and how thy Valleys lie;
From those clear pearly Cleeves which see the morning's pride,
And check the surly imps of *Neptune* when they chide,
Unto the big-swoll'n waves in the *Iberian*[1] stream,
Where *Titan* still unyokes his fiery-hooféd team,   20
And oft his flaming locks in luscious nectar steeps,
When from *Olympus'* top he plungeth in the deeps:
That from th' *Armoric*[2] sands, on surging *Neptune's* leas,
Through the Hibernic Gulf (those rough Vergivian seas)
My verse with wings of skill may fly a lofty gait,   25
§ As *Amphitrite* clips this Island Fortunate,
Till through the sleepy main to *Thuly*[3] I have gone,
And seen the frozen Isles, the cold *Deucalidon*,[4]
Amongst whose iron rocks grim *Saturn* yet remains,
Bound in those gloomy caves with adamantine chains.   30
  Ye sacred Bards,[5] that to your harps' melodious strings
Sung th' ancient Heroes' deeds (the monuments of Kings)
And in your dreadful verse ingrav'd the prophecies,
The agéd world's descents, and genealogies;
If, as those *Druids*[6] taught, which kept the British rites, 35
And dwelt in darksome groves, there counselling with sprites,

---

[1] The Western or Spanish Ocean.   [2] The coast of Little Britaine in
   [3] The furthest Isle in the British Ocean.   [France.
    [4] The Sea upon the North of Scotland.
    [5] The old British Poets.   [6] Priests among the ancient Britons.

(But their opinions fail'd, by error led awry,
As since clear truth hath shew'd to their posterity)
When these our souls by death our bodies do forsake,
§ They instantly again do other bodies take ;   40
I could have wish'd your spirits redoubled in my breast,
To give my verse applause, to time's eternal rest.

    Thus scarcely said the Muse, but hovering while she hung
Upon the Celtic [1] wastes, the Sea-Nymphs loudly sung :
O ever-happy Isles, your heads so high that bear,   45
By nature strongly fenc'd, which never need to fear
On *Neptune's* wat'ry realms when *Eolus* raiseth wars,
And ev'ry billow bounds, as though to quench the stars :
Fair *Jersey* first of these here scatt'red in the deep,
Peculiarly that boast'st thy double-hornéd sheep :   50
Inferior nor to thee, thou *Jernsey*, bravely crown'd
With rough-imbattl'd rocks, whose venom-hating ground
The hard'ned emeril hath, which thou abroad dost send :
Thou *Ligon*, her belov'd, and *Serk*, that dost attend
Her pleasure ev'ry hour ; as *Jethow*, them at need,   55
With pheasants, fallow deer, and conies, that dost feed :
Ye *Seven small sister Isles*, and *Sorlings*, which to see
The half-sunk seaman joys, or whatsoe'er you be,
From fruitful *Aurney*, near the ancient Celtic shore,
To *Ushant*, and the *Seams*, whereas those Nuns of yore   60
§ Gave answers from their caves, and took what shapes they
Ye happy Islands set within the British Seas,   [please :
With shrill and jocund shouts, th' unmeasur'd deeps awake,
And let the Gods of sea their secret bow'rs forsake,
Whilst our industrious Muse great *Britain* forth shall bring,
Crown'd with those glorious wreaths that beautify the
    Spring ;   66
And whilst green *Thetis'* Nymphs, with many an amorous lay
Sing our invention safe unto her long-wish'd Bay.

        [1] The French Seas.

Upon the utmost end of *Cornwall's* furrowing beak,
Where *Bresan* [1] from the land the tilting waves doth break ;
The shore let her transcend, the promont [2] to descry, 71
And view about the Point th' unnumb'red fowl that fly.
Some, rising like a storm from off the troubled sand,
Seem in their hovering flight to shadow all the land ;
Some, sitting on the beach to prune their painted breasts, 75
As if both earth and air they only did possess.
Whence, climbing to the cleeves, herself she firmly sets
The Bourns, the Brooks, the Becks, the Rills, the Rivelets,
Exactly to derive ; receiving in her way   [Bay,
That straight'ned tongue of land, where, at *Mount-Michael's*
Rude *Neptune*, cutting in, a cantle forth doth take ; 81
And, on the other side, *Hayle's* vaster mouth doth make
A chersonese thereof, the corner clipping in ;
Where to the industrious Muse the *Mount* doth thus begin :
Before thou further pass, and leave this setting shore, 85
§ Whose towns unto the Saints that livéd here of yore
(Their fasting, works, and pray'rs, remaining to our shames,)
Were rear'd, and justly call'd by their peculiar names,
The builders honour still ; this due and let them have,
As deign to drop a tear upon each holy grave ;   90
Whose charity and zeal instead of knowledge stood :
For surely in themselves they were right simply good.
If, credulous too much, thereby they offended heaven,
In their devout intents yet be their sins forgiven.
Then from his rugged top the tears down trickling fell ; 95
And, in his passion stirr'd, again began to tell   [pass,
Strange things, that in his days Time's course had brought to
That forty miles now sea, sometimes firm fore-land was ;
And that a forest then, which now with him is flood,
§ Whereof he first was call'd the *Hoar-Rock in the Wood ;* 100

[1] A small island upon the very point of *Cornwall.*
[2] A hill lying out, as an elbow of land, into the sea.

Relating then how long this soil had lain forlorn,
As that her *Genius* now had almost her forsworn,
And of their ancient love did utterly repent,
Sith to destroy herself that fatal tool she lent
By which th' insatiate slave her entrails out doth draw,   105
That thrusts his gripple hand into her golden maw;
And for his part doth wish, that it were in his pow'r
To let the ocean in, her wholly to devour.

  Which *Hayle* doth overhear, and much doth blame his rage,
And told him (to his teeth) he doted with his age.   110
For *Hayle* (a lusty Nymph, bent all to amorous play,
And having quick recourse into the *Severn* Sea,
With *Neptune's* pages oft disporting in the deep;
One never touch'd with care; but how herself to keep
In excellent estate) doth thus again intreat: 115
Muse, leave the wayward Mount to his distemp'red heat,
Who nothing can produce but what doth taste of spite:
I'll shew thee things of ours most worthy thy delight.
Behold our diamonds here, as in the quarrs they stand,
By Nature neatly cut, as by a skilful hand,   120
Who varieth them in forms, both curiously and oft;
Which for she (wanting pow'r) produceth them too soft,
That virtue which she could not liberally impart,
She striveth to amend by her own proper art.
Besides, the seaholm here, that spreadeth all our shore,   125
The sick consuming man so pow'rful to restore:
Whose root th' eringo is, the reins that doth inflame
So strongly to perform the *Cytheræan* game,
That, generally approv'd, both far and near is sought.
§ And our *Main-Amber* here, and *Burien* Trophy, thought   130
Much wrong'd, nor yet preferr'd for wonders with the rest.

  But the laborious Muse, upon her journey prest,
Thus uttereth to herself: To guide my course aright,
What mound or steady mere is offered to my sight

Upon this outstretch'd arm, whilst sailing here at ease,   135
Betwixt the Southern waste, and the *Sabrinian* seas,
I view those wanton brooks, that, waxing, still do wane ;
That scarcely can conceive, but brought to bed again ;
Scarce rising from the spring (that is their natural mother)
To grow into a stream, but buried in another ?   140
When *Chore* doth call her on, that wholly doth betake
Herself unto the *Loo ;* transform'd into a lake,
Through that impatient love she had to entertain
The lustful *Neptune* oft ; whom when his wracks restrain,
Impatient of the wrong, impetuously he raves ;   145
And in his rageful flow, the furious King of waves
Breaks foaming o'er the beach, whom nothing seems to cool,
Till he have wrought his will on that capacious pool :
Where *Menedge,* by his brooks a chersonese [1] is cast,
Widening the slender shore to ease it in the wast ;   150
A promont jutting out into the dropping South,
That with his threat'ning cleeves in horrid *Neptune's* mouth,
Derides him and his pow'r ; nor cares how him he greets.
Next *Roseland* (as his friend, the mightier *Menedge*) meets
Great *Neptune* when he swells, and rageth at the rocks   155
(Set out into those seas) inforcing through his shocks
Those arms of sea, that thrust into the tinny strand,
By their meand'red creeks indenting of that land,
Whose fame by ev'ry tongue is for her minerals hurl'd,
Near from the mid-day's point, throughout the Western world.
Here *Vale,* a lively flood, her nobler name that gives   161
To *Flamouth ;* [2] and by whom, it famous ever lives,
Whose entrance is from sea so intricately wound,
Her haven angled so about her harb'rous sound,
That in her quiet Bay a hundred ships may ride,   165
Yet not the tallest mast be of the tall'st descried ;

---

[1] A place almost invironed with water, well-nigh an island.
[2] The bravery of *Flamouth* (i.e. *Falmouth,*) Haven.

Her bravery to this Nymph when neighb'ring rivers told,
Her mind to them again she briefly doth unfold :
Let *Camell*[1] of her course and curious windings boast,
In that her greatness reigns sole mistress of that coast   170
'Twixt *Tamer* and that Bay, where *Hayle* pours forth her pride:
And let us (nobler Nymphs) upon the mid-day side,
Be frolic with the best.   Thou *Foy*, before us all,
By thine own naméd Town made famous in thy fall,
As *Low*, amongst us here ; a most delicious brook,   175
With all our sister Nymphs, that to the noon-sted look,
Which gliding from the hills, upon the tinny ore,
Betwixt your high-rear'd banks, resort to this our shore :
Lov'd streams, let us exult, and think ourselves no less
Than those upon their side, the setting that possess.   180

  Which *Camell* overheard : but what doth she respect
Their taunts, her proper course that loosely doth neglect ?
As frantic, ever since her British *Arthur's* blood
By *Mordred's* murtherous hand was mingled with her flood.
For, as that river best might boast that Conqueror's breath,
So sadly she bemoans his too untimely death ;   186
Who, after twelve proud fields against the *Saxon* fought,
Yet back unto her banks by fate was lastly brought :
As though no other place, on *Britain's* spacious earth,
§ Were worthy of his end, but where he had his birth :   190
And careless ever since how she her course do steer,
This mutt'reth to herself, in wand'ring here and there :
Ev'n in the agedst face, where beauty once did dwell,
And nature (in the least) but seeméd to excell,
Time cannot make such waste, but something will appear,
To show some little tract of delicacy there.   196
Or some religious work, in building many a day,
That this penurious age hath suffer'd to decay,

---

[1] This hath also the name of *Alan.*

Some limb or model, dragg'd out of the ruinous mass,
The richness will declare in glory whilst it was :   200
But time upon my waste committed hath such theft,
That it of *Arthur* here scarce memory hath left.
    The *Nine-ston'd Trophy* thus whilst she doth entertain,
Proud *Tamer* swoops along, with such a lusty train
As fits so brave a flood two Countries that divides :   205
So, to increase her strength, she from her equal sides
Receives their several rills ; and, of the Cornish kind,
First taketh *Atre* in ; and her not much behind
Comes *Kensey;* after whom, clear *Enian* in doth make,
In *Tamer's* roomthier banks their rest that scarcely take.   210
Then *Lyner,* though the while aloof she seem'd to keep,
Her Sovereign when she sees t'approach the surgeful deep,
To beautify her fall her plenteous tribute brings.
This honours *Tamer* much; that she whose plenteous springs,
Those proud aspiring hills, *Bromwelly* and his friend   215
High *Rowter,* from their tops impartially commend,
And is by *Carew's*[1] muse the river most renown'd,
Associate should her grace to the *Devonian* ground.
Which in those other brooks doth emulation breed.
Of which, first *Car* comes crown'd, with osier, segs, and reed :
Then *Lid* creeps on along, and, taking *Thrushel,* throws   221
Herself amongst the rocks ; and so incavern'd goes,
That of the blessèd light (from other floods) debarr'd,
To bellow under earth she only can be heard,
As those that view her tract seems strangely to affright: 225
So *Toovy* straineth in ; and *Plym,* that claims by right
The christ'ning of that Bay, which bears her nobler name.
Upon the British coast, what ship yet ever came,
That not of *Plymouth* hears,[2] where those brave Navies lie,
From cannons' thund'ring throats that all the world defy?

[1] A worthy gentleman, who writ the description of Cornwall.
[2] The praise of Plymouth.

Which, to invasive spoil when th' English list to draw,   231
Have check'd *Iberia's* pride, and held her oft in awe:
Oft furnishing our dames with *India's* rar'st devices,
And lent us gold, and pearl, rich silks, and dainty spices.
But *Tamer* takes the place, and all attend her here,   235
A faithful bound to both; and two that be so near
For likeliness of soil, and quantity they hold,
Before the Roman came; whose people were of old
§ Known by one general name, upon this point that dwell,
All other of this Isle in wrastling that excell: 240
With collars be they yok'd, to prove the arm at length,
Like bulls set head to head, with mere deliver strength:
Or by the girdles grasp'd, they practise with the hip,
The forward,[1] backward, falx, the mare, the turn, the trip,
When stript into their shirts, each other they invade   245
Within a spacious ring, by the beholders made
According to the law. Or when the ball to throw,
And drive it to the goal, in squadrons forth they go;
And to avoid the troops (their forces that fore-lay)
Through dikes and rivers make, in this robustious play;   250
By which the toils of war most lively are exprest.
   But Muse, may I demand, Why these of all the rest
(As mighty *Albion's* eld'st) most active are and strong?
From *Corin*[2] came it first, or from the use so long?
§ Or that this fore-land lies furth'st out into his sight,   255
Which spreads his vigorous flames on ev'ry lesser light?
With th' virtue of his beams, this place that doth inspire:
Whose pregnant womb prepar'd by his all-pow'rful fire,
Being purely hot and moist, projects that fruitful seed
Which strongly doth beget, and doth as strongly breed: 260
The well-disposéd heav'n here proving to the earth
A husband furthering fruit, a midwife helping birth.

---

[1] The words of art in wrastling.
[2] Our first great wrastler arriving here with Brute.

But whilst th' industrious Muse thus labours to relate
Those rillets that attend proud *Tamer* and her state,
A neighbourer of this Nymph's, as high in fortune's grace, 265
And whence calm *Tamer* trips, clear *Towridge* in that place
Is pouréd from her spring ; and seems at first to flow
That way which *Tamer* strains ; but as she great doth grow
Rememb'reth to fore-see what rivals she should find
To interrupt her course : whose so unsettled mind   270
Ock coming in perceives, and thus doth her persuade :
Now *Neptune* shield (bright Nymph) thy beauty should
          be made
The object of her scorn, which (for thou canst not be
Upon the Southern side so absolute as she)
Will awe thee in thy course.   Wherefore, fair flood, recoil ;
And, where thou may'st alone be sov'reign of the soil,   276
There exercise thy pow'r, thy braveries and display.
Turn *Towridge*, let us back to the *Sabrinian* sea,
Where *Thetis'* handmaids still in that recourseful deep
With those rough Gods of sea continual revels keep ;   280
There mayst thou live admir'd, the Mistress of the Lake.

Wise *Ock* she doth obey, returning, and doth take [gales,
The *Tawe :* which from her fount forc'd on with amorous
And eas'ly ambling down through the *Devonian* dales,
Brings with her *Moule* and *Bray*, her banks that gently
          bathe ;   285
Which on her dainty breast, in many a silver swathe,
She bears unto that Bay, where *Barstable* beholds
How her belovéd *Tawe* clear *Towridge* there enfolds.

The confluence of these brooks divulg'd in *Dertmoore*, bred
Distrust in her sad breast, that she, so largely spread, 290
And in this spacious Shire the neer'st the centre set
Of any place of note ; that these should bravely get
The praise from those that sprung out of her pearly lap ;
Which, nourish'd and bred up at her most plenteous pap,

No sooner taught to dade, but from their mother trip,　　205
And, in their speedy course, strive others to outstrip.
The *Yalme*, the *Awne*, the *Aume*, by spacious *Dertmoore* fed,
And in the Southern sea being likewise brought to bed ;
That these were not of pow'r to publish her desert,
Much griev'd the ancient Moor : which understood by *Dert*
(From all the other floods that only takes her name,　　301
And as her eld'st (in right) the heir of all her fame)
To shew her nobler spirit it greatly doth behove.　　[move :
Dear mother, from your breast this fear (quoth she) re-
Defie their utmost force : there's not the proudest flood,　305
That falls betwixt the *Mount* and *Exmore*, shall make good
Her royalty with mine, with me nor can compare :
I challenge any one, to answer me that dare ;
That was, before them all, predestinate to meet
My *Britain*-founding *Brute*, when with his puissant fleet　310
At *Totnesse* first he touch'd : which shall renown my stream
§ (Which now the envious world doth slander for a dream.)
Whose fatal flight from *Greece*, his fortunate arrive
In happy *Albion* here whilst strongly I revive,
Dear *Harburne* at thy hands this credit let me win,　　315
Quoth she, that as thou hast my faithful handmaid been ;
So now (my only brook) assist me with thy spring,
Whilst of the god-like *Brute* the story thus I sing :
When long-renownéd *Troy* lay spent in hostile fire,
And aged *Priam's* pomp did with her flames expire,　　320
Æneas (taking thence *Ascanius*, his young son,
And his most rev'rend sire, the grave *Anchises*, won [shores ;
From shoals of slaught'ring Greeks) set out from *Simois'*
And through the *Tyrrhene* Sea, by strength of toiling oars,
Raught *Italy* at last ; where King *Latinus* lent　　325
Safe harbour for his ships, with wrackful tempests rent :
When, in the Latin Court, *Lavinia* young and fair
(Her father's only child, and kingdom's only heir)

Upon the Troian lord her liking strongly plac'd,
And languish'd in the fires that her fair breast imbrac'd :
But *Turnus* (at that time) the proud *Rutulian* King,   331
A suitor to the maid, *Æneas* malicing,
By force of arms attempts his rival to extrude :
But, by the *Teucrian* pow'r courageously subdu'd,
Bright *Cytherea's* son the Latin crown obtain'd ;   335
And dying, in his stead his son *Ascanius* reign'd.
§ Next *Silvius* him succeeds, begetting *Brute* again :
Who in his mother's womb whilst yet he did remain,
The Oracles gave out, that next-born *Brute* should be
§ His parents' only death : which soon they liv'd to see.   340
For, in his painful birth his mother did depart ;
And ere his fifteenth year, in hunting of a hart,
He with a luckless shaft his hapless father slew :
For which, out of his throne, their king the Latins threw.
      Who, wand'ring in the world, to *Greece* at last doth get.   345
Where, whilst he liv'd unknown, and oft with want beset,
He of the race of *Troy* a remnant hapt to find,
There by the Grecians held ; which (having still in mind
Their tedious ten years' war, and famous heroes slain)
In slavery with them still those Troians did detain :   350
Which *Pyrrhus* thither brought (and did with hate pursue,
To wreak *Achilles'* death, at *Troy* whom *Paris* slew)
There by *Pandrasus* kept in sad and servile awe.
Who, when they knew young *Brute*, and that brave shape
      they saw,
They humbly him desire, that he a mean would be,   355
From those imperious Greeks, his countrymen to free.
      He, finding out a rare and sprightly youth, to fit
His humour ev'ry way, for courage, pow'r, and wit,
Assaracus (who, though that by his sire he were
A prince amongt the Greeks, yet held the Troians dear ;

Descended of their stock upon the mother's side :   361
For which he'by the Greeks his birth-right was denied)
Impatient of his wrongs, with him brave *Brute* arose,
And of the Troian youth courageous captains chose,
Rais'd earthquakes with their drums, the ruffling ensigns rear ;
And, gathering young and old that rightly Troian were,   366
Up to the mountains march, through straits and forests
          strong :
Where, taking-in the towns, pretended to belong
Unto that Grecian [1] lord, some forces there they put :
Within whose safer walls their wives and children shut,   370
Into the fields they drew, for liberty to stand.
    Which when *Pandrasus* heard, he sent his strict command
To levy all the pow'r he presently could make :
So to their strengths of war the Troians them betake.   374
    But whilst the Grecian guides (not knowing how or where
The Teucrians were entrench'd, or what their forces were)
In foul disord'red troops yet straggled, as secure,
This looseness to their spoil the Troians did allure,
Who fiercely them assail'd : where stanchless fury rap'd
The Grecians in so fast, that scarcely one escap'd :   380
Yea, proud *Pandrasus'* flight himself could hardly free.
Who, when he saw his force thus frustrated to be,
And by his present loss his passéd error found,
(As by a later war to cure a former wound)
Doth reinforce his pow'r to make a second fight.   385
When they whose better wits had over-match'd his might,
Loth what they got to lose, as politicly cast
His armies to entrap, in getting to them fast
Antigonus as friend, and *Anaclet* his pheere
(Surpris'd in the last fight) by gifts who hiréd were   390
Into the Grecian camp th' insuing night to go,
And feign they were stoln forth, to their allies to show

<hr>

[1] Assaracus.

How they might have the spoil of all the Troian pride;
And gaining them belief, the credulous Grecians guide
Into th' ambushment near, that secretly was laid :　　395
So to the Troians' hands the Grecians were betray'd ;
Pandrasus self surpris'd ; his crown who to redeem
(Which scarcely worth their wrong the Troian race esteem)
Their slavery long-sustain'd did willingly release :
And (for a lasting league of amity and peace)　　400
Bright *Innogen*, his child, for wife to *Brutus* gave,
And furnish'd them a fleet, with all things they could crave
To set them out to sea.　Who launching, at the last
They on *Lergecia* light, an isle ; and, ere they past,
Unto a temple, built to great *Diana* there,　　405
The noble *Brutus* went ; wise *Trivia* [1] to enquire,
To show them where the stock of ancient Troy to place.
　　The Goddess, that both knew and lov'd the Troian race,
Reveal'd to him in dreams, that furthest to the West,
§ He should descry the Isle of *Albion*, highly blest ;　　410
With Giants lately stor'd ; their numbers now decay'd :
By vanquishing the rest his hopes should there be stay'd :
Where, from the stock of Troy, those puissant kings should
　　rise,
Whose conquests from the West the world should scant suffice.
　　Thus answer'd, great with hope, to sea they put again,　　415
And, safely under sail, the hours do entertain
With sights of sundry shores, which they from far descry :
And viewing with delight th' *Azarian* Mountains high,
One walking on the deck unto his friend would say
(As I have heard some tell) ' So goodly *Ida* lay.'　　420
　　Thus talking mongst themselves, they sun-burnt *Afric* keep
Upon the lee-ward still, and (sulking up the deep)
For *Mauritania* make : where putting-in, they find
A remnant (yet reserv'd) of th' ancient *Dardan* kind,

　　　　　[1] One of the titles of *Diana*.

By brave *Antenor* brought from out the Greekish spoils   425
(O long renownéd *Troy !* of thee, and of thy toils,
What country had not heard?) which, to their General, then
Great *Corineus* had, the strong'st of mortal men :
To whom (with joyful hearts) *Diana's* will they show.
  Who eas'ly being won along with them to go,   430
They altogether put into the wat'ry plain :
Oft-times with pirates, oft with monsters of the main,
Distresséd in their way ; whom hope forbids to fear.
Those Pillars first they pass, which *Jove's* great son did rear,
And cuffing those stern waves,which like huge mountains roll,
(Full joy in ev'ry part possessing ev'ry soul)   436
In *Aquitaine* at last the *Ilion* race arrive.
Whom strongly to repulse, when as those recreants strive,
They (anchoring there at first but to refresh their fleet,
Yet saw those savage men so rudely them to greet)   440
Unshipp'd their warlike youth, advancing to the shore.
The dwellers, which perceiv'd such danger at the door,
Their King *Groffarius* get to raise his pow'rful force :
Who, must'ring up an host of mingled foot and horse,
Upon the Troians set ; when suddenly began   445
A fierce and dangerous fight : where *Corineus* ran
With slaughter through the thick-set squadrons of the foes,
And with his arméd axe laid on such deadly blows,
That heaps of lifeless trunks each passage stopp'd up quite.
  Groffarius having lost the honour of the fight,   450
Repairs his ruin'd pow'rs ; not so to give them breath :
When they, which must be freed by conquest or by death,
And conquering them before, hop'd now to do no less,
(The like in courage still) stand for the like success.
Then stern and deadly war put on his horrid'st shape ;   455
And wounds appear'd so wide, as if the grave did gape
To swallow both at once ; which strove as both should fall,
When they with slaughter seem'd to be encircled all :

Where *Turon* (of the rest) *Brute's* sister's valiant son,
(By whose approvéd deeds that day was chiefly won)   460
Six hundred slew outright through his peculiar strength :
By multitudes of men yet over-press'd at length.
His nobler uncle there, to his immortal name,
§ The city *Turon* built, and well-endow'd the same.
For *Albion* sailing then, they arrivéd quickly here   465
(O ! never in this world men half so joyful were,
With shouts heard up to heav'n, when they beheld the land)
And in this very place where *Totness* now doth stand,
First set their gods of *Troy*, kissing the blesséd shore ;
Then, foraging this Isle, long-promis'd them before,   470
Amongst the ragged cleeves those monstrous Giants sought :
Who, of their dreadful kind, t' appall the Troians, brought
Great *Gogmagog*, an oak that by the roots could tear :
§ So mighty were (that time) the men who livéd there :
But, for the use of arms he did not understand   475
(Except some rock or tree, that, coming next to hand,
He ras'd out of the earth to execute his rage)
He challenge makes for strength, and off'reth there his gage.
Which *Corin* taketh up, to answer by-and-by,
Upon this son of earth his utmost pow'r to try.   480
   All doubtful to which part the victory would go,
Upon that lofty place at *Plymouth* call'd the *Hoe*,
Those mighty wrastlers [1] met ; with many an ireful look
Who threat'ned, as the one hold of the other took :
But, grappled, glowing fire shines in their sparkling eyes.   485
And, whilst at length of arm one from the other lies,
Their lusty sinews swell like cables, as they strive :
Their feet such trampling make, as though they forc'd to drive
A thunder out of earth : which stagger'd with the weight :
Thus, either's utmost force urg'd to the greatest height.   490

---

[1] The description of the wrastling betwixt *Corineus* and *Gogmagog*.

Whilst one upon his hip the other seeks to lift,
And th' adverse (by a turn) doth from his cunning shift,
Their short-fetch'd troubled breath a hollow noise doth make,
Like bellows of a forge.   Then *Corin* up doth take
The Giant twixt the grayns ; and, voiding of his hold,   495
(Before his combrous feet he well recover could),
Pitch'd head-long from the hill ; as when a man doth throw
An axtree, that, with sleight deliver'd from the toe,
Roots up the yielding earth : so that his violent fall,   499
Strook *Neptune* with such strength, as shoulder'd him withall ;
That where the monstrous waves like mountains late did
       stand,
They leap'd out of the place, and left the baréd sand
To gaze upon wide heaven : so great a blow it gave.
For which, the conquering *Brute* on *Corineus* brave   504
This horn of land bestow'd, and mark'd it with his name ;
§ Of *Corin, Cornwall* call'd, to his immortal fame.

    Clear *Dert* delivering thus the famous *Brute's* arrive,
Inflam'd with her report, the straggling rivulets strive
So highly her to raise, that *Ting* (whose banks were blest
By her belovéd Nymph, dear *Leman*) which addrest   510
And fully with her self determinéd before
To sing the *Danish* spoils committed on her shore,
When hither from the East they came in mighty swarms,
Nor could their native earth contain their numerous arms,
Their surcrease grew so great, as forcéd them at last   515
To seek another soil (as bees do when they cast)
And by their impious pride how hard she was bested,
When all the country swam with blood of *Saxons* shed :
This River (as I said) which had determin'd long
§ The deluge of the *Danes* exactly to have song,   520
It utterly neglects ; and studying how to do
The *Dert* those high respects belonging her unto,

Inviteth goodly *Ex*, who from her full-fed spring
Her little *Barlee* hath, and *Dunsbrook* her to bring   524
From *Exmore:* when she yet hath scarcely found her course,
Then *Creddy* cometh in, and *Forto*, which inforce
Her faster to her fall ; as *Ken* her closely clips,
And on her Eastern side sweet *Leman* gently slips
Into her widen'd banks, her sovereign to assist ;
As *Columb* wins for *Ex*, clear *Wever* and the *Clist*,   530
Contributing their streams their Mistress' fame to raise.
As all assist the *Ex*, so *Ex* consumeth these ;
Like some unthrifty youth, depending on the Court,
To win an idle name, that keeps a needless port ;
And raising his old rent, exacts his farmers' store   535
The land-lord to enrich, the tenants wondrous poor ;
Who having lent him theirs, he then consumes his own,
That with most vain expense upon the Prince is thrown :
So these, the lesser brooks unto the greater pay ;
The greater, they again spend all upon the sea :   540
As, *Otrey* (that her name doth of the Otters take,
Abounding in her banks) and *Ax*, their utmost make
To aid stout *Dert*, that dar'd *Brute's* story to revive.
For, when the *Saxon* first the *Britons* forth did drive,
Some up into the hills themselves o'er *Severne* shut :   545
Upon this point of land, for refuge others put,
To that brave race of *Brute* still fortunate.   For where
Great *Brute* first disembark'd his wand'ring Troians, there
§ His offspring (after long expulst the inner land,
When they the *Saxon* power no longer could withstand)   550
Found refuge in their flight ; where *Ax* and *Otrey* first
Gave these poor souls to drink, oppress'd with grievous thirst.
   Here I'll unyoke awhile, and turn my steeds to meat :
The land grows large and wide : my team begins to sweat.

ILLUSTRATIONS.

F in prose and religion it were as justifiable, as in poetry and fiction, to invoke a *Local power* (for anciently both *Jews, Gentiles,* and *Christians* have supposed to every Country a singular *Genius*[1]) I would therein join with the Author. Howsoever, in this and all ἐκ διός ἀρχόμεθα:[*] and so I begin to you.

26. *As* Amphitrite *clips this* Island fortunate.

When Pope *Clement* VI. granted the *Fortunate Isles* to *Lewis* Earl of *Cleremont*, by that general name (meaning only the Seven *Canaries*, and purposing their Christian conversion) the English Ambassadors at Rome seriously doubted,[2] lest their own country had been comprised in the donation. They were *Henry* of *Lancaster* Earl of *Derby*, *Hugh Spenser, Ralph* Lord *Stafford*, the Bishop of *Oxford*, and others, agents there with the Pope, that he, as a private friend, not as a judge or party interested, should determine of *Edward* the *Third's* right to *France ;* where you have this

---

[1] Rabbin. ad 10. Dan. ; Macrob. Saturnal. 3 cap. 9. ; Symmach. Epist. 40. lib. 1.; D. Th. 2. dist. 10. art. 3.; alii.
[*] God afore.
[2] Rob. Avesburiens. A. xvii. Ed. III.

Embassage in *Walsingham*,[1] correct *Regnum Angliæ*, and
read *Franciæ*. *Britain's* excellence in earth and air (whence
the *Macares*,[2] and particularly *Crete*, among the Greeks, had
their title) together with the Pope's exactions, in taxing,
collating, and provising of benefices (an intolerable wrong
to lay-men's inheritances, and the Crown revenues) gave
cause of this jealous conjecture ; seconded in the conceit of
them which derive *Albion* from ὅλβιος ;* whereto the Author
in his title and this verse alludes. But of *Albion* more
presently.

29. *Amongst whose iron rocks grim* Saturn *yet remains.*

Fabulous *Jupiter's* ill dealing with his father *Saturn* is
well known ; and that after deposing him, and his privities
cut off, he perpetually imprisoned him. *Homer*[3] joins *Japet*
with him, living in eternal night about the utmost ends of
the earth : which well fits the more Northern climate of
these Islands. Of them (dispersed in the *Deucalidonian* Sea)
in one most temperate, of gentle air, and fragrant with
sweetest odours, lying towards the Northwest, it is
reported,[4] that *Saturn* lies bound in iron chains, kept by
Briareus, attended by spirits, continually dreaming of
Jupiter's projects ; whereby his ministers prognosticate the
secrets of Fate. Every thirty years, divers of the adjacent
Islanders, with solemnity for success of the undertaken
voyage, and competent provision, enter the vast seas, and
at last, in this *Saturnian* Isle (by this name the Sea[5] is called
also) enjoy the happy quiet of the place ; some in studies
of nature, and the mathematics, which continue ; others in

---

[1] Hypodigmatis Neustriæ locus emendatus, sub anno 1344.
[2] Pompon. Mela l. 2. c. 7.
* Happy.
[3] Iliad θ. et Hesiod. in Theogon.
[4] Plutar. de facie in Orbe Lunæ. et l. de defect Oracul.
[5] Κρόνιον πέλαγος.

sensuality, which after thirty years return perhaps to their first home. This fabulous relation might be, and in part is, by Chymiques as well interpreted for mysteries of their art, as the common tale of *Dædalus'* Labyrinth, *Jason* and his *Argonautics*, and almost the whole chaos of Mythic inventions. But neither Geography (for I guess not where or what this Isle should be, unless that *des Macræons*[1] which *Pantagruell* discovered) nor the matter-self permits it less poetical (although a learned Greek Father[2] out of some credulous Historian seems to remember it) than the *Elysian* fields, which, with this, are always laid by *Homer* about the νείατα πείρατα γαίης;* a place whereof too large liberty was given to feign, because of the difficult possibility in finding the truth. Only thus note seriously, that this revolution of thirty years (which with some latitude is *Saturn's* natural motion) is especially[3] noted for the longest period, or age also among our *Druids;* and that in a particular form, to be accounted yearly from the sixth moon, as their New-year's-day: which circuit of time, divers of the ancients reckon for their generations in chronology; as store[4] of authors show you.

40. *They instantly again do* other bodies *take.*

You cannot be without understanding of this *Pythagorean* opinion of *transanimation* (I have like liberty to naturalize that word, as *Lipsius* had to make it a Roman, by turning μετεμψύχωσις†) if ever you read any that speaks of *Pythagoras*

---

[1] Rabelais.

[2] Clem. Alexandrin. Stromat. 6. Odyss. δ. Iliad. θ.

* Utmost ends of the earth. Upon affinity of this with the Cape de Finisterre, Goropius thinks the Elysian fields were by that Promontory of Spain. vide Strab. lib. γ.

[3] Plin. Hist. Nat. 16. cap. 44.

[4] Eustat. ad Iliad α. Herodot. lib. α. Suid. in γενεά. Censorin. de. Die Nat. cap. 17.

† A passing of souls from one to another.

(whom, for this particular, *Epiphanius* reckons among his heretics) or discourse largely of philosophical doctrine of the soul. But especially, if you affect it tempered with inviting pleasure, take *Lucian's* Cock, and his *Negromancy;* if in serious discourse, *Plato's Phædon,* and *Phædrus* with his followers. *Lipsius* doubts[1] whether *Pythagoras* received it from the *Druids,* or they from him, because in his travels he conversed as well with *Gaulish* as *Indian* Philosophers. Out of *Cæsar* and *Lucan* inform yourself with full testimony of this their opinion, too ordinary among the heathen and Jews also, which thought our *Saviour*[2] to be *Jeremy* or *Elias* upon this error; irreligious indeed, yet such a one, as so strongly erected moving spirits, that they did never

—— *redituræ parcere vitæ,*[*]

but most willingly devote their whole selves to the public service : and this was in substance the politic envoyes wherewith *Plato* and *Cicero* concluded their Commonwealths, as *Macrobius* hath observed. The Author, with pity, imputes to them their being led away in blindness of the time, and errors of their fancies; as all other the most divine philosophers (not lightened by the true word) have been, although (mere human sufficiencies only considered) some of them were sublimate far above earthly conceit : as especially *Hermes, Orpheus, Pythagoras* (first learning the soul's immortality of *Phérecydes*[3] a *Syrian*), *Seneca, Plato,* and *Plutarch;* which last two, in a Greek hymn of an Eastern Bishop,[4] are commended to Christ for such as came nearest to holiness of any untaught Gentiles. Of the *Druids* more large in fitter place.

[1] Physiolog. Stoic. 1. 3. dissert. 12.
[2] Justin Martyr. dialog.
[*] Spare in spending their lives, which they hoped to receive again.
[3] Cicer. Tusculan. 1.
[4] Joann Euchaitens. jampridem Etoniæ Græcè editus.

61. *Gave answer from their caves, and took what shapes they please.*

In the *Seame* (an Isle by the coast of the *French Bretaigne*) Nine Virgins, consecrate to perpetual chastity, were priests of a famous oracle, remembered by *Mela.* His printed books have *Gallicenas vocant ;* where that great critic *Turneb* reads *Galli Zenas,* * or *Lenas vocant.* But *White* of *Basingstoke* will have it *Cenas,*† as interpreting their profession and religion, which was in an arbitrary metamorphosing themselves, charming the winds (as of later time the Witches of *Lapland* and *Finland*), skill in predictions, more than natural medicine, and such like ; their kindness being in all chiefly to sailors.[1] But finding that in the *Syllies* were also of both sexes such kind of professors, that there were *Samnitæ,*[2] strangely superstitious in their *Bacchanals,* in an Isle of this coast (as is delivered by *Strabo*), and that the *Gauls, Britons, Indians* (twixt both whom and *Pythagoras* is found no small consent of doctrine) had their philosophers (under which name both priests and prophets of those times were included) called *Samanæi,*[3] and *Semni,* and (perhaps by corruption of some of these) *Samothei,* which, to make it Greek, might be turned into *Semnothei :* I doubted whether some relic of these words remained in that of *Mela,*[4] if you read *Cenas* or *Senas,* as contracted from *Samanæi ;* which by deduction from a root of some Eastern tongue, might signify as much as what we call Astrologers. But of this too much.

86. *Whose towns unto the* Saints *that lived here of yore.*

Not only to their own country Saints (whose names are there very frequent) but also to the *Irish ;* a people

---

* The Gauls call them Jupiter's Priests or Bawds. † Vain.

[1] Solin. Polyhist. cap. 35.

[2] Ἀμνῖται Dionys. Afro in περιηγ. multis. n. pro arbitrio antiquorum S. litera adest vel abest. vide Casaubon. ad α. Strab.

[3] Origen. κατὰ Κελσ. lib. α. Clem. Alex. strom. α. & β. Diogen. Laert. lib. α. [4] Conjecture upon Mela.

anciently (according to the name of the *Holy Island*[1] given to *Ireland*) much devoted to, and by the *English* much respected for their holiness and learning. I omit their fabulous *Cæsara*, niece to Noah, their *Bartholan,*[2] their *Ruan*, who, as they affirm, first planted religion, before Christ, among them : nor desire I your belief of this *Ruan's* age, which by their account (supposing him living 300 years after the Flood, and christened by Saint *Patrick*) exceeded 1700 years, and so was elder than that impostor, whose[3] feigned continuance of life and restless travels, ever since the Passion, lately offered to deceive the credulous. Only thus I note out of *Venerable Bede*, that in the *Saxon* times, it was usual for the *English* and *Gaulish* to make *Ireland*, as it were, both their University and Monastery, for studies of learning and divine contemplation, as the life of *Gildas*[4] also, and other frequent testimonies discover.

100. *From which he first was call'd the* Hoar-rock in the wood.

That the ocean (as in many other places of other countries) hath eaten up much of what was here once shore, is a common report, approved in the *Cornish* name of S. *Michael's* Mount ; which is **Careg Cowz in Clowz**[5] *i.e.*, the hoar-rock in the wood.

130. *And our* Main-Amber *here, and* Burien *trophy——*

Main-Amber, i.e., Ambrose's stone (not far from *Pensans*), so great that many men's united strength cannot remove it,

[1] Festo Avieno Insula sacra dicta Hibernia.
[2] Girald. Cambrens. dist. 3. cap. 2.
[3] Assuerus Cordonnier (dictus in historiâ Gallicâ Victoris ante triennium editâ *de la paix,* &c.) cuius partes olim egisse videntur Josephus Chartophylacius (referente Episcopo Armeniaco apud Matth. Paris in Hen. 3.) et Joannes ille (Guidoni Bonato in Astrologiâ sic indigitatus) Butta-deus.
[4] In Bibliothec. Floriacens. edit. per Joann. à Bosco.
[5] Carew Descript. Corn. Lib. 2.

yet with one finger you may wag it. The *Burien* trophy is 19 stones, circularly disposed, and, in the middle, one much exceeding the rest in greatness: by conjecture of most learned *Camden*, erected either under the Romans, or else by King *Athelstan* in his conquest of these parts.

190. *Were worthy of his end, but where he had his birth.*

Near *Camel*, about *Cumblan*, was *Arthur** slain by *Mordred*, and on the same shore, East from the river's mouth, born in *Tintagel* castle. *Gorlois* Prince of *Cornwall* at *Uther-Pendragon's* coronation, solemnized in *London*, upon divers too kind passages and lascivious regards twixt the King and his wife *Igerne*, grew very jealous, in a rage left the court, committed his wife's chastity to this castle's safeguard; and to prevent the wasting of his country (which upon this discontent was threatened) betook himself in other forts to martial preparation. *Uther* (his blood still boiling in lust), upon advice of *Ulfin Rhicaradoch*, one of his knights, by *Ambrose Merlin's* magic personated like *Gorlois*, and *Ulfin* like one *Jordan*, servant to *Gorlois*, made such successful use of their imposture, that (the Prince in the mean time slain) *Arthur* was the same night begotten, and verified that Νόθοι τε πολλοὶ γνησίων ἀμείνονες;[1] although *Merlin* by the rule of *Hermes*, or astrological *direction*, justified that he was conceived three hours after *Gorlois'* death; by this shift answering the dangerous imputation of bastardy to the heir of a crown. For *Uther*, taking *Igerne* to wife, left *Arthur* his successor in the Kingdom. Here have you a *Jupiter*, an *Alcmena*, an *Amphitryo*, a *Sosias*, and a *Mercury;* nor wants there scarce anything, but that truth-passing reports of poetical bards have made the birth an *Hercules.*

* Dictus hinc in Merlini vaticinio, *Aper Cornubiæ.*
[1] Euripid. Andromach. Bastards are ofttimes better than legitimates.

230. *Known by* one general name *upon this point that dwell.*

The name *Dumnonii, Damnonii,* or *Danmonii,* in *Solinus* and *Ptolemy,* comprehended the people of *Devonshire and Cornwall :* whence the *Lizard-promontory* is called *Damnium* in[1] *Marcian Heracleotes;* and *William* of *Malmsbury, Florence* of *Worcester, Roger* of *Hoveden,* and others style *Devonshire* by name of *Domnonia,* perhaps all from 𝔇uff neint, *i.e.,* low valleys in *British ;* wherein are most habitations of the country, as judicious *Camden* teaches me.

255. *Or that this foreland lies* furth'st out *into his sight, Which spreads his vigorous flames*————:

Fuller report of the excellence in wrastling and nimbleness of body, wherewith this Western people have been, and are famous, you may find in *Carew's* description of his country. But to give reason of the climate's nature for this prerogative in them, I think as difficult as to show why about the *Magellanic Straits* they are so white, about the *Cape de Buon Speranza* so black,[2] yet both under the same Tropic ; why the *Abyssins* are but tawny Moors, when as in the East Indian Isles, *Zeilan* and *Malabar,* they are very black, both in the same parallel ; or why we that live in this Northern latitude, compared with the Southern, should not be like affected from like cause. I refer it no more to the Sun than the special horsemanship in our *Northern men,* the nimble ability of the *Irish,* the fiery motions of the *French, Italian* jealousy, *German* liberty, *Spanish* puffed-up vanity, or those different and perpetual carriages of state-government, *haste* and *delay,*[3] which, as in-bred qualities, were remarkable in the two most martial people of *Greece.* The cause of *Ethiopian* blackness and curled hair was long since judiciously

---

[1] τὸ δάμνιον ἄκρον.

[2] Ortelius theatro.

[3] Thucydid. α et passim, de Athen. et Lacedæm.; et de Thebis et Chalcide. v. Columell, ι. de Re Rustic. cap. 4.

fetched[1] from the disposition of soil, air, water, and singular operations of the heavens ; with confutation of those which attribute it to the Sun's distance. And I am resolved that every land hath its so singular self-nature, and individual habitude with celestial influence, that human knowledge, consisting most of all in universality, is not yet furnished with what is requisite to so particular discovery : but for the learning of this point in a special treatise *Hippocrates, Ptolemy, Bodin,* others, have copious disputes.

312. *Which now the* envious world *doth slander for* a dream.

I should the sooner have been of the Author's opinion (in more than poetical form, standing for *Brute*) if in any *Greek* or *Latin* story authentic, speaking of *Æneas* and his planting in *Latium,* were mention made of any such like thing. To reckon the learned men which deny him, or at least permit him not in conjecture, were too long a catalogue : and indeed, this critic age scarce any longer endures any nation their first supposed Author's name ; not *Italus* to the *Italian,* not *Hispalus* to the *Spaniard, Bato* to the *Hollander, Brabo* to the *Brabantine, Francio* to the *French, Celtes* to the *Celt, Galathes* to the *Gaul, Scota* to the *Scot ;* no, nor scarce *Romulus* to his *Rome,* because of their unlikely and fictitious mixtures : especially this of *Brute,* supposed long before the beginning of the *Olympiads* (whence all time backward is justly called by *Varro,*[2] unknown or fabulous) some 2,700 and more years since, about *Samuel's* time, is most of all doubted. But (reserving my censure) I thus maintain the Author : although nor *Greek* nor *Latin,* nor our country stories of *Bede* and *Malmesbury* especially, nor that fragment yet re-

---

[1] Onesicrit. ap. Strabon. lib. ıc.
[2] Ap. Censorin. de Die Nat. cap. 21. Christoph. Heluici Chronologiam sequimur, ut accuratiùs temporum subductioni hoc loci incumbamus res postulat ; verùm et ille satis accuratè, qui Samuelis præfecturam A.M. 3850. haùt iniquo computo posuit.

maining of *Gildas*, speak of him ; and that his name were
not published until *Geffrey* of *Monmouth's* edition of the
British story, which grew and continues much suspected, in
much rejected ; yet observe that *Taliessin*, a great Bard,[1]
more than 1,000 years since affirms it ; *Nennius* (in some copies
he is under name of *Gildas*) above 800 years past, and the
Gloss of *Samuel Beaulan*, or some other, crept into his text,
mention both the common report, and descent from *Æneas;*
and withal (which I take to be *Nennius's* own), make him
son to one *Isicio* or *Hesichio* (perhaps meaning *Aschenaz*, of
whom more to the Fourth Song) continuing a pedigree to
Adam, joining these words : *This Genealogy I found by tradition of the ancients, which were first inhabitants of Britain.*[2]
In a manuscript Epistle of *Henry* of *Huntingdon*[3] to one
Warin, I read the Latin of this English : " *You ask me, Sir,
why omitting the succeeding reigns from* Brute *to* Julius Cæsar,
I begin my story at Cæsar ? *I answer you, that neither by word
nor writing, could I find any certainty of those times ; although
with diligent search I oft inquired it, yet this year in my journey
towards Rome, in the Abbey of Beccensam, even with amazement,
I found the story of* Brute :" and in his own printed book he
affirms, that what *Bede* had in this part omitted, was supplied to him by other authors ; of which *Girald* seems to
have had use. The British story of *Monmouth* was a translation (but with much liberty, and no exact faithfulness) of
a Welsh book, delivered to *Geffrey* by one *Walter* Arch-
deacon of *Oxford*, and hath been followed (the translator
being a man of some credit, and Bishop of S. *Asaph's*, under
King *Stephen*) by *Ponticus Virunnius* an Italian ; most of our

---

[1] ˜Io. Pris. def. Hist. Brit.

[2] Ex vetustiss & perpulchrè MS. Nennio sub titulo Gildæ.

[3] Lib. de summitatibus rerum qui 10 est historiarum in MS. Huntingdon began his History at Cæsar, but upon better inquisition
added Brute. Librum illum, in quem ait se incidisse, Nennium fuisse
obsignatis fermè tabulis sum potis adserere.

Country Historians of middle times, and this age, speaking
so certainly of him, that they blazon his coat[1] to you, *Two
Lions combatant, and crowned, Or, in a field gules ;* others, *Or,
a Lion passant gules;* and lastly, by Doctor *White* of *Basingstoke,* lately living at *Doway,* a *Count Palatine,* according to
the title bestowed by the *Imperials*[2] upon their professors.
Arguments are there also drawn from some affinity of the
Greek[3] tongue, and much of *Troian* and *Greek* names, with
the British. These things are the more enforced by *Cambro-
Britons,* through that universal desire, bewitching our Europe,
to derive their blood from *Troians,* which for them might
as well be by[4] supposition of their ancestors' marriages with
the hither deduced *Roman* Colonies, who by original were
certainly Troian if their antiquities deceive not. You may
add this weak conjecture ; that in those large excursions of
the Gauls, *Cimmerians,* and *Celts* (among them I doubt not
but were many Britons, having with them community of
nation, manners, climate, customs ; and *Brennus* himself is
affirmed a Briton) which under indistinct names when this
Western world was undiscovered, overran *Italy, Greece,* and
part of *Asia,* it is reported[5] that they came to *Troy* for safeguard ; presuming perhaps upon like kindness, as we read
of twixt the *Troians* and *Romans,* in their wars with *Antio-
chus*[6] (which was loving respect through contingence of blood)
upon like cause remembered to them by tradition. Briefly,
seeing no national story, except such as *Thucydides, Xenophon, Polybius, Cæsar, Tacitus, Procopius, Cantacuzen,* the late
Guicciardin, Commines, Macchiavel, and their like, which
were employed in the state of their times, can justify themselves but by tradition ; and that many of the Fathers and
Ecclesiastical Historians,[7] especially the Jewish Rabbins

---

[1] Harding. Nich. Upton. de re militari. 2.
[2] C. tit. de professorib. l. unica.   [3] Girald descript. cap. 15.
[4] Camden.   [5] Agesianax ap. Strab. lib. ιγ.   [6] Trog. Pomp. lib. 31.
[7] Melchior Canus lib. 11. de Aut. Hist. Hum. de his plurima.

(taking their highest learning of *Cabala* but from antique
and successive report) have inserted upon tradition many
relations current enough, where Holy Writ crosses them
not : you shall enough please *Saturn* and *Mercury,* presidents
of antiquity and learning, if with the Author you foster this
belief.   Where are the authorities (at least of the names) of
Jannes and *Jambres,*[1] the writings of *Enoch,* and other such
like, which we know by divine tradition were ?   The same
question might be of that infinite loss of authors, whose
names are so frequent in *Stephen, Athenæus, Plutarch, Clemens, Polybius, Livy,* others.   And how dangerous it were to
examine antiquities by a foreign writer (especially in those
times) you may see by the Stories of the *Hebrews,* delivered
in *Justin, Strabo, Tacitus,* and such other, discording and contrary (beside their infinite omissions) to *Moses'* infallible
context.   Nay he with his successor *Joshua* is copious in
the Israelites entering, conquering, and expelling the Gerge-
sites,* Jebusites, and the rest out of the Holy Land; yet no
witness have they of their transmigration, and peopling of
Africa, which by testimony of two pillars,[2] erected and en-
graven at *Tingis* hath been affirmed.   But you blame me
thus expatiating.   Let me add for the Author, that our
most judicious antiquary of the last age. *John Leland,*[3] with
reason and authority hath also for *Brute* argued strongly.

337. *Next,* Sylvius *him succeeds*———
So goes the ordinary descent ; but some make *Sylvius* son
to *Æneas,* to whom the prophecy was given :

> *Serum   Lavinia coniunx*
> *Educet sylvis regem regúmque parentem.*[4]

As you have in *Virgil.*

---

[1] Origen. ad 35. Matth.   * See the Sixth Song.
[2] Procopius de Bell. Vandilic. lib. *δ.*   [3] Ad Cyg. Cant.
[4] Æneid. vi. et ibid. Serv. Honoratus.

> After thy death Lavinia brings
> A king born in the woods, father of kings.

340. *His parent's only death*———

From these unfortunate accidents, one[1] will have his name *Brotus*, as from the Greek βροτὸς, *i.e.*, mortal; but rather (if it had pleased him) from βροτόεις, *i.e.*, bloody.

410. *He should descry the Isle of* Albion, *highly blest;*

His request to *Diana* in an hexastich, and her answer in an ogdoastich, hexameters and pentameters, discovered to him in a dream, with his sacrifice and ritual ceremonies are in the British story: the verses are pure Latin, which clearly (as is written of *Apollo*[2]) was not in those times spoken by *Diana*, nor understood by *Brute:* therefore in charity, believe it a translation; by *Gildas* a British Poet, as *Virunnius* tells you. The Author takes a justifiable liberty, making her call it *Albion*, which was the old name of this Isle, and remembered in *Pliny*, *Marcian*, the book περὶ κόσμου, falsely attributed to *Aristotle*, *Stephen*, *Apuleius*, others; and our Monk of *Bury*[3] calls *Henry the Fifth*

———**Protectour of Brute's Albion,**

often using that name for the Island. From *Albina*, daughter to *Dioclesian*[4] King of *Syria*, some fetch the name: others from a lady of that name, one of the *Danaids;* affirming their arrival[5] here, copulation with spirits, and bringing forth Giants; and all this above 200 years before *Brute*. But neither was there any such King in *Syria*, nor had *Danaus* (that can be found) any such daughter, nor travelled they for adventures, but by their father were newly married,[6] after slaughter of their husbands: briefly, nothing can be written more impudently fabulous. Others

[1] Basingstoch. lib. 1. [2] Cicer. de Divinat. lib. 2.
[3] Io. Lidgat. lib. de Bell. Troian. 5. et alibi sæpius.
[4] Chronic. S. Albani. [5] Hugo de Genes. ap. Harding. cap. 3.
[6] Pausanias in Laconic.

from King *Albion, Neptune's* son; from the Greek ὅλβιος*
others, or from (I know not what) *Olibius* a Celtish King,
remembered by the false *Manethon.* Follow them rather,
which will it *ab albis rupibus,*† whereby it is specially conspicuous. So was an Isle in the Indian Sea called *Leuca,*
i.e., white, and another in *Pontus,*[1] supposed also fortunate
and a receptacle of the souls of those great heroes, *Peleus*
and *Achilles.* Thus was a place by *Tyber* called *Albiona,*[2]
and the very name of *Albion* was upon the *Alps,* which from
like cause had their denomination; *Alpum* in the *Sabin*
tongue (from the Greek ἄλφον), signifying *white.* Some
much dislike this derivation, because[3] it comes from a tongue
(suppose it either *Greek* or *Latin*) not anciently communi-
cated to this Isle. For my part, I think clearly (against
the common opinion) that the name of *Britain* was known
to strangers before *Albion.* I could vouch the finding[4] of
one of the masts of *Hiero's* Ship ἐν τοῖς ὄρεσι τῆς Βρετανίας,‡
if judicious correction admonished me not rather to read
Βρεττιανῆς, *i.e.,* the now lower *Calabria* in *Italy,* a place above
all other, I remember, for store of ship-timber, commended[5]
by *Alcibiades* to the *Lacedæmonians.* But with better surety
can I produce the express name of Βρετανικῶν νήσων,§ out of
a writer[6] that lived and travelled in warfare with *Scipio;*
before whose time *Scylax* (making a Catalogue of twenty
other Isles) and *Herodotus* (to whom these Western parts
were by his confession unknown) never so much as speak
of us by any name. Afterward was *Albion* imposed upon

---

* Happy.   † From White Cliffs.

[1] παρὰ τὴν λευκὴν ἀκτὴν uti Euripides in Andromachâ, magis
vellem, quàm οὕνεκα ὁι τὰ παρέστι κενώπε τὰ λευκὰ τέτυκται, quod
canit Dionysius Afer.

[2] Strabo lib. δ. et Sixt. Pompeius in Alpum.

[3] Humf. Lhuid. iu Breviar.   [4] Moschion ap. Athen. Deipnosoph. ε.

‡ In the Hills of Britany.   [5] Thucydid. Hist. 6.   § British Isles.

[6] Polyb. Hist, γ. qui Jul. Cæsarem 200. fermè annos antevertit.

the cause before touched, expressing the old *British* name
𝕴𝖓𝖎𝖘-𝖖𝖚𝖎𝖓 :* which argument moves me before all other, for
that I see it usual in antiquity to have names among
strangers in their tongue just significant with the same in
the language of the country to which they are applied ;
as the Red Sea is (in *Strabo, Curtius, Stephen,* others) named
from a King of that coast called *Erythræus* (for, to speak of
red sand, as some, or red hills, as an old writer,[1] were but
refuges of shameful ignorance), which was surely the same
with *Esau,* called in Holy Writ *Ædom ;*[2] both signifying
(the one in Greek, the other in Hebrew) *red.* So the River
Nile,[3] in Hebrew and Egyptian called שׁחור, *i.e., black,* is
observed by that mighty prince of learning's state, *Joseph
Scaliger,* to signify the same colour in the word Αἴγυπτιος,
used for it by *Homer ;*[4] which is inforced also by the black
Statues[5] among the *Greeks,* erected in honour of *Nile,* named
also expressly *Melas :*[6] so in proper names of men ; *Simon
Zelotes,*[7] in *Luke,* is but *Simon* the *Canaunite,* and Ὑδογενής in
Orpheus the same with *Moses ; Janus* with *Oenotrus :* and in
our times those Authors, *Melanchthon, Magirus, Theocrenus,
Pelargus,* in their own language but *Swertearth, Cooke, Foun-
tain de Dieu, Storke.* Divers such other plain examples
might illustrate the conceit ; but, these sufficient. Take
largest etymological liberty, and you may have it from
Ellan-ban,[8] *i.e., the White Isle,* in Scottish, as they call their
Albania ; and to fit all together, the name of *Britain* from
𝕭𝖗𝖎𝖙𝖍-𝖎𝖓𝖎𝖘, *i.e., the Coloured Isle* in Welsh ; twixt which and

---

* The White Isle.
[1] Uranius in Arabic. ap. Steph. περὶ πολ. in Ερυθρά.
[2] Gen. 36. Num. 20.　　　　[3] Jesai. 23. Jirm. 2.
[4] Odyss. δ.—Αἰγύπτοιο διιπετέος ποταμοῖο. fortè tamen, fluvius
Ægypti, ut Hebræis מצרים נחר Gen. 15. commat. 17.
[5] Pausan. Arcadic. ή.
[6] Festus in Alcedo.
[7] Nebrissens. in quinquagen. cap. 49.
[8] Camden.

the Greek Βρύτον,[1] or Βρύτιον (used for a kind of drink
nearly like our beer), I would with the *French Forcatulus*
think affinity (as *Italy* was called *Oenotria*, from the name
of wine) were it not for that Βρύτον may be had from an
ordinary primitive, or else from Βρίθυ, *i.e.*, *sweet* (as *Solinus*
teaches, making *Britomart* signify as much as Sweet Virgin)
in the *Cretic* tongue. But this is to play with syllables, and
abuse precious time.

404. *The City* Turon *built*———

Understand *Tours* upon *Loire* in France, whose name and
foundation the inhabitants refer[2] to *Turnus* (of the same
time with *Æneas*, but whether the same which *Virgil* speaks
of, they know not) : his funeral monuments they yet show,
boast of, and from him idly derive the word *Torneaments*.
The *British* story says *Brute* built it (so also *Nennius*) and
from one *Turon*, *Brute's* nephew there buried, gives it the
name. *Homer* is cited for testimony : in his works extant
it is not found. But, because he had divers others (which
wrongful time hath filched from us) as appears in *Herodotus*
and *Suidas*, you may in favour think it to be in some of
those lost; yet I cannot in conscience offer to persuade you
that he ever knew the continent of *Gaul* (now, in part,
France) although a learned German[3] endeavours by force of
wit and etymology, to carry *Ulysses* (which he makes of
Elizza in *Genesis*) into *Spain*, and others before him[4] (but
falsely) into the Northern parts of *Scotland*. But for *Homer's*
knowledge, see the last note to the Sixth Song.

---

[1] Vocabulo Βρύτον usi sunt Æschylus, Sophocles, Hellanicus, Ar-
chilochus, Hecatæus ap. Athenæum Deipnosoph. 10. ἀντὶ τοῦ κριθίνου
οἴνου ejusdem ferè naturæ cum Sytho & Curmithe apud Dioscoridem
lib. of cap. σϛζ & σϛή. fortè παρὰ τὸ βρύειν.

[2] Andrè du Chesne en les Recherchez des villes 1. ca. 122.

[3] Goropius in Hispanic. 4. vide Strab. Geograph. γ. et alios de Oly-
sippone.

[4] Solin. Polyhist. cap. 35.

474. *So* mighty *were* that time *the men that lived there :*

If you trust our stories, you must believe the land then peopled with Giants, of vast bodily composture. I have read of the *Nephilim,* the *Rephaiim, Anakim, Og, Goliath,* and other in Holy Writ : of *Mars, Tityus, Antæus, Turnus,* and the *Titans* in *Homer, Virgil, Ovid ;* and of *Adam's* stature (according to *Jewish* fiction[1]) equalling at first the world's diameter : yet seeing that Nature (now as fertile as of old) hath in her effects determinate limits of quantity, that in *Aristotle's* time[2] (near 2,000 years since) their beds were but six foot ordinarily (nor is the difference, twixt ours and Greek dimension, much) and that near the same length was our Saviour's Sepulchre, as *Adamnan* informed King *Alfrid ;*[3] I could think that there now are some as great statures as for the most part have been, and that Giants were but of a somewhat more than vulgar excellence[4] in body, and martial performance. If you object the finding of great bones, which, measured by proportion, largely exceed our times, I first answer, that in some singulars, as monsters rather than natural, such proof hath been ; but withal, that both now and of ancient time,[5] the eye's judgment in such like hath been, and is, subject to much imposture ; mistaking bones of huge beasts for human.[6] *Claudius* brought over his elephants hither, and perhaps *Julius Cæsar* some, (for I have read[7] that he terribly frighted the *Britons,* with sight of one at *Coway stakes*) and so may you be deceived. But this is no place to examine it.

---

[1] Rabbi Eleazar ap. Riccium in epit. Talmud. cæterum in hâc re allegoriam vide ap. D. Cyprianum Serm. de montib. Sina & Sion.

[2] Προβλημ. μηχ. κε.   [3] Bed. Hist. Ecclesiast. 5. cap. 17.

[4] 'Εὐμεγέθεις καὶ ἐπιστάμενοι πόλεμον. Baruch. cap. γ. Consule, si placet, Scaliger. Exercitat. Becan. becceselan. 2.; Augustin. Civ. Dei 15. cap. 23.; Clement. Rom. Recognit. 1.; Lactant.; &c.

[5] Sueton. Octav. cap. 72.

[6] Dio Cass. lib. ξ.

[7] Polyæn. Strategemat. η. in Cæsare.

506. *Of* Corin, Cornwall *call'd, to his immortal fame.*

So, if you believe the tale of *Corin,* and *Gogmagog :* but
rather imagine the name of *Cornwall* from this promontory
of the Land's End ; extending itself like a horn,[1] which in
most tongues is *Corn,* or very near.   Thus was a promontory in *Cyprus,*[2] called *Cerastes,* and in the now *Candy* or
Crete, and *Gazaria,* (the old *Taurica Chersonesus*) another
titled Κρϼοῦ μέτωπον,* and *Brundusium* in *Italy* had name from
Brendon or *Brention,*[3] *i.e., a Hart's-head,* in the *Messapian*
tongue, for similitude of horns.   But *Malmesbury*[4] thus :
They are called Cornewalshmen, *because being seated in the
Western part of* Britain, *they lie over against a horn* (a promontory) *of* Gaul.   The whole name is, as if you should
say *Corne-wales ;* for hither in the *Saxon* conquest the *British*
called *Welsh* (signifying the people, rather than strangers as
the vulgar opinion wills) made transmigration : whereof an
old Rhymer :[5]

𝕿𝖍𝖊 𝖇𝖊𝖇𝖊 𝖙𝖍𝖆𝖙 𝖇𝖊𝖗 𝖔𝖋 𝖍𝖔𝖒 𝖇𝖎𝖑𝖊𝖇𝖊𝖉, 𝖆𝖘 𝖎𝖓 𝕮𝖔𝖗𝖓𝖇𝖆𝖎𝖑𝖊 𝖆𝖓𝖉
        𝖂𝖆𝖑𝖎𝖘,
𝕭𝖗𝖚𝖙𝖔𝖓𝖘 𝖓𝖊𝖗 𝖓𝖆𝖒𝖔𝖗𝖊 𝖞𝖈𝖑𝖚𝖕𝖊𝖉, 𝖆𝖈 𝖂𝖆𝖑𝖊𝖞𝖘 𝖞𝖇𝖎𝖘.

Such was the language of your fathers between 300 and
400 years since : and of it more hereafter.

520. *The deluge of the* Dane *exactly to have song.*

In the fourth year of *Brithric,*[6] King of the West *Saxons,*
at *Portland,* and at this place (which makes the fiction
proper) three ships of *Danish* Pirates entered : the King's
Lieutenant offering inquisition of their name, state, and
cause of arrival, was the first *English* man, in this first

---

[1] Cornugallia dicta est Henrico Huntingdonio, aliis.
[2] Strabo lib. ζ. & ι.; Steph.; Mel.; Plin.; Geographi passim.
* Ram's head.
[3] Seleucus ap. Steph. Βρεντης. et Suid. in Βρενδ.
[4] De Gest. Reg. 2. cap. 6.   [5] Rob. Glocestrens.
[6] Anno 787.

Danish invasion, slain by their hand. Miserable losses and continual, had the English by their frequent irruptions from this time till the *Norman* Conquest ; twixt which intercedes 279 years : and that less account of 230,[1] during which space this land endured their bloody slaughters, according to some men's calculation, begins at King *Ethelulph ;* to whose time *Henry* of *Huntingdon,* and *Roger* of *Hoveden,* refer the beginning of the *Danish* mischiefs, continuing so intolerable, that under King *Ethelred* was there begun a tribute insupportable (yearly afterward exacted from the subjects) to give their King *Swain,* and so prevent their insatiate rapine. It was between 30 & 40 thousand pounds[2] (for I find no certainty of it, so variable are the reports) not instituted for pay of Garrisons, imployed in service against them (as upon the misunderstanding of the *Confessor's* Laws some ill affirm) but to satisfy the wasting enemy ; but so that it ceased not, although their spoils ceased, but was collected to the use of the Crown until King *Stephen* promised to remit it. For indeed S. *Edward* upon imagination of seeing a devil dancing about the whole sum of it lying .in his treasury, moved in conscience, caused it to be repaid, and released the duty, as *Ingulph* Abbot of *Crowland* tells you : yet observe him, and read *Florence* of *Worcester, Marian* the Scot, *Henry* of *Huntingdon,* and *Roger Hoveden,* and you will confess that what I report thus from them is truth, and different much from what vulgarly is received. Of the *Danish* race were afterward three Kings, *Cnut, Hardcnut,* and *Harold* the First.

549. *His* offspring *after long expuls'd the* inner land.

After some 1,500 years from the supposed arrival of the

---

[1] Audacter lege ducentos vice τοῦ trecentos in fol. 237. Hovedeni, cui prologum libro quinto H. Huntindon. committas licet. *Dangelt* showed against a common error, both in remission and institution.

[2] Mariano Scoto 36,000. libræ, et Florentio Wigorn.

Troians,* their posterity were by incroachment of *Saxons,
Jutes, Angles, Danes* (for among the *Saxons* that noble *Douz*[1]
wills that surely *Danes* were) *Frisians*[2] and *Franks* driven
into those Western parts of the now *Wales* and *Cornwales.*
Our stories have this at large, and the *Saxon* Heptarchy;
which at last by public edict of King *Ecbert* was called
Enƺle-lonꝺ.   But *John* Bishop of *Chartres*[3] saith it had that
name from the first coming of the *Angles;* others from
the name of *Hengist*[4] (a matter probable enough) whose
name, wars, policies, and government, being first invested
by *Vortigern* in *Kent,* are above all the other *Germans* most
notable in the *British* stories: and *Harding*

He calleꝺ it Engestes **lanꝺ,
Which afterwarꝺ was shorteꝺ, anꝺ calleꝺ England.**

Hereto accords that of one of our country old Poets :[5]

Engisti linguâ canit insula Bruti.†

If I should add the idle conceits of *Godfrey* of *Viterbo,* draw-
ing the name from I know not what *Angri,* the insertion of
L. for *R.* by Pope *Gregory,* or the conjectures of unlimitable
phantasy, I should unwillingly, yet with them impudently,
·err.

---

* Chronologiam hùc spectantem consulas in illustrat. ad. 4. Cant.
[1] Jan. Douz. Annal. Holland. 1. & 6.
[2] Procopius in frag. δ. lib. Gothic. ap. Camden. Name of England.
[3] Policratic. lib. 6. cap. 17.
[4] Chronic. S. Albani.; Hector. Boet. Scotor. Hist. 7.
[5] I. Gower Epigram. in Confess. Amantis.
† Britain sings in Hengist's tongue.

THE SECOND SONG.

MARCH strongly forth my Muse, whilst yet the tem-
    perate air
    Invites us, eas'ly on to hasten our repair. [great)
    Thou powerful God of flames (in verse divinely
Touch my invention so with thy true genuine heat,

That high and noble things I slightly may not tell,
Nor light and idle toys my lines may vainly swell ;
But as my subject serves, so high or low to strain,
And to the varying earth so suit my varying vein,
That Nature in my work thou may'st thy power avow ;
That as thou first found'st Art, and didst her rules allow, 10
So I, to thine own self that gladly near would be,
May herein do the best, in imitating thee :
As thou hast here a hill, a vale there, there a flood,
A mead here, there a heath, and now and then a wood,
These things so in my Song I naturally may show ; 15
Now, as the mountain high ; then, as the valley low ;
Here, fruitful as the mead ; there as the heath be bare ;
Then, as the gloomy wood, I may be rough, though rare.
 Through the *Dorsetian* fields that lie in open view,
My progress I again must seriously pursue, 20
From *Marshwood's* fruitful Vale my journey on to make :
(As *Phœbus* getting up out of the Eastern lake,
Refresh'd with ease and sleep, is to his labour prest ;
Even so the labouring Muse, here baited with this rest.)
Whereas the little *Lim* along doth eas'ly creep, 25
And *Car*, that coming down unto the troubled deep, [bank,
Brings on the neighbouring *Bert*, whose batning mellow'd
From all the British soils, for hemp most hugely rank
Doth bear away the best ; to *Bert-port* which hath gain'd
That praise from every place, and worthily obtain'd 30
Our cordage[1] from her store and cables should be made,
Of any in that kind most fit for marine trade :
Not sever'd from the shore, aloft where *Chesill* lifts [drifts,
Her ridgéd snake-like sands, in wrecks and smould'ring
Which by the South-wind rais'd, are heav'd on little hills :35
Whose valleys with his flows when foaming *Neptune* fills,

---

[1] By Act of Parliament, 21 Hen. 8.

Upon a thousand swans* the naked Sea-Nymphs ride
Within the oozy pools, replenish'd every tide :
Which running on, the Isle of *Portland* pointeth out
Upon whose moisted skirt with sea-weed fring'd about,   40
The bastard coral breeds, that, drawn out of the brack,
A brittle stalk becomes, from greenish turn'd to black :
§ Which th' ancients, for the love that they to *Isis* bare,
(Their Goddess most ador'd) have sacred for her hair.
Of which the *Naïdes*, and the blue *Nereids*[1] make   45
Them tawdries[2] for their necks : when sporting in the lake,
They to their secret bow'rs the Sea-gods entertain.
Where *Portland* from her top doth over-peer the main ;
Her rugged front empal'd (on every part) with rocks,
Though indigent of wood, yet fraught with woolly flocks : 50
Most famous for her folk excelling with the sling,
Of any other here this Land inhabiting ;
That therewith they in war offensively might wound,
If yet the use of shot invention had not found.   [path :
Where, from the neighbouring hills her passage *Wey* doth
Whose haven, not our least that watch the mid-day, hath 56
The glories that belong unto a complete Port ;
Though *Wey* the least of all the *Naïdes* that resort
To the *Dorsetian* sands from off the higher shore.

    The *Froome* (a nobler Flood) the Muses doth implore   60
Her mother *Blackmore's* state they sadly would bewail ;
Whose big and lordly oaks once bore as brave a sail
As they themselves that thought the largest shades to spread :
But man's devouring hand, with all the earth not fed,
Hath hew'd her timber down. Which wounded, when it fell,
By the great noise it made, the workmen seem'd to tell   66

---

* The beauty of the many swans upon the Chesills, noted in this poetical delicacy.
[1] Sea-Nymphs.
[2] A kind of necklaces worn by country wenches.

The loss that to the Land would shortly come thereby,
Where no man ever plants to our posterity :
That when sharp Winter shoots her sleet and hardned hail,
Or sudden gusts from sea the harmless deer assail,   70
The shrubs are not of pow'r to shield them from the wind.
　　Dear Mother, quoth the *Froome*, too late (alas) we find
The softness of thy sward continued through thy soil,
To be the only cause of unrecover'd spoil :
When scarce the *British* ground a finer grass doth bear ;   75
And wish I could, quoth she, (if wishes helpful were)
§ Thou never by that name of *White-hart* hadst been known,
But styléd *Blackmore* still, which rightly was thine own.
For why, that change foretold the ruin of thy state :
Lo, thus the world may see what 'tis to innovate.   80
　　By this, her own nam'd Town* the wand'ring *Froome* had
And quitting in her course old *Dorcester* at last,   [pass'd :
Approaching near the *Poole*, at *Warham* on her way,
As eas'ly she doth fall into the peaceful Bay,
Upon her nobler side, and to the Southward near,   85
Fair *Purbeck* she beholds, which nowhere hath her peer,
So pleasantly in-isl'd on mighty *Neptune's* marge,
A Forest-Nymph, and one of chaste *Diana's* charge,
Imploy'd in woods and launds her deer to feed and kill :
§ On whom the wat'ry God would oft have had his will ; 90
And often her hath woo'd, which never would be won ;
But, *Purbeck* (as profess'd a huntress and a nun)
The wide and wealthy Sea, nor all his power, respects :
Her marble-minded breast, impregnable, rejects
The ugly orks,[1] that for their lord the *Ocean* woo.   95
　　Whilst *Froome* was troubled thus where nought she hath
The *Piddle*, that this while bestirr'd her nimble feet, [to do,
In falling to the *Poole* her sister *Froome* to meet,

　　　* *Frampton.*
　　[1] Monsters of the sea, supposed Neptune's Guard.

And having in her train two little slender rills
(Besides her proper spring) wherewith her banks she fills,₁₀₀
To whom since first the world this later name her lent,
Who anciently was known to be instyléd *Trent*,¹
Her small assistant brooks her second name have gain'd.
Whilst *Piddle* and the *Froome* each other entertain'd,
Oft praising lovely *Poole*, their best-belovéd Bay,   105
Thus *Piddle* her bespake, to pass the time away :
When *Poole* (quoth she) was young, a lusty sea-born lass,
Great *Albion* to this Nymph an earnest suitor was ;
And bare himself so well, and so in favour came,
That he in little time, upon this lovely dame,   110
§ Begot three maiden Isles, his darlings and delight :
The eldest, *Brunksey* call'd ; the second, *Fursey* hight ;
The youngest and the last, and lesser than the other,
Saint *Helen's* name doth bear, the dilling of her mother.
And, for the goodly *Poole*² was one of *Thetis'* train,   115
Who scorn'd a Nymph of hers her virgin-band should
          stain,
Great *Albion* (that forethought, the angry Goddess would
Both on the dam and brats take what revenge she could)
I' th' bosom of the *Poole* his little children plac'd :
First *Brunksey ; Fursey* next ; and little *Helen* last ;   120
Then, with his mighty arms doth clip the *Poole* about,
To keep the angry Queen, fierce *Amphitrite*, out.
Against whose lordly might she musters up her waves ;
And strongly thence repuls'd (with madness) scolds and
          raves.
     When now, from *Poole*, the Muse (up to her pitch to get)
Herself in such a place from sight doth almost set,   126
As by the active pow'r of her commanding wings,
She (falcon-like) from far doth fetch those plenteous springs,

---

¹ The ancient name of *Piddle*.   ² The story of *Poole*.

Where *Stour** receives her strength from six clear fountains fed;
Which gathering to one stream from every several head, 130
Her new-beginning bank her water scarcely wields ;
And fairly ent'reth first on the *Dorsetian* fields :
Where *Gillingham* with gifts that for a god were meet,
(Enamell'd paths, rich wreaths, and every sov'reign sweet
The earth and air can yield, with many a pleasure mixt) 135
Receives her.   Whilst there pass'd great kindness them be-
The Forest her bespoke : How happy floods are ye, [twixt,
From our predestin'd plagues that privilegéd be ;
Which only with the fish which in your banks do breed,
And daily there increase, man's gourmandize can feed? 140
But had this wretched age such uses to imploy
Your waters, as the woods we lately did enjoy,
Your channels they would leave as barren by their spoil,
As they of all our trees have lastly left our soil.
Insatiable Time thus all things doth devour :   145
Whatever saw the sun, that is not in Time's pow'r ?
Ye fleeting streams last long, outliving many a day :
But, on more stedfast things Time makes the strongest prey.
    § Now tow'rds the *Solent* sea as *Stour* her way doth ply,
On *Shaftsbury* (by chance) she cast her crystal eye,   150
From whose foundation first, such strange reports arise
§ As brought into her mind the *Eagle's* prophecies ;
Of that so dreadful plague, which all great *Britain* swept,
From that which highest flew to that which lowest crept,
Before the *Saxon* thence the *Briton* should expell,   155
And all that thereupon successively befell.
    How then the bloody *Dane* subdued the *Saxon* race ;
And, next, the *Norman* took possession of the place :
Those ages, once expir'd, the Fates to bring about,
The *British* line restor'd ; the *Norman* linage out.   160

* *Stour* riseth from six fountains.

§ Then, those prodigious signs to ponder she began,
Which afterward again the *Britons'* wrack fore-ran ;
How here the owl at noon in public streets was seen,
As though the peopled towns had way-less deserts been.
And whilst the loathly toad out of his hole doth crawl,   165
And makes his fulsome stool amid the Prince's hall,
The crystal fountain turn'd into a gory wound,
And bloody issues brake (like ulcers) from the ground ;
The seas against their course with double tides return,
And oft were seen by night like boiling pitch to burn.   170
   Thus thinking, lively *Stour* bestirs her tow'rds the main ;
Which *Lidden* leadeth out : then *Dulas* bears her train
From *Blackmore*, that at once their wat'ry tribute bring :
When, like some childish wench, she loosely wantoning,
With tricks and giddy turns seems to in-isle the shore.   175
Betwixt her fishful banks, then forward she doth scour,
Until she lastly reach clear *Alen* in her race :
Which calmly cometh down from her dear mother Chase,[1]
Of *Cranburn* that is call'd ; who greatly joys to see
A riveret born of her, for *Stour's* should reckon'd be,   180
Of that renownéd flood, a favourite highly grac'd.
   Whilst *Cranburn*, for her child so fortunately plac'd,
With echoes every way applauds her *Alen's* state,
A sudden noise from *Holt*[2] seems to congratulate
With *Cranburn* for her brook so happily bestow'd :   185
Where to her neighb'ring Chase, the courteous Forest show'd
So just conceivéd joy, that from each rising hurst,[3]
Where many a goodly oak had carefully been nurst,
The *Sylvans* in their songs their mirthful meeting tell ;
And *Satyrs*, that in slades and gloomy dimbles dwell,   190
Run whooting to the hills to clap their ruder hands.
   As *Holt* had done before, so *Canford's* goodly launds

[1] *Cranburn* Chase.

[2] *Holt* Forest.   [3] A wood in English.

(Which lean upon the *Poole*) enrich'd with coppras veins,
Rejoice to see them join'd. When down from *Sarum* Plains
Clear *Avon* coming in, her sister *Stour* doth call,   195
§ And at *New-forest's* foot into the sea do fall,
Which every day bewail that deed so full of dread
Whereby she (now so proud) became first forested :
She now who for her sight even boundless seem'd to lie,
§ Her being that receiv'd by *William's* tyranny ;   200
Providing laws to keep those beasts here planted then,
Whose lawless will from hence before had driven men ;
That where the hearth was warm'd with Winter's feasting fires,
The melancholy hare is form'd in brakes and briars :
The agéd ranpick trunk where plow-men cast their seed,   205
And churches overwhelm'd with nettles, fern, and weed,
By Conquering *William* first cut off from every trade,
That here the *Norman* still might enter to invade ;
That on this vacant place, and unfrequented shore,
New forces still might land, to aid those here before.   210
But she, as by a King and Conqueror made so great,
By whom she was allow'd and limited her seat,
Into her own-self praise most insolently brake,
And her less fellow-Nymphs, *New-forest* thus bespake :
[1] Thou *Buckholt,* bow to me, so let thy sister *Bere ;*   215
Chute, kneel thou at my name on this side of the Shiere :
Where, for their goddess, me the *Dryads*[2] shall adore,
With *Waltham,* and the *Bere,* that on the sea-worn shore,
See at the Southern Isles the tides at tilt to run ;
And *Woolmer* placéd hence upon the rising sun,   220
With *Ashholt* thine ally (my Wood-Nymphs) and with you,
Proud *Pamber* tow'rds the North, ascribe me worship due.
Before my princely state let your poor greatness fall ;
And vail your tops to me, the Sov'reign of you all.

---

[1] The forests of Hampshire, with their situations.
[2] Nymphs that live and die with oaks.

Amongst the Rivers, so, great discontent there fell.   225
Th' efficient cause whereof (as loud report doth tell)
Was, that the sprightly *Test* arising up in *Chute*,
To *Itchin*, her ally, great weakness should impute,
That she, to her own wrong, and every other's grief,
Would needs be telling things exceeding all belief :   230
For, she had given it out *South-hampton* should not lose
§ Her famous *Bevis* so, wer't in her power to choose ;
§ And, for great *Arthur's* seat, her *Winchester* prefers,
Whose old *Round-table* yet she vaunteth to be hers :
And swore, th' inglorious time should not bereave her
     right :   235
But what it could obscure, she would reduce to light.
For, from that wondrous Pond [1] whence she derives her head,
And places by the way, by which she's honoréd ;
(Old *Winchester*, that stands near in her middle way,
And *Hampton*, at her fall into the *Solent* sea)   240
She thinks in all the Isle not any such as she,
And for a demi-god she would related be.
    Sweet sister mine (quoth *Test*) advise you what you
     do ;
Think this : For each of us, the Forests here are two :
Who, if you speak a thing whereof they hold can take,   245
Be't little, or be't much, they double will it make :
Whom *Humble* helpeth out ; a handsome proper Flood,
In courtesy well-skill'd, and one that knew her good.
    Consider, quoth this Nymph, the times be curious now,
And nothing of that kind will any way allow.   250
Besides, the Muse hath next the *British* cause in hand,
About things later done that now she cannot stand.
    The more they her persuade, the more she doth persist ;
Let them say what they will, she will do what she list.

[1] A pool near unto *Alresford*, yielding an unusual abundance of
water.

She styles herself their Chief, and swears she will com-
    mand ;   255
And, whatsoe'er she saith, for oracles must stand.
Which when the Rivers heard, they further speech forbare.
And she (to please herself that only seem'd to care)
To sing th' achievement great of *Bevis* thus began :
    Redoubted Knight (quoth she); O most renownéd
    man !   ·   260
Who, when thou wert but young, thy mother durst reprove
(Most wickedly seduc'd by the unlawful love
Of *Mordure*, at that time the *Almain* Emperor's son)
That she thy sire to death disloyally had done.
    Each circumstance whereof she largely did relate ;   265
Then, in her song pursu'd his mother's deadly hate ;
And how (by *Saber's* hand) when she suppos'd him dead,
Where long upon the Downs a shepherd's life he led ;
Till by the great recourse, he came at length to know
The country there-about could hardly hold the show   270
His mother's marriage feast to fair *South-hampton* drew,
Being wedded to that lord who late her husband slew :
Into his noble breast which pierc'd so wondrous deep,
That (in the poor attire he us'd to tend the sheep,
And in his hand his hook) unto the town he went ;   275
As having in his heart a resolute intent
Or manfully to die, or to revenge his wrong :
Where pressing at the gate the multitude among,
The porter at that place his entrance that forbad
(Supposing him some swain, some boist'rous country-lad) 280
Upon the head he lent so violent a stroke,
That the poor empty skull like some thin potsherd broke,
The brains and mingled blood were spertled on the wall.
Then hasting on he came into the upper hall,
Where murderous *Mordure* sate embracéd by his bride :   285

Who (guilty in himself) had he not *Bevis* spied,
His bones had with a blow been shatt'red : but, by chance
(He shifting from his place, whilst *Bevis* did advance
His hand, with greater strength his deadly foe to hit,
And missing him) his chair he all to shivers split :   290
Which strook his mother's breast with strange and sundry
      fears,
That *Bevis*, being then but of so tender years,
Durst yet attempt a thing so full of death and doubt.
And, once before deceiv'd, she newly cast about
To rid him out of sight ; and, with a mighty wage,   295
Won such, themselves by oath as deeply durst ingage,
To execute her will : who shipping him away
(And making forth their course into the mid-land sea)
As they had got before, so now again for gold
To an *Armenian* there that young *Alcides* sold :   300
Of all his gotten prize, who (as the worthiest thing,
And fittest where-withal to gratify his king)
Presented that brave youth ; the splendour of whose eye
A wondrous mixture show'd of grace and majesty :
Whose more than man-like shape, and matchless stature,
      took   305
The king ; that often us'd with great delight to look
Upon that English Earl.   But though the love he bore
To *Bevis* might be much, his daughter ten times more
Admir'd the god-like man : who, from the hour that first
His beauty she beheld, felt her soft bosom pierc'd   310
With *Cupid's* deadliest shaft ; that *Josian*, to her guest,
Already had resign'd possession of her breast.
    Then sang she, in the fields how as he went to sport,
And those damn'd *Paynims* heard, who in despiteful sort
Derided *Christ* the Lord ; for his Redeemer's sake   315
He on those heathen hounds did there such slaughter make,

That whilst in their black mouths their blasphemies they drew,
They headlong went to hell. As also how he slew
That cruel Boar, whose tusks turn'd up whole fields of grain,
(And, rooting, raiséd hills upon the level plain ;   320
Digg'd caverns in the earth, so dark and wond'rous deep
As that, into whose mouth the desperate *Roman** leap) :
And cutting off his head, a trophy thence to bear ;
The foresters that came to intercept it there,
How he their scalps and trunks in chips and pieces cleft, 325
And in the fields (like beasts) their mangled bodies left.
   As to his further praise, how for that dangerous fight
The great *Armenian* King made noble *Bevis* Knight :
And having raiséd pow'r, *Damascus* to invade,
The General of his force this English hero made.   330
Then, how fair *Josian* gave him *Arundell* his steed,
And *Morglay* his good sword, in many a gallant deed
Which manfully he tried.   Next, in a buskin'd† strain,
Sung how himself he bore upon *Damascus*' Plain
(That dreadful battle) where with *Bradamond* he fought ; 335
And with his sword and steed such earthly wonders wrought,
As even amongst his foes him admiration won ;
Incount'ring in the throng with mighty *Radison ;*
And lopping off his arms, th' imperial standard took.
At whose prodigious fall, the conquer'd foe forsook   340
The field ; where, in one day so many peers they lost,
So brave commanders, and so absolute an host,
As to the humbled earth took proud *Damascus* down,
Then tributary made to the *Armenian* Crown.
And how at his return, the king (for service done,   345
The honour to his reign, and to *Armenia* won)
In marriage to this Earl the Princess *Josian* gave ;

---

* *Curtius*, that for his country's sake so lavished his life.
† Lofty.

As into what distress him Fortune after drave,
To great *Damascus* sent ambassador again;
When, in revenge of theirs, before by *Bevis* slain,   350
(And now, at his return, for that he so despis'd
Those idols unto whom they daily sacrific'd :
Which he to pieces hew'd and scatt'red in the dust)
They, rising, him by strength into a dungeon thrust;
In whose black bottom, long two serpents had remain'd   355
(Bred in the common sewer that all the city drain'd)
Empois'ning with their smell; which seiz'd him for their
      prey :
With whom in struggling long (besmear'd with blood and
      clay)
He rent their squalid chaps, and from the prison 'scap'd.

As how adult'rous *Joure*, the King of *Mambrant*, rap'd 360
Fair *Josian* his dear love, his noble sword and steed :
Which afterward by craft, he in a palmer's weed
Recover'd, and with him from *Mambrant* bare away.

And with two lions how he held a desperate fray,
Assailing him at once, that fiercely on him flew :   365
Which first he tam'd with wounds, then by the necks them ·
      drew,
And 'gainst the hard'ned earth their jaws and shoulders
      burst;
And that (*Goliah*-like) great *Ascupart* inforc'd
To serve him for a slave, and by his horse to run.

At *Colein* as again the glory that he won   370
On that huge Dragon, like the country to destroy;
Whose sting strook like a lance : whose venom did destroy
As doth a general plague : his scales like shields of brass;
His body, when he mov'd, like some unwieldy mass,
Even bruis'd the solid earth. Which boldly having song, 375
With all the sundry turns that might thereto belong,
Whilst yet she shapes her course how he came back to show

                              4—2

What pow'rs he got abroad, how them he did bestow ;
In *England* here again, how he by dint of sword
Unto his ancient lands and titles was restor'd,   380
New-forest cried, enough : and *Waltham* with the *Bere*,
Both bade her hold her peace ; for they no more would hear.
And for she was a flood, her fellows nought would say ;
But slipping to their banks, slid silently away.

When as the pliant Muse, with fair and even flight,   385
Betwixt her silver wings is wafted to the *Wight :*[1]
That Isle, which jutting out into the sea so far,
Her offspring traineth up in exercise of war ;
Those pirates to put back that oft purloin her trade,
Or *Spaniards,* or the *French* attempting to invade.   390
Of all the Southern Isles she holds the highest place,
And evermore hath been the great'st in *Britain's* grace :
Not one of all her Nymphs her sov'reign favoreth thus,
Imbracéd in the arms of old *Oceanus.*
For none of her account so near her bosom stand,   395
'Twixt *Penwith's*[2] furthest point and *Goodwin's*[2] queachy sand,
Both for her seat and soil, that far before the other,
Most justly may account great *Britain* for her mother.
A finer fleece than hers not *Lemster's* self can boast,
Nor *Newport* for her mart, o'ermatch'd by any coast.   400
To these, the gentle South, with kisses smooth and soft,
Doth in her bosom breathe, and seems to court her oft.
Besides, her little rills, her in-lands that do feed,
Which with their lavish streams do furnish every need :
And meads, that with their fine soft grassy towels stand   405
To wipe away the drops and moisture from her hand,
And to the North, betwixt the fore-land and the firm,
She hath that narrow Sea,[3] which we the *Solent* term :

[1] Isle of *Wight.*   [2] The forelands of *Cornwall* and *Kent.*
[3] The *Solent.*

Where those rough ireful tides, as in her straits they meet,
With boist'rous shocks and roars each other rudely greet : 410
Which fiercely when they charge, and sadly make retreat,
Upon the bulwark'd forts of *Hurst* and *Calshot*[1] beat,
Then to *South-hampton* run : which by her shores supplied
(As *Portsmouth*[2] by her strength) doth vilify their pride ;
  Both roads that with our best may boldly hold their
      plea, 415
Nor *Plimmouth's* self hath born more braver ships than they ;
That from their anchoring bays have travailéd to find
Large *China's* wealthy realms, and view'd the either *Ind*,
The pearly rich *Peru ;* and with as prosperous fate,
Have borne their full-spread sails upon the streams of *Plate :*
Whose pleasant harbours oft the seaman's hope renew, 421
To rig his late-craz'd bark, to spread a wanton clue ;
Where they with lusty sack, and mirthful sailors' songs,
Defy their passéd storms, and laugh at *Neptune's* wrongs :
The danger quite forgot wherein they were of late ; 425
Who half so merry now as master and his mate ?
And victualling again, with brave and man-like minds
To seaward cast their eyes, and pray for happy winds.
But, partly by the floods sent thither from the shore,
And islands that are set the bord'ring coast before : 430
As one amongst the rest, a brave and lusty dame
Call'd *Portsey*, whence that Bay of *Portsmouth* hath her name :
By her, two little Isles, her handmaids (which compar'd
With those within the *Poole*, for deftness not out-dar'd)
The greater *Haling* hight : and fairest though by much, 435
Yet *Thorney* very well, but somewhat rough in touch.
Whose beauties far and near divulgéd by report,
And by the *Tritons*[3] told in mighty *Neptune's* court,

---

[1] Two castles in the sea.   [2] *Portsmouth.*
[3] Neptune's Trumpeters.

Old *Proteus*[1] hath been known to leave his finny herd,
And in their sight to sponge his foam-bespawléd beard   440
The sea-gods, which about the wat'ry kingdom keep,
Have often for their sakes abandonéd the deep ;
That *Thetis* many a time to *Neptune* hath complain'd,
How for those wanton Nymphs her ladies were disdain'd :
And there arose such rut th' unruly rout among,   445
That soon the noise thereof through all the ocean rong.

  § When *Portsey,* weighing well the ill to her might grow,
In that their mighty stirs might be her overthrow,
She strongly strait'neth-in the entrance to her Bay ;
That,[2] of their haunt debarr'd, and shut out to the sea   450
(Each small conceivéd wrong helps on distemper'd rage.)
No counsel could be heard their choler to assuage :
When every one suspects the next that is in place
To be the only cause and means of his disgrace.
Some coming from the East, some from the setting sun,   455
The liquid mountains still together mainly run ;
Wave woundeth wave again ; and billow billow gores ;
And topsy-turvy so, fly tumbling to the shores.
From hence the *Solent* sea, as some men thought, might stand
Amongst those things which we call *Wonders of our Land.*

  When towing up that stream,[3] so negligent of fame,   461
As till this very day she yet conceals her name ;
By *Bert* and *Waltham* both that's equally imbrac'd,
And lastly, at her fall, by *Tichfield* highly grac'd.
Whence, from old *Windsor* hill, and from the aged *Stone,*[4] 465
The Muse those Countries sees, which call her to be gone.
The Forests took their leave : *Bere, Chute,* and *Buckholt,* bid
Adieu ; so *Wolmer,* and so *Ashholt,* kindly did.

---

[1] *Proteus,* a Sea-god, changing himself into any shape.
[2] A poetical description of the *Solent* Sea.
[3] *Tichfield* River.
[4] Another little hill in *Hampshire.*

And *Pamber* shook her head, as grievéd at the heart ;
When far upon her way, and ready to depart,   470
As now the wand'ring Muse so sadly went along,
To her last farewell, the goodly Forests sung.   [brought,
   Dear Muse, to plead our right, whom time at last hath
Which else forlorn had lain, and banish'd every thought,
When thou ascend'st the hills, and from their rising shrouds
Our sisters shalt command, whose tops once touch'd the
            clouds ;   476
Old *Arden*[1] when thou meet'st, or dost fair *Sherwood*[2] see,
Tell them, that as they waste, so every day do we :
Wish them, we of our griefs may be each other's heirs ;
Let them lament our fall, and we will mourn for theirs. 480
   Then turning from the South which lies in public view,
The Muse an oblique course doth seriously pursue :
And pointing to the Plains, she thither takes her way ;
For which, to gain her breath she makes a little stay.

       [1] The great and ancient forest of *Warwickshire.*
       [2] The goodly forest by *Nottingham.*

ILLUSTRATIONS.

HE Muse, yet observing her began course of Chorographical longitude, traces Eastward the Southern shore of the Isle. In this second, sings *Dorset* and *Hantshire;* fitly here joined as they join themselves, both having their South limits washed by the *British* Ocean.

43. *Which th' Ancients, for the love that they to* Isis *bare.*

Juba remembers alike[1] coral by the *Troglodytic* Isles (as is here in this Sea) and styles it *Isidis plocamos.** True reason of the name is no more perhaps to be given, than why Adiantum is called *Capillus Veneris*, or Sengreene *Barba Jouis.* Only thus : You have in *Plutarch* and *Apuleius* such variety of *Isis'* titles, and, in *Clemens* of *Alexandria*, so large circuits of her travels, that it were no more wonder to hear of her name in this Northern climate than in *Ægypt :* especially, we having three rivers of note[2] synonymous with her. Particularly to make her a Sea-goddess, which the common story of her and *Osiris* her husband (son to *Cham*, and of whom *Bale* dares offer affirmance, that in his travelling over the world, he first taught the *Britons* to make beer

---

[1] Apud Plin. Hist. Nat. lib. 13. cap. 25. * Isis hair.
[2] Ouse. Leland. ad Cyg. Cant.

instead of wine) does not: *Isis Pelagia,** after *Pausanias'*
testimony, hath an old coin.[1] The special notice which
Antiquity took of her hair is not only shewed by her attribute[2] of Λυσίκομος,† but also in that her hair was kept as
a sacred relic in *Memphis*[3] as *Geryon's* bones at *Thebes*, the
Boar's skin at *Tegea*, and such like elsewhere. And after
this to fit our coral just with her colour, *Æthiopicis solibus
Isis furva*,‡ she is called by *Arnobius*.[4] Gentlewomen of
black hair§ (no fault with brevity to turn to them) have no
simple pattern of that part in this great Goddess, whose
name indeed comprehended whatsoever in the Deity was
feminine, and more too ; nor will I swear, but that *Ana-
creon* (a man very judicious in the provoking ·motives of
wanton love) intending to bestow on his sweet mistress that
one of the titles of women's special ornament, *Well-haired,*‖
thought of this, when he gave his Painter direction to
make her picture black-haired. But thus much out of
the way.

77. *Thou never by that name of* White-hart *hadst been known.*

Very likely from the soil was the old name *Blackmore*.
By report of this country, the change was from a white hart,
reserved here from chase, by express will of *Hen. III.* and
afterward killed by *Thomas de la Lynd*, a gentleman of
these parts. For the offence, a mulct imposed on the pos-
sessors of *Blackmore* (called *white-hart*[5] *silver*) is to this day
paid into the Exchequer. The destruction of woods¶ here
bewailed by the Muse, is (upon occasion too often given)

---

* Isis of the Sea.   [1] Goltz. Thes. Antiq.   † Loosehaired.
[2] Philostrat. in εἰκ.   [3] Lucian. in εἰκ.
‡ Æthiopian sun-burnt.   [4] Advers. Gent. 1.   § Black-hair.
‖ Καλλιπλόκαμος, and καλλίσφυρος, *i.e.*, well-haired, and pretty-
footed ; two special commendations, dispersed in Greek poets, joined
in Lucilius.
[5] Camden.   ¶ Destruction of woods.

often seconded : but while the Muse bewails them, it is
Marsyas and his countrymen that most want them.

90. *On whom the* wat'ry God *would oft have had his will.*

Purbecke (named, but indeed not, an Isle, being joined to
the firm land) stored with game of the forest.

Thence alluding to *Diana's* devotions, the Author well
calls her an *Huntress* and a *Nun.* Nor doth the embracing
force of the ocean (whereto she is adjacent) although very
violent, prevail against her stony cliffs. To this purpose
the Muse is here wanton with *Neptune's* wooing.

110. *That he in little time upon this lovely dame,'*
      Begat three maiden Isles, *his darlings and delight.*

Albion (son of *Neptune*) from whom the first name of this
Britain was supposed, is well fitted to the fruitful bed of
this *Poole,* thus personated as a Sea-Nymph. The plain
truth (as words may certify your eyes, saving all impro-
priety of object) is, that in the *Poole* are seated three Isles,
Brunksey, Fursey, and S. *Helen's,*[1] in situation and magnitude,
as I name them. Nor is the fiction of begetting the Isles
improper ; seeing Greek antiquities[2] tell us of divers in the
Mediterranean and the *Archipelago,* as *Rhodes, Delos, Hiera,*
the *Echinades,* and others, which have been, as it were,
brought forth out of the salt womb of *Amphitrite.*

149. *Now towards the* Solent *Sea, as* Stour *her way doth ply,*
      On Shaftesbury, *&c.*

The strait twixt the *Wight* and *Hantshire,* is titled
in *Bede's* story, *Pelagus latudinis* III *millium, quod vocatur,*
Solent ;[3] famous for the double, and thereby most violent

---

[1] Isles newly out of the Sea.
[2] Lucian Dialog.; Pindar. Olymp. ζ.; Strab.; Pausanias.
[3] A Sea three miles over, called *Solent:* Lib. 4. Hist. Eccles. cap. 16.

floods of the ocean (as *Scylla* and *Charybdis* twixt *Sicily* and *Italy* in *Homer*) expressed by the Author towards the end of this Song, and reckoned among our *British* wonders. Of it the Author tells you more presently. Concerning *Shaftesbury* (which, beside other names, from[1] the corpse of St. *Edward*, murdered in *Corfe* Castle through procurement of the bloody hate of his stepmother *Ælfrith*, hither translated, and some three years lying buried, was once called St. *Edward's*) you shall hear a piece out of *Harding :*

𝕮𝖆𝖎𝖗𝖊[2] 𝕻𝖆𝖑𝖆𝖉𝖔𝖚𝖗𝖊 𝖙𝖍𝖆𝖙 𝖓𝖔𝖜 𝖎𝖘 𝕾𝖍𝖆𝖋𝖙𝖊𝖘𝖇𝖚𝖗𝖞
𝖂𝖍𝖊𝖗𝖊 𝖆𝖓 𝕬𝖓𝖌𝖊𝖑𝖑 𝖘𝖕𝖆𝖐𝖊 𝖘𝖎𝖙𝖙𝖎𝖓𝖌 𝖔𝖓 𝖙𝖍𝖊 𝖜𝖆𝖑𝖑
𝖂𝖍𝖎𝖑𝖊 𝖎𝖙 𝖜𝖆𝖘 𝖎𝖓 𝖜𝖔𝖗𝖐𝖎𝖓𝖌 𝖔𝖇𝖊𝖗 𝖆𝖑𝖑.

Speaking of *Rudhudibras* his fabulous building it. I recite it, both to mend it,[3] reading 𝕬𝖎𝖌𝖑𝖊 for 𝕬𝖓𝖌𝖊𝖑𝖑, and also that it might then, according to the *British* story, help me explain the Author in this.

152. As brought into her mind the *Eagle's* prophecies.

This *Eagle* (whose prophecies among the *Britons*, with the later of *Merlin*, have been of no less respect than those of *Bacis* were to the Greeks, or the *Sybillines* to the *Romans*) foretold of a reverting of the Crown, after the *Britons*, *Saxons*, and *Normans*, to the first again, which in *Hen. VII.*, grandchild to *Owen Tyddour*, hath been observed[4] as fulfilled. This in particular is peremptorily affirmed by that *Count Palatine* of *Basingstoke*. *Et aperte dixit tempus aliquando fore ut Britannium imperium denuo sit ad veteres Britannos post Saxonas et Normannos rediturum,** are his words of this *Eagle*. But this prophecy in manuscript I have seen, and

[1] Malmes. 6. Lib. 2. de *Pontific. S. Edward's.* 979.
[2] Camden takes this Cair for *Bath.*
[3] Harding amended.
[4] Twin. in Albionic. 2. See the Fifth Song.
* He plainly said that there would be a time of this reverting of the Crown.

without the help of _Albertus'_ secret, _Canace's_ ring in _Chaucer,_
or reading over _Aristophanes'_ Comedy of _Birds,_ I understood
the language; neither find I in it any such matter expressly.
Indeed as in _Merlin_ you have in him the _White Dragon,_ the
Red Dragon, the _Black Dragon,_ for the _Saxons, Britons,_ Nor-
mans, and the _Fertile Tree,_ supposed for _Brute,_ by one that
of later time hath given his obscurities interpretation[1] : in
which, not from the _Eagle's,_ but from[2] an Angelical voice,
almost 700 years after Christ, given to _Cadwallader_ (whom
others call _Cedwalla_) that restitution of the Crown to the
Britons is promised, and grounded also upon some general
and ambiguous words in the _Eagle's_ text, by the Author
here followed ; which (provided your faith be strong) you
must believe made more than 2,500 years since. For a
corollary, in this not unfit place, I will transcribe a piece
of the Gloss out of an old copy, speaking thus upon a
passage in the prophecy: _Henricus IV._ (he means _Hen. III._
who, by the ancient account in regard of _Henry,_ son to
Henry Fitz-lempresse, crown'd in his father's life, is in _Bracton_
and others called _the Fourth_) _concessit omne jus et clameum,_
pro se et heredibus suis, quod habuit in Ducatu Normanniæ im-
perpetuam. Tunc fractum fuit ejus sigillum et mutatum ;
nam prius tenebat in sceptro gladium, nunc tenet virgam ; qui
gladius fuit de conquestu Ducis Willielmi Bastardi, et ideo dicit
Aquila, separabitur gladius à sceptro. Such good fortune
have these predictions, that either by conceit (although
strained) they are applied to accident, or else ever religiously expected ; as _Buchanan_ of _Merlin's._*

---

[1] Distinct. Aquil. Sceptoniæ.
[2] A prophecy of an angel to Cadwallader.
[3] A sceptre instead of a sword first in _Hen._ the _Third's_ seal, but
believe him not; the seals of those times give no warrant for it : and
even in _King Arthur's, Leland_ says, there was a fleury sceptre ; but
that perhaps as feigned, as this false.
* Hist. Scot. Lib. 5. in Congallo.

161. *Then those* prodigious signs *to ponder she began.*

I would not have you lay to the Author's charge a justification of these signs at those times: but his liberty herein it is not hard to justify,

Obseditque frequens castrorum limina bubo:

and such like hath *Silius Italicus* before the *Roman* overthrow at *Canna;* and Historians commonly affirm the like; therefore a Poet may well guess the like.

196. *And at* New-forest *foot into the sea doth fall.*

The fall of *Stour* and *Avon* into the ocean is the limit of the two shires, and here limits the Author's description of the first, his Muse now entering *New-forest* in *Hantshire.*

200. Her being that receiv'd by *William's* tyranny.

New-forest (it is thought the newest in *England,* except that of *Hampton Court,* made by *Hen. VIII.*) acknowledges *William* her maker, that is, the *Norman Conqueror.* His love to this kind of possession and pleasure was such, that he constituted loss of eyes[1] punishment for taking his Venery: so affirm expressly *Florence* of *Worcester, Henry* of *Huntingdon, Walter Mapes,* and others, although the Author of *Distinctio Aquilæ,* with some of later time, falsely laid it to *William Rufus* his charge. To justify my truth, and for variety, see these rhymes,[2] even breathing antiquity:

Game of houndes he louede inou, and of wild best,
And is* forest, and is wodes, and mest the niwe forest,
That is in Suthamtessire, bor thulke he lobede inow
And astored well mid† bestes, and lese‡ mid gret wou:

---

[1] Matth. Paris post Hen. Huntingdon. And under Will. II. it was capital to steal deer.
[2] Robert Glocestrens.   * His.   † With.   ‡ Pastures.

Uor he cast out of house and hom of men a great route,
And binom* their lond thritti mile and more thereaboute,
And made it all forest and lese the bests bor to fede,
Of pouer men diserited he nom let el hede :
Cheruore therein bell mony mischeuing,
And is sone was thercine issote William the red King,†
And is o‡ sone, that het Richard, caght there is deth also,
And Richard is o‡ neueu, brec there is neck thereto,
As he rod an honteth and perauntre his horse sprend,
The bnright ido to pouer men to such mesauntre trend.

But to quit you of this antique verse, I return to the
pleasanter Muse.

232. *Her famous* Bevis *so wert in her power to choose;*

About the *Norman* invasion was *Bevis* famous with title
of *Earl* of *Southampton ; Duncton* in *Wiltshire* known for his
residence. What credit you are to give to the hyperboles
of *Itchin* in her relation of *Bevis,* your own judgment, and
the Author's censure in the admonition of the other rivers
here personated, I presume, will direct. And it is wished
that the poetical Monks in celebration of him, *Arthur,* and
other such Worthies had contained themselves within bounds
of likelihood ; or else that some judges, proportionate to
those of the *Grecian* Games,[1] (who always by public authority pulled down the statues[2] erected, if they exceeded the
true symmetry of the victors) had given such exorbitant
fictions their desert. The sweet grace of an inchanting
Poem (as inimitable *Pindar* affirms[3]) often compels belief ;
but so far have the undigested reports of barren and Monkish invention expatiated out of the lists of Truth, that from

---

* Took. † Shot by *Walter Tirell.* ‡ His own.
[1] Ἑλλανοδίκαι. [2] Lucian. περὶ εἰκον.
[3] Olymp. α et Nem. ζ. σοφία δὲ κλέπτει παράγοισα μύθοις.

their intermixed and absurd fauxeties hath proceeded doubt; and, in some, even denial of what was truth. His sword is kept as a relic in *Arundel* Castle, not equalling in length (as it is now worn) that of *Edward* the *Third's* at *Westminster*.

233. *And for great* Arthur's *seat her* Winchester *prefers, Whose* old Round Table *yet, &c.*

For him, his Table, Order, Knights, and places of their celebration, look to the Fourth Song.

447. *When* Portsey *weighing well the ill to her might grow.*

Portsey an Island in a creek of the *Solent*, coming in by *Portsmouth*, endures the forcible violence of that troublesome sea, as the Verse tells you in this fiction of wooing.

THE THIRD SONG.

THE ARGUMENT.

P with the jocund lark (too long we take our rest)
    Whilst yet the blushing dawn out of the cheerful
       East
    Is ushering forth the day to light the Muse along ;
Whose most delightful touch, and sweetness of her song,

Shall force the lusty swains out of the country-towns,   5
To lead the loving girls in daunces to the downs.
The Nymphs, in *Selwood's* shades and *Braden's* woods that be,
Their oaken wreaths, O Muse, shall offer up to thee.
And when thou shap'st thy course tow'rds where the soil
     is rank,
The *Sommersetian* maids, by swelling *Sabryn's* bank   10
Shall strew the ways with flowers (where thou art com-
     ing on)
Brought from the marshy-grounds by aged *Avalon.*[1]
   § From *Sarum* thus we set, remov'd from whence it stood
By *Avon* to reside, her dearest lovéd Flood :
Where her imperious Fane[2] her former seat disdains,   15
And proudly overtops the spacious neighbouring *Plains.*
What pleasures hath this Isle, of us esteem'd most dear,
In any place, but poor unto the plenty here ?
The chalky *Chiltern*[3] fields, nor *Kelmarsh'* self compares
With *Everley*[4] for store and swiftness of her hares :   20
A horse of greater speed, nor yet a righter hound,
Not anywhere twixt *Kent* and *Calidon*[5] is found.
Nor yet the level South can shew a smoother race,
Whereas the ballow* nag outstrips the winds in chace ;
As famous in the West for matches yearly tried,   25
As *Garterley,*[6] possess'd of all the Northern pride :
And on his match as much the Western horseman lays,
As the rank-riding *Scots* upon their *Galloways.*[7]
   And as the Western soil as sound a horse doth breed,
As doth the land that lies betwixt the *Trent* and *Tweed :* 30

---

[1] *Glastenbury.*   [2] The goodly Church at *Salisbury.*
[3] Two places famous for hares, the one in *Buckinghamshire,* the other in *North-hamptonshire.*
[4] *Everley* warren of hares.   [5] The furthest part of *Scotland.*
* Gaunt.   [6] A famous *Yorkshire* horse-race.
[7] The best kind of *Scottish* nags.

No hunter, so, but finds the breeding of the West,
The only kind of hounds,[1] for mouth and nostril best ;
That cold doth seldom fret, nor heat doth over-hale ;
As standing in the flight, as pleasant on the trail ;
Free hunting, eas'ly check'd, and loving every chace ;   35
Straight running, hard, and tough, of reasonable pace :
Not heavy, as that hound which *Lancashire* doth breed ;
Nor as the Northern kind, so light and hot of speed,
Upon the clearer chase, or on the foiléd train,
Doth make the sweetest cry, in woodland, or on plain.   40
   Where she, of all the *Plains* of *Britain*, that doth bear
The name to be the first (renownéd everywhere)
§ Hath worthily obtained that *Stonendge* there should
   · stand :
She, first of *Plains ;* and that,[2] first Wonder of the Land.
She *Wansdike* also wins, by whom she is imbrac'd,   45
That in his aged arms doth gird her ampler waist :
Who (for a mighty Mound sith long he did remain
§ Betwixt the *Mercian's* rule, and the *West-Saxons'* reign,
And therefore of his place himself he proudly bare)
Had very oft been heard with *Stonendge* to compare ;   50
Whom for a paltry Ditch, when *Stonendge* pleas'd t' upbraid,
The old man taking heart, thus to that Trophy said :
   Dull heap, that thus thy head above the rest dost rear,
Precisely yet not know'st who first did place thee there ;
But traitor basely turn'd, to *Merlin's* skill dost fly,   55
And with his magiques dost thy Maker's truth belie :
Conspirator with Time, now grown so mean and poor,
Comparing these his spirits with those that went before ;
Yet rather art content thy builders' praise to lose,
Than passéd greatness should thy present wants disclose.   60
Ill did those mighty men to trust thee with their story,
That hast forgot their names, who rear'd thee for their glory :

---

[1] The Western hounds generally the best.
[2] *Stonendge* the greatest Wonder of *England.*

For all their wondrous cost, thou that hast serv'd them so,
What 'tis to trust to tombs, by thee we eas'ly know.
  In these invectives thus whilst *Wansdike* doth complain,₆₅
He interrupted is by that imperious *Plain*,[1]
§ To hear two crystal Floods to court her, that apply
Themselves, which should be seen most gracious in her eye.
  First, *Willy* boasts herself more worthy than the other,
And better far deriv'd ; as having to her mother   70
Fair *Selwood*,[2] and to bring up *Diver*[3] in her train ;
Which, when the envious soil would from her course restrain,
A mile creeps under earth, as flying all resort :
And how clear *Nader* waits attendance in her court ;
And therefore claims of right the *Plain* should help her
          dear,   75
Which gives that Town[4] the name; which likewise names the
  The Eastern *Avon* vaunts, and doth upon her take [Shire.
To be the only child of shadeful *Savernake* :[5]
As *Ambraye's* ancient flood ; herself and to enstyle
The *Stonendge's* best-lov'd, first wonder of the Isle ;   80
And what (in her behoof) might any want supply,
She vaunts the goodly seat of famous *Salsbury ;*
Where meeting pretty *Bourne*, with many a kind embrace,
Betwixt their crystal arm s they clip that lovéd place.
  Report, as lately rais'd, unto these Rivers came,   85
§ That *Bathe's* clear *Avon* (wax'd imperious through her
          fame)
Their dalliance should deride ; and that by her disdain,
Some other smaller Brooks, belonging to the *Plain*,
A question seem'd to make, whereas the Shire sent forth
Two *Avons*, which should be the Flood of greatest worth ; 90

----

[1] *Salisbury Plain.*
[2] A Forest betwixt *Wiltshire* and *Somersetshire.*
[3] Of diving under the earth.
[4] *Wilton* of *Willie,* and *Wiltshire* of *Wilton.*
[5] A Forest in *Wiltshire,* as the Map will tell you.

This stream, which to the South the *Celtick*[1] Sea doth get,
Or that which from the North saluteth *Somerset.*

  This when these Rivers heard, that even but lately strove
Which best did love the *Plain,* or had the *Plain's* best love,
They straight themselves combine: for *Willy* wisely weigh'd,
That should her *Avon* lose the day for want of aid,   96
If one so great and near were overpress'd with pow'r,
The foe (she being less) would quickly her devour.
As two contentious Kings, that, on each little jar,
Defiances send forth, proclaiming open war,   100
Until some other realm, that on their frontier lies,
Be hazarded again by other enemies,
Do then betwixt themselves to composition fall,
To countercheck that sword, else like to conquer all:
So falls it with these Floods, that deadly hate do bear.   105
And whilst on either part strong preparations were,
It greatly was suppos'd strange strife would there have been,
Had not the goodly *Plain* (plac'd equally between)
Forewarn'd them to desist, and off their purpose brake:
When in behalf of *Plains* thus (gloriously) she spake :   110
  [2] Away ye barb'rous Woods ; how ever ye be plac'd
On mountains, or in dales, or happily be grac'd
With floods, or marshy fells,* with pasture, or with earth
By nature made to till, that by the yearly birth
The large-bay'd barn doth fill, yea though the fruitfull'st
      ground.   115
For, in respect of *Plains,* what pleasure can be found
In dark and sleepy shades? where mists and rotten fogs
Hang in the gloomy thicks, and make unstedfast bogs,
By dropping from the boughs, the o'ergrown trees among,
With caterpillars' kells, and dusky cobwebs hung.   120

[1] The French Sea, as you have in the note before.
[2] The *Plain* of *Salisbury's* speech in defence of all *Plains.*
* Boggy places. A word frequent in *Lancashire.*

The deadly screech-owl sits, in gloomy covert hid :
Whereas the smooth-brow'd *Plain*, as liberally doth bid
The lark to leave her bow'r, and on her trembling wing
In climbing up tow'rds heav'n, her high-pitch'd hymns to
    sing
Unto the springing day ; when 'gainst the sun's arise   125
The early dawning strews the goodly Eastern skies
With roses everywhere : who scarcely lifts his head
To view this upper world, but he his beams doth spread
Upon the goodly *Plains ;* yet at his noonsted's height,
Doth scarcely pierce the brake with his far-shooting sight. 130
    The gentle shepherds here survey their gentler sheep :
Amongst the bushy woods luxurious *Satyrs* keep.
To these brave sports of field, who with desire is won,
To see his greyhound course, his horse (in diet) run,
His deep-mouth'd hound to hunt, his long-wing'd hawk to fly,
To these most noble sports his mind who doth apply,   136
Resorts unto the *Plains.* And not a foughten Field,
Where Kingdoms' rights have lain upon the spear and
    shield,
But *Plains* have been the place; and all those trophies high
That ancient times have rear'd to noble memory ;   140
As, *Stonendge*, that to tell the *British* Princes slain
By those false *Saxons*' fraud, here ever shall remain.
It was upon the *Plain* of *Mamre* (to the fame
Of me and all our kind) whereas the Angels came
To *Abraham* in his tent, and there with him did feed ;   145
To *Sara* his dear wife then promising the Seed
By Whom all nations should so highly honor'd be,
In which the Son of God they in the flesh should see.
But Forests, to your plague there soon will come an Age,
In which all damnéd sins most vehemently shall rage.   150
An Age ! what have I said ? nay, Ages there shall rise,
So senseless of the good of their posterities,

That of your greatest groves they scarce shall leave a tree
(By which the harmless deer may after shelter'd be)
Their luxury and pride but only to maintain,   155
And for your long excess shall turn ye all to pain.

 Thus ending; though some hills themselves that do apply
To please the goodly *Plain*, still standing in her eye,
Did much applaud her speech (as *Haradon*,[1] whose head
Old *Ambry* still doth awe, and *Bagden* from his stead   160
Surveying of the *Vies*, whose likings do allure
Both *Ouldbry* and *Saint Anne;* and they again procure
Mount *Marting-sall:* and he those hills that stand aloof,
Those brothers *Barbury* and *Badbury*, whose proof
Adds much unto her praise) yet in most high disdain   165
The Forests take her words, and swear the prating.*Plain*,
Grown old, began to dote : and *Savernake* so much
Is gallèd with her taunts (whom they so nearly touch)
That she in spiteful terms defies her to her face ;
And *Aldburne* with the rest, though being but a Chace,   170
At worse than nought her sets : but *Bradon* all-afloat
When it was told her, set open such a throat,
That all the country rang.   She calls her barren jade,
Base quean, and riv'ld witch, and wish'd she could be made
But worthy of her hate (which most of all her grieves)   175
The basest beggar's bawd, a harbourer of thieves.
Then *Peusham*, and with her old *Blackmore* (not behind)
Do wish that from the seas some sultry Southern wind,
The foul infectious damps and pois'ned airs would sweep,
And pour them on the *Plain*, to rot her and her sheep.   180

 But whilst the sportive Muse delights her with these
She strangely taken is with those delicious springs [things,
Of *Kennet* rising here, and of the nobler stream
Of *Isis* setting forth upon her way to *Tame*,   184

---

[1] Divers hills near and about *Salisbury Plain*.

§ By *Greeklade;* whose great name yet vaunts that learned
Where to great *Britain* first the sacred Muses song; [tong,
Which first were seated here, at *Isis'* bounteous head,
As telling that her fame should through the world be spread;
And tempted by this flood, to *Oxford* after came,
There likewise to delight her bridegroom, lovely *Tame:* 190
Whose beauty when they saw, so much they did adore,
That *Greeklade* they forsook, and would go back no more.

   Then *Bradon* gently brings forth *Avon* from her source :
Which Southward making soon in her most quiet course,
Receives the gentle *Calne:* when on her rising side, 195
First *Blackmoore* crowns her bank, as *Peusham* with her pride
Sets out her murmuring shoals, till (turning to the West)
Her *Somerset* receives, with all the bounties blest
That Nature can produce in that *Bathonian* Spring, 199
Which from the sulphury mines her med'cinal force doth
     bring ;
As Physic hath found out by colour, taste, and smell,
Which taught the world at first the virtue of the Well ;
What quickliest it could cure : which men of knowledge
     drew
From that first mineral cause : but some that little knew
(Yet felt the great effects continually it wrought) 205
§ Ascrib'd it to that skill, which *Bladud* hither brought,
As by that learned King the Baths should be begun ;
Not from the quick'ned mine, by the begetting sun
Giving that natural pow'r, which by the vig'rous sweat,
Doth lend the lively Springs their perdurable heat 210
In passing through the veins, where matter doth not need ;
Which in that minerous earth insep'rably doth breed :
So Nature hath purvey'd, that during all her reign
The *Baths* their native power for ever shall retain :
Where Time that City built, which to her greater fame, 215
Preserving of that Spring, participates her name ;

The tutelage whereof (as those past worlds did please)
[1] Some to *Minerva* gave, and some to *Hercules:*
Proud *Phœbus'* lovéd Spring, in whose diurnal course,
§ When on this point of earth he bends his greatest force,
By his so strong approach, provokes her to desire ;   221
Stung with the kindly rage of love's impatient fire :
Which boiling in her womb, projects (as to a birth)
Such matter as she takes from the gross humorous earth ;
Till purg'd of dregs and slime, and her complexion clear, 225
She smileth on the light, and looks with mirthful cheer.
    Then came the lusty *Froome*, the first of Floods that met
Fair *Avon* ent'ring into fruitful *Somerset,*
With her attending Brooks ; and her to *Bath* doth bring,
Much honoured by that place, *Minerva's* sacred Spring.   230
To noble *Avon*, next, clear *Chute* as kindly came,
[2] To *Bristow* her to bear, the fairest seat of Fame :
To entertain this Flood, as great a mind that hath,
And striving in that kind far to excel the *Bath.*
As when some wealthy lord prepares to entertain   235
A man of high account, and feast his gallant train,
Of him that did the like, doth seriously enquire
His diet, his device, his service, his attire ;
That varying everything (exampled by his store)
He every way may pass what th' other did before :   240
Even so this City doth ; the prospect of which place
To her fair building adds an admirable grace ;
Well-fashion'd as the best, and with a double wall,
As brave as any town ; but yet excelling all
For easement, that to health is requisite and meet ;   245
Her piléd shores, to keep her delicate and sweet :
Hereto, she hath her tides ; that when she is opprest
With heat or drought, still pour their floods upon her breast.

---

[1] Minerva and Hercules, the protectors of these fountains.
[2] The delicacies of *Bristow.*

To *Mendip* then the Muse upon the South inclines,
Which is the only store, and coffer of her mines :   250
Elsewhere the fields and meads their sundry traffics suit :
The forests yield her wood, the orchards give her fruit.

   As in some rich man's house his several charges lie,
There stands his wardrobe, here remains his treasury ;
His large provision there, of fish, of fowl, and neat ;   255
His cellars for his wines, his larders for his meat ;
There banquet-houses, walks for pleasure ; here again
Cribs, graners, stables, barns, the other to maintain :
So this rich country hath, itself what may suffice ;
Or that which through exchange a smaller want supplies. 260
   Yet *Ochy's* dreadful Hole still held herself disgrac'd,
§ With th' wonders* of this Isle that she should not be
      plac'd :
But that which vex'd her most, was, that the *Peakish Cave*[1]
Before her darksome self such dignity should have ;
And th' *Wyches*[2] for their salts such state on them should take ;
Or *Cheshire* should prefer her sad *Death-boding-lake ;*[3]   266
And *Stonendge* in the world should get so high respect,
Which imitating Art but idly did erect :
And that amongst the rest, the vain inconstant *Dee*,[4]
By changing of his fords, for one should reckon'd be ;   270
As of another sort, wood turn'd to stone ;[5] among,
Th' anatomizéd fish,[6] and fowls[7] from planchers sprong :
And on the *Cambrian* side those strange and woudrous
      Springs ;[8]
Our beasts[9] that seldom drink ; a thousand other things

---

* A catalogue of many wonders of this Land.
[1] The Devil's Arse. [2] The salt-wells in *Cheshire*.
[3] *Bruerton's* Pond.   [4] A river by *Westchester*.
[5] By sundry soils of *Britain*.
[6] Our pikes, ripped and sewed-up, live.
[7] Barnacles, a bird breeding upon old ships.
[8] Wondrous Springs in Wales.   [9] Sheep.

Which *Ochy* inly vex'd, that they to fame should mount, 275
And greatly griev'd her friends for her so small account;
That there was scarcely rock, or river, marsh, or mere
That held not *Ochy's* wrongs (for all held *Ochy* dear)
§ In great and high disdain : and *Froome* for her disgrace
Since scarcely ever wash'd the coal-sleck from her face ; 280
But (melancholy grown) to *Avon* gets a path,
Through sickness forc'd to seek for cure unto the *Bath :*
§ And *Chedder,* for mere grief his teen he could not wreak,
Gush'd forth so forceful streams, that he was like to break
The greater banks of *Ax,* as from his mother's cave 285
He wand'red towards the sea ; for madness who doth rave
At his drad mother's wrong : but who so woe begone
For *Ochy,* as the Isle of ancient *Avalon ?*
Who having in herself, as inward cause of grief,
Neglecteth yet her own, to give her friend relief. 290
The other so again for her doth sorrow make,
And in the Isle's behalf the dreadful Cavern spake :
   O three times famous Isle, where is that place that might
Be with thyself compar'd for glory and delight,
Whilst *Glastenbury* stood ? exalted to that pride, 295
Whose Monastery seem'd all other to deride ?
O who thy ruin sees, whom wonder doth not fill
With our great fathers' pomp, devotion, and their skill ?
Thou more than mortal pow'r (this judgment rightly weigh'd)
Then present to assist, as that foundation laid ; 300
On whom, for this sad waste, should Justice lay the crime ?
Is there a pow'r in Fate, or doth it yield to Time ?
Or was their error such, that thou could'st not protect
Those buildings which thy hand did with their zeal erect ?
To whom didst thou commit that monument to keep, 305
That suff'reth with the dead their memory to sleep ?
§ When not great *Arthur's* Tomb, nor holy *Joseph's*[1] Grave,
From sacrilege had power their sacred bones to save ;

----

[1] *Joseph* of *Arimathæa.*

He who that God-in-man to his sepulchre brought,
Or he which for the faith twelve famous battles fought.   310
What? Did so many Kings do honour to that place,
For avarice at last so vilely to deface?
For rev'rence to that seat which hath ascribéd been,
Trees[1] yet in winter bloom, and bear their summer's green.
   This said, she many a sigh from her full stomach cast,   315
Which issued through her breast in many a boist'rous blast;
And with such floods of tears her sorrows doth condole,
As into rivers turn within that darksome hole:
Like sorrow for herself, this goodly Isle doth try;
§ Imbrac'd by *Selwood's* son, her flood the lovely *Bry*,   320
On whom the Fates bestow'd (when he conceivéd was)
He should be much belov'd of many a dainty lass;
Who gives all leave to like, yet of them liketh none:
But his affection sets on beauteous *Avalon;*   [do prove
Though many a plump-thigh'd moor, and full-flank'd marsh
To force his chaste desires, so dainty of his love.   326
First [2]*Sedgemore* shews this flood her bosom all unbrac'd,
And casts her wanton arms about his slender waist:
Her lover to obtain, so amorous *Audry* seeks:
And *Gedney* softly steals sweet kisses from his cheeks.   330
One takes him by the hand, intreating him to stay:
Another plucks him back, when he would fain away:
But, having caught at length, whom long he did pursue,
Is so intranc'd with love, her goodly parts to view,
That alt'ring quite his shape, to her he doth appear,   335
And casts his crystal self into an ample mere:
But for his greater growth when needs he must depart,
And forc'd to leave his love (though with a heavy heart)
As he his back doth turn, and is departing out,
The batning marshy *Brent* environs him about: 340

[1] The wondrous tree at *Glastenbury*.
[2] Fruitful Moors on the banks of *Bry*.

But loathing her imbrace, away in haste he flings,
And in the *Severne* sea surrounds his plenteous springs.

 But, dallying in this place, so long why dost thou dwell,
So many sundry things here having yet to tell?
Occasion calls the Muse her pinions to prepare.   345
Which (striking with the wind the vast and open air)
Now, in the finny heaths, then in the champains roves;
Now, measures out this plain; and then surveys those groves;
The batfull pastures fenc'd, and most with quickset mound,
The sundry sorts of soil, diversity of ground;   350
Where ploughmen cleanse the earth of rubbish, weed, and filth,
And give the fallow lands their seasons and their tilth:
Where best for breeding horse; where cattle fitt'st to keep:
Which good for bearing corn; which pasturing for sheep:
The lean and hungry earth, the fat and marly mould,   355
Where sands be always hot, and where the clays be cold;
With plenty where they waste, some others touch'd with want:
Here set, and there they sow; here proin, and there they plant.

 As *Wiltshire* is a place best pleas'd with that resort
Which spend away the time continually in sport;   360
So *Somerset* herself to profit doth apply,
As given all to gain, and thriving housewifry.
For, whereas in a land one doth consume and waste,
'Tis fit another be to gather in as fast:
This liketh moory plots, delights in sedgy bow'rs,   365
The grassy garlands loves, and oft attir'd with flow'rs
Of rank and mellow glebe: a sward as soft as wool,
With her complexion strong, a belly plump and full.

 Thus whilst the active Muse strains out these various things,
Clear *Parret* makes approach, with all those plenteous springs
Her fruitful banks that bless; by whose monarchal sway, 371
She fortifies herself against that mighty day
Wherein her utmost power she should be forc'd to try.
For, from the *Druids'* time there was a prophecy,

That there should come a day (which now was near at hand
By all forerunning signs) that on the Eastern strand,   376
If *Parret*[1] stood not fast upon the English side,
They all should be suppress'd : and by the *British* pride
In cunning overcome ; for why, impartial Fate
(Yet constant always to the *Britons'* crazéd state)   380
Forbad they yet should fall ; by whom she meant to show
How much the present Age, and after-times should owe
Unto the line of *Brute*.   Clear *Parret* therefore press'd
Her tributary streams, and wholly her address'd
Against the ancient foe : First, calling to her aid   385
Two Rivers of one name;[2] which seem as though they stay'd
Their empress as she went, her either hand that take.
The first upon the right, as from her source doth make
Large *Muchelney* an Isle, and unto *Ivell* lends
Her hardly-rend'red name : That on her left, descends   390
From *Neroch's* neighbouring woods ; which, of that forest
Her rival's proffer'd grace opprobriously doth scorn. [born,
She by her wand'ring course doth *Athelney* in-isle :
And for the greater state, herself she doth instile
§ The nearest neighbouring flood to *Arthur's* ancient seat, 395
Which made the *Britons'* name through all the world so
Like *Camelot*, what place was ever yet renown'd ?   [great.
Where, as at *Carlion*, oft, he kept the *Table-round*,
Most famous for the sports at *Pentecost* so long,   [sprong.
From whence all knightly deeds, and brave achievements
As some soft-sliding rill, which from a lesser head   401
(Yet in his going forth, by many a fountain fed)
Extends itself at length unto a goodly stream ;
So, almost through the world his fame flew from this realm ;
That justly I may charge those ancient *Bards* of wrong, 405
So idly to neglect his glory in their song.

[1] A supposed prophecy upon *Parret*.
[2] *Ivel :* from which the town *Ivel* is denominated.

For some abundant brain, O there had been a story
Beyond the Blind-man's[1] might to have inhanc'd our glory.
  Tow'rds the *Sabrinian* sea then *Parret* setting on,
To her attendance next comes in the beauteous *Tone*,   410
Crown'd with embroid'red banks, and gorgeously array'd
With all th' enamell'd flowers of many a goodly mead :
In orchards richly clad ; whose proud aspiring boughs
Even of the tallest woods do scorn a jot to lose,
Though *Selwood's* mighty self, and *Neroch* standing by :   415
The sweetness of her soil through every coast doth fly.
What ear so empty is, that hath not heard the sound
Of *Taunton's* fruitful *Deane ?*[2] not match'd by any ground ;
By *Athelney*[3] ador'd, a neighbourer to her land :
Whereas those higher hills to view fair *Tone* that stand,   420
Her coadjuting Springs with much content behold :
Where sea-ward *Quantock* stands as *Neptune* he controll'd,
And *Blackdown* inland born, a Mountain and a Mound,
As though he stood to look about the country round :
But *Parret* as a Prince, attended here the while,   425
Inrich'd with every Moor, and every inland Isle,
Upon her taketh state, well forward tow'rds her fall :
Whom lastly yet to grace, and not the least of all,
Comes in the lively *Carre*, a Nymph most lovely clear,
From *Somerton* sent down the Sovereign of the Shire ;   430
Which makes our *Parret* proud.   And wallowing in excess,
Whilst like a Prince she vaunts amid the wat'ry press,
The breathless Muse awhile her wearied wings shall ease,
To get her strength to stem the rough *Sabrinian* seas.

---

[1] *Homer.*   [2] One of the fruitful places of this land.
[3] Interpreted the Noble Isle.

ILLUSTRATIONS.

ISCONTINUING her first course, the Muse returns to *Somerset* and *Wiltshire*, which lie twixt the *Severne* and *Hantshire;* as the song here joins them.

13. *From* Sarum *thus we set*, remov'd *from whence it stood.*

Old *Salisbury* seated North-east from the now famous *Salisbury*, some mile distant, about *Richard Cœur de Lion's* time had her name and inhabitants hither translated, upon the meeting of *Avon* and *Aderborn;* where not long after she enjoyed, among other, that glorious title of admiration for her sumptuous Church-buildings. Of that, one of my authors[1] thus :

————in the peare of grace
Twelf hundred and to and twenti in the baire place
Of the noble Munstre of Salesburi hii leide the berste
stone
That me not in Christindom bairore work non.
Ther was Pandulf the Legat, and as hept of echon,
Ke leide biue the berste stones : as bor the Pope put on,

[1] Rob. Glocestrens.

Che other bor bre* ȝonge Ḳing, the thriꝺꝺe as me seȝe
Ꝼor the goꝺe Erle of Salisburi Williamꞇ the Longespei,
Che berth bor the Contesse, the bifte he leiꝺe tho
Ꝼor the Bishopꞇ of Salesburi, anꝺ he ne leiꝺe na mo.

This work then began, was by *Robert* of *Bingham*, next succeeding Bishop to that excellency, prosecuted.

43. *Hath worthily obtain'd that* Stonehenge *there should stand.*

Upon *Salisbury* Plain stones of huge weight and greatness,
some in the earth pitched, and in form erected, as it were
circular; others lying cross over them, as if their own poise
did no less than their supporters give them that proper
place, have this name of *Stone-henge;*

> *But so confus'd that neither any eye*
> *Can count them just, nor reason reason try,*
> *What force brought them to so unlikely ground.*

As the noble *Sidney*[1] of them.

No man knows, saith *Huntingdon*[2] (making them the first
wonder of this Land, as the Author doth) how, or why,
they came here. The cause thus take from the *British*
story: *Hengist* under colour of a friendly treaty with *Vortigern* at *Amesbury*, his falsehood's watchword to his *Saxons*
(provided there privily with long knives) being Nimeþ youþ
ꝛexeꝛ,[3] there traitorously slew 660 noble *Britons*, and kept
the King prisoner. Some thirty years after King *Ambros*
(to honour with one monument the name of so many murdered Worthies) by help of *Uter-pen-dragon's* forces and
Merlin's magic, got them transported from off a plain (others
say a hill) near *Naas*[4] in *Kildare* in *Ireland*, hither, to re-

---

* Hen. III.   † Wilhelm. de longâ spathâ.   ‡ Richard Poore.
[1] In his Sonnets.   [2] Histor. lib. 1.   [3] *i.e.*, Take your swords.
[4] Girald. Cambrensis Topograph. Hib. dist. 2. cap. 18. *Chorea
gigantum.*

main as a trophy, not of victory, but of wronged innocency.
This *Merlin* persuaded the King that they were medicinal,
and first brought out of the utmost parts of *Afrique* by
Giants which thence came to inhabit *Ireland.* *Non est ibi
lapis qui medicamento caret,*[1] as in *Merlin's* person *Geffrey* of
Monmouth speaks ; whose authority in this treacherous
slaughter of the *Britons,* I respect not so much as *Nennius,
Malmesbury, Sigebert, Matthew* of *Westminster,* and others,
who report it as I deliver. Whether they be naturally solid,
or with cement artificially composed, I will not dispute.
Although the last be of easier credit ; yet I would, with
our late Historian *White,* believe the first sooner, than that
Ulysses' ship was by *Neptune* turned into one stone, as it is
in the *Odyssees,* and that the *Ægyptian* King *Amasis* had a
house cut out in one marble (which, by *Herodotus'* description, could not after the workmanship have less content
than 2,394 solid cubits, if my Geometry fail me not) or
that which the *Jews*[2] are not ashamed to affirm of a stone,
with which King *Og* at one throw from his head purposed
to have crushed all the *Israelites,* had not a lapwing strangely
pecked such a hole through it, that it fell on his shoulders,
and by miracle his upper teeth suddenly extended, kept it
there fast from motion. It is possible they may be of some
such earthy dust as that of *Puzzolo,* and by *Ætna,* which
cast into the water turns stony, as *Pliny* after *Strabo* of
them and other like remembers. And for certain[3] I find it
reported, that in *Cairnarvan* upon *Snowdon* Hills is a stone
(which miraculously somewhat more than sixty years since,
raised itself out of a lake at the hill's foot) equalling a large
house in greatness, and supposed not moveable by a thousand
yoke of oxen. For the form of bringing them, your opinion

[1] Not one of the stones but is good for somewhat in Physic.
[2] Apud Munster. ad Deuter. 3. If among them there be a whet-
stone, let the Jew have it.
[3] Powel ad lib. 2. cap. 9. Girald. Itinerarii.

may take freedom. That great one which *Hercules*[1] is wondered at for the carriage was but a cartload,[2] which he left for a monument in *Otranto* of *Italy*: and except *Geffrey* of *Monmouth*, with some which follow him, scarce any affirm or speak of it, nor *Nennius*, nor *Malmesbury*; the first living somewhat near the supposed time.

48. *Betwixt the* Mercian *rule, and the* West-Saxons' *reign.*

So thinks our Antiquary and Light of this Kingdom; that, to be a limit of those two ancient states, sometime divided by *Avon*, which falls into *Severne*, *Wansdike* crossing the Shire Westward over the Plain was first cast up. [3]*Wodensdike*, the old name, is supposed from *Woden;* of no less (if not greater) esteem to the *Saxons*, than *Arsaces*, *Pelops*, *Cadmus*, and other such, to their posterity; but so that I guess it went but for their greatest God *Mercury* (he is called rather *Wonden* from *Win*, that is, *gain*, by *Lipsius*[4]) as the *German* and *English* antiquities discover. And very likely, when this limit was made, that in honour of him, being by name President of ways, and by his office of Heraldship *Pacifex*, *i.e.*, Peacemaker,[5] as an old stamp titles him, they called it *Wodensdike;* as not only the *Greeks*[6] had their Ἑρμαῖ ἐνόδιοι τετραγλωχῖνες (statues erected) for limits and direction of ways, and the *Latins* their *Terminus*, but the ancient *Jews* also, as upon interpretation of במרגמה[7] in the Proverbs, *i.e.*, *into an heap of Mercury* (in the Vulgate) for a heap of stones in that sense, *Goropius* in his hieroglyphics affirms, somewhat boldly deriving *Mercury* from **Herr,** which signifies a limit in his and our tongue, and so fits this place in name and nature. *Stonhenge* and it not im-

---

[1] Aristot. περὶ θαυμ. ἀκουσμ.   [2] ἀμαξαῖος.
[3] Woden or Wonden.   [4] Ad Germ. Tacit.
[5] Iþmunꝯull. Sax. Mercury. Adam Bremens. cap. 5. and hence *Irmingstreate.*
[6] Pausan. saepiùs; et Theocrit. εἰδ. κε.   [7] Proverbs 26. v. 8.

properly contend, being several works of two several
nations anciently hateful to each other ; *Britons* and *Saxons.*

67. *To hear* two crystal floods *to court her which apply.*

Willibourne (by the old name the Author calls her *Willy*)
derived from near *Selwood* by *Warmister*, with her creeky
passage, crossing to *Wilton*, naming both that town and the
shire, and on the other side *Avon* taking her course out of
Sarernake by *Marleborow* through the shire Southward,
washing *Ambresbury* and the *Salisburies* (New *Salisbury* being
her Episcopal city) both watering the Plain, and furnished
with these reasons, are fitly thus personated, striving to en-
dear themselves in her love : and prosecuting this fiction,
the Muse thus adds :

86. *How that* Bathe's Avon *wax'd imperious through her fame.*

Divers rivers of that name have we ; but two of eminent
note in *Wiltshire :* one is next before shewed you, which
falls through *Dorset* into the Ocean ; the other here mentioned hath her head in the edge of *Glocester :* and with her
snaky course, visiting *Malmesbury, Chippenham, Bradford,*
and divers towns of slight note, turns into *Somerset,* passes
Bath, and casts herself into *Severne* at *Bristow.*   This com-
pendious contention (whose proportionate example is a
special elegancy for the expressing of diversity, as in the
Pastorals of *Theocritus* and *Virgil*) is aptly concluded with
that point of ancient politic observation,[1] that *Outward common fear is the surest band of friendship.*

185. *To* Greeklade *whose great name yet vaunts that learned tong.*

The History of *Oxford* in the Proctors' book, and certain
old verses,[2] kept somewhere in this tract, affirm, that with
Brute came hither certain *Greek* Philosophers, from whose

---

[1] In Thucydid. et Liv.   [2] Leland. ad Cyg. Cant. in Iside.

name and profession here it was thus called, and as an
University afterward translated to *Oxford* (upon like notation a company of Physicians retiring to *Lechlade*[1] in this
shire, gave that its title, as *I. Rous* adds in his story to
Hen. VII.). But *Godwin* and a very old *Anonymus*, cited
by *Br. Twine*, refer it to *Theodore* of *Tarsus* in *Cilicia* (made
Archbishop of *Canterbury* by *Pope Vitalian* under *Ecgbert*, King
of *Kent*) very skilful in both tongues, and an extraordinary
restorer of learning to the *English-Saxons ;* That he had
(among other) *Greek* schools, is certain by *Bede's* affirmation
that some of his scholars understood both *Greek* and *Latin*
as their mother language. *Richard* of the *Vies*[2] will that
Penda, King of *Mercland*, first deduced a colony of *Cambridge*
men hither, and calls it *Crekelade*, as other *Kirklade* with
variety of names : but I suspect all ; as well for omission of
it in best authorities, as also that the name is so different
in itself. *Grecolade* was never honoured with *Greek* schools,
as the ignorant multitude think, saith *Leland*,[3] affirming it
should be rather *Creclade*, *Lechelade*, or *Lathlade*. Nor me-
thinks (of all) stands it with the *British* story,* making the
tongue then a kind of *Greek* (a matter, that way reasonable
enough, seeing it is questionless that colonies anciently derived out of the Western *Asia*, *Peloponnesus*, *Hellas*, and
those Continents into the coast whence *Brute* came, transported the *Greek* with them) that profession of *Grecians*
should make this so particular a name.

266. Ascrib'd *to that high skill which learned* Bladud *brought*.

You are now in *Somersetshire*. I doubt not but the true
cause is that which is ordinary of other hot springs ; not

---

[1] *i.e.*, The Physician's lake.
[2] Apud. Cai. de antiq. Cantabrig. lib. 2. et Cod. Nig. Cantabr.
apud aut. assert. antiq. Oxon.
[3] Ad Cyg. Cant. in Iside et Isid. vad.
* Curvus Græcus sermo Britannicus. Galfred. Monumeth. lib. 1.

the sun's heat (saving the Author's opinion, which hath warrant enough in others) or agitation of wind, as some will ; but either passage through metallic, bituminous, and sulphurous veins, or rather a real subterranean fire, as *Empedocles*[1] first thought, and with most witty arguments (according to the poetical conceit of *Typhon*,[2] buried in *Prochyta;* whereto *Strabo* refers the best Baths in *Italy*) my learned and kind friend Mr. *Lydiat,* that accurate Chronologer, in his ingenious Philosophy, hath lately disputed. But, as the Author tells you, some *British* vanity imputes it to *Bladud's* art, which in a very ancient fragment of rhymes[3] I found expressed: and if you can endure the language and fiction you may read it, and then laugh at it.

> Two tunne there beth of bras,
> And other two imaked of glas
> Seue seats there buth inne
> And other thing imaked with ginne :
> Quick brimston in them also,
> With wild fier imaked thereto :
> Sal gemmæ and sal petræ,
> Sal armonak there is eke
> Sal albrod and sal alkine
> Sal Geminæ is minged with him.
> Sal Comin and sal almetre bright
> That borneth both day and night,
> Al this is in the tonne ido
> And other things many mo,
> And borneth both night and day,
> That neuer quench it ne may
> In bour welsprings the tonnes liggeth[4]
> As the Philosophers vs siggeth

[1] Senec. Natural. Quæst. lib. 3. cap. 24.
[2] Pindar. Pyth. α.   [3] Ex antiq. sched.
[4] See the Author's Eighth Song.

The hete within, the water without,
Maketh it hot al about
The two welsprings earneth mere
And the other two beth inner clere.
There is maked full this
That Kings hath icluped is.
The rich King Bladud
The Kings sonne' Lud
And when he maked that bath hot
And if him failed ought
Of that that should thereto,
Perkeneth what he would do
From Bath to London he would flee
And thulke' day selfe againe bee
And fetch that thereto biuel,
He was quicke, and swith fell
Tho the master was ded
And is soule wend to the Qued
For god ne was not put ybore
Nor deth suffred him biuore.

I will as soon believe all this, as that S. *Devi*[1] or *Julius
Cæsar*[2] (who never came near it) was author of it, or that
he made Knights of the Bath. They are not wanting which
have durst say so.

220. *When on this point of earth he bends his* greatest force.

From eight in the morning till three (within which time
the sunbeams make their strongest angles of incidence) it
purges itself (as boiling) of unclean excrements, nor then
doth any enter it ; which the Muse here expresses in a fervent sympathy of love twixt the Water and the Sun, and

---

[1] Bal. cent. 1.   [2] Malmesbury, lib. 2. Pontific.

the more properly because it had ·the name of[1] *Aquæ Solis.*[*]

262. *With th' wonders of the Isle that she should not be plac'd.*

Wockey hole[+] (so called in my conceit, from þocȝ,[2] which is the same with þic, signifying a *hollow* or *creeky passage*) in *Mendip* Hills by *Wells*, for her spacious vaults, stony walls, creeping labyrinths, unimaginable cause of posture in the earth, and her neighbours' report (all which almost equal her to that *Grotta della Sibylla*[3] in the *Apenin* of *Marca An-conitana*, and the Dutch song of little *Daniel*) might well wonder she had not place among her country wonders.[4] One that seems to increase *Samuel Beaulan* upon *Nennius*, reckons thirteen by that name, but with ·vain and false reports (as that of the *Bath* to be both hot and cold, accord-ing to the desire of him that washes) and in some the Author of *Polychronicon* follows him; neither speaking of this.   But the last, and *Henry* of *Huntingdon*, reckon only four remarkable; the *Peake*, *Stonhenge*, *Chederhole*, and a hill out of which it rains.   That wonder of human excel-lence, *Sir Philip Sidney*, to fit his Sonnet, makes six; and to fit that number conceitedly adds a froward, but chaste, Lady for the seventh.   And the Author here tells you the chiefest.

279.   ———*that* Froome *for her disgrace*
     Since scarcely ever wash'd the coalsleck *from her face.*

Out of *Mendip* Hills *Froome* springeth, and through the Coalpits after a short course Eastward turns upward to *Bathe's Avon.*   The fiction of her besmeared face happens the better, in that *Froome*, after our old mother language,

---

[1] Antoninus in Itinerario.   [*] Waters of the Sun.
[+] Or, *Ochy.*   [2] Beat. Rhenan. lib. 2. Rer. Germanic.
[3] Ortelius Theat. Mundi.   [4] The wonders of *England.*

signifies *fair*, as that paradoxical *Becanus*,[1] in exposition of the *Egyptian Pyromis* in *Herodotus*,[2] would by notation teach us.

283. *And* Chedder *for mere grief his teen he could not wreak.*

Near *Axbridge*, *Chedder Cleeves*, rocky and vaulted, by continual distilling, is the fountain of a forcible stream (driving twelve mills within a mile's quartèr of its head) which runs into *Ax* derived out of *Wockey*.

307. *When not great* Arthur's *Tomb, nor holy* Joseph's *Grave.*

Henry the *Second* in his expedition towards *Ireland* entertained by the way in *Wales* with *Bardish* songs, wherein he heard it affirmed that in *Glastenbury* (made almost an Isle by the River's embracements) *Arthur* was buried twixt two pillars, gave commandment to *Henry* of *Blois* then Abbot, to make search for the corpse: which was found in a wooden coffin (*Girald* saith oaken, *Leland* thinks alder) some sixteen foot deep; but after they had digged nine foot, they found[3] a stone on whose lower side was fix'd a leaden cross (crosses fixed upon the tombs of old Christians were in all places ordinary) with his name inscribed, and the letter side of it turned to the stone. He was then honoured with a sumptuous monument, and afterward the sculls of him and his wife *Guinever* were taken out (to remain as separate relics and spectacles) by *Edward Longshanks* and *Elianor*. Of this, *Girald*, *Leland*, *Prise*, divers others (although *Polydore* made slight of it) have more copious testimony. The *Bards'* Songs suppose, that after the Battle of *Camlan* in *Cornwall*, where traitorous *Mordred* was slain, and *Arthur* wounded, *Morgain le Fay*, a great *Elfin* Lady (supposed his near kinswoman) conveyed the body hither to cure it: which done, *Arthur* is to return (yet expected) to the rule of his country.

[1] Hermathen. lib. 5.   [2] Euterpe.   [3] Chronicon. Glasconiens.

Read these attributed to the best[1] of the *Bards*, expressing
as much:

>————*Morgain suscepit honore,*
> *Inque suis thalamis posuit super aurea regem*
> *Fulcra, manuque sibi detexit vulnus honestâ,*
> *Inspexitque diù: tandemque redire salutem*
> *Posse sibi dixit, si secum tempore longo*
> *Esset, et ipsius vellet medicamine fungi.*

English in metre for me thus by the Author:

>————*Morgain* with honour took,
> And in a chair of State doth cause him to repose;
> Then with a modest hand his wounds she doth unclose:
> And having search'd them well, she bad him not to doubt,
> He should in time be cur'd, if he would stay it out,
> And would the med'cine take that she to him would give.

The same also in effect, an excellent Poet[2] of his time
thus singing it.

> He is a King crouned in Fairie,
> With Scepter and sword and with his regally
> Shall resort as Lord and Soueraigne
> Out of Fairie and reigne in Britaine:
> And repaire againe the Round Table
> By prophesy Merlin set the date,
> Among Princes King incomparable
> His seat againe to Carlion to translate
> The Parchas suffren sponne to his fate
> His Epitaph* recordeth so certaine
> Here lieth K. Arthur that shall raigne againe.

[1] Taliessin. ap. Pris. defens. hist. Brit.
[2] Dan Lidgat. lib. 8. vers. Boccat. cap. 24. Nænias ad has refert
Alanus de Insulis illud Merlini vaticinium. Exitus ejus dubius erit.
* *Hic jacet Arthurus, Rex quondam, Rexque futurus.*

Worthily famous was the Abbey also from *Joseph* of *Arimathea* (that, Εὐσχήμων βουλευτής,* as S. *Mark* calls him) here buried, which gives proof of *Christianity* in the Isle before our *Lucius.*[1] Hence in a Charter of liberties by *Hen. II.* to the Abbey (made in presence of *Heraclius* Patriarch of *Jerusalem*, and others) I read, *Olim à quibusdam mater sanctorum dicta est, ab aliis tumulus sanctorum,†quam ab ipsis discipulis Domini edificatam et ab ipso Domino dedicatam primò fuisse venerabilis habet antiquorum authoritas.* It goes for current truth that a Hawthorn thereby on Christmas day always blossometh:[2] which the Author tells you in that, *Trees yet in winter, &c.* You may cast this into the account of your greatest Wonders.

320. *Imbrac'd by* Selwood's *son her flood the lovely* Bry.

Selwood sends forth *Bry*, which after a winding course from *Bruton*, (so called of the River) through part of *Sedgmore*, and *Andremore*, comes to *Glastenbury*, and almost inisles it; thence to *Gedney* Moor, and out of *Brent marsh* into *Severne*.

335. *The nearest neighbouring floods to* Arthur's *ancient seat.*

By South *Cadbury* is that *Camelot*; a hill of a mile compass at the top, four trenches circling it, and twixt every of them an earthen wall; the content of it, within, about twenty acres, full of ruins and relics of old buildings. Among *Roman* coins there found, and other works of antiquity, *Stow* speaks of a silver Horseshoe there digged up in the memory of our fathers: *Dii boni* (saith Leland) *quot hic profundissimarum fossarum! quot hic egestæ terræ valla! quæ demùm præcipitia! atque ut paucis finiam, videtur*

---

* Noble Counsellor.
[1] First Christianity in *Britain:* but see the Eighth Song.
† It was called the mother and tomb of the Saints.
[2] A Hawthorn blossoming in Winter.

mihi quidem esse et Artis et Naturæ miraculum.* Antique report makes this one of *Arthur's* places of his Round Table, as the Muse here sings. But of this more in the next Canto.

  * The workmanship of the Ditches, Walls, and strange steepness of them, makes it seem a wonder of Art and Nature.

THE FOURTH SONG.

THE ARGUMENT.

England and Wales *strive, in this Song,*
To whether Lundy *doth belong:*
When either's Nymphs, to clear the doubt,
By Music mean to try it out.
Of mighty Neptune *leave they ask:*
Each one betakes her to her task;
The Britons, *with the Harp and Crowd:*
The English, *both with still and loud.*
The Britons *chaunt King* Arthur's *glory:*
The English *sing their* Saxons' *story.*   10
The Hills of Wales *their weapons take,*
And are an uproar like to make,
To keep the English *part in awe.*
There's heave and shove, and hold and draw;
That Severne *can them scarce divide,*   15
Till Judgment may the Cause decide.

THIS while in *Sabrin's* Court strong factions strangely
    grew,
    Since *Cornwall* for her own, and as her proper due,
    Claim'd *Lundy*, which was said to *Cambria* to
    belong,
Who oft had sought redress for that her ancient wrong:

But her inveterate foe, borne-out by *England's* might, 5
O'ersways her weaker pow'r ; that (now in either's right)
As *Severne* finds no Flood so great, nor poorly mean,
But that the natural Spring (her force which doth main-
tain)
From this[1] or that she takes ; so from this faction free
(Begun about this Isle) not one was like to be. 10
   This *Lundy* is a Nymph to idle toys inclin'd ;
And, all on pleasure set, doth wholly give her mind
To see upon her shores her fowl and conies fed,
§ And wantonly to hatch the birds of *Ganymed*.
Of traffic or return she never taketh care : 15
Not provident of pelf, as many Islands are :
A lusty black-brow'd Girl, with forehead broad and high,
That often had bewitch'd the Sea-gods with her eye.
Of all the inlaid Isles her sovereign *Severne* keeps,
That bathe their amorous breasts within her secret deeps, 20
(To love her *Barry*[2] much and *Silly* though she seem,
The *Flat Holme* and the *Steep* as likewise to esteem)
This noblest *British* Nymph* yet likes her *Lundy* best,
And to great *Neptune's* grace prefers before the rest.
   Thus, *Cambria*[3] to her right that would herself restore, 25
And rather than to lose *Loëgria*,[4] looks for more ;
The Nymphs of either part, whom passion doth invade,
To trial straight will go, though *Neptune* should dissuade :
But of the weaker sex, the most part full of spleen,
And only wanting strength to wreak their angry teen, 30
For skill their challenge make, which every one profest,
And in the learned Arts (of knowledges the best,
And to th' heroic spirit most pleasing under sky)
Sweet Music, rightly match'd with heavenly Poësy,

[1] From England or Wales.
[2] Certain little Isles lying within *Severne*.   * *Severne.*
[3] Wales.   [4] England.

In which they all exceed : and in this kind alone 35
They conquerors vow to be, or lastly overthrown.

Which when fair *Sabrine* saw (as she is wondrous wise)
And that it were in vain them better to advise,
Sith this contention sprang from countries like allied,
That she would not be found t' incline to either side, 40
To mighty *Neptune* sues to have his free consent
Due trial they might make : When he incontinent
His *Tritons* sendeth out the challenge to proclaim.

No sooner that divulg'd in his so dreadful name,
But such a shout was sent from every neighb'ring Spring, 45
That the report was heard through all his Court to ring :
And from the largest Stream unto the lesser Brook,
Them to this wondrous task they seriously betook :
They curl their ivory fronts ; and not the smallest Beck
But with white pebbles makes her tawdries for her neck ; 50
Lay forth their amorous breasts unto the public view,
Enamelling the white, with veins that were as blue ;
Each Moor, each Marsh, each Mead, preparing rich array
To set their Rivers forth against this general day. [shove
'Mongst Forests, Hills, and Floods, was ne'er such heave and
Since *Albion* wielded arms against the son of *Jove.*[1] 56

When as the English part their courage to declare,
Them to th' appointed place immediately prepare.
A troop of stately Nymphs proud *Avon* with her brings
(As she that hath the charge of wise *Minerva's* Springs[2]) 60
From *Mendip* tripping down, about the tinny Mine.
And *Ax*, no less imploy'd about this great design,
Leads forth a lusty rout ; when *Bry*, with all her throng
(With very madness swoll'n that she had stay'd so long)
Comes from the boggy meres and queachy fens below : 65
That *Parret* (highly pleas'd to see the gallant show)

---

[1] *Albion, Neptune's* son, warred with *Hercules.*
[2] The Baths. All these Rivers you may see in the Third Song.

Set out with such a train as bore so great a sway,
The soil but scarcely serves to give her hugeness way.

Then the *Devonian Tawe*, from *Dertmore* deck'd with pearl,
Unto the conflict comes: with her that gallant Girl   70
§ Clear *Towridge*, whom they fear'd would have estrang'd her
Whose coming, lastly, bred such courage in them all, [fall:
As drew down many a Nymph from the *Cornubian* shore,
That paint their goodly breasts with sundry sorts of ore.

The *British*, that this while had stood a view to take   75
What to her utmost pow'r the public foe could make,
But slightly weigh their strength : for by her natural kind,
As still the *Briton* bears a brave and noble mind ;
So, trusting to their skill, and goodness of their cause,
For speedy trial call, and for indifferent laws.   80

At length, by both allow'd, it to this issue grew ;
To make a likely choice of some most expert crew,
Whose number coming near unto the others dower,
The *English* should not urge they were o'erborne by power.
§ Yet hardly upon *Powse* they dare their hopes to lay,   85
For that she hath commerce with *England* every day :
§ Nor *Rosse ;* for that too much she aliens doth respect ;
And following them, foregoes her ancient dialect.
The *Venedotian* Floods,[1] that ancient *Britons* were,
The Mountains kept them back, and shut them in the rear:
But *Brecknock*, long time known a country of much worth,[91]
Unto this conflict brings her goodly Fountains forth :
For almost not a Brook of *Morgany*, nor *Gwent*,[2]
But from her fruitful womb do fetch their high descent.
For *Brecan*, was a Prince once fortunate and great   95
(Who dying, lent his name to that his nobler seat)
With twice twelve daughters blest, by one and only wife :
Who for their beauties rare, and sanctity of life,

---

[1] Floods of North Wales.   [2] *Glamorgan* and *Monmouth Shires.*

To Rivers were transform'd;* whose pureness doth declare
How excellent they were, by being what they are :   100
Who dying virgins all, and Rivers now by fate,
To tell their former love to the unmarried state,   [bear ;
To *Severne* shape their course, which now their form doth
Ere she was made a flood, a virgin as they were.
And from the *Irish* seas with fear they still do fly :   105
So much they yet delight in maiden company.

    Then most renownèd *Wales*, thou famous ancient place,
Which still hast been the Nurse of all the *British* race,
Since Nature thee denies that purple-cluster'd vine,
Which others' temples chafes with fragrant sparkling wine ;
And being now in hand, to write thy glorious praise,   111
Fill me a bowl of *meath*, my working spirit to raise :
And ere Seven Books have end, I'll strike so high a string,
Thy *Bards* shall stand amaz'd with wonder whilst I sing ;
§ That *Taliessen*, once which made the Rivers dance,   115
And in his rapture rais'd the Mountains from their trance,
Shall tremble at my verse, rebounding from the skies,
Which like an earthquake shakes the tomb wherein he lies.

    First our triumphing Muse of sprightly *Uske* shall tell,
And what to every Nymph attending her befell :   120
Which *Cray* and *Camlas* first for Pages doth retain ;
With whom the next in place comes in the tripping *Breane*,
With *Isker ;* and with her comes *Hodny* fine and clear,
Of *Brecknock* best belov'd, the Sovereign of the Sheere :
And *Grony*, at an inch, waits on her Mistress' heels.   125
And ent'ring (at the last) the *Monumethian* fields,
Small *Fidan*, with *Cledaugh*, increase her goodly menie,
Short *Kebby*, and the Brook that christ'neth *Abergeny*.

    With all her wat'ry train, when now at last she came
Unto that happy Town† which bears her only name,   130

---

* A supposed metamorphosis of *Brecan's* daughters.
† Monmouth.

Bright *Birthin*, with her friend fair *Olwy*, kindly meet her :
Which for her present haste, have scarcely time to greet
   her :
But earnest on her way, she needsly will be gone ;
So much she longs to see the ancient *Curleon*.
When *Avon* cometh in, than which amongst them all 135
A finer is not found betwixt her head and fall.
Then *Ebwith*, and with her slides *Srowy ;* which forelay
Her progress, and for *Uske* keep entrance to the sea.
 When *Munno*, all this while, that (for her own behoof)
From this their great recourse had strangely stood aloof, 140
Made proud by *Monmouth's* name appointed her by Fate,
Of all the rest herein observéd special state.
For once the *Bards* foretold she should produce a King,[1]
Which everlasting praise to her great name should bring,
Who by his conquering sword should all the land surprise,
Which twixt the *Penmenmaur*[2] and the *Pyreni*[3] lies : 146
She therefore is allow'd her leisure ; and by her
They win the goodly *Wye*, whom strongly she doth stir
Her powerful help to lend : which else she had denied,
Because herself so oft to *England* she allied : 150
But being by *Munno* made for *Wales*, away she goes.
Which when as *Throggy* sees, herself she headlong throws
Into the wat'ry throng, with many another Rill,
Repairing to the Welch, their number up to fill.
That *Remny* when she saw these gallant Nymphs of *Gwent*,
On this appointed match, were all so hotly bent, 156
Where she of ancient time had parted, as a mound,
The *Monumethian* fields, and *Glamorganian* ground,
Intreats the *Taffe* along, as gray as any glass :
With whom clear *Cunno* comes, a lusty *Cambrian* lass : 160

[1] *Henry* the Fifth, styled of Monmouth.
[2] A maritime hill in *Caernarvan* Shire.
[3] Hills dividing *Spain* and *France.*

Then *Elwy*, and with her *Ewenny* holds her way,
And *Ogmore*, that would yet be there as soon as they,
By *Avon* calléd in : when nimbler *Neath* anon   [known ;
(To all the neighbouring Nymphs for her rare beauties
Besides her double head, to help her stream that hath   165
Her handmaids, *Melta* sweet, clear *Hepsey*, and *Tragath*)
From *Brecknock* forth doth break; then *Dulas* and *Cledaugh*,
By *Morgany*** do drive her through her wat'ry saugh[1] ;
With *Taury*, taking part t' assist the *Cambrian* power :
§ Then *Lhu* and *Logor*, given to strengthen them by *Gower*.
  'Mongst whom, some *Bards* there were, that in their
      sacred rage   171
Recorded the descents, and acts of every Age.   [string ;
Some with their nimbler joints that strook the warbling
In fing'ring some unskill'd, but only us'd to sing
Unto the other's harp : of which you both might find   175
Great plenty, and of both excelling in their kind,
§ That at the *Stethva* oft obtain'd a victor's praise,
Had won the *Silver Harp*, and worn *Apollo's* bays :
Whose verses they deduc'd from those first golden times,
Of sundry sorts of feet, and sundry suits of rhymes.   180
In *Englins*[2] some there were that on their subject strain ;
Some Makers that again affect the loftier vein,
Rehearse their high conceits in *Cowiths :* other-some
In *Owdells* theirs express, as matter haps to come ;
So varying still their moods, observing yet in all   185
Their quantities, their rests, their ceasures metrical :
For to that sacred skill they most themselves apply,
Addicted from their births so much to poësy,
That in the mountains those who scarce have seen a book,
Most skilfully will make, as though from Art they took. 190

  * *Glamorgan.*   [1] A kind of trench.
  [2] **Englins, Cowiths, and Awdells,** British forms of verses.
See the Illustrations. A word, used by the Ancients, signifying to
versify.

And as *Loëgria* spares not anything of worth
That any way might set her goodly Rivers forth,
As stones by nature cut from the *Cornubian* strond,
Her *Dertmore* sends them pearl; *Rock-vincent* diamond :
So *Cambria* of her Nymphs especial care will have.   195
For *Conwy* sends them pearl to make them wondrous brave;
The sacred *Virgin's-well*,[1] her moss most sweet and rare,
Against infectious damps for pomander to wear :
And *Goldcliff*[2] of his ore in plenteous sort allows,
To spangle their attires and deck their amorous brows.   200
     And lastly, holy *Dee* (whose pray'rs were highly pris'd,
As one in heavenly things devoutly exercis'd :
Who, changing of his fords,[3] by divination had
Foretold the neighbouring folk of fortune good or bad)
In their intended course sith needs they will proceed,   205
His benediction sends in way of happy speed.
And though there were such haste unto this long-look'd hour,
Yet let they not to call upon th' Eternal Pow'r.
For, who will have his work his wishéd end to win,
Let him with hearty prayer religiously begin.   210
Wherefore the *English* part, with full devout intent,
In meet and godly sort to *Glastenbury* sent,
Beseeching of the Saints in *Avalon* that were,
There off'ring at their Tombs for every one a tear.
§ And humbly to Saint *George* their Country's Patron pray,
To prosper their design now in this mighty day.   216
     The *Britons*, like devout, their messengers direct
To *David*, that he would their ancient right protect.
'Mongst *Hatterill's* lofty hills, that with the clouds are crown'd,
The Valley *Ewias*[4] lies, immur'd so deep and round,   220
As they below that see the mountains rise so high,
Might think the straggling herds were grazing in the sky :

---

[1] Saint *Winifrid's* Well.   [2] A glistering Rock in *Monmouthshire.*
[3] See the Eighth Song.   [4] In *Monmouthshire.*

Which in it such a shape of solitude doth bear,
As Nature at the first appointed it for pray'r :
Where, in an aged Cell, with moss and ivy grown, 225
In which not to this day the sun hath ever shone,
That reverend *British* Saint, in zealous ages past,
To contemplation liv'd ; and did so truly fast,
As he did only drink what crystal *Hodney* yields,
And fed upon the Leeks he gather'd in the fields. 230
In memory of whom, in the revolving year,
The Welch-men on his day that sacred herb do wear :
Where, of that holy man, as humbly they do crave,
That in their just defence they might his furtherance have.

 Thus either, well-prepar'd the other's pow'r before, 235
Conveniently being plac'd upon their equal shore ;
The *Britons*, to whose lot the onset doth belong,
Give signal to the foe for silence to their song.

 To tell each various strain and turning of their rhymes,
How this in compass falls, or that in sharpness climbs, 240
(As where they rest and rise, how take it one from one,
As every several chord hath a peculiar tone)
Even Memory herself, though striving, would come short :
But the material things Muse help me to report.

 As first, t' affront the Foe, in th' ancient *Britons*' right, 245
With *Arthur* they begin, their most renownéd Knight ;
The richness of the arms their well-made Worthy[1] wore,
The temper of his sword (the tried *Escalaboure*)
The bigness and the length of *Rone*, his noble spear ;
With *Pridwin* his great shield, and what the proof could bear;
His baudric how adorn'd with stones of wondrous price, 251
§ The sacred Virgin's shape he bore for his device ;
These monuments of worth the ancient *Britons* song. [long,
 Now, doubting lest these things might hold them but too

---

[1] *Arthur,* one of the Nine Worthies.

His wars they took to task ; the land then overlaid   255
With those proud *German* powers : when, calling to his aid
His kinsman *Howell*, brought from *Brittany* the Less,
Their armies they unite, both swearing to suppress
The *Saxon*, here that sought through conquest all to gain.
On whom he chanc'd to light at *Lincolne:* where the plain   260
Each-where from side to side lay scatter'd with the dead.
And when the conquer'd Foe, that from the conflict fled,
Betook them to the woods, he never left them there
Until the *British* earth he forc'd them to forswear.
And as his actions rose, so raise they still their vein   265
In words, whose weight best suit a sublimated strain.
  § They sung how he himself at *Badon* bore that day,
When at the glorious goal his *British* sceptre lay :
Two days together how the battle strongly stood :
Pendragon's worthy son,[1] who waded there in blood,   270
Three hundred *Saxons* slew with his own valiant hand.
  And after (call'd the *Pict* and *Irish* to withstand)
How he by force of arms *Albania* overran,
Pursuing of the *Pict* beyond Mount *Calidon :*
There strongly shut them up whom stoutly he subdu'd.   275
  How *Gillamore* again to *Ireland* he pursu'd,
So oft as he presum'd the envious *Pict* to aid :
And having slain the King, the Country waste he laid.
  To *Goth-land* how again this Conqueror maketh forth
With his so prosp'rous pow'rs into the farthest North :   280
Where, *Iseland* first he won, and *Orkney* after got.
  To *Norway* sailing next, with his dear Nephew *Lot*,
By deadly dint of sword did *Ricoll* there defeat :
And having plac'd the Prince on that *Norwegian* seat,
How this courageous King did *Denmarke* then control :   285
That scarcely there was found a Country to the Pole

[1] King *Arthur.*

That dreaded not his deeds, too long that were to tell.

And after these, in *France* th' adventures him befell
At *Paris*, in the lists, where he with *Flollio* fought ;
The Emperor *Leon's* power to raise his siege that brought. 290

Then bravely set they forth, in combat how these Knights
On horseback and on foot perform'd their several fights :
As with what marvellous force each other they assail'd,
How mighty *Flollio* first, how *Arthur* then prevail'd ;
For best advantaged how they traversèd their grounds, 295
The horrid blows they lent, the world-amazing wounds,
Until the Tribune, tir'd, sank under *Arthur's* sword.

Then sing they how he first ordain'd the Circled-board,
The Knights whose martial deeds far fam'd that *Table-round;*
Which, truest in their loves; which, most in arms renown'd:
The Laws, which long upheld that Order, they report ; 301
§ The *Pentecosts* prepar'd at *Carleon* in his Court,
That Table's ancient seat ; her Temples and her Groves,
Her Palaces, her Walks, Baths, Theatres, and Stoves :
Her Academy, then, as likewise they prefer : 305
Of *Camilot* they sing, and then of *Winchester.*
The feasts that underground the Faërie did him make,
And there how he enjoy'd the Lady of the Lake.

Then told they, how himself great *Arthur* did advance,
To meet (with his allies) that puissant force in *France*, 310
By *Lucius* thither led ; those armies that while-ere
Affrighted all the world, by him strook dead with fear :
Th' report of his great acts that over Europe ran,
In that most famous Field he with the Emperor wan :
As how great *Rython's* self he slew in his repair, 315
Who ravish'd *Howell's* niece, young *Helena* the fair ;
And for a trophy brought the Giant's coat away
Made of the beards of Kings.   Then bravely chanted they
The several twelve pitch'd Fields he with the *Saxons* fought:
The certain day and place to memory they brought ; 320

Then by false *Mordred's* hand how last he chanc'd to fall,
The hour of his decease, his place of burial.
　　When out the *English* cried, to interrupt their song :
But they, which knew to this more matter must belong,
Not out at all for that, nor any whit dismay'd,　　　　325
But to their well-tun'd Harps their fingers closely laid :
Twixt ev'ry one of which they plac'd their country's *Crowd,*
And with courageous spirits thus boldly sang aloud ;
How *Merlin* by his skill, and magic's wondrous might,
From *Ireland* hither brought the *Stonendge* in a night :　330
§ And for *Carmarden's* sake, would fain have brought to
About it to have built a wall of solid brass :　　　　[pass,
And set his Fiends to work upon the mighty frame ;
Some to the anvil : some, that still inforc'd the flame :
But whilst it was in hand, by loving of an Elfe　　　　335
(For all his wondrous skill) was cos'ned by himself.
For, walking with his *Fay,* her to the rock he brought,
In which he oft before his nigromancies wrought :
And going in thereat his magic to have shown,
She stopp'd the cavern's mouth with an inchanted stone : 340
Whose cunning strongly crost, amaz'd whilst he did stand,
She captive him convey'd unto the *Fairie* Land.
　　Then, how the laboring spirits, to rocks by fetters bound,
With bellows' rumbling groans, and hammers' thund'ring
A fearful horrid din still in the earth do keep,　　　[sound,
Their Master to awake, suppos'd by them to sleep ;　　346
As at their work how still the grievéd spirits repine,
Tormented in the fire, and tiréd at the mine.
　　When now the *British side* scarce finishéd their song,
But th' *English* that repin'd to be delay'd so long,　　350
All quickly at the hint, as with one free consent,
Strook up at once and sung each to the instrument ;
(Of sundry sorts that were, as the musician likes)
On which the practis'd hand with perfect'st fing'ring strikes,

Whereby their height of skill might liveliest be exprest. 355
The trembling *Lute*[1] some touch, some strain the *Viol* best
In sets which there were seen, the music wondrous choice:
Some likewise there affect the *Gamba* with the voice,
To shew that *England* could variety afford.
Some that delight to touch the sterner wiry *Chord*, 360
The *Cythron*, the *Pandore*, and the *Theorbo* strike:
The *Gittern* and the *Kit* the wand'ring Fiddlers like,
So were there some again, in this their learned strife
Loud Instruments that lov'd; the *Cornet* and the *Fife*,
The *Hoboy*, *Sagbut* deep, *Recorder*, and the *Flute:* 365
Even from the shrillest *Shawm* unto the *Cornamute.*
Some blow the *Bagpipe* up, that plays the *Country-round:*
The *Taber* and the *Pipe* some take delight to sound.
    Of *Germanie* they sung the long and ancient fame,
From whence their noble Sires the valiant *Saxons* came, 370
Who sought by sea and land adventures far and near;
And seizing at the last upon the *Britons* here,
Surpriz'd the spacious Isle, which still for theirs they hold:
As in that Country's praise how in those times of old,
§ *Tuisco*, *Gomer's* son, from unbuilt *Babel** brought 375
His people to that place, with most high knowledge fraught,
And under wholesome laws establish'd their abode;
Whom his *Tudeski* since have honor'd as a God:
Whose clear creation made them absolute in all,
Retaining till this time their pure original. 380
And as they boast themselves the Nation most unmix'd,
Their language as at first, their ancient customs fix'd,
The people of the world most hardy, wise and strong;
So gloriously they show, that all the rest among
The *Saxons* of her sorts the very noblest were: 385
And of those crooked skaines they us'd in war to bear,

---

[1] The sundry Musics of England.   * Gen. xi. 8, 9.

Which, in their thund'ring tongue, the *Germans, Handseax*
   name,
§ They *Saxons* first were call'd : whose far-extended fame
For hardiness in war, whom danger never fray'd,
§ Allur'd the *Britons* here to call them to their aid :   390
From whom they after reft *Loëgria* as their own,
Brute's offspring then too weak to keep it being grown.
   This told : the Nymphs again, in nimble strains of wit,
Next neatly come about, the *Englishmen* to quit
Of that inglorious blot by *Bastard William* brought   395
Upon this conquered Isle : than which Fate never wrought
A fitter mean (say they) great *Germany* to grace ;
To graft again in one two remnants of her race :
Upon their several ways, two several times that went
To forage for themselves. The first of which she sent   400
§ To get their seat in *Gaul :* which on *Nuestria* light,
And (in a famous war the *Frenchmen* put to flight)
Possess'd that fruitful place, where only from their name
§ [1] Call'd *North-men* (from the North of *Germany* that came,
Who thence expell'd the *Gauls*, and did their rooms supply)
This, first *Nuestria* nam'd, was then call'd *Normandy*.   405
That by this means, the less (in conquering of the great)
Being drawn from their late home unto this ampler seat,
Residing here, resign'd what they before had won ;
§ [2] That as the Conqueror's blood, did to the conquer'd run
So kindly being mix'd, and up together grown,   411
As sever'd, they were hers ; united, still her own.
   But these mysterious things desisting now to show
(The secret works of heaven) to long descents they go :
How *Egelred* (the Sire of *Edward* the last King   415
Of th' English *Saxon* Line) by nobly marrying

[1] The Normans and the Saxons of one blood.
[2] The Normans lost that name, and became English.

With hardy *Richard's* heir, the *Norman Emma*, bred
Alliance in their bloods. Like Brooks that from one head
Bear several ways (as though to sundry seas to haste)
But by the varying soil, int' one again are cast :   420
So chancèd it in this the nearness of their blood.
For when as *England's* right in question after stood,
Proud *Harould*, *Goodwin's* heir, the sceptre having won
From *Edgar Etheling* young, the outlaw'd *Edward's* son ;
The valiant *Bastard* this his only colour made,   425
With his brave *Norman* powers this kingdom to invade.
Which leaving, they proceed to pedigrees again,
Their after-Kings to fetch from that old *Saxon* strain ;
From *Margarit* that was made the *Scottish Malcom's* Bride,
Who to her Grandsire had courageous *Ironside :*   430
Which outlaw'd *Edward* left ; whose wife to him did bring
This *Margarit* Queen of *Scots*, and *Edgar Etheling :*   [gave
That *Margarit* brought forth *Maud ;* which gracious *Malcolme*
To *Henry Beauclark's* bed (so Fate it pleas'd to have) [spare :
§ Who him a daughter brought ; which heaven did strangely
And for the special love he to the mother bare,   436
Her *Maude* again he nam'd, to th' *Almain* Emperor wed :
Whose Dowager whilst she liv'd (her puissant *Cæsar* dead)
She th' Earl of *Anjou* next to husband doth prefer.
The Second *Henry* then by him begot of her,   440
Into the *Saxon* Line the sceptre thus doth bring.
    Then presently again prepare themselves to sing
The sundry foreign Fields the *Englishmen* had fought.
Which when the Mountains saw (and not in vain) they thought
That if they still went on as thus they had begon,   445
Then from the *Cambrian* Nymphs (sure) *Lundy* would be won.
And therefore from their first they challeng'd them to fly ;
And (idly running on with vain prolixity)
A larger subject took than it was fit they should.   [hold,
    But, whilst those would proceed, these threat'ning them to

Black-Mountain[1] for the love he to his Country bare,   451
As to the beateous *Uske*, his joy and only care,
(In whose defence t' appear more stern and full of dread)
Put on a helm of clouds upon his rugged head.
Mounchdeny doth the like for his belovéd *Tawe :*   455
Which quickly all the rest by their example draw :
As *Hatterell* in the right of ancient *Wales* will stand.
To these three Mountains, first of the *Brekinnian* band,
The *Monumethian* Hills, like insolent and stout,
On lofty tip-toes then began to look about ;   460
That *Skeridvaur* at last (a Mountain much in might,
In hunting that had set his absolute delight)
Caught up his Country-hook ;[2] nor cares for future harms,
But irefully enrag'd, would needs to open arms :
Which quickly put *Penvayle*[3] in such outrageous heat,   465
That whilst for very teen his hairless scalp doth sweat,
The *Blorench* looketh big upon his baréd crown :
And tall *Tomberlow* seems so terribly to frown,
That where it was suppos'd with small ado or none
Th' event of this debate would eas'ly have been known,   470
Such strange tumultuous stirs upon this strife ensue,
As where all griefs should end, old sorrows still renew :
That *Severne* thus forewarn'd to look unto the worst
(And finds the latter ill more dang'rous than the first)
The doom she should pronounce yet for awhile delay'd,   475
Till these rebellious routs by justice might be stay'd ;
A period that she put to my discourse so long,
To finish this debate the next ensuing Song.

[1] These and the rest following, the famousest Hills in *Brecknocke*, *Glamorgan*, and *Monmouth*.
[2] Welch-hook.   [3] So named of his bald head.

ILLUSTRATIONS.

OVER *Severne* (but visiting *Lundey*, a little Isle twixt *Hartland* and *Goven* Point) you are transported into *Wales.* Your travels with the Muse are most of all in *Monmouth*, *Glamorgan*, and the South maritime Shires.

14. *And wantonly to hatch the* Birds *of* Ganymed.

Walter Baker a Canon of *Osney* (interpreter of *Thomas de la Moore's* Life of *Edward* the Second) affirms, that it commonly breeds Conies, Pigeons, *et struconas, quos vocat Alexander Nechamus* (so you must read,[1] not *Nechristum*, as the *Francfort* print senselessly mistook, with *Conday* for *Lundey*) *Ganymedis ares.* What he means by his Birds of *Ganymed*, out of the name, unless Eagles or Ostriches (as the common fiction of the *Catamite's* ravishment, and this French Latin word of the Translator, would) I collect not. But rather read also *Palamedis aves, i.e.,* Cranes) of which *Necham*[2] indeed hath a whole chapter: what the other should be, or whence reason of the name comes, I confess I am ignorant.

---

[1] Tho. de la Moore emendatus.   [2] De rerum naturâ. lib. 1.

71. *Clear* Towridge *whom they fear'd would have estrang'd her*
fall.

For she rising near *Hartland*, wantonly runs to *Hatherlay*
in *Devon*, as if she would to the Southern Ocean ; but returning, there at last is discharged into the *Severne* Sea.

85. *Yet hardly upon* Powse *they dare their hopes to lay.*

Wales had her three parts,[1] *Northwales, Southwales,* and
Powis.[2] The last, as the middle twixt the other, extended
from *Cardigan* to *Shropshire;* and on the English side from
Chester to *Hereford* (being the portion of *Anarawd,* son to
great *Roderique*) bears this accusation, because it compre-
hends, for the most, both Nations and both tongues. But
see for this division to the Seventh Song.

87. *Nor* Rosse *for that too much she* aliens *doth respect.*

Under *Henry* I. a Colony of *Flemings* driven out of their
country by inundation, and kindly received here in respect
of that alliance which the King had with their Earl (for
his mother *Maude,* wife to the *Conqueror,* was daughter to
Baldwin Earl of *Flanders*) afterward upon difference 'twixt
the King and Earl *Robert,* were out of divers parts, but
especially *Northumberland,* where they most of all (as it
seems by *Hoveden*) had residence, constrained into *Rosse**
in *Penbroke,* which retains yet in name and tongue express
notes of being aliens to the *Cambro-Britons.* See the Author
in his next Song.

115. *That* Taliessen *once which made the Rivers dance.*

Taliessin (not *Telesin,* as *Bale* calls him) a learned *Bard,*

---

[1] Girald. Descript. cap. 2. et Powel ad Caradoc. Lancharuan.
[2] Tripartite division of *Wales.*
* So called perhaps because it is almost inisled within the Sea, and
Lhogor as *Rosay* in *Scotland,* expressing almost an Isle. Buchanan.
Hist. 5. in Eugenio 4.

styled **Ben Beirꝺh**,[1] *i.e., the Chiefest of the Bards*, Master to *Merlin Sylvester*, lived about *Arthur's* reign, whose acts his Muse hath celebrated.

170. *With* Lhu *and* Lhogor *given, to strengthen them by* Gower.

Twixt *Neth* and *Lhogor* in *Glamorgan* is this *Gower*, a little province, extended into the sea as a chersonese ; out of it on the West, rise these two Rivers meant by the Author.

177. *That at the* Stethva *oft obtained a* victor's *praise.*

Understand this *Stethva* to be the meeting of the *British Poets* and *Minstrels* for trial[2] of their Poems and Music sufficiencies, where the best had his reward, *a Silver Harp.* Some example is of it under *Rees ap Griffith*, Prince of *South-wales*, in the year 1176. A custom so good, that, had it been judiciously observed, truth of Story had not been so uncertain : for there was, by suppose, a correction of what was faulty in form or matter, or at least a censure[3] of the hearers upon what was recited. As (according to the *Roman* use) it is noted,[4] that *Girald* of *Cambria*, when he had written his *Topography of Ireland*, made at three several days several recitals of his three distinctions in *Oxford ;* of which course some have wished a recontinuance, that either amendment of opinion, or change of purpose in publishing, might prevent blazoned errors. The sorts of these Poets and Minstrels out of Doctor *Powel's* interserted annotations upon *Caradoc Lhancaruan*, I note to you ; first *Beirdhs*, otherwise *Pryduids* (called in *Athenæus*, *Lucan*, and others,

---

[1] Pris. in descript. Walliæ.
[2] Antiquis hujusmodi certamina fuisse docemur à scholiast. Aristoph. et D. Cypriano Serm. de aleator.
[3] Censure upon books published.
[4] Camd. in Epist. Fulconi Grevil. ad edit. Anglic. Norm., &c.

Bards) who, somewhat like the 'Ραψῳδοὶ among the Greeks,
*fortia virorum illustrium facta heroicis composita versibus cum
dulcibus lyræ modulis cantitarunt,*[1] which was the chiefest form
of the ancientest music among the Gentiles, as *Zarlino*[2] hath
fully collected. Their charge also as heralds, was to describe
and preserve pedigrees, wherein their line ascendent went
from the *Petruccius* to *B. M.*, thence to *Sylvius* and *Ascanius*,
from them to *Adam*. Thus *Girald* reporting, hath his *B.M.* in
some copies by transcription[3] of ignorant monks (forgetting
their tenent of perpetual virginity, and that[4] relation of *Theo-
dosius*) turned into *Beatam Mariam*†, whereas it stands for
Belinum Magnum (that was *Heli*, in their writers, father to
Lud and *Cassibelin*) to whom their genealogies had always
reference. [5]The second are which play on the *Harp* and
Crowd ; their music, for the most part, came out of *Ireland*
with *Gruffith ap Conan* Prince of *Northwales*, about King
Stephen's time. This *Gruffith* reformed the abuses of those
Minstrels by a particular statute, extant to this day. The
third are called *Atcaneaid ;* they sing to instruments played
on by others. For the 𝕰𝖓𝖌𝖑𝖞𝖓𝖘, 𝕮𝖔𝖇𝖎𝖙𝖍𝖘 and 𝕬𝖇𝖚𝖔𝖑𝖘;[6] the
first are couplets interchanged of sixteen and fourteen feet,
called 𝕻𝖆𝖑𝖆𝖉𝖎𝖗𝖎𝖊𝖘 and 𝕻𝖊𝖓𝖘𝖊𝖑𝖘, the second of equal tetra-
meters, the third of variety in both rhyme and quantity.
Subdivision of them, and better information may be had
in the elaborate institution of the *Cumraeg* language by
David ap Rees. [7]Of their music anciently, out of an old

---

* Did sing the valiant deeds of famous men to the sweet melody
of the Harp.
  [1] Ammian Marcelin. Hist. 15.   [2] Parte seconda, cap. 4 et 5.
  [3] Dav. Powel. ad Girald. descript. cap. 3.
  [4] Suid. in Ιησ.   † *S. Mary.*
  [5] For the *Harp* and other music instruments, their form and
antiquity, see to the Sixth Song ; whether a special occasion compelled it.
  [6] Quantity of the *Bards'* verses.
  [7] Form of the *British* Music.

writer read this: *Non uniformiter, ut alibi, sed multipliciter multisque modis et modulis cantilenas emittunt, adeò ut, turbâ canentium, quot videas capita tot audias carmina, discriminaque vocum varia, in unam denique, sub B. mollis dulcedine blandâ, consonantiam et organicam convenientia melodiam.* A good musician will better understand it, than I that transcribe it. But by it you see they especially affected the mind-composing *Doric* (which is shewed in that of an old author,[1] affirming that ἡμερώσεως χάριν* the Western people of the world constituted use of music in their assemblies), though the *Irish*[2] (from whence they learned) are wholly for the sprightful *Phrygian.* See the next Canto.

215. *And humbly to S. George their Country's Patron pray.*

Our Author (a judgement-day thus appointed twixt the Water-Nymphs) seems to allude to the course used of old with us, that those which were to end their cause by combat, were sent to several Saints for invocation, as in our Law-annals[3] appears. For *S. George,*† that he is patron to the *English,* as S. *Denis,* S. *James,* S. *Patrick,* S. *Andrew,* S. *Antony,* S. *Mark,* to the *French, Spanish, Irish, Scotish, Italian, Venetian,* scarce any is that knows not. Who he was, and when the *English* took him, is not so manifest. The old Martyrologies give, with us, to the honor of his birth the 23rd of April. His passion is supposed in *Diocletian's* persecution. His country *Cappadoce.* His acts are divers and strange, reported by his servant *Pasicrates, Simeon Metaphrastes,* and lately collected by *Surius.* As for his Knightly form, and the Dragon under him, as he is

---

[1] Marcian. Heracleot. in περιηγήσει.
* To make them gentle-natured.
[2] Girald. Topog. dist. 3. cap. 11.
[3] 30 Ed. III. fol. 20.
† Tropelophorus dictus in Menologio Græco apud Baronium, fortè ῾Ροπαλοφόρος sive Τροπαιοφόρος, quid n. Tropelophorus?

pictured in *Beryth*, a City of *Cyprus*, with a young maid
kneeling to him, an unwarrantable report goes that it was
for his martial delivery of the King's daughter from the
Dragon, as *Hesione* and *Andromeda* were from the Whales by
Hercules and *Perseus*. Your more neat judgements, finding
no such matter in true antiquity, rather make it symbolical
than truly proper. So that some account him an allegory
of our Saviour Christ; and our admired *Spenser*[1] hath made
him an emblem of Religion. So *Chaucer* to the Knights of
that Order.

> ————but for ⍟ods pleasance
> And his mother, and in signifiance
> That ye ben of S. Georges liuerie
> Doeth him seruice and Knightly obeisance
> For Christs cause is his, well knowen yee.

Others interpret that picture of him as some country or city
(signified by the Virgin) imploring his aid against the Devil,
charactered in the Dragon. Of him you may particularly
see, especially in *Usuard's* Martyrology, and *Baronius* his
annotations upon the *Roman* Calendar, with *Erhard Celly*
his description of *Frederick* Duke of *Wittemberg's* installation
in the Garter by favour of our present Sovereign. But
what is delivered of him in the legend, even the Church of
Rome[2] hath disallowed in these words; *That not so made as
any scandal may rise in the Holy Roman Church, the passions
of S.* George, *and such like, supposed to be written by heretics,
are not read in it.* But you may better believe the Legend,
than that he was a *Coventry* man born, with his *Caleb* Lady
of the woods, or that he descended from the *Saxon* race,
and such like; which some *English* fictions deliver. His
name (as generally[3] also S. *Maurice* and S. *Sebastian*) was
anciently called on by Christians as an advocate of victory

[1] Faery Q. lib. 1.
[2] C. Sancta Rom. Eccles. 3. dist. 15. Gelasius PP.
[3] Ord. Rom. de divin. officiis apud *Baronium* in Martyrolog.

(when in the Church that kind of doctrine was) so that our particular right to him (although they say King *Arthur*[1] bare him in one of his Banners) appears not until *Edward* III. consecrated to S. *George* the Knightly *Order* of the *Garter*, soon after the victory at *Calais* against the *French*,[2] in which his invocation was 𝕳𝖆 𝕾. 𝕰𝖉𝖜𝖆𝖗𝖉, 𝕳𝖆 𝕾. 𝕲𝖊𝖔𝖗𝖌𝖊. Some authority[3] refers this to *Richard Cœur de Lion*, who supposed himself comforted by S. *George* in his wars against the *Turks* and *Hagarens*. But howsoever, since that he hath been a Patron among others, as in that of *Frederic* III.'s institution[4] of the quadripartite Society of S. *George's shield*, and more of that nature, you find. And under *Hen.* VIII. it was enacted,[5] that the *Irish* should leave their 𝕮𝖗𝖔𝖒𝖆𝖇𝖔𝖔 and 𝕭𝖚𝖙𝖑𝖊𝖗𝖆𝖇𝖔𝖔, words of unlawful patronage, and name themselves as under S. *George* and the *King of England*. More proper is S. *Dewy* (we call him S. *David*) to the *Welsh*. Reports of him affirm that he was of that country, uncle to King *Arthur* (*Bale* and others say, gotten upon Melaria *a Nun, by* Xantus *Prince of Cardigan*) and successor to *Dubrice* Archbishop of *Caer-leon* upon *Uske* (whereto a long time the *British* Bishoprics as to their Metropolitic See were subject) and thence translated with his nephew's consent the Primacy to *Menevia*, which is now S. *Devies* in *Penbroke*.[6] He was a strong oppugner of the *Pelagian* heresy. To him our country Calendars give the 1st of March, but in the old Martyrologies I find him not remembered : yet I read that *Calixtus* II.[7] first canonized him. See him in the next Canto.

[1] Harding, cap. 72.

[2] Th. de Walsing. an. 1350, and 24 Ed. III. *Fabian* puts it before this year, but erroneously.

[3] Ex antiq. MS. ap. Camd. in Berkscir.

[4] 1488. 𝕯𝖎𝖊 𝖌𝖊 𝖘𝖈𝖊𝖎𝖘𝖈𝖍 𝖆𝖋𝖙 𝕾. 𝕲𝖊𝖔𝖗𝖌𝖊𝖓 𝖘𝖈𝖍𝖎𝖑𝖙𝖘. Martin. Crus. Annal. Suevic. part. 3. lib. 9.

[5] 10 Hen. VIII. in Statutis Hibernicis.

[6] Polychronic. lib. 1. cap. 52.

[7] Bal. Cent. 1.

8—2

252. *The* sacred Virgin's shape *he bare for his device.*

Arthur's shield[1] *Pridwen* (or his Banner) had in it the picture of *Our Lady,* and his helm an ingraven *Dragon.* From the like form was his father called *Uter-pen-dragon.* To have terrible crests or ingraven beasts of rapine (*Herodotus* and *Strabo* fetch the beginning of them, and the bearing of arms from the *Carians*) hath been from inmost antiquity continued;[2] as appears in that epithet of Γοργολόφας, proper to *Minerva,* but applied to others in *Aristophanes,* and also in the *Theban* war.[3] Either hence may you derive the *English* Dragon[4] now as a supporter, and usually pitched in fields by the *Saxon, English,* and *Norman* Kings for their Standard (which is frequent in *Hoveden, Matthew Paris,* and *Florilegus*) or from tho *Romans,* who after the *Minotaur, Horse, Eagle,* and other their antique ensigns took this beast; or else imagine that our Kings joined in that general consent, whereby so many nations bare it. For by plain and good authority, collected by a great critic,[5] you may find it affirmed of the *Assyrians, Indians, Scythians, Persians, Dacians, Romans;* and of the *Greeks* too for their shields, and otherwise: wherein *Lipsius* unjustly finds fault with *Isidore,* but forgets that in a number of Greek authors[6] is copious witness of as much.

267. *They sing how he himself at* Badon *bare the day.*

That is *Baunsedowne* in *Somerset* (not *Blackmore* in *Yorkshire,* as *Polydore* mistakes) as is expressly proved out of a *MS. Gildas,*[7] different from that published by *Josselin.*

---

[1] Nennius. Histor. Galfred. lib. 6. cap. 2. et lib. 7. cap. 2.
[2] Beginning of arms and crests.
[3] Æschyl. Sept. c. Theb.; Euripid. in Phœniss.
[4] The Dragon supporter and *Standard* of *England.*
[5] Lips. Com. ad Polyb. 4. dissert. 5.
[6] Pindar. Pythionic. ειδ. η.; Homer. Iliad. λ.; Suid Epaminond.; Hesiod. Scut. Herc.; Plutarch. Lysand.; Euripid. in Iph. in Aul.
[7] Camden.

286. *That scarcely there was found a* country *to the* pole.

Some, too hyperbolic, stories make him a large conqueror on every adjacent country, as the Muse recites : and his seal, which *Leland* says he saw in *Westminster* Abbey, of red wax pictured with a *Mound*, bearing a *Cross* in his left hand (which was first *Justinian's*[1] device ; and surely, in later time, with the seal counterfeited and applied to *Arthur :* no King of this Land, except the *Confessor*, before the Conquest[2] ever using in their Charters more than subscription of *name* and *crosses*) and a *Sceptre fleury* in his right, calls him *Britanniæ, Galliæ, Germaniæ, Daciæ Imperator.*[*] The *Bards'* songs have with this kind of unlimited attribute so loaden him, that you can hardly guess what is true of him. Such indulgence to false report hath wronged many Worthies, and among them even that great *Alexander* in prodigious suppositions (like *Stichus*[3] his Geography, laying *Pontus* in *Arabia*) as *Strabo* often complains ; and some idle Monk of middle time is so impudent to affirm, that at *Babylon* he erected a column, inscribed with *Latin* and *Greek* verses, as notes of his victory ; of them you shall taste in these two :

> *Anglicus et Scotus Britonum superque caterva*
> *Irlandus, Flander,* Cornwallis, *et quoque* Norguey.

Only but that *Alexander* and his followers were no good Latinists (wherein, when you have done laughing, you may wonder at the *decorum*) I should censure my lubberly versifier to no less punishment than *Marsyas* his excoriation. But for *Arthur*, you shall best know him in this elogy.

---

[1] Suid. in Justinian.   [2] No seals before the Conquest.
[3] Ingulphus.
[*] Emperor of *Britain, Gaul, Germany,* and *Danmarke ;* for so they falsely turned *Dacia.*
[3] Plaut. in Sticho.

'*This is that* Arthur *of whom the* Britons *even to this day speak so idly; a man right worthy to have been celebrated by true story, not false tales, seeing it was he that long time upheld his declining country, and even inspired martial courage into his countrymen;*' as the Monk of *Malmesbury* of him:

302. *The* Pentecost *prepar'd at* Caer-leon *in his Court.*

At *Caer-leon* in *Monmouth*, after his victories, a pompous celebration was at Whitsontide, whither were invited divers Kings and Princes of the neighbouring coasts; he, with them, and his Queen *Guinever*, with the ladies, keeping those solemnities in their several conclaves.[1] For so the *British* story makes it according to the *Troian* custom, that in festival solemnities both sexes should not sit together. Of the *Troians* I remember no warrant for it : but among the *Greeks* one *Sphyromachus*[2] first instituted it. Torneaments and jousts were their exercises, nor vouchsafed any lady to bestow her favour on him which had not been thrice crowned with fame of martial performance. For this order (which herein is delineated) know, that the old *Gauls* (whose customs and the *British* were near the same) had their Orbicular[3] tables to avoid controversy of precedency (a form much commended by a late writer[4] for the like distance of all from the salt, being centre, first, and last of the furniture) and at them every Knight attended by his Esquire (ὁπλοφοροῦντες* *Athenæus*[5] calls them) holding his shield. Of the like in *Hen. III.* Matthew Paris, of *Mortimer's* at *Kelingworth*, under *Edw. I.* and that of *Windsor*, celebrated by *Edw. III. Walsingham* speaks. Of the *Arthurian* our

---

[1] Knights and Ladies sate in several rooms.
[2] Scholiast. ad Aristophan. Eccles.; et Suidas.
[3] Round Tables.   [4] Gemos. Halograph. lib. 3. cap. 9.
* Armigeri, which is expressed in the word *Schilpors* in Paul Warnfred. lib. 2. de gest. Longobard. cap. 28.
[5] Deipnosoph. lib. 4.

Histories have scarce mention. But *Hawillan's Architrenius*, *Robert* of *Gloucester*, *John Lidgat* Monk of *Bury*, and English rhymes in divers hands sing it. It is remembered by *Leland*, *Camden*, *Volateran*, *Philip* of *Bergomo*, *Lily*, *Aubert Mirec*, others, but very diversely. *White* of *Basingstoke* defends it, and imagines the original from an election by *Arthur* and *Howell* King of *Armoric Britain* of six of each of their worthiest Peers to be always assistant in council. The antiquity of the Earldom of *Mansfeld*[1] in old *Saxony* is hence affirmed, because *Heger* Earl thereof was honoured in *Arthur's* Court with this order; [2]places of name for residence of him and his Knights were this *Caer-leon*, *Winchester* (where his Table is yet supposed to be, but that seems of later date) and *Camelot* in *Somerset*. Some put his number twelve. I have seen them anciently pictured twenty-four in a poetical story of him; and in *Denbighshire*, *Stow* tells us, in the parish of *Lansannan* on the side of a stony hill is a circular plain, cut out of a main rock, with some twenty-four seats unequal, which they call *Arthur's Round Table*. Some Catalogues of arms have the coats of the Knights blazoned; but I think with as good warrant as *Rablais*[3] can justify, that Sir *Lancelot du Lac* flays horses in hell, and that *Tous les chevaliers de la Table ronde estoient poures gaigne-deniers tirans la rame pur passer les rivers de Cocyte, Phlegeton, Styx, Acheron, et Lethe quand Messieurs les diables se veulent esbatre sur l'eau come font les Basteliers de Lyon et Gondoliers de Venise. Mais pour chacune passade ils n'ont qu'un nazarde et sur le soir quelque morceau de pain chaumeny.** Of them, their

---

[1] *Hoppenrod* et *Spangberg.* apud Ortelium in *Mansfeld.*

[2] Many places in Wales in hills and rocks, honoured with *Arthur's* name. Pris. Defens. Hist. Brit. &c. ꞓꜵꝹꜳꞮꝛ Ꜳꞃꞇꜧꞟꞃ, *i.e.*, *Arthur's* Chair in *Brecknock.* Girald. Itin. Camb. cap. 2. &c. Ꜳꞃꞇꜧꞟꞃꞅ Ꝏꞗꞧꞟ in *Stirling* of *Scotland.*   [3] Livre 2. chapit. 30.

* The Knights of the Round Table use to ferry spirits over Styx, Acheron, and other rivers, and for their fare have a fillip on the nose and a piece of mouldy bread.

number, exploits, and prodigious performances you may read *Caxton's* published volume, digested by him into twenty-one books, out of divers *French* and *Italian* fables. From such I abstain, as I may.

331. *And for* Caermardhin's *sake*————————

Two *Merlins*[1] have our stories: One of *Scotland* commonly titled *Sylvester,* or *Caledonius,* living under *Arthur;* the other *Ambrosius* (of whom before) born of a Nun (daughter to the King of *Southwales*) in *Caermardhin,* not naming the place (for rather in *British* his name is *Merdhin*) but the place (which in *Ptolemy* is *Maridunum*) naming him ; begotten, as the vulgar, by an *Incubus.* For his burial (in supposition as uncertain as his birth, actions, and all of those too fabulously mixed stories) and his *Lady* of the *Lake,* it is by liberty of profession laid in *France* by that *Italian Ariosto*[2] *:* which perhaps is as credible as some more of his attributes, seeing no persuading authority, in any of them, rectifies the uncertainty. But for his birth see the next Song, and, to it, more.

375. Tuisco *Gomer's son from unbuilt* Babel *brought.*

According to the text,[3] the *Jews* affirm that *all the sons of* Noah *were dispersed through the earth, and every one's name left to the land which he possessed.* Upon this tradition, and false *Berosus'* testimony, it is affirmed that *Tuisco* (son of *Noah,* gotten with others after the Flood[4] upon his wife *Arezia*) took to his part the coast about *Rhine,* and that thence came the name of *Teutschland* and *Teutsch,* which we call *Dutch,* through *Germany.* Some[5] make him the same with *Gomer,* eldest son to *Japhet* (by whom these parts of *Europe* were peopled) out of notation of his name, deriving *Tuiscon* or *Tuiston* (for so *Tacitus* calls him) from 𝕿𝖍𝖊=𝖍𝖔𝖔𝖉𝖙=𝖘𝖔𝖓,

---

[1] Girald. Itiner. Camb. 3. cap. 8.
[2] Orland. Furios. cant. 3. See Spenser's Faery Q. lib. 3. cant. 3.
[3] Gen. 10. [4] Munster. Cosm. lib. 3. [5] Goropius in Indoscythic.

i.e., **the eldest sonne.** Others (as the Author here) suppose him son to *Gomer*, and take[1] him for *Aschenaz* (remembered by *Moses* as first son to *Gomer*, and from whom the *Hebrews* call the *Germans Aschenazim*[2]) whose relics probably indeed seem to be in *Tuisco*, which hath been made of *Aschen* either by the *Dutch* prepositive article **die** or **lie**, as our *the* (according to *Derceto* for *Atergatis*,[3] which should be *Adardaga* in *Ctesias;* and *Danubius* for *Adubenus* in *Festus*, perhaps therein corrupted, as *Joseph Scaliger* observes; as *Theudibald* for *Ildibald* in *Procopius;* and *Diceneus* for *Ceneus* among the *Getes*) or through mistaking of א for ט or ת in the Hebrew, as in *Rhodanim* ר for ד[4] being *Dodanim*, and in *Chalibes* and *Alybes* for *Thalybes* from *Tubal* by taking ה or א for ת; for in ruder manuscripts by an imperfect reader, the first mistaking might be as soon as the rest. I conjecture it the rather, for that in most Histories diversity with affinity twixt the same-meant proper names (especially Eastern as this was) is ordinary; as *Megabyzus* in *Ctesias* is *Bacabasus* in *Justin*, who calls *Aaron*, *Arcas*, and *Herodotus's Smerdis*, *Mergidis; Asarhadon, Corus* and *Esther* in the Scriptures, are thus *Sardanapalus, Cyrus*, and *Amestris* in the Greek stories; *Eporedorix, Ambiorix, Ariminius*, in *Cæsar*, and *Sueton*, supposed to have been *Frederique, Henry, Herman:* divers like examples occur; and in comparison of *Arrian* with *Q. Curtius* very many; like as also in the life of *S. John* the Evangelist, anciently written[5] in *Arabic* you have *Asubasianvusu, Thithimse, Damthiancusu* for *Vespasian, Titus, Domitian*, and in our stories *Androgeus* for *Cæsar's Mandubratius*. From *Tuisco* is our name of *Tuesday;* and in that too,

---

[1] Jodoc. Willich. Comm. ad Tacit. Germaniam. et Pantaleon lib. 1. Prosopograph.
[2] Elias Levit. in Thisb.; Arias. Mont. in Peleg.
[3] Strab. lib. ζ. ιϛ́. et ιϛ́. de aliis quæ hic congerimus.
[4] Broughton in concent. præf.
[5] Pet. Kirstenius Grammaticæ Arabicæ subjunxit.

taking the place of *Mars* (the most fiery Star, and observe withal that against the vulgar opinion the planetary account of days is very ancient[1]) discovers affinity with *Aschenaz*, in whose notation (as somebody[2] observes) **שא** signifies fire.

> ass. *They* Saxons *first were call'd*———

So a Latin rhyme in *Engelhuse*[3] also ;

> *Quippe brevis gladius apud illos* Saxa *vocatur,*
> *Unde sibi* Saxo *nomen traxisse putatur.*

Although from the *Sacans* or *Sagans* a populous nation in *Asia* (which were also *Scythians*, and of whom an old Poet,[4] as most others in their epithets and passages of the *Scythians*,

> Τόξα Σάκαι φορέοντες ἃ μηκέτις ἄλλος ἐλέγχοι
> Τοξευτής, οὐ γάρ σφι θέμις ἀνεμώλια βάλλειν.*

A faculty for which the *English*[5] have had no small honour in their later wars with the *French*) both *Goropius* with long argument in his *Becceselana*, our judicious *Camden* and others will have them, as it were, *Sacai's-sons*. According hereto is that name of *Sacasena*,[6] which a colony of them gave to part of *Armenia* and the *Sasones*[7] in *Scythia* on this side of *Imaus*. Howsoever, the Author's conceit thus chosen is very apt, nor disagreeing to this other, in that some community was twixt the name of *Sacœ* or *Sagœ*, and a certain sharp weapon called *Sagaris*, used by the *Amazons, Sacans,* and *Persians,* as the Greek stories[8] inform us.

---

[1] Scalig. in prolegom. ad Emendat. Temp.
[2] Melancthon ap. Becan. in Indoscyth.
[3] Ap. Camdenum.   [4] Dionys. Afer. in Perieg. 750.
  * The shooting *Sacœ* none can teach them Art :
    For what they loos'd at, never 'scapes their dart.
[5] The English from their original, excellent Archers. See the Eighth Song.
[6] Strabo, lib. ια.   [7] Ptolem. Geograph. lib. ϛ. cap. ιδ.
[8] Herodot. Polyhymn.; Xenoph. Anab. 4.; Strabo, lib. ι.ε.

390. *The* Britons *here* allur'd *to call them to their* aid.

[1]Most suppose them sent to by the *Britons* much subject to the irruptions of *Picts* and *Scots*, and so invited hither for aid : but the stories of *Gildas* and *Nennius* have no such thing, but only that there landed of them (as banished their country, which *Geffrey* of *Monmouth* expresses also) three long boats in Kent with *Horse* and *Hengist* Captains. They afterward were most willingly requested to multiply their number by sending for more of their countrymen to help King *Vortigern*, and under that colour, and by *Ronix* (daughter to *Hengist*, and wife to *Vortigern*) her womanish subtlety, in greater number were here planted. Of this, more large in every common story. But to believe their first arrival rather for new place of habitation, than upon embassage of the *Britons*, I am persuaded by this, that[2] among the *Cimbrians, Gauls, Goths, Dacians, Scythians*, and especially the *Sacans* (if *Strabo* deceive not ; from whom our *Saxons*) with other Northern people, it was a custom upon numerous abundance to transplant colonies : from which use the *Parthians* (sent out of *Scythia*, as the *Romans* did their *Ver Sacrum*[3]) retain that name, signifying banished (says *Trogus;*) not unlikely, from the Hebrew *Paratz*,[4] which is to *separate*, and also to *multiply* in this kind of propagation, as it is used in the promise to *Abraham*, and in *Isay's* consolation to the Church. Here being the main change of the *British* name and State, a word or two of the time and year is not untimely. Most put it under 449 (according to *Bede's* copies and their followers) or 450 of Christ ; whereas indeed by apparent proof it was in 428 and the 4th of *Valentinian* the Emperor. So *Prise* and *Camden* (out of an old fragment

[1] See the Eighth Song.
[2] Justin. lib. 24. et 41.; Herodot. Clio.; Walsingh. Hypodig. Neust.; Gemeticens. lib. 1. cap. 4. Sabinis et Græcis morem hunc fuisse memini legisse me apud Varronem et Columellam.
[3] Festus in eod. et Mamertinis.   [4] פרץ. Gen. 28. 14.; Jesai. 54. 3.

annexed to *Nennius*) and, before them, the Author of *Fasci-
culus Temporum* have placed it. The error I imagine to be
from restoring of worn-out times in *Bede* and others, by
those which fell into the same error with *Florence* of *Worcester* and *Marian* the *Scot*, who begin the received Christian
accompt but twelve years before the Passion, thereby omitting twenty-two. For although *Marian's* published Chronicle (which is but a defloration[1] by *Robert* of *Lorraine*
Bishop of *Hereford* under *Hen. I.* and an epitome of *Marian*)
goes near from the ordinary time of Incarnation under
Augustus, yet he lays it also, according to the *Roman* Abbot
Dionysius, in the twenty-third year following, which was
rather by taking advantage of *Dionysius* his error than
following his opinion.[2] For when he (about *Justinian's* time)
made his period of 532 years of the Golden Number and
cycle of the Sun multiplied, it fell out so in his computation
that the fifteenth Moon following the *Jews'* Passover, the
Dominical letter, Friday, and other concurrents according
to Ecclesiastical tradition supposed for the Passion could
not be but in the twelfth year[3] after his birth (a lapse by
himself much repented) and then supposing Christ lived
thirty-four years, thirty-two must needs be omitted ; a col-
lection directly against his meaning, having only forgotten
to fit those concurrents. This accompt (in itself. and by
the Abbot's purpose, as our vulgar is now, but with some
little difference) erroneously followed, I conjecture, made
them, which too much desired correction, add the supposed
Evangelical twenty-two years to such times as were before
true ; and so came 428 to be 449 and 450 which *White* of
Basingstoke (although aiming to be accurate) unjustly follows.
Subtraction of this number, and, in some, addition (of addition you shall have perhaps example in amendment of the 156

[1] Malmesb. lib. 4. de Pontificib.
[2] Mistaking in our Chronologies.
[3] Paul. de Midleburgo. part 2. lib. 5.

year for King *Lucius* his letters to *PP. Eleutherius*) will rec-
tify many gross absurdities in our Chronologies, which are
by transcribing, interpolation, misprinting, and creeping in
of anti-chronisms, now and then strangely disordered.

401. *To get their seat in* Gaul *which on* Nuestria *light.*
And a little after,
Call'd Northmen *from the* North *of* Germany *that came.*

What is now *Normandy* is, in some, styled *Neustria* and
Nuestria corruptly, as most think, for *Westria*, that is 𝕎𝕖𝕤𝕥=
𝕣𝕚𝕔𝕙,* *i.e.*, the West Kingdom (confined anciently twixt the
Mense and the *Loire*), in respect of 𝔸𝕦𝕤𝕥𝕣𝕚𝕔𝕙 or 𝕆𝕠𝕤𝕥𝕣𝕚𝕔𝕙,
i.e., the East Kingdom, now *Lorraine*, upon such reason as
the Archdukedom hath his name at this day. *Rollo*, son of
a *Danish* Potentate, accompanied with divers *Danes*, *Nor-
wegians, Scythians, Goths*, and a supplement of *English*, which
he had of King *Athelstan*, about the year 900, made transmigration into *France*, and there, after some martial discords, honored in holy tincture of Christianity with the
name of *Robert*, received[1] of *Charles the Simple* with his
daughter (or sister) *Gilla* this Tract as her dower containing (as before) more than *Normandy*. It is reported,[2] that
when the Bishops at this donation required him to kiss the
King's foot for homage, after scornful refusal, he commanded
one of his Knights to do it; the Knight took up the King's
leg, and in straining it to his mouth, overturned him[3]; yet
nothing but honourable respect followed on either part.

410. *That as the* Conqueror's *blood did to the* conquered *run.*

Our Author makes the *Norman* Invasion a re-uniting of
severed kindred, rather than a conquest by a mere stranger,
taking argument as well from identity of countryship (being
all *Germans* by original, and the people of the *Cimbrica Cher-*

---

* Westrich.   [1] Paul. Æmilius, Hist. Franc. 3.
[2] Guil. Gemiticens. lib. 2, cap. 17.   [3] An unmannerly homage.

soncsus,[1] now *Danmarch,* anciently called *Saxons*), as from
contingency of blood twixt the *Anglo-Saxon* Kings, and the
Norman Dukes thus expressed :*—

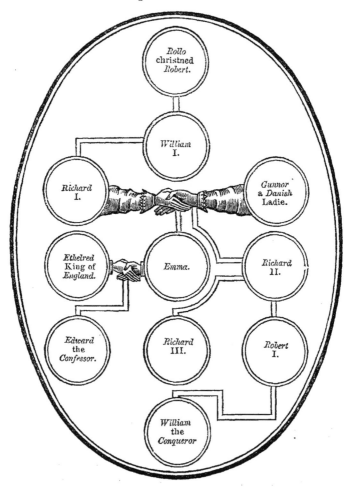

[1] Marcian. Heracleot. in περιπλ β.
* Gemiticens. lib. 7. cap. 36. et lib. 3. cap. 18.

Object not that Duke *Robert* got the Conqueror upon *Ar-letta* (from whom perhaps came our name of *Harlot*) his Con-cubine, nor that [1] *Consanguinitatis et adgnationis jura à patre tantum et legitimis nuptiis oriuntur,** as the *Civil* Law, and upon the matter the *English* also, defines; but rather allow it by law of Nature and Nobility, which justifies the bastard's bearing of his father's coat, distinguished with a bend sinis-ter: *Nicholas Upton* calls it *Fissura, eò quod finditur à patriâ hæreditate;* [2] which is but his conceit: and read *Heuter's* tract *de liberâ hominis nativitate,* where you shall find a kind of legitimation of that now disgraceful name *Bastard;* which in more antique times was, as a proud title, inserted in the style of great and most honourable Princes. Pretending this consanguinity, S. *Edward's* adoption, and King *Harold's* oath, aided by successful arms, the *Norman* acquired the *English* Crown [3]; although *William* of *Poitiers* [4] affirms, that on his death-bed he made protestation, that his right was not hereditary, but by effusion of blood, and loss of many lives.

433. *Who him a daughter brought, which* Heaven *did strangely spare.*

After composition of *French* troubles *Hen. I.,* returning into *England,* the ship, wherein his sons *William* and *Richard* were, twixt *Barbefleu* and *South-hampton* was cast away, so that Heaven only spared him this issue *Maude* the *Empress,* married, at last, to *Geffrey Plantagenest* Earl of *Anjou,* from whom in a continued race through *Hen. II.* (son to this *Maude*) until *Rich. III.* that most noble surname [5] possessed the royal Throne of *England.*

---

[1] ff. unde cognati, 1. 4. spurius. et tit. de grad. affin. 1. 4. non facile. § 8. sciendum.
* Right of blood and kindred comes only by lawful marriage.
[2] A division, because he is separated from his father's inheritance.
[3] 1066. [4] Histor. Cadomens. [5] Plantagenest.

THE FIFTH SONG.

THE ARGUMENT.

In this Song, Severne *gives the doom*
What of her Lundy *should become.*
And whilst the nimble Cambrian *Rills*
Dance hy-day-gies amongst the Hills,
The Muse them to Carmarden *brings ;*   5
Where Merlin's *wondrous birth she sings.*
From thence to Penbrooke *she doth make,*
To see how Milford *state doth take :*
The scattered Islands there doth tell :
And, visiting Saint David's *Cell,*   10
Doth sport her all the shores along,
Preparing the ensuing Song.

OW *Sabrine,* as a Queen, miraculously fair,
Is absolutely plac'd in her Emperial Chair
Of crystal richly wrought, that gloriously did shine,
Her grace becoming well, a creature so divine :
And as her god-like self, so glorious was her throne,   5
In which himself to sit great *Neptune* had been known ;
Whereon there were ingrav'd those Nymphs the God had
    wooed,
And every several shape wherein for love he sued ;
Each daughter, her estate and beauty, every son ;
What Nations he had rul'd, what Countries he had won. 10

No fish in this wide waste but with exceeding cost
Was there in antique work most curiously imbost.
She, in a watchet weed, with many a curious wave,
Which as a princely gift great *Amphitrite* gave;
Whose skirts were to the knee, with coral fring'd below   15
To grace her goodly steps.   And where she meant to go,
The path was strew'd with pearl : which though they orient
          were,
Yet scarce known from her feet, they were so wondrous clear :
To whom the Mermaids hold her glass, that she may see
Before all other Floods how far her beauties be :   20
Who was by *Nereus* taught, the most profoundly wise,
That learnéd her the skill of hidden prophecies,
By *Thetis'* special care ; as *Chiron* [1] erst had done
To that proud bane of Troy, her god-resembling son.
For her wise censure now, whilst every list'ning Flood   25
(When reason some-what cool'd their late distemp'red mood)
Incloséd *Severne* in ; before this mighty rout,
She sitting well-prepar'd, with count'nance grave and stout,
Like some great learnéd Judge, to end a weighty cause,
Well-furnish'd with the force of arguments and laws,   30
And every special proof that justly may be brought ;
Now with a constant brow, a firm and settled thought,
And at the point to give the last and final doom :
The people crowding near within the pest'red room
. A slow soft murmuring moves amongst the wond'ring throng,
As though with open ears they would devour his tongue : 35
So *Severne* bare herself, and silence so she wan,
When to th' assembly thus she seriously began :
    My near and lovéd Nymphs, good hap ye both betide :
Well *Britons* have ye sung ; you *English*, well replied :   40
Which to succeeding times shall memorise your stories
To either Country's praise, as both your endless glories.

----

[1] *Chiron* brought up *Achilles*, son to *Thetis*.

And from your list'ning ears, sith vain it were to hold
What all-appointing Heaven will plainly shall be told,
Both gladly be you pleas'd : for thus the Powers reveal, 45
That when the *Norman* Line in strength shall lastly fail
(Fate limiting the time) the ancient *Briton* race
Shall come again to sit upon the sovereign place.
A branch sprung out of *Brute*, th' imperial top shall get,
Which grafted in the stock of great *Plantagenet*, 50
The Stem shall strongly wax, as still the Trunk doth wither:
That power which bare it thence, again shall bring it thither
By *Tudor*, with fair winds from Little *Britaine* driven,
§ To whom the goodly Bay of *Milford* shall be given ;
As thy wise Prophets, *Wales*, fore-told his wish'd arrive, 55
§ And how *Lewellin's* Line in him should doubly thrive.
For from his issue sent to *Albany* before,
Where his neglected blood his virtue did restore,
He first unto himself in fair succession gain'd
The *Stewards'* nobler name ; and afterward attain'd 60
The royal *Scottish* wreath, upholding it in state.
This Stem, to *Tudor's*[1] join'd (which thing all-powerful Fate
So happily produc'd out of that prosperous Bed,
Whose marriages conjoin'd the White-rose and the Red)
Suppressing every Plant, shall spread itself so wide, 65
As in his arms shall clip the Isle on every side.
By whom three sever'd Realms in one shall firmly stand,
As *Britain*-founding *Brute* first monarchiz'd the Land :
And *Cornwall*, for that thou no longer shalt contend,
But to old *Cambria* cleave, as to thy ancient friend, 70
Acknowledge thou thy brood of *Brute's* high blood to be ;
And what hath hapt to her, the like t' have chanc'd to thee ;
The *Britons* to receive, when Heaven on them did low'r,
Loegria forc'd to leave ; who from the *Saxons'* pow'r

---

[1] *James* the Fourth, sirnamed *Steward*, married *Margaret*, eldest
daughter to *Henry* the Seventh, King of England.

Themselves in deserts, creeks, and mount'nous wastes be-
    stow'd,   75
Or where the fruitless rocks could promise them abode :
Why strive ye then for that, in little time that shall
(As you are all made one) be one unto you all ;
Then take my final doom pronouncéd lastly, this ;
That *Lundy* like allied to *Wales* and *England* is.   80
    Each part most highly pleas'd, then up the session brake :
When to the learnéd Maids again Invention spake :
O ye *Pegasian* Nymphs, that, hating viler things,
Delight in lofty Hills, and in delicious Springs,
That on *Piërus*[1] born, and naméd of the place,   85
The Thracian *Pimpla* love, and *Pindus* often grace ;
In *Aganippa's* Fount, and in *Castalia's* brims,
That often have been known to bathe your crystal limbs;
Conduct me through these brooks, and with a fast'ned clue,
Direct me in my course, to take a perfect view   90
Of all the wand'ring streams, in whose entrancing gyres,
Wise Nature oft herself her workmanship admires
(So manifold they are, with such meanders wound,
As may with wonder seem invention to confound)
That to those *British* names, untaught the ear to please, 95
Such relish I may give in my delicious lays,
That all the arméd orks of *Neptune's* grisly band,
With music of my verse, amaz'd may list'ning stand ;
As when his Tritons' trumps do them to battle call
Within his surging lists to combat with the whale.   100
    Thus, have we over-gone the *Glamorganian Gowre*,
Whose promontory (plac'd to check the Ocean's pow'r)
Kept *Severne* yet herself, till, being grown too great,
She with extended arms unbounds her ancient seat :
And turning lastly sea,[2] resigns unto the main   105
What sovereignty herself but lately did retain.

    [1] The Seats of the Muses.   [2] *Severne* turned sea.

Next, *Loghor* leads the way, who with a lusty crew
(Her wild and wand'ring steps that ceaselessly pursue)
Still forward is inforc'd : as, *Amond* thrusts her on,
And *Morlas* (as a maid she much relies upon)   110
Intreats her present speed ; assuring her withall,
Her best-belovéd Isle, *Bachannis*, for her fall
Stands specially prepar'd, of everything supplied.

When *Guendra* with such grace deliberately doth glide
As *Tory* doth entice : who setteth out prepar'd   115
At all points like a Prince, attended with a Guard :
Of which, as by her name, the near'st to her of kin
Is *Toothy*, tripping down from *Verwin's* rushy lin,[1]
Through *Rescob* running out, with *Pescover* to meet
Those Rills that Forest loves ; and doth so kindly greet, 120
As to intreat their stay she gladly would prevail.
Then *Tranant* nicely treads upon the wat'ry trail :
The lively skipping *Brane*, along with *Gwethrick* goes ;
In *Tory's* wand'ring banks themselves that scarcely lose,
But *Mudny*, with *Cledaugh*, and *Sawthy*, soon resort,   125
Which at *Langaddock* grace their Sovereign's wat'ry Court.

As when the servile world some gathering man espies,
Whose thriving fortune shows, he to much wealth may rise,
And through his Prince's grace his followers may prefer,
Or by revenue left by some dead ancester ;   130
All lowting low to him, him humbly they observe,
And happy is that man his nod that may deserve :
To *Tory* so they stoop, to them upon the way
Which thus displays the Spring within their view that lay.

Near *Denevoir*, the seat of the *Demetian* King,*   135
Whilst *Cambria* was herself, full, strong, and flourishing,
There is a pleasant Spring, that[2] constant doth abide
Hard-by these winding shores wherein we nimbly slide;

---

[1] A pool or watery moor.   * Of *South-wales.*
[2] Ebbing and flowing with the Sea.

Long of the Ocean lov'd, since his victorious hand
First proudly did insult upon the conquer'd Land.   140
And though a hundred Nymphs in fair *Demetia* be,
Whose features might allure the Sea-gods more than she,
His fancy takes her form, and her he only likes
(Whoe'er knew half the shafts wherewith blind *Cupid* strikes?)
Which great and constant faith, show'd by the God of Sea,
This clear and lovely Nymph so kindly doth repay,   146
As suff'ring for his sake what love to lover owes,
With him she sadly ebbs, with him she proudly flows,
To him her secret vows perpetually doth keep,
Observing every law and custom of the Deep.   150
  Now *Tovy* toward her fall (*Langaddock* overgone)
Her *Dulas* forward drives: and *Cothy* coming on
The train to overtake, the nearest way doth cast
Ere she *Carmarden* get: where *Gwilly*, making haste,
Bright *Tovy* entertains at that most famous Town   155
Which her great Prophet[1] bred, who *Wales* doth so renown:
And taking her a harp, and tuning well the strings,
To princely *Tovy* thus she of the Prophet sings:
  Of *Merlin* and his skill what region doth not hear?
The world shall still be full of *Merlin* everywhere.   160
A thousand lingering years his prophecies have run,
And scarcely shall have end till Time itself be done:
Who of a *British* Nymph was gotten, whilst she play'd
With a seducing Spirit, which won the goodly maid;
(As all *Demetia* through, there was not found her peer)   165
Who, being so much renown'd for beauty far and near,
Great Lords her liking sought, but still in vain they prov'd:
§ That Spirit (to her unknown) this Virgin only lov'd;
Which taking human shape, of such perfection seem'd,
As (all her suitors scorn'd) she only him esteem'd.   170
Who, feigning for her sake that he was come from far,

___
[1] *Merlin*, born in *Caer-merd-hin*.

And richly could endow (a lusty batcheler)
On her that Prophet got, which from his Mother's womb
Of things to come foretold until the general Doom.

But, of his feignèd birth in sporting idly thus,   175
Suspect me not, that I this dreamèd *Incubus*
By strange opinions should licentiously subsist ;
Or, self-conceited, play the humorous *Platonist,*
Which boldly dares affirm, that Spirits themselves supply
With bodies, to commix with frail mortality,   180
And here allow them place, beneath this lower Sphere
Of the unconstant Moon, to tempt us daily here.
Some, earthly mixture take ; as others, which aspire,
Them subtler shapes resume, of water, air, and fire,
Being those immortals long before the heaven that fell,   185
Whose deprivation thence determinèd their hell :
And losing through their pride that place to them assign'd,
Predestinèd that was to man's regenerate kind,
They, for th' inveterate hate to his election, still
Desist not him to tempt to every damnèd ill :   190
And to seduce the spirit, oft prompt the frailer blood,
Inveigling it with tastes of counterfeited good,
And teach it all the sleights the soul that may excite
To yield up all her power unto the appetite.
And to those curious wits if we ourselves apply,   195
Which search the gloomy shades of deep Philosophy,
They Reason so will clothe, as well the mind can show,
That contrary effects from contraries may grow ;
And that the soul a shape so strongly may conceit,
As to herself the-while may seem it to create ;   200
By which th' abusèd Sense more easily oft is led
To think that it enjoys the thing imaginèd.

But, toil'd in these dark tracts with sundry doubts repleat,
Calm shades, and cooler streams must quench this furious
        heat :

Which seeking, soon we find where *Cowen* in her course, ₂₀₅
Tow'rds the *Sabrinian* shores, as sweeping from her source,
Takes *Towa,* calling then *Karkenny* by the way,
Her through the wayless woods of *Cardiffe* to convey;
A Forest, with her floods inviron'd so about,
That hardly she restrains th' unruly wat'ry rout, ₂₁₀
When swelling, they would seem her Empire to invade :
And oft the lustful Fauns and Satyrs from her shade
Were by the streams entic'd, abode with them to make.
Then *Morlas* meeting *Taw,* her kindly in doth take :
Cair coming with the rest, their wat'ry tracts that tread, ₂₁₅
Increase the *Cowen* all ; that as their general head
Their largess doth receive, to bear out his expence :
Who to vast *Neptune* leads this Courtly confluence.

To the *Penbrokian*[1] parts the Muse her still doth keep,
Upon that utmost point to the *Iberian* Deep, ₂₂₀
By *Cowdra* coming in : where clear delightful air
(That Forests most affect) doth welcome her repair ;
The Heliconian Maids in pleasant groves delight :
(Floods cannot still content their wanton appetite)
And wand'ring in the woods, the neighbouring hills below,
With wise *Apollo* meet (who with his ivory bow, ₂₂₆
Once in the paler shades, the Serpent *Python* slew)
And hunting oft with him, the heartless deer pursue ;
Those beams then laid aside he us'd in heaven to wear.
Another Forest Nymph is *Narber,* standing near ; ₂₃₀
That with her curléd top her neighbour would astound,
Whose Groves once bravely grac'd the fair *Penbrokian* ground,
When *Albion* here beheld on this extended land,
Amongst his well-grown woods, the shag-hair'd Satyrs stand,
(The *Sylvans'* chief resort) the shores then sitting high, ₂₃₅
Which under water now so many fadoms lie :
And wallowing porpice sport and lord it in the flood,

[1] Passage into *Penbrokeshire.*

Where once the portly oak, and large-limb'd poplar stood:
Of all the forest's kind these two now only left.
But Time, as guilty since to man's insatiate theft,   240
Transferr'd the *English* names of Towns and households
      hither,
With the industrious *Dutch* since sojourning together.
  When wrathful Heaven the clouds so liberally bestow'd,
The Seas (then wanting roomth to lay their boist'rous load)
Upon the *Belgian* Marsh their pamp'red stomachs cast,   245
That peopled Cities sank into the mighty waste.
The *Flemings* were inforc'd to take them to their oars,
To try the setting Main to find out firmer shores;[1]
When as this spacious Isle them entrance did allow,
To plant the *Belgian* stock upon this goodly brow: 250
These Nations, that their tongues did naturally affect,
Both generally forsook the *British* Dialect:
As when it was decreed by all-foredooming Fate,
That ancient *Rome* should stoop from her emperious state,
With Nations from the North then altogether fraught,   255
Which to her civil bounds their barbarous customs brought,
Of all her ancient spoils and lastly be forlorn,
From *Tyber's* hallowed banks to old *Byzantium*[2] borne:
Th' abundant Latin then old *Latium* lastly left,
Both of her proper form and elegancy reft,   260
Before her smoothest tongue, their speech that did prefer,
And in her tables fixt their ill-shap'd character.
  A divination strange the Dutch made-English have,
Appropriate to that place (as though some Power it gave)
§ By th' shoulder of a Ram from off the right side par'd,   265
Which usually they boil, the spade-bone being bar'd:
Which then the Wizard takes, and gazing thereupon,
Things long to come foreshows, as things done long agone;

---

[1] The Colony of *Flemings* here planted. See to the Fourth Song.
[2] Now *Constantinople.*

Scapes secretly at home, as those abroad, and far;
Murders, adulterous stealths, as the events of war,   275
The reigns and death of Kings they take on them to know:
Which only to their skill the shoulder-blade doth show.
  You goodly sister Floods, how happy is your state!
Or should I more commend your features, or your fate;
That *Milford*, which this Isle her greatest Port doth call,   275
Before your equal Floods is lotted to your fall?
Where was sail ever seen, or wind hath ever blown,
Whence *Penbrooke* yet hath heard of Haven like her own?
She bids *Dungleddy* dare *Iberia's** proudest Road,
And chargeth her to send her challenges abroad   280
Along the coast of *France*, to prove if any be
Her *Milford* that dare match: so absolute is she.
And *Clethy* coming down from *Wrenyvaur* her Sire
(A hill that thrusts his head into th' etherial fire)
Her sister's part doth take and dare avouch as much: 285
And *Percily* the proud, whom nearly it doth touch,
Said, he would bear her out; and that they all should know.
And therewithal he struts, as though he scorn'd to show
His head below the heaven, when he of *Milford* spake:
But there was not a Port the prize durst undertake.   290
So highly *Milford* is in every mouth renown'd,
No Haven hath ought good, in her that is not found
Whereas the swelling surge, that, with his foamy head,
The gentler-looking land with fury menaced,
With his encount'ring wave no longer there contends;   295
But sitting mildly down like perfect ancient-friends,
Unmov'd of any wind which way soe'er it blow,
And rather seem to smile, than knit an angry brow.
The ships with shatt'red ribs scarce creeping from the seas,
On her sleek bosom ride with such deliberate ease,   300
As all her passéd storms she holds but mean and base,

* *Spain.*

So she may reach at length this most delightful place,
By nature with proud cleeves invironéd about,
§ To crown the goodly Road: where builds the Falcon stout,
Which we the Gentle call: whose fleet and active wings, 305
It seems that Nature made when most she thought on Kings:
Which manag'd to the lure, her high and gallant flight
The vacant sportful man so greatly doth delight,
That with her nimble quills his soul doth seem to hover,
And lie the very pitch that lusty bird doth cover; 310
That those proud eyries,[1] bred whereas the scorching sky
Doth singe the sandy wilds of spiceful *Barbary;*
Or underneath our Pole, where *Norway's* Forests wide
Their high cloud-touching heads in Winter snows do hide,
Out-brave not this our kind in mettle, nor exceed 315
The Falcon, which sometimes the *British* cleeves do breed:
Which prey upon the Isles in the *Vergivian* waste,
That from the *British* shores by *Neptune* are imbrac'd ;
Which stem his furious tides when wildliest they do rave,
And break the big-swoln bulk of many a boist'rous wave; 320
As, calm when he becomes, then likewise in their glory
Do cast their amorous eyes at many a promontory
That thrust their foreheads forth into the smiling South ;
As *Rat* and *Sheepy,* set to keep calm *Milford's* mouth,
Expos'd to *Neptune's* power. So *Gresholme* far doth stand: 325
Scalme, Stockholme, with Saint *Bride,* and *Gatholme,*[2] nearer
          land,
(Which with their veiny breasts entice the Gods of sea,
That with the lusty Isles do revel every day)
As crescent-like the land her breadth here inward bends,
From *Milford,* which she forth to old *Menevia* sends ; 330
Since, holy *David's* seat; which of especial grace
Doth lend that nobler name to this unnobler place.

---

[1] The places from whence the highest-flying Hawks are brought.
[2] The Islands upon the point of *Penbrookeshire.*

Of all the holy men whose fame so fresh remains,
To whom the *Britons* built so many sumptuous Fanes,
This Saint before the rest their Patron still they hold :   335
§ Whose birth, their ancient Bards to *Cambria* long foretold;
And seated here a See, his Bishopric of yore,
Upon the farthest point of this unfruitful shore ;
Selected by himself, that far from all resort
With contemplation seem'd most fitly to comport ;   340
That, void of all delight, cold, barren, bleak, and dry,
No pleasure might allure, nor steal the wand'ring eye :
Where *Ramsey* with those Rocks, in rank that ord'red stand
Upon the furthest point of *David's* ancient Land,
Do raise their rugged heads (the seaman's noted marks) 345
Call'd, of their mitred tops, *The Bishop and his Clarks ;*
Into that channel cast, whose raging current roars
Betwixt the *British* sands and the *Hibernian* shores :
Whose grim and horrid face doth pleaséd heaven neglect,
And bears bleak Winter still in his more sad aspéct :   350
Yet *Gwin* and *Nevern* near, two fine and fishful Brooks,
Do never stay their course, how stern soe'er he looks ;
Which with his shipping once should seem to have commerst,
Where *Fiscard* as her flood doth only grace the first.
To *Newport* falls the next : there we awhile will rest·;   355
Our next ensuing Song to wondrous things addrest.

ILLUSTRATIONS.

I F you ever read of, or vulgarly understand, the form of the *Ocean*, and affinity twixt it and Rivers, you cannot but conceive this poetical description of *Severne;* wherein *Amphitrite* is supposed to have given her a precious robe : very proper in the matter-self, and imitating that Father of the Muses[1] which derives *Agamemnon's* Sceptre to him by descent joined with gift from *Jupiter*, *Achilles'* armor from *Vulcan's* bounty, *Helen's Nepenthe* from the *Egyptian Polydamna*, and such like, honoring the possessor with the giver's judgment, as much as with the gift possessed.

54. *To whom the goodly Bay of* Milford *should be given.*

At *Milford* Haven arrived *Henry* Earl of *Richmont*, aided with some forces and sums of money by the *French Charles* VIII. but so entertained and strengthened by divers of his friends, groaning under the tyrannical yoke of *Rich.* III. that, beyond expectation, at *Bosworth* in *Leicester*, the day and Crown was soon his. Every Chronicle tells you more largely.

---

[1] Iliad. β. et σ.; Odyss. δ.

56.· *And how* Lhewelin's *line in him should* doubly *thrive.*

Turn to the *Eagle's* prophecies in the Second Song, where the first part of this relation is more manifested. For the rest, thus : About our Confessor's time, *Macbeth* King of *Scotland*[1] (moved by predictions, affirming that, his line extinct, the posterity of *Banqhuo*, a noble Thane of *Loqhua-brie*, should attain and continue the *Scottish* reign) and, jealous of others' hoped-for greatness, murdered *Banqhuo*, but missed his design ; for one of the same posterity, *Fleanch* son to *Banqhuo*, privily fled to *Gryffith* ap *Lhewelin* then Prince of *Wales*, and was there kindly received. To him and *Nesta* the Prince's daughter was issue one *Walter.* He (afterward for his worth favourably accepted, and through stout perform-ance honourably requited by *Malcolmb* III.) was made Lord High *Stewart* of *Scotland ;* out of whose loins *Robert* II. was derived : since whom that royal name hàth long continued, descending to our mighty Sovereign, and in him is joined with the commixed Kingly blood of *Tyddour* and *Plantagenest.* These two were united, with the *White* and *Red Roses,** in those auspicious nuptials of *Henry* the Seventh and *Eliza-beth* daughter to *Edward* IV. and from them, through the Lady *Margaret* their eldest daughter, married to *James* the Fourth, his Majesty's descent and spacious Empire observed easily shows you what the Muse here plays withal. The rest alludes to that ; Cambria *shall be glad,* Cornwall *shall flourish, and the Isle shall be styled with* Brute's *name, and the*

---

[1] Hector Boet. lib. 12 et Buchanan. in reg. 85. et 86. lib. 7. qui eosdem ævo citeriori *Stuartos* ait dictos, quos olim *Thanos* nuncupa-bant. *Thani* verò quæstores erant regii per interpretationem, uti Boetius. Certè in Chartâ illâ quâ jure clientelari se *Henrico* II. ob-strinxit *Willielmus* Scotorum Rex, leguntur inter testes *Willielmus de Curcy* Seneschallus, *Willielmus* Filius *Aldelmi* Seneschallus, *Aluredus* de Sancto *Martino* Seneschallus, *Gilbertus Malet* Seneschallus, unde honorarium fuisse hoc nomen paret. Horum bini desunt apud Hove-denum, verum ex vetustiss. anonymo MS. excerpsi.

* York and Lancaster.

name of strangers shall perish: as it is in *Merlin's* prophecies.

108. *That* Spirit *to her unknown this* Virgin *only lov'd.*

So is the vulgar tradition of *Merlin's* conception. Untimely it were, if I should slip into discourse of spirits' faculties in this kind. For my own part, unless there be some creatures of such middle nature, as the *Rabbinic* conceit[1] upon the Creation supposes; and the same with *Hesiod's* Nymphs, or *Paracelsus* his *Non-adams*, I shall not believe that other than true bodies on bodies can generate, except by swiftness of motion in conveying of stolen seed some unclean spirit might arrogate the improper name of generation. Those which S. *Augustine*[2] calls *Dusii,** in *Gaul*, altogether addicted to such filthiness, *Fauns, Satyrs* and *Sylvans* have had as much attributed to them. But learn of this, from divines upon the *Beni-haelohim* in Holy Writ,[3] passages of the Fathers upon this point, and the later authors of disquisitions in Magic and Sorcery, as *Bodin, Wier, Martin del Rio*, others. For this *Merlin* (rather *Merdhin*, as you see to the Fourth Song, his true name being *Ambrose*) his own answer to *Vortigern* was, that his father was a *Roman Consul*[4] (so *Nennius* informs me) as perhaps it might be, and the fact palliated under name of a spirit; as in that of *Ilia* supposing, to save her credit, the name of *Mars* for *Romulus* his Father. But to enterlace the polite Muse with what is more harsh, yet even therein perhaps not displeasing, I offer you this antique passage of him.

[1] Rabbi Abraham in Zerror Hammor ap. Munst. ad 2. Genes.
[2] Lib. 15. de Civ. Dei cap. 23.
* Forte Drusii (quod vult Bodinus lib. 2. cap. 7. Dæmonoman.) quasi Sylvani. aut Dryades.   [3] Gen. 6. 2.
[4] Illustres sæpiùs viros indigetant historici nostri *Consules*, unde et *Ætium* adloquuntur *Saxones* Cos., quem tametsi Consulem fuisse haut asserent Fasti, illustriss. tamen et in republicâ nobilissimum Procopii aliorumque Historiæ Gothicæ produnt.

————¹the messagers to Kermerdin come
And hou children biuore the yate pleyde hii toke gome
Tho sede on to another,* Merlin wat is the
Thou faderlese ssrewe,† wy misdostou me   [fille
Uor icham of Kinges icome and thou nart nought worth a
Uor thou naddest neuere namne fader, thereuore hold the
Tho the messagers hurde this hii astunte there   [stille
And essie at men aboute wat the child were
Me sede that he ne had neuere fader that me mighte
            bnderstonde
And is moder au Kings doughter was of thulke lond
And woned at S. Petres in a nonnerie there.

His mother (a Nun, daughter to *Pubidius* King of *Mathraval*,
and called *Matilda*, as by poetical authority[2] only I find
justifiable) and he being brought to the King, she colours
it in these words :

————whanne ich ofte was
In chambre mid mine fellawes, there come to me bi cas
A suithe bair man mid alle, and bi clupt me wel softe,
And semblance made baire ynou, and cust me well ofte.

and tells on the story which should follow so kind a preface.
But enough of this.

265. ‡*By th'* shoulder *of a* Ram *from off the right side par'd.*

Take this as a taste of their art in old time. Under
Hen. II. one *William Mangunel,*[3] a Gentleman of those parts,
finding by his skill of prediction that his wife had played

---

[1] See to the Tenth Song.   * Durbitius dictus Galfredo.
† *Shrew* now a word applied to the shrewish sex, but in *Chaucer,*
Lidgat, and *Gower,* to the quieter also.
[2] *Spenser's* Faery Q. lib. 3. cant. 3.   ‡ Osteomantie.
[3] Girald. Itin. 1. cap. 11.
            ————Quæ te dementia cepit,
        Quærere sollicitè quod reperire times?
                            Th. Mor. Epig.

false with him, and conceived by his own nephew, formally dresses the shoulder-bone of one of his own rams ; and sitting at dinner (pretending it to be taken out of his neighbour's flock) requests his wife. (equalling him in these divinations) to give her judgment ; she curiously observes, and at last with great laughter casts it from her : the Gentleman, importuning her reason of so vehement an affection, receives answer of her, that, his wife, out of whose flock the ram was taken, had by incestuous copulation with her husband's nephew fraughted herself with a young one. Lay all together, and judge, Gentlewomen, the sequel of this cross accident. But why she could not as well divine of whose flock it was, as the other secret, when I have more skill in *Osteomanty*, I will tell you. Nor was their report less in knowing things to come, than past ; so that jealous *Panurge* in his doubt *de la Coquage*** might here have had other manner of resolution than *Rondibilis*, *Hippothade*, *Bridoye*, *Trovillogan*, or the Oracle itself, were able to give him. Blame me not, in that, to explain my author, I insert this example.

304. *To crown the goodly Road, where built that* Falcon *stout.*

In the rocks of this maritime coast of *Penbroke* are eyries of excellent Falcons.[1] *Henry* the Second here passing into *Ireland*, cast off a *Norway* Goshawk at one of these : but the Goshawk taken at the source by the Falcon, soon fell down at the King's foot, which performance in this ramage, made him yearly afterward send hither for *Eyesses*, as *Girald* is author. Whether these here are the *Haggarts* (which they call *Peregrins*) or *Falcon-gentles*, I am no such falconer to argue ; but this I know, that the reason of the name of *Peregrins* is given, for that they come from remote

---

* Of Cuckoldry. *Rablais.*   [1] Hawks.

and unknown places,[1] and therefore hardly fits these : but also I read in no less than Imperial authority,[2] that *Peregrins* never bred in less latitude than beyond the seventh climate, *Dia Riphœos*, which permits them this place ; and that, of true Falcons-gentle an eyrie is never found but in a more Southern and hotter parallel : which (if it be true) excludes the name of *Gentle* from ours, breeding near the ninth, *per Rostochium*. And the same authority makes them (against common opinion) both of one kind, differing rather in local and outward accidents than in self-nature.

836. *Whose birth the ancient* Bards *to Cambria long* foretold.

Of S. *Dewy* and his Bishopric you have more to the Fourth Song. He was prognosticated[3] above thirty years before his birth; which with other attributed miracles (after the fashion of that credulous age) caused him be almost paralleled in Monkish zeal with that Holy *John* which, unborn, sprang at presence of the Incarnate Author of our Redemption. The translation of the Archbishopric was also foretold in that of *Merlin :*[4] Menevia *shall put on the Pall of* Caer-leon ; *and the Preacher of* Ireland *shall wax dumb by an infant growing in the womb*. That was performed when S. *Patrick*, at presence of *Melaria* then with child, suddenly lost use of his speech ; but recovering it after some time made prediction of *Dewy's* holiness, joined with greatness, which is so celebrated. Upon my Author's credits only believe me.

[1] Albert. de Animal. 23. cap. 8.
[2] Frederic. II. lib. 2. de arte Venand. cap. 4.
[3] Monumeth. lib. 8, cap. 8.; Girald. Itin. 2. cap. 1.; Bal. cent. 1. Vita S. *Dewy*.
[4] Alan. de Insul. 1 ad. Proph. Merlin.

THE SIXTH SONG.

THE ARGUMENT.

With Cardigan *the Muse proceeds,*
And tells what rare things Tivy *breeds:*
Next, proud Plynillimon *she plyes;*
Where Severne, Wy, *and* Rydoll *rise.*
With Severne *she along doth go,*   5
Her Metamorphosis to show;
And makes the wand'ring Wy *declaim*
In honour of the British *name:*
Then musters all the wat'ry train
That those two Rivers entertain: 10
And viewing how those Rillets creep
From shore to the Vergivian *Deep,*
By Radnor *and* Mountgomery *then*
To Severne *turns her course again:*
And bringing all their Riverets in,   15
There ends; a new Song to begin.

ITH I must stem thy stream, clear *Tivy*, yet before
The Muse vouchsafe to seize the *Cardiganian* shore,
She of thy source will sing in all the *Cambrian* coast;
    Which of thy *castors* once, but now canst only boast
The *salmons*, of all Floods most plentiful in thee.   5
Dear Brook, within thy banks if any Powers there be;

Then *Naiads*, or ye Nymphs of their like wat'ry kind,
(Unto whose only care, great *Neptune* hath assign'd
The guidance of those Brooks wherein he takes delight)
Assist her: and whilst she your dwelling shall recite,   10
Be present in her work: let her your graces view,
That to succeeding times them lively she may show;
As when great *Albion's* sons, which him a Sea-Nymph brought
Amongst the grisly rocks, were with your beauties caught,
(Whose only love surpris'd those of the *Phlegrian*[1] size,   15
The *Titanois*, that once against high Heaven durst rise)
When as the hoary woods, the climbing hills did hide,
And cover'd every vale through which you gently glide;
Ev'n for those inly heats which through your loves they felt,
That oft in kindly tears did in your bosoms melt,   20
To view your secret bow'rs, such favour let her win.
   Then *Tivy* cometh down from her capacious lin,
Twixt *Mirk* and *Brenny* led, two handmaids, that do stay
Their Mistress, as in state she goes upon her way.
   Which when *Lanbeder* sees, her wondrously she likes: 25
Whose untam'd bosom so the beauteous *Tivy* strikes,
As that the Forest fain would have her there abide.
But she (so pure a stream) transported with her pride,
The offer idly scorns; though with her flattering shade
The *Sylvan* her entice with all that may persuade   30
A Water-Nymph; yea, though great *Thetis'* self she were:
But nothing might prevail, nor all the pleasures there
Her mind could ever move one minute's stay to make.
   Mild *Mathern* then, the next, doth *Tivy* overtake:
Which instantly again by *Dittor* is supplied.   35
Then, *Keach* and *Kerry* help: twixt which on either side,
To *Cardigan* she comes, the Sovereign of the Shere.
Now *Tivy* let us tell thy sundry glories here.
   When as the salmon seeks a fresher stream to find

---

[1] Giants.

(Which hither from the sea comes yearly by his kind,   40
As he in season grows) and stems the wat'ry tract
Where *Tivy*, falling down, doth make a cataract,*
Forc'd by the rising rocks that there her course oppose,
As though within their bounds they meant her to inclose ;
Here, when the labouring fish doth at the foot arrive,
And finds that by his strength but vainly he doth strive,
His tail takes in his teeth ; and bending like a bow,
That's to the compass drawn, aloft himself doth throw :
Then springing at his height, as doth a little wand,
That bended end to end, and flerted from the hand,   50
Far off itself doth cast ; so doth the salmon vaut.
And if at first he fail, his second summersaut[1]
He instantly assays ; and from his nimble ring,
Still yarking, never leaves, until himself he fling
Above the streamful top of the surrounded heap.   55
    More famous long agone, than for the salmons' leap,
For *bearers Tivy* was, in her strong banks that bred,
Which else no other brook of *Britain* nourishéd :
Where Nature, in the shape of this now-perish'd beast
His property did seem t' have wondrously exprest ;   60
Being bodied like a boat, with such a mighty tail
As serv'd him for a bridge, a helm, or for a sail,
When kind did him command the architect to play,
That his strong castle built of branchéd twigs and clay :
Which, set upon the deep, but yet not fixéd there,   65
He eas'ly could remove as it he pleas'd to steer
To this side or to that ; the workmanship so rare,
His stuff wherewith to build, first being to prepare,
A foraging he goes, to groves or bushes nigh,
And with his teeth cuts down his timber: which laid-by,   70
He turns him on his back, his belly laid abroad,

* Falling of water.
[1] The word in tumbling, when one casteth himself over and over.

When with what he hath got, the other do him load,
Till lastly by the weight, his burthen he have found.
Then, with his mighty tail his carriage having bound
As carters do with ropes, in his sharp teeth he gript　　75
Some stronger stick : from which the lesser branches stript,
He takes it in the midst ; at both the ends, the rest
Hard holding with their fangs, unto the labour prest,
Going backward, tow'rds their home their loaded carriage led,
From whom, those first here born, were taught the useful
　　　　sled.　　　　　　　　　　　　　　　　　　80
Then builded he his fort with strong and several fights ;
His passages contriv'd with such unusual sleights,
That from the hunter oft he issued undiscern'd,
As if men from this beast to fortify had learn'd ;
§ Whose kind, in her decay'd, is to this Isle unknown.　85
Thus *Tivy* boasts this beast peculiarly her own.
　　But here why spend I time these trifles to areed ?
Now, with my former task my Muse again proceed,
To show the other Floods from the *Cerettick*[1] shore
To the *Vergivian* Sea contributing their store :　　　90
With *Bidder* first begin, that bendeth all her force
The *Arron* to assist, *Arth* holding on her course
The way the other went, with *Werry* which doth win
Fair *Istwid* to her aid ; who kindly coming in,
Meets *Rydoll* at her mouth, that fair and princely maid,　95
Plynillimon's dear child, deliciously array'd,
As fits a Nymph so near to *Severne* and her Queen.
Then come the sister *Salks*, as they before had seen
Those delicater Dames so trippingly to tread :
Then *Kerry ; Cletur* next, and *Kinver* making head　　100
With *Enion*, that her like clear *Levant* brings by her.
　　Plynillimon's high praise no longer Muse defer :
What once the *Druids* told, how great those Floods should be

[1] Of *Cardigan.*

That here (most mighty Hill) derive themselves from thee.
The Bards with fury rapt, the *British* youth among,   105
§ Unto the charming Harp thy future honor song
In brave and lofty strains ; that in excess of joy,
The beldam and the girl, the grandsire and the boy,
With shouts and yearning cries, the troubled air did load
(As when with crownéd cups unto the *Elian*[1] God   110
Those Priests his orgies held ; or when the old world saw
Full *Phœbe's* face eclips'd, and thinking her to daw,
Whom they supposéd fall'n in some inchanted swound,
Of beaten tinkling brass still ply'd her with the sound)
That all the *Cumbrian* hills, which high'st their heads do bear
With most obsequious shows of low subjected fear,   115
Should to thy greatness stoop : and all the Brooks that be
Do homage to those Floods that issued out of thee :
To princely *Severne* first ; next, to her sister *Wye*,
Which to her elder's Court her course doth still apply.   120
But *Rydoll*, young'st, and least, and for the other's pride
Not finding fitting roomth upon the rising side,
Alone unto the West directly takes her way.
So all the neighboring Hills *Plynillimon* obey.
For, though *Moylvadian* bear his craggy top so high,   125
As scorning all that come in compass of his eye,
Yet greatly is he pleas'd *Plynillimon* will grace
Him with a cheerful look : and, fawning in his face,
His love to *Severne* shows as though his own she were,
Thus comforting the Flood : *O ever-during heir   130
Of *Sabrine*, *Locrine's* child (who of her life bereft,
Her ever-living name to thee fair River left)
Brute's first begotten son, which *Gwendolin* did wed ;
But soon th' unconstant Lord abandonéd her bed
(Through his unchaste desire) for beauteous *Elstred's* love.   135
Now, that which most of all her mighty heart did move,

---

[1] *Bacchus.*   * The Story of *Severne.*

Her father, *Cornwall's* Duke, great *Corineus* dead,
Was by the lustful King unjustly banishéd.
When she, who to that time still with a smoothéd brow
Had seem'd to bear the breach of *Locrine's* former vow,　140
Perceiving still her wrongs insufferable were ;
Grown big with the revenge which her full breast did bear,
And aided to the birth with every little breath
(Alone she being left the spoil of love and death,
In labour of her grief outrageously distract,　145
The utmost of her spleen on her false lord to act)
She first implores their aid to hate him whom she found ;
Whose hearts unto the depth she had not left to sound.
To *Cornwall* then she sends (her country) for supplies :
Which all at once in arms with *Gwendolin* arise.　150
Then with her warlike power, her husband she pursu'd,
Whom his unlawful love too vainly did delude.

　The fierce and jealous Queen, then void of all remorse,
As great in power as spirit, whilst he neglects her force,
Him suddenly surpris'd, and from her ireful heart　155
All pity clean exil'd (whom nothing could convert)
The son of mighty *Brute* bereavéd of his life ;
Amongst the *Britons* here the first intestine strife,
Since they were put a-land upon this promis'd shore.
Then crowning *Madan* King, whom she to *Locrine* bore,　160
And those which serv'd his Sire to his obedience brought ;
Not so with blood suffic'd, immediately she sought
The mother and the child : whose beauty when she saw,
Had not her heart been flint, had had the power to draw
A spring of pitying tears ; when, dropping liquid pearl,　165
Before the cruel Queen, the Lady and the Girl
Upon their tender knees begg'd mercy.　Woe for thee,
Fair *Elstred*, that thou should'st thy fairer *Sabrine* see,
As she should thee behold the prey to her stern rage,
Whom kingly *Locrine's* death suffic'd not to assuage :　170

Who from the bord'ring cleeves thee with thy mother cast
Into thy christ'ned flood, the whilst the rocks aghast
Resounded with your shrieks ; till in a deadly dream
Your corses were dissolv'd into that crystal stream,
Your curls to curléd waves, which plainly still appear   175
The same in water now, that once in locks they were :
And, as you wont to clip each others neck before,
Ye now with liquid arms embrace the wand'ring shore.

But leave we *Severne* here, a little to pursue
The often wand'ring *Wye* (her passages to view,   180
As wantonly she strains in her lascivious course)
And muster every flood that from her bounteous source
Attends upon her stream, whilst (as the famous bound
Twixt the *Brecknokian* earth, and the *Radnorian* ground)
She every Brook receives. First, *Clarwen* cometh in,   185
With *Clarwy :* which to them their consort *Eland* win
To aid their goodly *Wye ;* which, *Ithon* gets again :
She *Dulas* draws along : and in her wat'ry train
Clowedock hath recourse, and *Comran ;* which she brings
Unto their wand'ring flood from the *Radnorian* Springs : 190
As *Edwy* her attends, and *Matchwy* forward heaves
Her Mistress. When, at last the goodly *Wye* perceives
She now was in that part of *Wales*, of all the rest
Which (as her very waist) in breadth from East to West,
In length from North to South, her midst is every way,   195
From *Severne's* bord'ring banks unto the either Sea,
And might be term'd her heart. The ancient *Britons* here
The River calls to mind, and what those *British* were
Whilst *Britain* was herself, the Queen of all the West.

To whose old Nation's praise whilst she herself addrest, 200
From the *Brecknokian* bound when *Irvon* coming in,
Her *Dulas*, with *Commarch*, and *Wevery* that doth win,
Persuading her for them good matter to provide.
The Wood-Nymphs so again, from the *Radnorian* side,

As *Radnor,* with *Blethaugh,* and *Knuckles* Forests, call   205
To *Wye,* and bad her now bestir her for them all :
For, if she stuck not close in their distressèd case,
The *Britons* were in doubt to undergo disgrace.
That strongly thus provok'd, she for the *Britons* says :
What spirit can lift you up, to that immortal praise   210
§ You worthily deserve? by whom first *Gaul* was taught
Her knowledge : and for her, what nation ever wrought
The conquest you achiev'd? And, as you were most drad,
So ye (before the rest) in so great reverence had
Your Bards which sung your deeds, that where stern hosts
          have stood   215
With lifted hands to strike (in their inflamèd blood)
§ One Bard but coming in, their murd'rous swords hath staid;
In her most dreadful voice as thund'ring Heaven had said,
Stay *Britons :* when he spake, his words so pow'rful were.
    So to her native Priests, the dreadless *Druids* here,   220
The nearest neighboring *Gaul,* that wisely could discern
Th' effect their doctrine wrought, it for their good to learn,
Her apt and pregnant Youth sent hither year by year,
Instructed in our Rites with most religious fear.
And afterward again, when as our ancient seat   225
Her surcrease could not keep, grown for her soil too great,
(But like to casting bees, so rising up in swarms)
§ Our *Cymbri* with the *Gauls,* that their commixèd arms
Join'd with the *German* Powers (those Nations of the North
Which overspread the world) together issued forth :   230
§ Where, with our brazen swords, we stoutly fought, and long ;
And after conquests got, residing them among,
First planted in those parts our brave courageous brood,
Whose natures so adher'd unto their ancient blood,
As from them sprang those Priests, whose praise so far did
          sound,   .   235
Through whom that spacious *Gaul* was after so renown'd.

Nor could the *Saxons'* swords (which many a ling'ring year
Them sadly did afflict, and shut us *Britons* here
Twixt *Severne* and this Sea) our mighty minds deject ;
But that even they which fain'st our weakness would detect,
Were forcéd to confess, our wildest beasts that breed   241
Upon our mighty wastes, or on our mountains feed,
Were far more sooner tam'd, than here our Welch-men were :
Besides, in all the world no Nation is so dear
As they unto their own ; that here within this Isle,   245
Or else in foreign parts, yea, forcéd to exile,
The noble *Briton* still his countryman relieves ;
A Patriot, and so true, that it to death him grieves
To hear his *Wales* disgrac'd : and on the *Saxons'* swords
Oft hazardeth his life, ere with reproachful words   250
His Language or his Leek he'll stand to hear abus'd.
Besides, the *Briton* is so naturally infus'd
With true poetic rage, that in their[1] measures, art
Doth rather seem precise, than comely ; in each part
Their metre most exact, in verse of th' hardest kind.   255
And some to rhyming be so wondrously inclin'd,
Those numbers they will hit, out of their genuine vein,
Which many wise and learn'd can hardly e'er attain.
   O memorable Bards, of unmix'd blood, which still
Posterity shall praise for your so wond'rous skill,   260
That in your noble Songs, the long descents have kept
Of your great Heroes, else in *Lethe* that had slept,
With theirs whose ignorant pride your labours have disdain'd ;
How much from time, and them, how bravely have you gain'd !
Musician, Herald, Bard, thrice may'st thou be renown'd,   265
And with three several wreaths immortally be crown'd ;
Who, when to *Penbrooke* call'd before the English King,
And to thy powerful Harp commanded there to sing,

---

[1] See to the Fourth Song.

Of famous *Arthur* told'st, and where he was interr'd ;
In which, those retchless times had long and blindly err'd,
And ignorance had brought the world to such a pass   271
As now, which scarce believes that *Arthur* ever was.
But when King *Henry*[1] sent th' reported place to view,
He found that man of men; and what thou said'st was true.
  Here then I cannot choose but bitterly exclaim   275
Against those fools that all Antiquity defame,
Because they have found out, some credulous ages lay'd
Slight fictions with the truth, whilst truth on rumour stay'd;
And that one forward Time (perceiving the neglect
A former of her had) to purchase her respect,   280
With toys then trimm'd her up, the drowsy world t' allure,
And lent her what it thought might appetite procure
To man, whose mind doth still variety pursue ;
And therefore to those things whose grounds were very true,
Though naked yet and bare (not having to content   285
The wayward curious ear) gave fictive ornament ;
And fitter thought, the truth they should in question call,
Than coldly sparing that, the truth should go and all.
And surely I suppose, that which this froward time
Doth scandalize her with to be her heinous crime,   290
That hath her most preserv'd : for, still where wit hath found
A thing most clearly true, it made that fiction's ground :
Which she suppos'd might give sure colour to them both:
From which, as from a root, this wond'red error grow'th
At which our Critics gird, whose judgments are so strict,   295
And he the bravest man who most can contradict
That which decrepit Age (which forcéd is to lean
Upon Tradition) tells ; esteeming it so mean,
As they it quite reject, and for some trifling thing
(Which Time hath pinn'd to Truth) they all away will fling.

[1] *Henry* the Second.

These men (for all the world) like our Precisians be,   301
Who for some Cross or Saint they in the window see
Will pluck down all the Church: Soul-blinded sots that creep
In dirt, and never saw the wonders of the deep.
Therefore (in my conceit) most rightly serv'd are they   305
§ That to the *Roman* trust (on his report that stay)
Our truth from him to learn, as ignorant of ours
As we were then of his ; except 'twere of his powers :
Who our wise *Druids* here unmercifully slew ;
Like whom, great Nature's depths no men yet ever knew,   310
Nor with such dauntless spirits were ever yet inspir'd ;
Who at their proud arrive th' ambitious *Romans* fir'd
When first they heard them preach _the soul's immortal
          state ;
And ev'n in *Rome's* despite, and in contempt of Fate,
Grasp'd hands with horrid death: which out of hate and
          pride   315
They slew, who through the world were rev'rencéd beside.
   To understand our state, no marvel then though we
Should so to *Cæsar* seek, in his reports to see
What anciently we were ; when in our infant war,
Unskilful of our tongue but by interpreter,   320
He nothing had of ours which our great Bards did sing,
Except some few poor words ; and those again to bring
Unto the Latin sounds, and easiness they us'd,
By their most filéd speech, our *British* most abus'd.
But of our former state, beginning, our descent,   325
The wars we had at home, the conquests where we went,
He never understood. And though the *Romans* here
So noble trophies left, as very worthy were
A people great as they, yet did they ours neglect,
Long-rear'd ere they arriv'd. And where they do object,   330
The ruins and records we show, be very small
To prove ourselves so great : ev'n this the most of all

('Gainst their objection) seems miraculous to me,
That yet those should be found so general as they be;
The *Roman*, next the *Pict*, the *Saxon*, then the *Dane*,   335
All landing in this Isle, each like a horrid rain
Deforming her; besides the sacrilegious wrack
Of many a noble book, as impious hands should sack
The centre, to extirp all knowledge, and exile
All brave and ancient things, for ever from this Isle :   340
Expressing wondrous grief, thus wand'ring *Wye* did sing.

But, back, industrious Muse; obsequiously to bring
Clear *Severne* from her source, and tell how she doth strain
Down her delicious dales; with all the goodly train,
Brought forth the first of all by *Brugan :* which to make 345
Her party worthy note, next, *Dulas* in doth take.
Moylvadian his much love to *Severne* then to show,
Upon her Southern side, sends likewise (in a row)
Bright *Biga*, that brings on her friend and fellow *Floyd ;*
Next, *Dungum ; Bacho* then is busily imploy'd,   350
Tarranon, Carno, Hawes, with *Becan*, and the *Rue*,
In *Severne's* sovereign banks that give attendance due.

Thus as she swoops along, with all that goodly train,
Upon her other bank by *Newtowne :* so again
§ Comes *Dulas* (of whose name so many Rivers be,   355
As of none others is) with *Mule*, prepar'd to see
The confluence to their Queen, as on her course she makes :
Then at *Mountgomery* next clear *Kennet* in she takes;
Where little *Fledding* falls into her broader bank;
Fork'd *Vurnway,* bringing *Tur*, and *Tanot :* growing rank, 360
She plies her towards the *Poole*, from the *Gomerian* fields ;
Than which in all our *Wales*, there is no country yields
An excellenter horse, so full of natural fire,
As one of *Phœbus'* steeds had been that stallion's sire,
Which first their race begun; or of th' *Asturian* kind,   365
§ Which some have held to be begotten by the wind,

Upon the mountain mare ; which strongly it receives,
And in a little time her pregnant part upheaves.

But, leave we this to such as after wonders long :
The Muse prepares herself unto another Song.   370

ILLUSTRATIONS.

FTER *Penbroke* in the former Song, succeeds here *Cardigan;* both washed by the *Irish* Seas. But, for intermixture of rivers, and contiguity of situation, the inlands of *Montgomery, Radnor,* and *Brecknocke* are partly infolded.

85. *Whose* kind, *in her* decay'd, *is to this Isle unknown.*

That these Beavers were in *Tivy* frequent, anciently is testified by *Sylvester Girald*,[1] describing the particulars, which the Author tells you, both of this, and the *Salmons;* but that here are no *Beavers* now, as good authority of the present time[2] informs you.

106. *Unto the* charming Harp *thy future honor song.*

Of the *Bards,* their Singing, Heraldship, and more of that nature, see to the Fourth Song. *Ireland* (saith one[3]) *uses the Harp and Pipe,* which he calls *tympanum :* Scotland *the Harp, Tympan, and Chorus ;* Wales *the Harp, Pipe, and Chorus.* Although *Tympanum* and *Chorus* have other signi-fications, yet, this *Girald* (from whom I vouch it) using

---

[1] Topograph. Hib. dist. 1. cap. 21. Itin. Cam. 2. cap. 3.
[2] Powel. et Camden.　　[3] Girald Topograph. 3. dist. cap. 11.

these words as received, I imagine, of S. *Hierome's* Epistle
to *Dardanus*, according to whom, for explanation, finding
them pictured in *Ottomar Luscinius* his *Musurgy*, as several
kind of Pipes, the first dividing itself into two at the end,
the other spread in the middle, as two segments of a circle,
but one at both ends, I guess them intended near the same.
But I refer myself to those that are more acquainted with
these kind of *British* fashions. For the Harp his word is
Cithara, which (if it be the same with *Lyra*, as some think,
although urging reason and authority are to the contrary)
makes the *Bards'* music, like that expressed in the Lyric[1] :

> ———*bibam,*
> *Sonante mistum tibiis carmen lyrâ,*
> *Hâc Dorium, illis Barbarum.*

Apply it to the former notes, and observe with them, that
the *Pythagoreans*[2] used, with music of the Harp (which in
those times, if it were *Apollo's*, was certainly but of seven
strings[3]) when they went to sleep, to charm (as the old
Scots were wont to do, and do yet in their Isles, as *Buchanan*[4]
affirms) and compose their troubled affections. Which I
cite to this purpose, that in comparing it with the *British*
music, and the attributes thereof before remembered out of
Heracleotes and *Girald*, you may see conveniency of use in
both, and worth of antiquity in ours ; and as well in *Pipes*
as *Harp*, if you remember the poetic story of *Marsyas*. And
withal forget not that in one of the oldest coins that have
been made in this Kingdom, the picture of the reverse is
Apollo having his Harp incircled with *Cunobelin's* name, then

---

[1] Horat. Epod. 9.   [2] Plutarch. de Isid. et Osiride.
[3] Horat. Carm. III. od. 11; Homer in Hym. ad Herm; Serv. Hono-
rat. ad IV. Æneid. (ubi testudinem primò trium chordarum, quam à
Mercurio Caducei pretio emisse Apollinem, septémque discrimina
vocum addidisse, legimus, et videndus Diodor. Sicul. lib. α.) unde
'Επτάγλωσσος, 'Επταφθογγος, etc. dicitur Græcis.
[4] Hist. Scot. 4. in Fethelmacho.

chief King of the *Britons*; and for *Belin* and *Apollo*, see to
the Eighth Song.

211.　*By whom first* Gaul *was* taught *her* knowledge.

Understand the knowledge of those great Philosophers,
Priests, and Lawyers called *Druids* (of whom to the Tenth
Song largely). Their discipline was first found out in this
Isle, and afterward transferred into *Gaul;* whence their
youth were sent hither as to an University for instruction
in their learned professions : *Cæsar*[1] himself is author of as
much. Although, in particular law-learning, it might seem
that *Britain* was requited, if the Satirist[2] deceive not in
that ;

> Gallia *causidicos docuit facunda* Britannos.*

Which, with excellent *Lipsius*,[3] I rather apply to the dis-
persion of the *Latin* tongue through *Gaul* into this Province,
than to any other language or matter. For also in *Agricola's*
time, somewhat before, it appears that matter of good literature was here in a far higher degree than there, as *Tacitus*
in his life hath recorded. Thus hath our Isle been as
Mistress to *Gaul* twice. First in this *Druidian* doctrine,
next in the institution of their now famous University of
Paris; which was done by *Charlemaine*,[4] through aid and
industry of our learned *Alcuin* (he is called also *Albin*, and
was first sent Embassador to the Emperor by *Offa* King of
Mercland) seconded by those *Scots, John Mailros, Claudius
Clement*, and *Raban Maurus*.[5] But I know great men permit
it not ; nor can I see any very ancient authority for it, but
infinite of later times; so that it goes as a received opinion;

---

[1] Comment. 6.　　　　　[2] Juvenal. Satir. 15.
　　　* Eloquent *Gaul* taught the *British* Lawyers.
[3] De pronuntiat. rect. Lat. ling. cap. 3. v. Viglium ad instit.
Justin. tit. quib. non est permiss. fac. test.
[4] University of *Paris* instituted. Circa 790.　　　[5] Balæus cent. 1.

therefore without more examination in this no more fit passage, I commit it to my Reader.

217. *One* Bard *but coming in their* murd'rous swords *hath* staid.

Such strange assertion find I in story of these *Bards'* powerful enchantments, that with the amazing sweetness of their delicious harmonies,[1] not their own only, but withal their enemies', armies have suddenly desisted from fierce encounters ; *so,* as my author says, *did* Mars *reverence the Muses.* This exactly continues all fitness with what is before affirmed of that kind of Music ; twixt which (and all other by authentic affirmance) and the mind's affections there are certain[2] Μιμήματα,* as in this particular example is apparant. But how agreeth this with that in *Tacitus*[3] which calls a musical incentive to war among the *Germans, Barditus ?* Great critics would there read *Barrhitus,*[4] which in *Vegetius* and *Ammian* especially, is a peculiar name for those stirring up alarms before the battle used in *Roman* assaults (equal in proportion to the *Greeks'* ἀλαλαγμός, the *Irish* Kerns' *Pharroh,* and that *Roland's* Song of the *Normans,* which hath had his like also in most nations). But, seeing *Barrhitus* (in this sense) is a word of later time, and scarce yet, without remembrance of his naturalization, allowed in the *Latin ;* and, that this use was notable in those *Northerns* and *Gauls,* until wars with whom, it seems *Rome* had not a proper word for it (which appears by *Festus Pompeius,* affirming that the cry of the army was called *Barbaricum*) I should think somewhat confidently, that *Barditus* (as the common copies are) is the truest reading ;[5] yet so, that *Bar-*

---

[1] Diodor. Sicul. de gest. fabulos. antiq. lib. 6.
[2] Aristot. Polit. η. cap. ς.　　　* Imitations.
[3] Locus Taciti in de morib. Germ.
[4] Lips. ad Polyb. 4. Dialog. 11.
[5] Bardus *Gallicè* et *Britannicè* Cantor. Fest. et vide Bodin.' Meth. Hist. cap. 9. qui *Robartum Dagobartum* et similia vocabula hinc (malè verò) deducit.

rhitus formed by an unknowing pronunciation is, and, by
original, was the self-same.   For that *Lipsius*, mending the
place, will have it from 𝕭𝖆𝖗𝖊𝖓 in Dutch, which signifies, *To
cry out*, or from *Har Har* (which is as *Haron* in the *Norman*
customs and elsewhere) or from the word 𝕭𝖊𝖆𝖗𝖊 for imitation of that beast's cry, I much wonder, seeing *Tacitus* makes
express mention of verses harmonically celebrating valiant
performers, recital whereof hath that name *Barditus*, which
to interpret we might well call *Singing*.   But to conjoin
this fiery office with that quenching power of the *Bards*,
spoken of by the Author, I imagine that they had also for
this martial purpose skill in that kind of music which they
call *Phrygian*, being (as *Aristotle* says) 'Οργιαστική, Παθητική,
και 'Ενθουσιαστική, *i.e.*, as it were, madding the mind with
sprightful motion.   For so we see that those which sing the
tempering and mollifying *Pœans*[1] to *Apollo*, the τήνελλα and
καλλίνικος after victory, did among the *Greeks* in another
strain move with their *Pœans* to *Mars*, their "Ορθια, and
provoking charms before the encounter; and so meets this
in our *Bards* dispersed doubtless (as the *Druids*) through
Britain, Gaul, and part of *Germany*, which three had especially in warfare much community.

228. *Our* Cimbri *with the* Gauls————

National transmigrations touched to the Fourth Song
give light hither.   The name of *Cimbri* (which most of the
learned in this later time have made the same with *Cimmerians, Cumerians, Cambrians*, all coming from *Gomer*[2]
Japhet's son, to whom with his posterity was this North-
Western part of the world divided) expressing the *Welsh*,
calling themselves also 𝕶𝖚𝖒𝖗𝖞.   The Author alludes here
to that *British* army, which in our story is conducted under
Brennus and *Belinus* (sons to *Molmutius*) through *Gaul*, and

---

[1] Suid. in Παιαν.   [2] Genes. 10.

thence prosecuted, what in the Eighth Song and my notes there more plainly.

231. *Where, with our brazen swords*————

The Author thus teaches you to know, that, among the ancients, Brass, not Iron, was the metal of most use. In their little scythes, wherewith they cut[1] their herbs for inchantments, their Priests' razors, plowshares for describing the content of plotted cities, their music instruments, and such like, how special this metal was, it is with good warrant delivered : Nor with less, how frequent in the making of swords, spears, and armour in the Heroic times, as among other authorities that in the encounter of *Diomedes* and *Hector*[2] manifesteth :

$$————\pi\lambda\acute{\alpha}\gamma\chi\theta\eta\ \delta'\ \dot{\alpha}\pi\grave{o}\ \chi\alpha\lambda\varkappa\acute{o}\varphi\iota\ \chi\alpha\lambda\varkappa\acute{o}\varsigma.*$$

Which seems in them to have proceeded from a willingness of avoiding instruments too deadly in wounding ; For from a styptic faculty in this, more than in Iron, the cure of what it hurts is affirmed more easy, and the metal itself φαρμαχώδης† as *Aristotle*[3] expresses. But that our *Britons* used it also it hath been out of old monuments by our most learned Antiquary[4] observed.

306. *That to the* Roman trust (*on his report that stay*).

For indeed many are which the author here impugns, that dare believe nothing of our story, or antiquities of more ancient times ;[5] but only *Julius Cæsar*, and other about or since him. And surely his ignorance of this Isle

---

[1] Sophocles; Carminius; Virgil. ap. Macrobium Saturnal. lib. 5. cap. 19.; Pausan. in Laconic. γ. et Arcadic. η.; Samuel. lib. 1. cap. 17.
[2] Iliad. λ.   * Brass rebounds from Brass.
† Of remedial power.   [3] Problem. α. Sect. λε.
[4] Camd. in Cornub.   [5] See for this more in the Tenth Song.

was great, time forbidding him language or conversation
with the *British*. Nor was any before him of his country,
that knew or meddled in relation of us. The first of them
hat once to letters committed any word deduced from
Britain's name was a philosophical Poet[1] (flourishing some
fifty years before *Cæsar*) in these verses :

> *Nam quid* Britannum *cœlum differre putamus,*
> *Et quod in Ægypto'st quà mundi claudicat axis ?*

In the somewhat later Poets that lived about *Augustus*, as
Catullus, Virgil, and *Horace,* some passages of the name
have you, but nothing that discovers any monument of this
Island proper to her inhabitants. I would not reckon *Cornelius Nepos* among them,[2] to whose name is attributed, in
print, that polite Poem (in whose composition *Apollo* seems
to have given personal aid) of the *Troian* war, according to
Dares the *Phrygian's* story ; where, by poetical liberty, the
Britons are supposed to have been with *Hercules* at the rape
of *Hesione :* I should so, besides error, wrong my country,
to whose glory the true author's name of that book will
among the worthies of the Muses ever live. Read but these
of his verses, and then judge if he were a *Roman :*

> ————*Sine remigis usu*
> *Non nosset Memphis Romam, non Indus Hiberum,*
> *Non Scytha Cecropidem, non* Nostra Britannia *Gallum.*

And in the same book to *Baldwin* Archbishop of Canterbury:

> *At tu dissimulis longè cui fronte serená*
> *Sanguinis egregii lucrum, pacemque litatá*
> *Emptam animá Pater ille pius, summumque cacumen*
> *In curam venisse velit, cui cederet ipse*
> *Prorsus, vel proprias lætus sociaret habenas.*

---

[1] Lucret. de Rer. Nat. 6.
[2] *Cornelius Nepos* challenged to an *English* wit.

Of him a little before :

> ————*quo præside floret*
> *Cantia,* et in priscas respirat libera leges.*

Briefly thus : the Author was *Joseph* of *Excester* (afterward Archbishop of *Bourdeaux*) famous in this and other kind of good learning, under *Hen. II.* and *Rich. I.* speaking among those verses in this form :

> *Te sacræ assument acies divinaque bella.*
> *Tunc dignum majore tubâ, tunc pectore toto*
> *Nitar, et immensum mecum spargêre per orbem.*

Which must (as I think) be intended of *Baldwin* whose undertaking of the Cross and voyage with *Cœur de Lion* into the Holy Land, and death there, is in our Stories[1] ; out of which you may have large declaration of this holy father (so he calls *Tho. Becket*) that bought peace with price of his life; being murdered in his house at *Canterbury*, through the urging grievances intolerable to the King and laity, his diminution of common law liberties, and endeavoured derogation, for maintenance of *Romish* usurped supremacy. For these liberties, see *Matthew Paris* before all other, and the Epistles of *John* of *Salisbury*,[2] but lately published ; and, if you please, my *Janus Anglorum,* where they are restored from senseless corruption, and are indeed more themselves than in any other whatsoever in print. But thus too much of this false *Cornelius.* Compare with these notes what is to the First Song of *Britain* and *Albion ;* and you shall see that in *Greek* writers mention of our Land is long before any in the *Latin :* for *Polybius* that is the first which men-

---

* Ita legendum, non *Tantia* aut *Pontia*, uti ineptiunt qui *Josepho* nostro merenti suam inviderunt coronam in Codice typis excuso.

[1] Chronicis adde et Girald. Itin. Camb. 2. cap. 14.

[2] Sarisburiens. Epist. 159. 210. 220. et 268.

tions it, was more than one hundred years before *Lucretius.*
The Author's plainness in the rest of *Wie's* Song to this
purpose discharges my further labour.

355. *Comes* Dulas, *of whose name so* many rivers *be.*

As in *England* the names of *Avon, Ouse, Stoure,* and some
other; so in *Wales,* before all, is *Dulas,* a name very often
of rivers in *Radnor, Brecknock, Caermardhin,* and elsewhere.

366. *Which some have held to be begotten of the wind.*

In those Western parts of *Spain, Gallicia, Portugal,* and
Asturia many Classic testimonies, both Poets, as *Virgil,*
Silius Italicus, Naturalists, Historians, and Geoponics, as
Varro, Columel, Pliny, Trogus, and *Solinus,* have remembered
these mares, which conceive through fervent lust of Nature,
by the West wind; without copulation with the male (in
such sort as the *Ova subventanea*[1] are bred in hens) but so
that the foals live not over some three years. I refer it as
an Allegory[2] to the expressing only of their fertile breed
and swiftness in course; which is elegantly to this purpose
framed by him that was the father[3] of this conceit to his
admiring posterity, in these speaking of *Xanthus* and *Balius,*
two of *Achilles'* horses:—

$$\text{———}τὼ\ ἅμα\ πνοιῇσι\ πετέσθην·$$
$$Τοὺς\ ἔτεκε\ Ζεφύρῳ\ ἀνέμῳ\ "Αρπυια\ Ποδάργη,$$
$$Βοσκομένη\ λειμῶνι\ παρὰ\ ῥόον\ 'Ωκεανοῖο.*$$

*Whence withal you may note, that *Homer* had at least
heard of these coasts of *Spain,* according as upon the con-

---

[1] ἱππηνίμια, windy eggs, bred without a Cock.
[2] Justin. Hist. lib. 44.
[3] Iliad. xvi. 150.
* These did fly like the wind, which swift *Podarge* foaled to their
sire *Zephyrus,* feeding in a meadow by the ocean.

jectures on the name of *Lisbon*, the *Elysians*, and other such you have in *Strabo*.[1]   But for *Lisbon*, which many will have from *Ulysses*, and call it *Ulixbon*, being commonly written *Olisippo* or *Ulisippo* in the ancients, you shall have better etymology, if you hence derive and make it Ὅλος ἵππων,* as it were, that the whole tract is a Seminary of Horses, as a most learned man[2] hath delivered.

[1] Geograph. α.
* Ὅλιος Ἵππων. Ptolemæo. iota sublato, vera restat lectio.
[2] Paul. Merul. Cosmog. part 2. lib. 2. cap. 26.

THE SEVENTH SONG.

THE ARGUMENT.

The Muse from Cambria *comes again,*
To view the Forest of fair Deane ;
Sees Severne ; *when the* bigre *takes her,*
How fever-like the sickness shakes her ;
Makes mighty Malverne *speak his mind*   5
In honour of the Mountain-kind ;
Thence wafted with a merry gale,
Sees Lemster, *and the* Golden Vale ;
Sports with the Nymphs, themselves that ply
At th' wedding of the Lug *and* Wy;   10
Viewing the Herefordian *pride*
Along on Severne's *setting side,*
That small Wigornian *part surveys :*
Where for awhile herself she stays.

IGH matters call our Muse, inviting her to see
As well the lower Lands, as those where lately she
The *Cumbrian* Mountains clome, and (looking from
    aloft)
Survey'd coy *Severne's* course : but now to shores more soft
She shapes her prosperous sail ; and in this lofty Song,   5
The *Herefordian* Floods invites with her along,   [waste,
§ That fraught from plenteous *Powse*, with their superfluous
Manure the batfull *March*, until they be imbrac'd

In *Sabrin's* sovereign arms : with whose tumultuous waves
§ Shut up in narrower bounds, the *higre* wildly raves ;   10
And frights the straggling flocks, the neighbouring shores to
Afar as from the main it comes with hideous cry,   [fly,
And on the angry front the curléd foam doth bring,
The billows 'gainst the banks when fiercely it doth fling ;
Hurls up the slimy ooze, and makes the scaly brood   15
Leap madding to the land affrighted from the flood ;
O'erturns the toiling barge, whose steersman doth not lanch,
And thrusts the furrowing beak into her ireful panch :
As[1] when we haply see a sickly woman fall
Into a fit of that which we the Mother call,   20
When from the grievéd womb she feels the pain arise,
Breaks into grievous sighs, with intermixéd cries,
Bereavéd of her sense ; and struggling still with those
That 'gainst her rising pain their utmost strength oppose,
Starts, tosses, tumbles, strikes, turns, touses, spurns, and
        sprawls,   25
Casting with furious limbs her holders to the walls ;
But that the horrid pangs torment the grievéd so,
One well might muse from whence this sudden strength
        should grow.
   Here (Queen of Forests all, that West of *Severne* lie)
Her broad and bushy top *Deane* holdeth up so high,   30
The lesser are not seen, she is so tall and large.
And standing in such state upon the winding marge,
§ Within her hollow woods the *Satyrs* that did won
In gloomy secret shades, not pierc'd with summer's sun,
Under a false pretence the Nymphs to entertain,   35
Oft ravishéd the choice of *Sabrin's* wat'ry train ;
And from their Mistress' banks them taking as a prey,
Unto their woody caves have carried them away :

----

[1] A Simile expressing the *bore* or *higre.*

Then from her inner groves for succour when they cried,
She retchless of their wrongs (her *Satyrs'* scapes to hide) 40
Unto their just complaint not once her ear inclines :
So fruitful in her woods, and wealthy in her mines,
That *Leden* which her way doth through the desert make,
Though near to *Deane* allied, determin'd to forsake
Her course, and her clear limbs amongst the bushes hide, 45
Lest by the *Sylvans* (should she chance to be espied)
She might unmaid'ned go unto her Sovereign Flood :
So many were the rapes done on the wat'ry brood,
That *Sabrine* to her Sire (great *Neptune*) forc'd to sue,
The riots to repress of this outrageous crew, 50
His arméd orks he sent her milder stream to keep,
To drive them back to *Deane* that troubled all the deep.
§ Whilst *Malverne* (king of Hills) fair *Severne* overlooks
(Attended on in state with tributary Brooks)
And how the fertile fields of *Hereford* do lie, 55
And from his many heads, with many an amorous eye
Beholds his goodly site, how towards the pleasant rise,
Abounding in excess, the Vale of *Eusham* lies,
The Mountains every way about him that do stand,
Of whom he's daily seen, and seeing doth command ; 60
On tiptoes set aloft, this proudly uttereth he :
    Olympus, fair'st of Hills, that Heaven art said to be,
I not envy thy state, nor less myself do make ;
Nor to possess thy name, mine own would I forsake :
Nor would I, as thou dost, ambitiously aspire 65
To thrust my forkéd top into th' etherial fire.
For, didst thou taste the sweets that on my face do breathe,
Above thou wouldst not seek what I enjoy beneath :
Besides, the sundry soils I everywhere survey,
Make me, if better not, thy equal every way. 70
And more, in our defence, to answer those, with spite
That term us barren, rude, and void of all delight ;

We Mountains, to the land, like warts or wens to be,
By which, fair'st living things disfigur'd oft they see ;
This strongly to perform, a well-stuff'd brain would need.   75
And many Hills there be, if they this cause would heed,
Having their rising tops familiar with the sky
(From whence all wit proceeds) that fitter were than I
The task to undertake.   As not a man that sees
Mounchdeany, Blorench Hill, with *Breedon,* and the *Clees,*   80
And many more as great, and nearer me than they,
But thinks, in our defence they far much more could say.
Yet, falling to my lot, This stoutly I maintain   [Plain,
'Gainst Forests, Valleys, Fields, Groves, Rivers, Pasture,
And all their flatter kind (so much that do rely   85
Upon their feedings, flocks, and their fertility)
The Mountain is the King : and he it is alone
Above the other soils that Nature doth inthrone.
For Mountains be like Men of brave heroic mind,
With eyes erect to heaven, of whence themselves they find ; 90
Whereas the lowly Vale, as earthly, like itself,
Doth never further look than how to purchase pelf.
And of their batfull sites, the Vales that boast them thus,
Ne'er had been what they are, had it not been for us :
For, from the rising banks that strongly mound them in,   95
The Valley (as betwixt) her name did first begin :
And almost not a Brook, if she her banks do fill,
But hath her plenteous spring from Mountain or from Hill.
If Mead, or lower Slade, grieve at the room we take,
Know that the snow or rain, descending oft, doth make   100
The fruitful Valley fat, with what from us doth glide,
Who with our Winter's waste maintain their Summer's pride.
And to you lower Lands if terrible we seem,
And cover'd oft with clouds ; it is your foggy steam
The powerful Sun exhales, that in the cooler day   105
Unto this region com'n, about our tops doth stay.

And, what's the Grove, so much that thinks her to be grac'd,
If not above the rest upon the Mountain plac'd,
Where she her curléd head unto the eye may show?
For, in the easy Vale if she be set below,   110
What is she but obscure? and her more dampy shade
And covert, but a den for beasts of ravin made?
Besides, we are the marks, which looking from an high,
The traveller beholds; and with a cheerful eye
Doth thereby shape his course, and freshly doth pursue   115
The way which long before lay tedious in his view.
   What Forest, Flood, or Field, that standeth not in awe
Of *Sina*, or shall see the sight that Mountain saw?
To none but to a Hill such grace was ever given:
As on his back, 'tis said, great *Atlas* bears up heaven.   120
   So *Latmus* by the wise *Endymion*[1] is renown'd;
That Hill, on whose high top he was the first that found
Pale *Phœbe's* wand'ring course; so skilful in her sphere,
As some stick not to say that he enjoy'd her there.
   And those Chaste Maids, begot on Memory by *Jove*,   125
Not *Tempe* only love delighting in their Grove;
Nor *Helicon* their Brook, in whose delicious brims,
They oft are us'd to bathe their clear and crystal limbs;
But high *Parnassus* have, their Mountain, whereon they
Upon their golden lutes continually do play.   130
Of these I more could tell, to prove the place our own,
Than by his spacious Maps are by *Ortellius* shown.
   For Mountains this suffice.   Which scarcely had he told;
Along the fertile fields, when *Malverne* might behold
The *Herefordian* Floods, far distant though they be: 135
For great men, as we find, a great way off can see.
First, *Frome* with forehead clear, by *Bromyard* that doth glide;
And taking *Loden* in, their mixéd streams do guide,

------

[1] *Endymion* found out the course of the Moon.

To meet their Sovereign *Lug,* from the *Radnorian* Plain
At *Prestayn* coming in ; where he doth entertain   140
The *Wadell,* as along he under *Derfold* goes :
Her full and lusty side to whom the Forest shows,
As to allure fair *Lug,* abode with her to make.

    Lug little *Oney* first, then *Arro* in doth take,
At *Lemster,* for whose wool whose staple doth excell,   145
And seems to overmatch the golden *Phrygian* fell.
Had this our *Colchos* been unto the Ancients known,
When Honor was herself, and in her glory shown,
He then that did command the Infantry of *Greece,*
Had only to our Isle adventur'd for this Fleece.   150
    Where lives the man so dull, on *Britain's* further shore,
To whom did never sound the name of *Lemster* Ore ?[1]
That with the silkworm's web for smallness doth compare :
Wherein the winder shows his workmanship so rare
As doth the fleece excel, and mocks her looser clew ;   155
As neatly bottom'd up as Nature forth it drew ;
Of each in high'st accompt, and reckonéd here as fine,
§ As there th' *Apulian* fleece, or dainty *Tarentyne.*
From thence his lovely self for *Wye* he doth dispose,
To view the goodly flocks on each hand as he goes ;   160
And makes his journey short, with strange and sundry tales
Of all their wondrous things ; and, not the least, of *Wales;*
Of that prodigious Spring (him neighbouring as he past)
That little fishes' bones continually doth cast.
Whose reason whilst he seeks industriously to know,   165
A great way he hath gone, and *Hereford* doth show
Her rising spires aloft ; when as the princely *Wye,*
Him from his Muse to wake, arrests him by and by.
Whose meeting to behold, with how well-ord'red grace
Each other entertains, how kindly they embrace ;   170

---

[1] The excellency of *Lemster* wool.

For joy, so great a shout the bordering City sent,
That with the sound thereof, which thorough *Haywood* went,
The Wood-Nymphs did awake that in the forest won ;
To know the sudden cause, and presently they ron
With locks uncomb'd, for haste the lovely *Wye* to see   175
(The Flood that grac'd her most) this day should married be
To that more lovely *Lug ;* a River of much fame,
That in her wandering banks should lose his glorious name.
For *Hereford,* although her *Wye* she hold so dear,
Yet *Lug* (whose longer course doth grace the goodly Sheere,
And with his plenteous stream so many Brooks doth bring)
Of all hers that be North is absolutely King.   182

   But *Marcely,* griev'd that he (the nearest of the rest,
And of the Mountain-kind) not bidden was a guest
Unto this nuptial feast, so hardly it doth take,   185
As (meaning for the same his station to forsake)
§ Inrag'd and mad with grief, himself in two did rive ;
The trees and hedges near, before him up doth drive,
And dropping headlong down, three days together fall :
Which, bellowing as he went, the rocks did so appall,   190
That they him passage made, who cotes and chapels crush'd;
So violently he into his valley rush'd.
But *Wye* (from her dear *Lug* whom nothing can restrain,
In many a pleasant shade, her joy to entertain)
To *Rosse* her course directs ; and right her name* to show,
Oft windeth in her way, as back she meant to go.   196
Meander, who is said so intricate to be,
Hath not so many turns, nor crankling nooks as she.

   The *Herefordian* fields when well-near having pass'd,
As she is going forth two sister Brooks at last   200
That soil her kindly sends, to guide her on her way ;
Neat *Gamar,* that gets in swift *Garran :* which do lay

---

* *Wye* or *Gwy,* so called (in the *British*) of her sinuosity, or turning.

Their waters in one bank, augmenting of her train,
To grace the goodly *Wye*, as she doth pass by *Deane*.
   Beyond whose equal spring unto the West doth lie   205
The goodly *Golden Vale*, whose luscious scents do fly
More free than *Hybla's* sweets; and twixt her bordering hills,
The air with such delights and delicacy fills,
As makes it loth to stir, or thence those smells to bear.
Th' *Hesperides* scarce had such pleasures as be there: 210
Which sometime to attain, that mighty son of *Jove*
One of his Labors made, and with the Dragon strove,
That never clos'd his eyes, the golden fruit to guard;
As if t' enrich this place, from others, Nature spar'd:
Banks crown'd with curlèd Groves, from cold to keep the
     Plain,   215
Fields batfull, flow'ry Meads, in state them to maintain;
Floods, to make fat those Meads, from marble veins that
     spout,
To show the wealth within doth answer that without.
So brave a Nymph she is, in every thing so rare,
As to sit down by her, she thinks there's none should dare.
And forth she sends the *Doire*, upon the *Wye* to wait.   221
Whom *Munno* by the way more kindly doth intreat
(For *Eskle*, her most lov'd, and *Olcon's* only sake)
With her to go along, till *Wye* she overtake.
To whom she condescends, from danger her to shield,   225
That th' *Monumethian* parts from th' *Herefordian* field.
   Which manly *Malvern* sees from furthest of the Sheere,
On the *Wigornian* waste when Northward looking near,
On *Corswood* casts his eye, and on his home-born Chase,[1]
Then constantly beholds, with an unusual pace   230
Teame with her tribute come unto the *Cambrian* Queen,[2]
Near whom in all this place a River's scarcely seen,

---

    [1] *Malvern* Chase.   [2] *Severne*.

That dare avouch her name; *Teame* scorning any spring
But what with her along from *Shropshire* she doth bring,
Except one nameless stream that *Malvern* sends her in,   235
And *Laughern* though but small; when they such grace that
    win,
There thrust in with the Brooks incloséd in her bank.
Teame lastly thither com'n with water is so rank,
As though she would contend with *Sabrine*, and doth crave
Of place (by her desert) precedency to have: 240
Till chancing to behold the other's godlike grace,
So strongly is surpris'd with beauties in her face
By no means she could hold, but needsly she must show
Her liking; and herself doth into *Sabrine* throw.

  Not far from him again when *Malvern* doth perceive   245
Two hills, which though their heads so high they do not
    heave,
Yet duly do observe great *Malvern*, and afford
Him reverence: who again, as fits a gracious Lord,
Upon his subjects looks, and equal praise doth give
That *Woodberry* so nigh and neighbourly doth live   250
With *Abberley* his friend, deserving well such fame
That *Saxton* in his Maps forgot them not to name:
Which, though in their mean types small matter doth appear,
Yet both of good account are reckon'd in the Sheere,
And highly grac'd of *Teame* in his proud passing by.   255

  When soon the goodly *Wyre*, that wonted was so high
Her stately top to rear, ashaméd to behold
Her straight and goodly woods unto the fornace sold
(And looking on herself, by her decay doth see
The misery wherein her sister Forests be)   260
Of *Erisicthon's* end begins her to bethink,[1]
And of his cruel plagues doth wish they all might drink

---

[1] A Fable in Ovid's Mm.

That thus have them despoil'd : then of her own despight;
That she, in whom her Town fair *Beudley* took delight,
And from her goodly seat conceiv'd so great a pride,   265
In *Severne* on her East, *Wyre* on the setting side,
So naked left of woods, of pleasure, and forlorn,
As she that lov'd her most, her now the most doth scorn;
With endless grief perplex'd, her stubborn breast she strake,
And to the deafened air thus passionately spake :   270
You *Dryades*, that are said with oaks to live and die,
Wherefore in our distress do you our dwellings fly,
Upon this monstrous Age and not revenge our wrong?
For cutting down an oak that justly did belong
To one of *Ceres'* Nymphs, in *Thessaly* that grew   275
In the *Dodonean* Grove (O Nymphs!) you could pursue
The son of *Perops* then, and did the Goddess stir
That villainy to wreak the Tyrant did to her :
Who with a dreadful frown did blast the growing grain,
And having from him reft what should his life maintain,   280
She unto *Scythia* sent, for Hunger him to gnaw,
And thrust her down his throat, into his stanchless maw :
Who, when nor sea nor land for him sufficient were,
With his devouring teeth his wretched flesh did tear.
   This did you for one Tree: but of whole Forests they   285
That in these impious times have been the vile decay
(Whom I may justly call their Country's deadly foes)
'Gainst them you move no Power, their spoil unpunish'd goes.
How many grievéd souls in future time shall starve,
For that which they have rapt their beastly lust to serve!   290
   We, sometime that the state of famous *Britain* were,
For whom she was renown'd in Kingdoms far and near,
Are ransack'd; and our Trees so hack'd above the ground,
That, where their lofty tops their neighbouring Countries
       crown'd,
Their trunks (like aged folks) now bare and naked stand,   295

As for revenge to heaven each held a withered hand :
And where the goodly herds of high-palm'd harts did gaze
Upon the passer-by, there now doth only graze
The gall'd-back carrion jade, and hurtful swine do spoil
Once to the Sylvan Powers our consecrated soil.　　300
　　This utter'd she with grief: and more she would have spoke:
When the *Salopian* Floods her of her purpose broke,
And silence did enjoin ; a list'ning ear to lend
To *Severne*, which was thought did mighty things intend.

ILLUSTRATIONS.

HE Muse yet hovers over *Wales*, and here sings the inner territories, with part of the *Severne* story, and her *English* neighbours.

7. *That fraught from plenteous* Powse *with their superfluous waste Manure the batfull* March——

Wales (as is before touched) divided into three parts, *North-Wales*, *South-Wales*, and *Powise*;[1] this last is here meant, comprising part of *Brecknock*, *Radnor*, and *Montgomery*. The division hath its beginning attributed to the three sons of *Roderic the Great*,[2] *Mervin*, *Cadelh*, and *Anarawt*, who possessed them for their portions hereditary, as they are named. But out of an old book of *Welsh* laws, *David Powel* affirms those tripartite titles more ancient. I know that the division and gift is different in *Caradoc Lhancarvan* from that of *Girald ;* but no great consequence of admitting either here. Those three princes were called in *British* 𝕽 trtbwysoc Talaethíoc,* because[3] every of them ware upon his bonnet or helmet, a coronet of gold, being a broad lace

---

[1] Tripartite division of *Wales*.
[2] Girald. Camb. Descript. cap. 2. DCCC.LXX.VI.
* The three crowned Princes.
[3] D. Powel. ad Caradoc. Lhancarvan.

or head-band, indented upward, set and wrought with precious stones, which in *British* or *Welsh* is call'd **Talaeth,**
which name Nurses give to the upper band on a child's head.
Of this form (I mean of a band or wreath) were the ancientest
of crowns,[1] as appears in the description of the *Cidaris,* and
Tiara of the *Persians* in *Ctesias, Q. Curtius,* and *Xenophon,* the
crowns of *oak, grass, parsley, olives, myrtle,* and such, among
the *Greeks* and *Romans,* and in that express name of *Diadema,*
signifying a *Band,* of which, whether it have in our tongue
community with that *Banda,* derived out of the *Carian*[2] into
Italian, expressing victory, and so, for ominous good words,
is translated to Ensigns and Standards (as in Oriental Stories
the words Βάνδα and Βανδοφόρος often show) I must not here
inquire. *Molmutius* first[3] used a golden Crown among the
British, and, as it seems by the same authority, *Athelstan*
among the *Saxons.* But I digress. By the *March* understand those limits between *England* and *Wales,* which continuing from North to South, join the *Welsh* Shires to *Here-*
ford, Shropshire, and the *English* part, and were divers
Baronies, divided from any Shire until *Hen.* VIII.[4] by Act of
Parliament annexed some to *Wales,* other to *England.* The
Barons that lived in them were called Lord *Marchers,* and
by the name of *Marchiones,*[5] *i.e., Marquesses.* For so *Roger*
of *Mortimer,*[6] *James* of *Audeleg, Roger* of *Clifford, Roger* of
Leiburn, Haimo L'Estrange, Hugh of *Turbervil* (which by sword
adventured the ransom of *Henry* III. out of *Simon* of *Mont-*
fort his treacherous imprisonment, after the Battle of *Lewes*)
are called *Marchiones Walliæ;** and *Edward* III. created

---

[1] Crowns, Diadems, Band.
[2] Stephan. περὶ πολ. 'Αλάβανδα. v. Gorop. Becceselan. 2. et Pet.
Pithæi Adversar. 2. c. 20. de *Bandá,* cui et *Andatem* apud Dionem
conferas, et videsis si in altero alterius reliquiæ.
[3] Galfred. Monumeth. lib. 1. et 9.
[4] 27. *Hen.* 8. cap. 26. v. 28. *Ed.* 3. cap. 2.
[5] Lib. Rub. Scaccar.   [6] Matth. Westmonast. lib. 2.
* Marquesses, or Lord Marchers of *Wales.*

Roger of *Mortimer* Earl of *March*, as if you should say, of the
Limits twixt *Wales* and *England*, **Marc,** or **Merc,** signifying
a bound or limit ;[1] as to the Third Song more largely. And
hence is supposed the original of that honorary title of *Mar-
quess*, which is as much as a Lord of the Frontiers, or such
like ; although I know divers other are the derivations
which the *Feudists*[2] have imagined. These *Marchers* had
their laws in their Baronies, and for matter of suit, if it had
been twixt Tenants holding of them, then was it commenced
in their own Courts and determined ; if for the Barony
itself, then in the King's Court at *Westminster,* by Writ
directed to the Sheriff of the next *English* Shire adjoining,
as *Glocester, Hereford,* and some other. For the King's Writ*
did not run in *Wales* as in *England,* until by Statute the
Principality was incorporated with the Crown ; as appears
in an old Report[3] where one was committed for esloigning a
ward into *Wales, extra potestatem Regis* under *Hen.* III.
Afterward *Edw.* I.[4] made some Shires in it, and altered the
customs, conforming them in some sort to the *English,* as in
the Statute of *Ruthlan* you have it largely, and under *Edw.* II.
to a Parliament[5] at *Yorke* were summoned twenty-four out
of *North-Wales,* and as many out of *South-Wales.* But not-
withstanding all this, the *Marches* continued as distinct ; and
in them were, for the most part, those controverted titles,
which in our Law-annals are referred to *Wales.* For the
divided Shires were, as it seems, or should have been subject to the *English* form ; but the particulars hereof are unfit
for this room : if you are at all conversant in our law, I send
you to my margin ;[6] if not, it scarce concerns you.

[1] For the Limits see to the next Song.
[2] Ad Const. Feud. 2. tit. quis dicatur Dux et Jurisconsulti sæpius.
* But see to the Ninth Song more particularly.
[3] 13. *Hen.* 3. tit. Gard. 147.   [4] Stat. Ruthland. 12. *Ed.* 1.
[5] 14. *Ed.* 2. dors. claus. mem. 13.
[6] Vid. 18. *Ed.* 2. tit. Assise 382. 13. *Ed.* 3. Jurisdict. 23. 6. *Hen.* 5.
b. 34. 1. *Ed.* 3. f. 14. et sæpius in annalibus Juris nostri.

10. ———— *the* higre *wildly raves.*

This violence of the waters' madness, declared by the Author, is so expressed in an old Monk,[1] which about four hundred years since, says it was called the *Higre* in *English*. To make more description of it, were but to resolve the Author's poem.

33. *Within her hollow woods the* Satyrs *that did won.*

By the *Satyrs* ravishing the Sea-Nymphs into this maritime Forest of *Deane* (lying between *Wye* and *Severne* in *Glocester*), with *Severne's* suit to *Neptune*, and his provision of remedy, you have, poetically described, the rapines which were committed along that shore, by such as lurked in these shady receptacles, which he properly titles *Satyrs*, that name coming from an Eastern* root, signifying *to hide*, or *lie hid*, as that all-knowing† *Isaac Casaubon* hath at large (among other his unmeasurable benefits to the state of learning) taught us. The *English* were also ill-intreated by the *Welsh* in their passages here, until by Act of Parliament remedy was given; as you may see in the Statute's[2] preamble, which satisfies the fiction.

53. *Whilst* Malverne *King of Hills fair* Severne overlooks.

Hereford and *Worcester* are by these hills seven miles in length confined; and rather, in respect of the adjacent vales, than the hill's self, understand the attribute of excellency. Upon these is the supposed Vision of *Piers Plowman*, done, as is thought, by *Robert Langland*,[3] a *Shropshire* man, in a kind of *English* metre: which for discovery of the infecting corruptions of those times, I prefer before many more seemingly

---

[1] Guil. Malmesbur. lib. 4. de Gest Pontificum.   * סתר.

† Πανεπιστήμων. lib. de Satyra. Meritò indigetatur hoc epitheto longè doctissimus à doctissimo Dan. Heinsio in annot. ad Horatium.

[2] Stat. 9. *Hen.* 6. cap. 5.   [3] About time of *Edward* III.

serious invectives, as well for invention as judgment. But I have read that the author's name was John *Malverne*, a Fellow of Oriel College in Oxford, who finished it in xvi. *Edw.* III.

155. *As there th' Apulian fleece, or dainty Tarentine.*

In *Apuglia* and the upper *Calabria* of *Italy*, the Wool hath been ever famous for finest excellence :[1] insomuch that for preserving it from the injury of earth, bushes, and weather, the shepherds used to clothe their sheep with skins; and indeed was so chargeable in these and other kind of pains about it, that it scarce requited cost.

157. ———— *himself in two did rive.*

Alluding to a prodigious division of *Marcly* hill, in an earthquake of late time ;[2] which most of all was in these parts of the Island.

[1] Varr. de Re Rustic. 2. cap. 2. ; Columell. lib. 7. cap. 4.　　[2] 1575.

THE EIGHTH SONG.

THE ARGUMENT.

The goodly Severne *bravely sings*
The noblest of her British *Kings;*
At Cæsar's *landing what we were,*
And of the Roman *Conquests here:*
Then shows, to her dear Britons' *fame,*
How quickly christned they became;
And of their constancy doth boast,
In sundry fortunes strangely tost:
Then doth the Saxons' *landing tell,*
And how by them the Britons *fell;*   10
Cheers the Salopian *Mountains high,*
That on the West of Severne *lie:*
Calls down each Riveret from her spring,
Their Queen upon her way to bring:
Whom down to Bruge *the Muse attends:*   15
Where, leaving her, this Song she ends.

O *Salop* when herself clear *Sabrine* comes to show,
And wisely her bethinks the way she had to go,
South-westward casts her course; and with an
amorous eye
Those Countries whence she came, surveyeth (passing by)
Those lands in ancient times old *Cambria* claim'd her due,   5
For refuge when to her th' oppresséd *Britons* flew;

By *England* now usurp'd, who (past the wonted meres,
Her sure and sovereign banks) had taken sundry Sheeres,
Which she her Marches made : whereby those Hills of fame
And Rivers stood disgrac'd ; accounting it their shame,   10
§ That all without that Mound which *Mercian Offa* cast
To run from North to South, athwart the *Cambrian* waste,
Could *England* not suffice, but that the straggling *Wye*,
Which in the heart of *Wales* was sometime said to lye,
Now only for her bound proud *England* did prefer.   15
That *Severne*, when she sees the wrong thus off'red her,
Though by injurious Time deprivéd of that place
Which anciently she held : yet loth that her disgrace
Should on the *Britons* light, the Hills and Rivers near
Austerely to her calls, commanding them to hear   20
In her dear children's right (their ancestors of yore,
Now thrust betwixt herself, and the *Virgivian* shore,
§ Who drave the Giants hence that of the earth were bred,
And of the spacious Isle became the sovereign head)
What from authentic books she liberally could say.   25
Of which whilst she bethought her, Westward every way,
The Mountains, Floods, and Meres, to silence them betake :
When *Severne* lowting low, thus gravely them bespake :

How mighty was that man, and honour'd still to be,
That gave this Isle his name, and to his children three   30
Three Kingdoms in the same ! which, time doth now deny,
With his arrival here, and primer monarchy.

Loëgria,[1] though thou canst thy *Locrine* eas'ly lose,
Yet *Cambria*,[2] him, whom Fate her ancient Founder chose,
In no wise will forego ; nay, should *Albania*[3] leave   35
§ Her *Albanact* for aid, and to the *Scythian* cleave.
And though remorseless *Rome*, which first did us enthrall,
As barbarous but esteem'd, and stick'd not so to call ;

---

[1] *England.*   [2] *Wales.*   [3] *Scotland.*

The ancient *Britons* yet a sceptred King obey'd
§ Three hundred years before *Rome's* great foundation laid; 40
And had a thousand years an Empire strongly stood,
Ere *Cæsar* to her shores here stemm'd the circling flood;
§ And long before, borne arms against the barbarous *Hun,*
Here landing with intent the Isle to over-run :
And following them in flight, their General *Humber* drown'd
In that great arm of sea, by his great name renown'd ;   46
And her great Builders had, her Cities who did rear
With Fanes unto her Gods, and Flamins[1] everywhere.
Nor *Troynovant* alone a City long did stand ;
But after, soon again by *Ebrank's* pow'rful hand   50
Yorke lifts her Towers aloft : which scarcely finish'd was,
But as they, by those Kings ; so by *Rudhudibras,*
Kent's first and famous Town,[1] with *Winchester,* arose :
And other, others built, as they fit places chose.

So *Britain* to her praise, of all conditions brings ;   55
The warlike, as the wise. Of her courageous Kings,
Brute Green-shield : to whose name we providence impute,
Divinely to revive the Land's first Conqueror, *Brute.*

So had she those were learn'd, endu'd with nobler parts :
As, he from learnéd *Greece,* that (by the liberal Arts)   60
§ To *Stamford,* in this Isle, seem'd *Athens* to transfer ;
Wise *Bladud,* of her Kings that great *Philosopher ;*
Who found our boiling Baths ; and in his knowledge high,
Disdaining human paths, here practiséd to fly.

Of justly-vexéd *Leire,* and those who last did tug   65
In worse than civil war, the sons[3] of *Gorboduq*
(By whose unnatural strife the Land so long was tost)
I cannot stay to tell, nor shall my *Britain* boast ;
But, of that man which did her Monarchy restore,
Her first imperial Crown of gold that ever wore,   70

---

[1] Priests among idolatrous *Gentiles.*   [2] *Canterbury.*
[3] *Ferrex* and *Porrex.*

And that most glorious type of sovereignty regain'd ;
Mulmutius: who this Land in such estate maintain'd
As his great bel-sire *Brute* from *Albion's* heirs it won.
  § This grand-child, great as he, those four proud Streets
          begun
That each way cross this Isle, and bounds did them allow. 75
Like privilege he lent the Temple and the Plow :
So studious was this Prince in his most forward zeal
To the Celestial power, and to the Public weal.
  Belinus he begot, who *Dacia* proud subdu'd ;
And *Brennus,*[1] who abroad a worthier war pursu'd,   80
Asham'd of civil strife ; at home here leaving all :
And with such goodly Youth, in *Germany* and *Gaul*
As he had gather'd up, the *Alpine* Mountains pass'd
And bravely on the banks of fatal *Allia* chas'd
The *Romans* (that her stream distainéd with their gore)   85
And through proud *Rome,* display'd his *British* ensign bore:
  § There, balancing his sword against her baser gold,
The Senators for slaves he in her *Forum* sold.
At last, by pow'r expell'd, yet proud of late success,
His forces then for *Greece* did instantly address ;   90
And marching with his men upon her fruitful face,
Made *Macedon* first stoop ; then *Thessaly,* and *Thrace;*
His soldiers there enrich'd with all *Peonia's* spoil ;
And where to *Greece* he gave the last and deadliest foil,
In that most dreadful fight, on that more dismal day,   95
O'erthrew their utmost prowess at sad *Thermopylœ ;*
And daring of her Gods, adventur'd to have ta'en
Those sacred things enshrin'd in wise *Apollo's* Fane : [word,
To whom when thund'ring Heaven pronounc'd her fearfull'st
  § Against the *Delphian* Power he shak'd his ireful sword. 100
    As of the *British* blood, the native *Cambri* here
(So of my *Cambria* call'd) those valiant *Cymbri* were

----

[1] Belinus and Brennus.

(When *Britain* with her brood so peopled had her seat.
The soil could not suffice, it daily grew so great)
Of *Denmarke* who themselves did anciently possess,   105
And to that strait'ned point, that utmost chersoness,
§ My Country's name bequeath'd; whence *Cymbrica* it took:
Yet long were not compris'd within that little nook,
But with those *Almaine* pow'rs this people issued forth :
And like some boist'rous wind arising from the North,   110
Came that unwieldy host; that, which way it did move,
The very burthenous earth before it seem'd to shove,
And only meant to claim the Universe its own.
In this terrestrial Globe, as though some world unknown,
By pampered Nature's store too prodigally fed   115
(And surfeiting there-with) her surcrease vomited,
These roaming up and down to seek some settling room,
First like a deluge fell upon *Illyricum*,
And with his *Roman* pow'rs *Papyrius* over-threw ;
Then, by great *Belus** brought against those Legions, slew   120
Their forces which in *France Aurelius Scaurus* led ;
And afterward again, as bravely vanquishéd
The Consuls *Cœpio* and stout *Manlius*, on the Plain,
Where *Rhodanus* was red with blood of *Latins* slain. ·

   In greatness next succeeds *Belinus'* worthy son,   125
Gurgustus : who soon left what his great Father won,
To *Guynteline* his heir : whose Queen,[1] beyond her kind,
In her great husband's peace, to shew her upright mind,
§ To wise *Molmutius'* laws, her *Martian* first did frame :
From which we ours derive, to her eternal fame.   130

   So *Britain* forth with these, that valiant Bastard brought,
Morindus, Danius' son, which with that Monster[2] fought
His subjects that devour'd ; to shew himself again
Their *Martyr*, who by them selected was to reign.

---

* A great General of those Northern Nations.   [1] Martia.
[2] A certain Monster often issuing from the Sea, devoured divers
of the *British* people.

So *Britain* likewise boasts her *Elidure* the just,   135
Who with his people was of such especial trust,
That (*Archigallo* fall'n into their general hate,
And by their powerful hand depriv'd of kingly state)
Unto the Regal Chair they *Elidure* advanc'd :
But long he had not reign'd, ere happily it chanc'd,   140
In hunting of a hart, that in the forest wild,
The late deposéd King, himself who had exil'd
From all resort of men, just *Elidure* did meet ;
Who much unlike himself at *Elidurus'* feet,
Him prostrating with tears, his tender breast so strook,   145
That he (the *British* rule who lately on him took
At th' earnest people's pray'rs) him calling to the Court,
There *Archigallo's* wrongs so lively did report,
Relating (in his right) his lamentable case,
With so effectual speech imploring their high grace,   150
That him they re-inthron'd ; in peace who spent his days.
   Then *Elidure* again, crown'd with applausive praise,
As he a brother rais'd, by brothers was depos'd,
And put into the Tow'r : where miserably inclos'd,
Out-living yet their hate, and the Usurpers dead,   155
Thrice had the *British* Crown set on his reverend head.
   When more than thirty Kings in fair succession came
Unto that mighty *Lud*, in whose eternal name
§ Great *London* still shall live (by him rebuilded) while
To Cities she remains the Sovereign of this Isle.   160
   And when commanding *Rome* to *Cæsar* gave the charge,
Her Empire (but too great) still further to enlarge
With all beyond the Alps ; the aids he found to pass
From these parts into *Gaul*, shew'd here some Nation was
Undaunted that remain'd with *Rome's* so dreadful name,   165
That durst presume to aid those she decreed to tame.
Wherefore that matchless man, whose high ambition wrought
Beyond her Empire's bounds, by shipping wisely sought

(Here prowling on the shores) this Island to descry,
What people her possess'd, how fashion'd she did lie :⠀⠀170
Where scarce a stranger's foot defil'd her virgin breast,
Since her first Conqueror *Brute* here put his powers to rest ;
Only some little boats, from *Gaul* that did her feed
With trifles, which she took for niceness more than need :
But as another world, with all abundance blest,⠀⠀175
And satisfied with what she in herself possest ;
Through her excessive wealth (at length) till wanton grown,
Some Kings (with other lands that would enlarge their own)
By innovating arms an open passage made
For him that gap'd for all (the *Roman*) to invade.⠀⠀180
Yet with grim-visag'd war when he her shores did greet,
And terriblest did threat with his amazing fleet,
Those *British* bloods he found, his force that durst assail,
And pouréd from the cleeves their shafts like show'rs of hail
Upon his helméd head ; to tell him as he came,⠀⠀185
That they (from all the world) yet feared not his name :
Which their undaunted spirits soon made that Conqueror
⠀⠀feel,
Oft vent'ring their bare breasts 'gainst his oft-bloodied steel ;
And in their chariots charg'd : which they with wondrous
⠀⠀skill
Could turn in their swift'st course upon the steepest hill, 190
And wheel about his troops for vantage of the ground,
Or else disrank his force where entrance might be found :
And from their arméd seats their thrilling darts could throw ;
Or nimbly leaping down, their valiant swords bestow,
And with an active skip remount themselves again,⠀⠀195
Leaving the *Roman* horse behind them on the plain,
And beat him back to *Gaul* his forces to supply ;
As they the Gods of *Rome* and *Cæsar* did defy.
⠀⠀*Cassibalan* renown'd, the *Britons'* faithful guide,
Who when th' *Italian* pow'rs could no way be denied,⠀⠀200

But would this Isle subdue ; their forces to fore-lay,
Thy forests thou didst fell, their speedy course to stay :
§ Those arméd stakes in *Tames* that stuck'st, their horse to
Which boldly durst attempt to forage on thy shore :   [gore
Thou such hard entrance here to *Cæsar* didst allow,   205
To whom (thyself except) the Western world did bow.
§ And more than *Cæsar* got, three Emperors could not win,
Till the courageous sons of our *Cunobelin*
Sunk under *Plautius*' sword, sent hither to discuss
The former *Roman* right, by arms again, with us.   210
Nor with that Consul join'd, *Vespasian* could prevail
In thirty several fights, nor make them stoop their sail.
Yea, had not his brave son, young *Titus*, past their hopes,
His forward Father fetch'd out of the *British* troops,
And quit him wondrous well when he was strongly charg'd,
His Father (by his hands so valiantly enlarg'd)   216
Had never more seen *Rome ;* nor had he ever spilt
The Temple that wise son of faithful *David* built,
Subverted those high walls, and laid that City waste
Which God, in human flesh, above all other grac'd.   220
     No marvel then though *Rome* so great her conquest thought,
In that the Isle of *Wight* she to subjection brought,
Our *Belgæ** and subdued (a people of the West)
That latest came to us, our least of all the rest ;
When *Claudius*, who that time her wreath-imperial wore, 225
Though scarce he shew'd himself upon our Southern shore,
It scorn'd not in his style ; but, due to that his praise,
Triumphal arches claim'd, and to have yearly plays ;
The noblest naval crown, upon his palace pitch'd ;
As with the *Ocean's* spoil his *Rome* who had enrich'd.   230
     Her *Caradock* (with cause) so *Britain* may prefer ;
Than whom, a braver spirit was ne'er brought forth by her :

---

* A people then inhabiting *Hamp, Dorset, Wilt,* and *Somerset* shires.

For whilst here in the West the *Britons* gather'd head,
This General of the rest, his stout *Silures*[1] led
Against *Ostorius*, sent by *Cæsar* to this place   235
With *Rome's* high fortune (then the high'st in Fortune's
    grace)
A long and doubtful war with whom he did maintain,
Until that hour wherein his valiant *Britons* slain,
He grievously beheld (o'erprest with *Roman* pow'r)
Himself well-near the last their wrath did not devour.   240
When (for revenge, not fear) he fled (as trusting most,
Another day might win, what this had lately lost)
To *Cartismandua*, Queen of *Brigants*[2] for her aid,
He to his foes, by her, most falsely was betray'd.
Who, as a spoil of war, t' adorn the Triumph sent   245
To great *Ostorius* due, when through proud *Rome* he went,
That had herself prepar'd (as she had all been eyes)
Our *Caradock* to view; who in his country's guise,
§ Came with his body nak'd, his hair down to his waist,
Girt with a chain of steel ; his manly breast inchas'd   250
With sundry shapes of beasts. And when this *Briton* saw
His wife and children bound as slaves, it could not awe
His manliness at all : but with a settled grace,
Undaunted with her pride, he look'd her in the face :
And with a speech so grave as well a prince became,   255
Himself and his redeem'd, to our eternal fame.
    Then *Rome's* great Tyrant* next, the last's adopted heir,
That brave *Suetonius* sent, the *British* coasts to clear ;
The utter spoil of *Mon*[3] who strongly did pursue
(Unto whose gloomy strengths, th' revolted *Britons* flew) 260
There ent'ring, he beheld what strook him pale with dread:
The frantic *British* froes, their hair dishevelléd,

---

[1] Those of *Monmouth*, and the adjacent Shires.
[2] Those of *Yorkshire*, and thereby.   * Nero.
[3] *Anglesey*, the chief place of residence of the *Druids.*

With fire-brands ran about, like to their furious eyes;
And from the hollow woods the fearless *Druides;*
Who with their direful threats, and execrable vows,   265
Inforc'd the troubled heaven to knit her angry brows.
  And as here in the West the *Romans* bravely wan,
So all upon the East the *Britons* over-ran :
§ The Colony long kept at *Mauldon,* overthrown,
Which by prodigious signs was many times fore-shown,   270
And often had dismay'd the *Roman* soldiers : when
Brave *Foxilicia* made with her resolved'st men
To *Virolam ;*[1] whose siege with fire and sword she plied,
Till levell'd with the earth.   To *London* as she hied,
The Consul coming in with his auspicious aid,   275
The Queen (to quit her yoke no longer that delay'd)
Him dar'd by dint of sword, it hers or his to try,
With words that courage show'd, and with a voice as high
(In her right hand her launce, and in her left her shield,
As both the battles stood prepared in the field)   280
Incouraging her men : which resolute, as strong,
Upon the *Roman* rush'd ; and she, the rest among,
Wades in that doubtful war : till lastly, when she saw
The fortune of the day unto the *Roman* draw,
The Queen (t' out-live her friends who highly did disdain,
And lastly, for proud *Rome* a Triumph to remain)   286
§ By poison ends her days, unto that end prepar'd,
As lavishly to spend what *Suetonius* spar'd.
  Him scarcely *Rome* recall'd, such glory having won,
But bravely to proceed, as erst she had begun,   290
Agricola here made her great Lieutenant then :
Who having settled *Mon,* that man of all her men,
Appointed by the powers apparently to see
The wearied *Britons* sink, and eas'ly in degree

────────

[1] By Saint *Alban's.*

Beneath his fatal sword the *Ordovies*[1] to fall   295
Inhabiting the West, those people last of all
Which stoutl'est him with-stood, renown'd for martial worth.
    Thence leading on his powers unto the utmost North,
When all the Towns that lay betwixt our *Trent* and *Tweed*,
Suffic'd not (by the way) his wasteful fires to feed,   300
He there some *Britons* found, who (to rebate their spleen,
As yet with grievéd eyes our spoils not having seen)
Him at *Mount Grampus*[2] met: which from his height beheld
Them lavish of their lives ; who could not be compell'd
The *Roman* yoke to bear : and *Galgacus* their guide   305
Amongst his murthered troops there resolutely died.
    Eight *Roman* Emperors reign'd since first that war began ;
Great *Julius Cæsar* first, the last *Domitian.*
A hundred thirty years the Northern *Britons* still,
That would in no wise stoop to *Rome's* imperious will,   310
Into the strait'néd land with theirs retiréd far,
In laws and manners since from us that different are ;
And with the *Irish Pict*, which to their aid they drew
(On them oft breaking in, who long did them pursue)
§ A greater to us in our own bowels bred,   315
Than *Rome*, with much expense that us had conqueréd.
    And when that we great *Rome's* so much in time were
                                                          grown,
That she her charge durst leave to Princes of our own,
(Such as, within ourselves, our suffrage should elect)
§ *Arriragus*, born ours, here first she did protect ;   320
Who faithfully and long, of labour did her ease.
    Then he, our Flamins' seats who turn'd to Bishops' sees ;
Great *Lucius*, that good King : to whom we chiefly owe
§ This happiness we have, Christ Crucified to know.
    As *Britain* to her praise receiv'd the Christian faith,   325
After (that Word-made Man) our dear Redeemer's death

---

¹ *North-wales* men.   ² In the midst of *Scotland.*

Within two hundred years; and His Disciples here,
By their Great Master sent to preach Him everywhere,
Most reverently receiv'd, their doctrine and preferr'd;
Interring him, who[1] erst the Son of God interr'd.   330

So *Britain's* was she born, though *Italy* her crown'd,
Of all the Christian world that Empress most renown'd,
§ *Constantius'* worthy wife; who scorning worldly loss,
Herself in person went to seek that Sacred Cross,
Whereon our Saviour died: which found, as it was sought,
From *Salem*[2] unto *Rome* triumphantly she brought.   336

As when the Primer Church her Councils pleas'd to call,
Great *Britain's* Bishops there were not the least of all;
§ Against the *Arian* Sect at *Arles* having room,
At *Sardica* again, and at *Ariminum*.   340

Now, when with various fate five hundred years had past,
And *Rome* of her great charge grew weary here at last;
The *Vandals*, *Goths*, and *Huns*, that with a powerful head
All *Italy* and *France* had well-near over-spread,
To much endanger'd *Rome* sufficient warning gave,   345
Those forces that she held, within herself to have.
The *Roman* rule from us then utterly remov'd.

Whilst, we, in sundry Fields our sundry fortunes prov'd
With the remorseless *Pict*, still wasting us with war.
And 'twixt the froward sire, licentious *Vortiger*,   350
And his too froward son, young *Vortimer*, arose
Much strife within ourselves, whilst here they interpose
By turns each other's reigns; whereby, we weak'néd grew.
The warlike *Saxon* then into the land we drew;
A nation nurs'd in spoil, and fitt'st to undergo   355
Our cause against the *Pict*, our most inveterate foe.

When they, which we had hir'd for soldiers to the shore,
Perceiv'd the wealthy Isle to wallow in her store,

---

[1] *Joseph* of *Arimathea*.   [2] *Jerusalem*.

And subtly had found out how we infeebléd were ;
They, under false pretence of amity and cheer,   360
The *British* Peers invite, the *German* healths to view
At *Stonehenge ;* where they them unmercifully slew.
    Then, those of *Brute's* great blood, of *Armorick* possest,
Extremely griev'd to see their kinsmen so distrest,
Us off'red to relieve, or else with us to die :   365
We, after, to requite their noble curtesie,
§ Eleven thousand maids sent those our friends again,
In wedlock to be link'd with them of *Brute's* high strain ;
That none with *Brute's* great blood, but *Britons* might be
      mixt :
Such friendship ever was the stock of *Troy* betwixt.   370
Out of whose ancient race, that warlike *Arthur* sprong :
Whose most renownéd Acts shall sounded be as long
As *Britain's* name is known : which spread themselves so wide,
As scarcely hath for fame left any roomth beside.
    My *Wales*, then hold thine own, and let thy *Britons* stand
Upon their right ; to be the noblest of the land.   376
Think how much better 'tis, for thee, and those of thine,
From Gods, and Heroes old, to draw your famous line,
§ Than from the *Scythian* poor ; whence they themselves
      derive
Whose multitudes did first you to the mountains drive.   380
Nor let the spacious Mound[1] of that great *Mercian* King
(Into a lesser roomth thy burliness to bring)
Include thee ; when myself, and my dear brother *Dee*,[1]
By nature were the bounds first limited to thee.   [near,
    Scarce ended she her speech, but those great Mountains
Upon the *Cambrian* part that all for *Brutus* were,   386
With her high truths inflam'd, look'd every one about
To find their several Springs ; and bade them get them out,

---

[1] The ancient bounds of *Wales*.

And in their fulness wait upon their sovereign Flood,
In *Britain's* ancient right so bravely that had stood.   390

    When first the furious *Teame*, that on the *Cambrian* side
Doth *Shropshire* as a meere from *Hereford* divide,
As worthiest of the rest ; so worthily doth crave
That of those lesser Brooks the leading she might have ;
The first of which is *Clun*, that to her mistress came ;   395
Which of a Forest* born that bears her proper name,
Unto the *Golden Vale* and anciently allied,
Of everything of both, sufficiently supplied,
The longer that she grows, the more renown doth win :
And for her greater state, next *Bradfield* bringeth in,   400
Which to her wider banks resigns a weaker stream.

    When fiercely making forth, the strong and lusty *Teame*
A friendly Forest-Nymph (nam'd *Mocktry*) doth imbrace,
Herself that bravely bears; twixt whom and *Bringwood-Chase*,
Her banks with many a wreath are curiously bedeckt,   405
And in their safer shades they long-time her protect.

    Then takes she *Oney* in, and forth from them doth fling :
When to her further aid, next *Bowe*, and *Warren*, bring
Clear *Quenny ;* by the way, which *Stradbrooke* up doth take :
By whose united powers, their *Teame* they mightier make :
Which in her lively course to *Ludlowe* comes at last,   411
Where *Corve* into her stream herself doth head-long cast.
With due attendance next, comes *Ledwich* and the *Rhea.*

    Then speeding her, as though sent post unto the Sea,
Her native *Shropshire* leaves, and bids those Towns adieu, 415
Her only sovereign Queen, proud *Severne* to pursue.

    When at her going-out, those Mountains of command
(The *Clees*, like loving twins, and *Stitterston* that stand)
Trans-Severnéd, behold fair *England* tow'rds the rise,
And on their setting side, how ancient *Cumbria* lies.   420

* *Clun* Forest.

Then *Stipperston* a hill, though not of such renown
As many that are set here tow'rds the going down,
To those his own allies, that stood not far away,
Thus in behalf of *Wales* directly-seem'd to say :
 Dear *Corndon*, my delight, as thou art lov'd of me, 425
And *Breedon*, as thou hop'st a *Briton* thought to be,
To *Cortock* strongly cleave, as to our ancient friend,
And all our utmost strength to *Cambria* let us lend.
For though that envious Time injuriously have wrong
From us those proper names did first to us belong, 430
Yet for our Country still, stout Mountains let us stand.
 Here, every neighbouring Hill held up a willing hand,
As freely to applaud what *Stipperston* decreed :
And *Hockstow* when she heard the Mountains thus proceed,
With echoes from her Woods, her inward joys exprest, 435
To hear that Hill she lov'd, which likewise lov'd her best,
Should in the right of *Wales*, his neighbouring Mountains
  stir,
So to advance that place which might them both prefer ;
That she from open shouts could scarce herself refrain.
 When soon those other Rills to *Severne* which retain, 440
And 't ended not on *Teame*, thus of themselves do show
The service that to her they absolutely owe.
First *Camlet* cometh in, a *Mountgomerian* maid,
Her source in *Severne's* banks that safely having laid,
Mele, her great Mistress, next at *Shrewsbury* doth meet, 445
To see with what a grace she that fair Town doth greet ;
Into what sundry gyres her wondered self she throws,
And oft in-isles the shore, as wantonly she flows ;
Of it oft taking leave, oft turns it to imbrace ;
As though she only were enamour'd of that place, 450
Her fore-intended course determinéd to leave,
And to that most-lov'd Town eternally to cleave :
With much ado at length, yet bidding it adieu,

Her journey towards the Sea doth seriously pursue.
Where, as along the shores she prosperously doth sweep,   455
Small *Marbrooke* maketh-in, to her inticing deep.
And as she lends her eye to *Bruge's** lofty sight,
That Forest-Nymph mild *Morffe* doth kindly her invite
To see within her shade what pastime she could make:
Where she, of *Shropshire ;* I my leave of *Severne* take.   460

* *Bruge-North.*

ILLUSTRATIONS.

TILL are you in the *Welsh* March, and the Chorography of this Song includes itself, for the most, within *Shropshire's* part over *Severne*.

11. *That all without the* Mound *that* Mercian Offa *cast.*

Of the *Marches* in general you have to the next before. The[1] particular bounds have been certain parts of *Dee, Wye, Severne,* and *Offa's* Dike. The ancientest is *Severne*, but a later is observed in a right line from *Strigoil*-Castle* upon *Wye,* to *Chester* upon *Dee,* which was so naturally a Mere between these two Countries *Wales* and *England,* that by apparant change of its channel towards either side superstitious judgment was used to be given of success in the following year's battles of both nations; whence perhaps came it to be called *Holy Dee,* as the Author also often uses. Twixt the mouths of *Dee* and *Wye* in this line (almost one hundred miles long) was that *Offa's*† Dike cast, after such time as he had besides his before-possessed *Mercland,* acquired by conquest even almost what is now *England.* King

---

[1] Caradoc Lhancarvan in *Conan Tindaethwy.* Girald. Itinerar. 2. cap. 11. et Descript. cap. 15.
* By *Chepstow* in *Monmouth.*
† **Claudh-Offa.** See to the Tenth Song for *Dee.* A.D. 780.

Harold[1] made a law, that whatsoever *Welsh* transcended this Dike with any kind of weapon should have, upon apprehension, his right hand cut off; *Athelstan* after conquest of *Howel Dha*, King of *Wales*, made *Wye* limit of *North-Wales*, as in regard of his chief territory of West *Saxony* (so affirms *Malmesbury*), which well-understood impugns the opinion received for *Wye's* being a general Mere instituted by him, and withal shows you how to mend the Monk's published text, where you read *Ludwalum regem omnium Wallensium, et Constantinum regem Scotorum, cedere regnis compulit.** For plainly this *Ludwal* (by whom he means *Howel Dha*, in other Chronicles called *Huwal*) in *Athelstan's* lifetime was not King of all *Wales*, but only of the *South* and *Western* parts with *Powis*, his cousin *Edwall Voel* then having *North-Wales;* twixt which and the part of *Howell* conquered, this limit was proper to distinguish. Therefore either read *Occidentalium Wallensium*† (for in *Florence* of *Worcester* and *Roger* of *Hoveden* that passage is with *Occidentalium Britonnum*‡) or else believe that *Malmesbury* mistook *Howel* to be in *Athelstan's* time, as he was after his death, sole Prince of all *Wales*. In this conjecture I had aid from *Lhancarvan's* History, which in the same page (as learned *Lhuid's* edition in *English* is) says, that *Athelstan* made the River *Cambia*§ the frontier towards *Cornwall:* but there, in requital, I correct him, and read *Tambra, i.e., Tamar,* dividing *Devonshire* and *Cornwall;* as *Malmesbury* hath it expressly, and the matter-self enough persuades.

23. *Who drave the* Giants *hence, that of the* earth *were* bred.

Somewhat of the Giants to the First Song; fabulously

---

[1] Higden. in Polychronic. 1. cap. 43.

* He compelled *Ludwall* King of *All Wales,* and *Constantine* King of *Scots* to leave their Crowns. Emendatio Historiæ Malmesburiensis lib. 2. cap. 6.

† *West-Wales.* 926.

‡ *West-Britons.* Caratacus Lancarbensis in *Edwall. Voel* Correctus.

§ *Cambalan* or *Camel.*

supposed begotten by Spirits upon *Dioclesian's* or *Danaus'* daughters. But here the Author aptly terms them *bred of the earth*, both for that the antiquities of the *Gentiles* made the first inhabitants of most countries as produced out of the soil, calling them *Aborigines* and Αὐτόχθονες, as also for imitation of those epithets of Γηγενεῖς, and Πηλογόνοι[1] among the *Greeks*, *Terræ filii* among the *Latins*, the very name of Giants being thence[2] derived,—

Οὕνεκα γῆς ἐγένοντο καὶ αἵματος οὐρανίοιο.[*]

Which misconceit I shall think abused the Heathen upon their ill-understanding of *Adam's* creation[3] and allegoric greatness, touched before out of *Jewish* Fiction.

36. *Her* Albanact; *for aid, and to the* Scythian *cleave.*

Britain's tripartite division by *Brute's* three sons, *Logrin*, *Camber* and *Albanact*, whence all beyond *Severne* was styled *Cambria*, the now *England Loegria*, and *Scotland Albania*, is here showed you : which I admit, but as the rest of that nature, upon credit of our suspected Stories followed with sufficient justification by the Muse ; alluding here to that opinion which deduces the *Scots* and their name from the *Scythians*. Arguments of this likelihood have you largely in our most excellent Antiquary. I only add, that by tradition of the *Scythians* themselves, they had very anciently a general name, titling them *Scolots*[4] (soon contracted into *Scots*), whereas the *Græcians* called the Northern all *Scythians*,[5] perhaps the original of that name being from *Shooting;* for which they were especially through the world famous, as you may see in most passages of their name in old Poets ;

---

[1] Callimach. in Hymn. Jovis.
[2] Orpheus ap. Nat. Com. Mytholog. 6. cap. 21.
[*] Because they were bred of earth, and the dew of heaven.
[3] אדמה *terra*.   [4] Herodot. Melpomene. δ.
[5] Ephor. ap. Strab. a.   See to the Fourth Song.

and that *Lucian's* title of *Toxaris*, is, as if you should say, an *Archer*. For, the word *shoot* being at first of the *Teutonic* (which was very likely dispersed largely in the Northern parts) anciently was written nearer *Schyth*, as among other testimonies, the name of Scÿce ꝼınȝeꝼ,[1] *i.e.*, *the shooting finger*, for the forefinger among our *Saxons*.[2]

40. *Three hundred years before* Rome's *great foundation laid.*

Take this with latitude: for between *Æneas Sylvius* King of the *Latins*, under whose time *Brute* is placed, to *Numitor*, in whose second year *Rome* was built, intercedes above three hundred and forty, and with such difference understand the thousand until *Cæsar*.

43. *And long before borne arms against the barbarous* Hun.

Our stories tell you of *Humber* King of *Huns* (a people, that being *Scythian*, lived about those parts[3] which you now call *Mar delle Zabach*) his attempt and victory against *Albanact*, conflict with *Logrin*, and death in this River, from whence they will the name. Distance of his country, and the unlikely relation weakens my historical faith. Observe you also the first transmigration of the *Huns*, mentioned by *Procopius*, *Agathias*, others, and you will think this very different from truth. And well could I think by conjecture (with a great Antiquary[4]) that the name was first (or thence derived) 𝕳abren or 𝕬ber,* which in *British*, as appears by the names *Abergevenni*, *Abertewi*, *Aberhodni*, signifying the fall of the River *Gevenni*, *Tewi*, *Rhodni*, is as much as a River's [5]*mouth* in *English*, and fits itself specially, in that

[1] In τῶ Scÿce forsan reliquiæ vocabuli ꝛwp, i.e., *arcus*, et punctorum variatione, *Sagittarius.* v. Goropium Becceselan. 8. sive Amazonic.

[2] Alured. leg. cap. 40.

[3] Agathias lib. ε. Mæotidis Palus.

[4] Leland. ad Cyg. Cant. in Hull.

* *Abus* dictum isthoc æstuarium Ptolemæo.

[5] Girald. Itinerar. cap. 2 et 4.

most of the *Yorkshire* Rivers here cast themselves into one confluence for the Ocean. Thus perhaps was *Severne* first *Hafren*, and not from the maid there drowned, as you have before; but for that, this no place.

61. *To* Stamford *in this Isle seem'd* Athens *to transfer.*

Look to the Third Song for more of *Bladud* and his Baths. Some testimony is,[1] that he went to *Athens*, brought thence with him four Philosophers, and instituted by them a University at *Stanford* in *Lincolnshire;* But, of any persuading credit I find none. Only of later time, that profession of learning was there, authority is frequent. For when through discording parts among the Scholars (reigning *Ed.* III.) a division in *Oxford* was into the *Northern* and *Southern* faction, the *Northern* (before under *Hen.* III. also was the like to *Northampton*) made secession to this *Stamford*, and there professed, until upon humble suit by *Robert* of *Stratford*, Chancellor of *Oxford*, the King[2] by edict, and his own presence, prohibited them; whence, afterward, also was that Oath taken by *Oxford* Graduates, that they should not profess at *Stamford*. *White* of *Basingstoke* otherwise guesses at the cause of this difference, making it the *Pelagian* heresy, and of more ancient time, but erroneously. Unto this refer that supposed prophecy of *Merlin:*—

> *Doctrinæ studium quod nunc viget ad Vada Boum**
> *Ante finem sæcli celebrabitur ad Vada Saxi.†*

Which you shall have *Englished* in that solemnized marriage of *Thames* and *Medway*, by a most admired Muse[3] of our nation, thus with advantage :

[1] Merlin. apud Hard. cap. 25. ex iisdem et Balæus.
[2] Jo. Cai. Antiq. Cant. 2. Br. Twin. lib. 3. Apolog. Oxon. §. 115. et seqq.   * *Oxen-ford.*   † *Stane-ford.*
[3] Spens. *Faery Q.* lib. 4. Cant. 11. Stanz. 35.

And after him the fatall Welland *went,*
That, if old sawes prove true (which God forbid)
Shall drowne all Holland * *with his excrement,*
And shall see Stamford, *though now homely hid,*
Then shine in learning more than ever did
Cambridge *or* Oxford, England's *goodly beames.*

Nor can you apply this but to much younger time than
Bladud's reign.

74. —— *As he those* four *proud* Streets *began.*

Of them you shall have better declaration to the Six-
teenth Song.

87. *There* balancing *his* sword *against her baser* gold.

In that story, of *Brennus* and his *Gauls* taking *Rome,* is
affirmed, that by Senatory authority *P. Sulpitius* (as a Tribune) was Committee to transact with the enemy for leaving
the *Roman* territory; the price was[1] agreed one thousand
pounds of gold; unjust weights were offered by the *Gauls,*
which *Sulpitius* disliking, so far were those insolent conquerors from mitigation of their oppressing purpose, that
(as for them all) *Brennus* to the first unjustice of the balance
added the poise of his Sword also, whence, upon a murmuring complaint among the *Romans,* crying *Væ victis,*† came
that to be as proverb applied to the conquered.

100. *Against the* Delphian *power yet shak'd his ireful sword.*

Like liberty as others, takes the Author in affirming that
Brennus, which was General to the *Gauls* in taking *Rome,* to

---

* The maritime part of *Lincolnshire,* where, *Welland* a River.
[1] Liv. dec. lib. 5.; Plutarch. in Camillo.
† *Woe to the conquered.* v. verò Stephan. Forcatulum lib. 2. de Gall.
Philosoph. qui hæc inter examinandum fœdè, ast cum aliis, in historiâ
lapsus est.

be the same which overcame *Greece*, and assaulted the
Oracle. But the truth of story stands thus : *Rome* was
afflicted by one *Brennus* about the year[1] 360 after the building, when the *Gauls* had such a *Cadmeian* victory of it, that
fortune converted by martial opportunity, they were at last
by *Camillus* so put to the sword, that a reporter of the
slaughter was not left, as *Livy* and *Plutarch* (not impugned
by *Polybius*, as *Polydore* hath mistaken) tell us.[2] About one
hundred and ten years after, were tripartite excursions of
the *Gauls;* of an army under *Cerethrius* into *Thrace;* of the
like under *Belgius* or *Bolgius* into *Macedon* and *Illyricum;* of
another under one *Brennus* and *Acichorius* into *Pannonia.*
What success *Belgius* had with *Ptolemy*, surnamed Κέραυνος,[*]
is discovered in the same authors[3] which relate to us *Brennus*
his wasting of *Greece*, with his violent, but somewhat voluntary, death; but part of this army, either divided by mutiny,
or left, after *Apollo's* revenge, betook them to habitation in
Thrace about the now *Constantinople*, where first under their
King *Comontorius* (as *Polybius*, but *Livy* saith under *Lutatius*
and *Lomnorius*, which name perhaps you might correct by
Polybius) they ruled their neighbouring States with imposi-
tion of tribute, and at last, growing too populous, sent (as
it seems) those colonies into *Asia*, which in *Gallogræcia*[4] left
sufficient steps of their ancient names. My compared classic
authors[5] will justify as much; nor scarce find I material oppo-
sition among them in any particulars; only *Trogus*, epito-
mized by *Justin*, is therein, by confusion of time and actions,

---

[1] Halicarnass. ἀρχ. α.; Liv. 5.
[2] Vid. Jo. Pris. Defens. Hist. Brit. qui nimiùm hîc errore involutus.
[*] Thunderbolt. [3] Pausanias in Phocic. [4] Strab. lib. ιβ.
[5] Polyb. l. ά, β, δ. et θ. et Liv. dec. 1. lib. 5. dec. 4. lib. 8.; Strab.
δ.; Pausan. Phocic. 1.; Appian. Illyric.; Justin. lib. 24 et 25.; Plutarch. Camillo. Cæterùm plerisque *Delphis* injectâ à Phœbo grandine
peremptis, qui fuerunt, reliquos in Ægyptum conductos sub stipen-
diis Ptolemæi Philadelphi meruisse ait vetus *Scholiastes* Græc. ad
Hymn. *Callimach*. in Delum.

somewhat abused; which hath caused that error of those
which take historical liberty (poetical is allowable) to affirm
Brennus which sacked *Rome,* and him that died at *Delphos,*
the same. Examination of time makes it apparently false;
nor indeed doth the *British* Chronology endure our *Brennus*
to be either of them, as *Polydore* and *Buchanan* have observed. But want of the *British* name moves nothing
against it; seeing the people of this Western part were all,
until a good time after those wars, styled by the name of
Gauls or *Celts;* and those which would have ransacked the
Oracle are said by *Callimachus* to have come

———— ἀφ Ἑσπέρου ἐσχατόωντος.*

Which as well fits us as *Gaul.* And thus much also observe,
that those names of *Brennus* and *Belinus,* being of great
note, both in signification and personal eminency; and,
likely enough, there being many of the same name in *Gaul*
and *Britain,* in several ages such identity made confusion in
story. For the first, in this relation appears what variety
was of it; as also **Urenhin** and **Brennin** in the *British* are
but significant words for *King;* and peradventure almost as
ordinary a name among these Westerns, as *Pharaoh* and
Ptolemy in *Ægypt, Agag* among the *Amalekites, Arsaces,
Nicomedes, Alerada, Sophi, Cæsar, Oiscing,* among the *Parthians, Bithynians, Thessalians, Persians, Romans,* and our
Kentish Kings, which the course of History shows you. For
the other, you may see it usual in names of their old Kings,
as *Cassi-Belin* in *Cæsar, Cuno-Belin* and *Cym-Belin* in *Tacitus*
and *Dio,* and perhaps *Cam-Baules* in *Pausanias,* and *Belin*
(whose steps seem to be in *Abellius*[1] a *Gaulish,* and *Bela-*

---

* From the utmost West.

[1] Vet. Inscript. in *Cumbria,* et apud Jos. Scalig. ad Auson. 1. cap.
9. et vid, Rhodigin. lib. 17. cap. 28. Plura de *Belino,* sive *Beleno,* i.e.,
Apolline Gallico, Pet. Pithæus Advers. Subsec. lib. 1. cap. 3. qui Bele-
num παρὰ τὸ Ἐκηβόλος Phœbi epitheton autumat. vide notas Camd.
ad Numismata; et nos ad Cant. IX.

tucadre a *British,* God) was the name among them of a wor-
shipped Idol, as appears in *Ausonius;* and the same with
Apollo, which also by a most ancient *British* coin, stamped
with *Apollo* playing on his Harp, circumscribed with
C V N O - B E L I N, is showed to have been expressly
among the *Britons.* Although I know, according to their
use, it might be added to *Cuno* (which was the first part of
many of their regal names, as you see in *Cuneglas, Cynyeto-
rix, Congolitan,* and others) to make a significant word, as if
you should say, *the yellow King;* for *Belin* in *British* is *yellow.*
But seeing the very name of their *Apollo* so well-fitted with
that colour, which to *Apollo** is commonly attributed (and
observe that their names had usually some note of colour in
them, by reason of their custom of painting themselves) I
suppose they took it as a fortunate concurrence to bear an
honored Deity in their title, as we see in the names of
Merodach and *Evil-Merodach* among the *Babylonian* Kings
from *Merodach,*[1] one of their false gods; and like examples
may be found among the old Emperors. Observe also that
in *British* genealogies, they ascend always to *Belin* the Great
(which is supposed *Heli,* father to *Lud* and *Cassibelin*) as you
see to the Fourth Song; and here might you compare that
of *Hel*[2] in the *Punic* tongue, signifying *Phœbus,* and turned
into *Belus;* but I will not therewith trouble you. Howsoever, by this I am persuaded (whensoever the time were of
our *Belinus*) that *Bolgus* in *Pausanias,* and *Belgius* in *Justin*
were mistook for *Belinus,* as perhaps also *Prausus* in *Strabo*
(π. supplying[3] ofttimes the room of β.) generated of *Brennus*
corrupted. In the story I dare follow none of the modern
erroneously-transcribing relaters or seeming correctors, but

---

* Ξανθὸς ᾽Απόλλων.   [1] Jirme. cap. 50.
[2] Cæl. Rhodig. Antiq. Lect. 1. cap. 6.
[3] Eustath. ad Dionys. Perieg. uti Αμπραξ, ἀντὶ τοῦ ῎Αμβραξ et
Νῆσοι Πρεταννικαὶ ἀντὶ τοῦ Βρεταννικαί.

have, as I might, took it from the best self-fountains, and only upon them, for trial, I put myself.

107. ———*whence* Cymbrica *it took.*

That Northern promontory now *Jutland*, part of the *Danish* Kingdom, is called in Geographers *Cymbrica Cherso-nesus*, from name of the people inhabiting it. And those which will the *Cymbrians*, *Cambrians*, or *Cumrians*, from *Camber*, may, with good reason of consequence, imagine that the name of this *Chersonese* is thence also, as the Author here, by liberty of his Muse. But if, with *Goropius*, *Camden*, and other their followers, you come nearer truth and derive them from *Gomer*,* son to *Japhet*, who, with his posterity, had the North-western part of the world; then shall you set, as it were, the accent upon *Chersonese* giving the more significant note of the Country; the name of *Cymbrians*, *Cimmerians*, *Cambrians*, and *Cumrians*, all as one in substance, being very comprehensive[1] in these climates; and perhaps, because this promontory lay out so far, under near sixty degrees latitude (almost at the utmost of *Ptolemy's* geography) and so had the first Winter days no longer than between five and six hours, therein somewhat (and more than other neighbouring parts of that people, having no particular name) agreeing with *Homer's*[2] attribute of darkness to the *Cimmerians*, it had more specially this title.

129. *To wise* Molmutius' *laws her* Martian *first did frame.*

Particulars of *Molmutius'* laws, of Church-liberty, freedom of ways, husbandry, and divers other, are in the *British* story, affirming also that *Q. Martia* made a Book of Laws,

---

* Transmutation of *G.* into *C.* was, anciently, often and easy, as *Lipsius* shews. lib. de pronunciat. Ling. Latin. cap. 13.
[1] Plutarch. in Mario.; et Herodot. lib. δ.
[2] Odyss. λ. Ἠέρι καὶ νεφέλῃ κεκαλυμμένοι.———

translated afterward, and titled by King *Alfred* Mepcenlaʒe.[1]
Indeed it appears that there were three sorts of laws* in
the *Saxon* Heptarchy, Mepcen-laʒe, Dan-laʒe ꝺpeꞃꞇꞃaxen-laʒe
i.e., the *Mercian, Danish,* and *West-Saxon* law ; all which
three had their several territories, and were in divers things
compiled into one volume by *Cnut,* and examined in that
Norman constitution of their new Common-wealth.   But
as the *Danish* and *West-Saxon* had their name from particular people; so it seems, had the *Mercian* from that Kingdom
of *Mercland,* limited with the *Lancashire* River *Mersey* toward *Northumberland,* and joining to *Wales,* having either
from the River that name, or else from the word Mapc,†
because it bounded upon most of the other Kingdoms ; as
you may see to the Eleventh Song.

15s.   ———*in whose eternal name,*
              Great London *still shall live*———

King *Lud's* re-edifying *Troynovant* (first built by *Brute*)
and thence leaving the name of *Caer Lud,* afterward turned
(as they say) into *London,* is not unknown, scarce to any
that hath but looked on *Ludgate's* inner frontispice ; and
in old rhymes[2] thus I have it expressed :

𝕸𝖆𝖑𝖑𝖘‡ 𝖍𝖊 𝖑𝖊𝖙𝖊 𝖒𝖆𝖐𝖊 𝖆𝖑 𝖆𝖇𝖔𝖚𝖙𝖊 𝖆𝖓𝖉 𝖞𝖆𝖙𝖊𝖘 𝖚𝖕 𝖆𝖓𝖉 𝖉𝖔𝖚𝖓
𝕬𝖓𝖉 𝖆𝖋𝖙𝖊𝖗 𝕷𝖚𝖉 𝖙𝖍𝖆𝖙 𝖜𝖆𝖘 𝖎𝖘 𝖓𝖆𝖒𝖊 𝖍𝖊 𝖈𝖑𝖚𝖕𝖊𝖉𝖊 𝖎𝖙 𝕷𝖚𝖉𝖘 𝖙𝖔𝖜𝖓𝖊.
𝕿𝖍𝖊 𝖍𝖊𝖗𝖙𝖊 𝖞𝖆𝖙𝖊 𝖔𝖋 𝖙𝖍𝖊 𝖙𝖔𝖚𝖓 𝖙𝖍𝖆𝖙 𝖞𝖚𝖙 𝖘𝖙𝖔𝖓𝖙 𝖙𝖍𝖊𝖗𝖊 𝖆𝖓𝖉 𝖎𝖘
𝕴𝖊 𝖑𝖊𝖙 𝖍𝖎𝖙 𝖈𝖑𝖚𝖕𝖎𝖊 𝕷𝖚𝖉𝖌𝖆𝖙𝖊 𝖆𝖋𝖙𝖊𝖗 𝖎𝖘 𝖔𝖜𝖊 𝖓𝖆𝖒𝖊 𝖎𝖜𝖎𝖘.
𝕴𝖊 𝖑𝖊𝖙 𝖍𝖎𝖒 𝖙𝖍𝖔 𝖍𝖊 𝖜𝖆𝖘 𝖉𝖊𝖉 𝖇𝖚𝖗𝖎𝖊 𝖆𝖙 𝖙𝖍𝖚𝖑𝖐𝖊 𝖞𝖆𝖙𝖊
𝕮𝖍𝖊𝖗𝖊𝖚𝖔𝖗𝖊 𝖞𝖚𝖙 𝖆𝖋𝖙𝖊𝖗 𝖍𝖎𝖒 𝖒𝖊 𝖈𝖑𝖚𝖕𝖊𝖙𝖍 𝖎𝖙 𝕷𝖚𝖉𝖊𝖌𝖆𝖙𝖊.

[1] Gervas. Tilburiensis de Scaccario.
* Look to the Eleventh Song.
† A limit or bound.   [2] Rob. Glocestrens.
‡ But it is affirmed that King *Coil's* daughter, mother to *Constantine* the Great, walled this first, and *Colchester* also.   Huntingdon
lib. 1. et Simon Dunelmens. ap. Stow. in notitiâ Londini.   I shall
presently speak of her also.

𝕮𝔥𝔢 𝔱𝔬𝔲𝔫 𝔪𝔢 𝔠𝔩𝔲𝔭𝔢𝔱𝔥 𝔱𝔥𝔞𝔱 𝔦𝔰 𝔴𝔦𝔡𝔢 𝔠𝔬𝔲𝔱𝔥
𝔄𝔫𝔡 𝔫𝔬𝔴 𝔪𝔢 𝔠𝔩𝔲𝔭𝔢𝔱𝔥 𝔦𝔱 London 𝔱𝔥𝔞𝔱 𝔦𝔰 𝔩𝔦𝔤𝔥𝔱𝔢𝔯 𝔦𝔫 𝔱𝔥𝔢 𝔪𝔬𝔲𝔱𝔥.
𝔄𝔫𝔡 new Troy 𝔦𝔱 𝔥𝔢𝔱 𝔢𝔯𝔢, 𝔞𝔫𝔡 𝔫𝔬𝔲 𝔦𝔱 𝔦𝔰 𝔰𝔬 𝔞𝔤𝔬
𝕿𝔥𝔞𝔱 London 𝔦𝔱 𝔦𝔰 𝔫𝔬𝔴 𝔦𝔠𝔩𝔲𝔭𝔢𝔡 𝔞𝔫𝔡 𝔴𝔬𝔯𝔱𝔥 𝔢𝔲𝔢𝔯𝔢 𝔪𝔬.

Judicious reformers of fabulous report I know have more
serious derivations of the name : and seeing conjecture is
free, I could imagine, it might be called at first 𝕷𝔥𝔞𝔫 𝕭𝔦𝔢𝔫,
i.e., the Temple of Diana, as 𝕷𝔥𝔞𝔫-𝕯𝔢𝔴𝔦, 𝕷𝔥𝔞𝔫 𝕾𝔱𝔢𝔭𝔥𝔞𝔫,
𝕷𝔥𝔞𝔫 𝕻𝔞𝔡𝔢𝔯𝔫 𝕮𝔞𝔲𝔴𝔯, 𝕷𝔥𝔞𝔫 𝕮𝔞𝔦𝔯, *i.e., S. Dewy's, S. Stephan's,
S. Patern* the Great, *S. Mary ;* and *Verulam* is by *H. Lhuid,*
derived from 𝕮𝔢𝔯-𝔩𝔥𝔞𝔫, *i.e., the Church upon the River Ver,*
with divers more such places in *Wales :* and so afterward
by strangers turned into *Londinium,*[1] and the like.   For,
that *Diana* and her brother *Apollo* (under name of *Belin*)
were two great Deities among the *Britons,* what is read
next before, *Cæsar's* testimony of the *Gauls ;* and that she
had her Temple there where *Paul's* is, relation in *Camden*
discloses to you.   Now, that the antique course was to title
their Cities ofttimes by the name of their power adored in
them, is plain by *Beth-el* among the *Hebrews, Heliopolis*
(which in Holy Writ[2] is call'd בית-שמש) in *Ægypt,* and the
same in *Greece, Phœnicia,* elsewhere ; and by *Athens* named
from *Minerva.*   But especially from this supposed deity of
Diana (whom in substance *Homer* no less gives the epithet
of 'Εργσίπτολις* than to *Pallas*) have divers had their titles :
as *Artemisium* in *Italy,* and *Eubœa,* and that *Bubastis*[3] in
Ægypt, so called from the same word, signifying in *Ægyptian,*
both a *Cat* and *Diana.*

203. *Those* arméd stakes *in* Thames———

He means that which now we call *Coway stakes* by *Ote-*

---

[1] *London* derived.   [2] Jirme. cap. 43. comm. ult.
* Patron of Cities. v. Homer. Hymn. ad. Dian.
[3] Stephan. περι πολ. in Βουβάς.   Herodot. lib. β.

lands, where only, the *Thames* being without boat passable, the *Britons* fixed both on the bank of their side, and in the water, sharp[1] stakes, to prevent the Romans coming over ; but in vain, as the stories tell you.

207. *And more than* Cæsar *got, three* Emperors *could not win.*

Understand not that they were resisted by the *Britons,* but that the three successors of *Julius, i.e., Augustus, Tiberius,* and *Caligula,* never so much as with force attempted the Isle, although the last after King *Cunobelin's son Adminius* his traitorous revolting to him, in a seeming martial vehemency, made[2] all arm to the *British* voyage, but suddenly in the *German* shore (where he then was) like himself, turned the design to a jest, and commanded the army to gather cockles.

249. *Came with his* body nak'd, *his* hair *down to his waist.*

In this *Caradoc* (being the same which at large you have in *Tacitus* and *Dio,* under name of *Caratacus* and *Cataracus* and is by some *Scottish* Historians drawn much too far Northward) the author expresses the ancient form of a *Briton's* habit. Yet I think not that they were all naked, but, as is affirmed[3] of the *Gauls,* down only to the navel ; so that on the discovered part might be seen (to the terror of their enemies) those pictures of beasts, with which[4] they painted themselves. It is justifiable by *Cæsar,* that they used to shave all except their head and upper lip, and wore very long hair ; but in their old coins I see no such thing warranted : and in later times[5] about 400 years since, it is especially attributed to them that they always cut their heads close for avoiding *Absalon's* misfortune.

---

[1] Bed. lib. 1. cap. 2.
[2] Sueton. lib. 4. cap. 44. et 46.; et Dio Cassius.
[3] Polybius Hist. γ.   [4] Solin. Polyhist. cap. 35.
[5] Girald. Descript. cap. 10.

269. *The Colony long kept at* Maldon——

Old Historians and Geographers call this *Camalodunum*, which some[1] have absurdly thought to be *Camelot* in the *Scottish* Shrifedom of *Stirling*, others have sought it elsewhere : but the *English* Light of antiquity (*Camden*) hath surely found it at this *Maldon* in *Essex*, where was a *Romish* Colony, as also at *Glocester*, *Chester*, *York*, and perhaps at *Colchester*,[2] which proves expressly (against vulgar allowance) that there was a time when in the chiefest parts of this Southern *Britany* the *Roman* laws were used,[3] as every one that knows the meaning of a Colony (which had all their rights and institutions deduced[4] with it) must confess. This was destroyed upon discontentment taken by the *Icens* and *Trinobants* (now *Norfolk*, *Suffolk*, *Middlesex*, and *Essex* men) for intolerable wrongs done to the wife and posterity of *Prasutagus* King of the *Icens* by the *Romans*,[5] which the King (as others in like form) thought, but vainly, to have prevented by instituting *Nero*, then Emperor, his heir. The signs, which the Author speaks of, were, a strange, and, as it were, voluntary falling down of the Goddess *Victory's* statue, erected by the *Romans* here ; women, as distracted, singing their overthrow ; the ocean looking bloody ; uncouth howlings in their assemblies, and such like. *Petilius Cerealis*, Lieutenant of the Ninth Legion, coming to aid, lost all his foot-men, and betook himself with the rest to his fortified tents. But for this read the history.

277. *By* poison *end her days*——

So *Tacitus ;* but *Dio*, that she died of sickness.   Her

---

[1] Hector. Boet. lib. 3.   [2] Antiq. Inscript. Lapideæ. et Numm.
[3] V. Fortescut. de laud. Leg. Ang. cap. 17. et Vitum Basingstoch. lib. 4. not. 36.   *Roman* laws used in *Britain*.
[4] Agellius lib. 16. cap. 13.   [5] Tacitus. Annal. 14. ; Dio. lib. ξ.

name is written diversely *Voadicia, Boodicia, Bunduica,* and *Boudicea :* she was wife to *Prasutagus,* of whom last before.

305. *A greater foe to us in our own bowels bred.*

Every story[1] of the declining *British* state will tell you what miseries were endured by the hostile irruptions of *Scots* and *Picts* into the Southern part. For the passage here of them, know, that the *Scottish* stories, which begin their continued Monarchic government at *Ferguze,* affirm the *Picts* (from the *Scythian* territories) to have arrived in the now *Jutland,* and thence passed into *Scotland* some 250 years after the *Scots* first entering *Britain,* which was, by account, about 80 years before our Saviour's birth, and thence continued these a State by themselves, until King *Kenneth* about 840 years after Christ utterly supplanted them. Others, as *Bede* and his followers, make them elder in the Isle than the *Scots,* and fetch them out of *Ireland ;* the *British* story (that all may be discords) says, they entered *Albania* under conduct of one *Roderic* their King (for so you must read in *Monmouth** and not *Londric,* as the print in that and much other mistakes) and were valiantly opposed by *Marius* then King of *Britons, Roderic* slain, and *Cathenes* given them for habitation. This *Marius* is placed with *Vespasian,* and the gross differences of time make all suspicious : so that you may as well believe none of them, as any one. Rather adhere to learned *Camden,* making the *Picts* very genuine *Britons,* distinguished only by accidental name, as in him you may see more largely.

---

[1] Pictorum in Britannia (potius Pictonum, ita nam legitur) primus meminit Romanorum Panegyristes ille inter alios, qui Constantinum encomiis adloquitur, et, si placet, adeas Humfred. Lhuid. Brev. Brit. et Buchanan. lib. 2. Rer. Scotic. aut Camdeni Scotos et Pictos. Rob. Glocestrensi dicuntur Ƿٜۃars.

* Galfredus Monumethensis correctus, et ibidem vice τοῦ *Maesmarius* lege *Vestmaria.*

310. Arviragus *of ours first taking to protect.*

His marriage with (I know not what) *Genissa,* daughter
to *Claudius,* the habitude of friendſhip twixt *Rome* and him,
after composition with *Vespasian* then, under the Emperor,
employed in the *British* war, the common story relates.
This is *Armitagus,* which *Juvenal*[1] speaks of. *Polydore* refers
him to *Nero's* time, others rightly to *Domitian,* because indeed the Poet[2] then flourished. That fabulous *Hector Boetius*
makes him the same with *Phasuiragus,* as he calls him, in
Tacitus; he means *Prasutagus,* having mis-read *Tacitus* his
copy.

314. *This happiness we have* Christ Crucified to know.

Near 180 after Christ (the chronology of *Bede* herein is
plainly false, and observe what I told you of that kind to
the Fourth Song) this *Lucius* upon request to Pope *Eleutherius* received at the hands of *Fugatius*[3] and *Damianus,*
Holy Baptism; yet so, that by *Joseph* of *Arimathea* (of
whom to the Third Song) seeds of true Religion were here
before sown: by some I find it, without warrant,[4] affirmed
that he converted *Arviragus,*

And gaue him then a shilde of siluer white,
A Crosse[5] endlong and ouerthwart full perfect,
These armes were used through all Britaine
For a common signe each man to know his nation
From enemies, which now we call certaine,
S. Georges armes———

But thus much collect, that, although until *Lucius* we had
not a Christian King (for you may well suspect, rather

---

[1] Satir. 4.   [2] Suidas in Juvenali.
[3] These names are very differently written.
[4] Ex Nennio Harding. cap. 48. Ast Codices ii, quos consuluisse
me *Nennii* antiquos contigit, huiusce rei parùm sunt memores.
[5] S. *George's* cross.

deny, for want of better authority, this of *Arviragus*) yet
(unless you believe the tradition of *Gundaser*[1] King of *Indy*,
converted[2] by S. *Thomas*, or *Abagar*[3] King of *Edessa*, to
whom those letters written, as is supposed, by our Saviour's
own hand, kept as a precious relic in *Constantinople*[4] until
the Emperor *Isaacius Angelus*, as my authors say, were sent)
it is apparent that *this Island had the first Christian King in
the world*, and clearly in *Europe*, for that you cite not *Tiberius* his private seeming Christianity (which is observed out
of *Tertullian*) even in whose time also *Gildas* affirms, *Britain*
was comforted with wholesome beams of religious Light.
Not much different from this age was *Donald* first King
Christian of the *Scots;* so that if priority oft-time swayed
it, and not custom (derived from a communicable attribute
given by the Popes) that name of *Most Christian* should
better fit our Sovereigns than the *French.* This *Lucius*, by
help of those two Christian aids, is said to have, in room
of three Arch-*Flamins* and twenty-eight *Flamins* (through
whose doctrine, polluting sacrifices and idolatry reigned
here instead of true service) instituted three Archbishoprics
at *London*, *York*, and *Caer-leon* upon *Usk*, and twenty-eight
Bishoprics ; of them, all beyond *Humber* subject to *York;*
all the now *Wales* to *Caer-leon;* to *London*, the now *England*
with *Cornwall.* And so also was the custom in other
Countries, even grounded upon S. *Peter's* own command, to
make substitution of Arch-bishops or Patriarchs to Arch-
Flamins, and Bishops to *Flamins*, if you believe a Pope's[5]
assertion. For *York*, there is now a Metropolitan See ;
Caer-leon had so until the change spoken of to the Fifth
Song ; and *London*, the *Cathedral* Church being at S. *Peter's*

[1] First *Christian King* in the world.
[2] Abdias Hist. Apostolic. lib. 9. Euseb. lib. 1. cap. 13.
[3] Nicet. Choniat. in Andronic. Comnen. lib. 2.
[4] Nicephor. Callist. lib. 2. cap. 7. et 8.
[5] Distinct. 80 c. in illis. Clemens PP.

in *Cornhill*, until translation of the pall[1] to *Canterbury* by
Augustine, sent hither by *Gregory* the First under King
Ethelbert, according to a prophecy of *Merlin*, that *Christianity
should fail, and then revive when the See of* London *did adorn*
Canterbury, as, after coming of the *Saxons*, it did. This
moved that ambitious *Gilbert* of *Folioth* Bishop of *London* to
challenge the Primacy of *England ;* for which he is bitterly
taxed by a great Clerk[2] of the same time. If I add to the
British glory that this *Lucius* was cause of like conversion
in *Bavaria* and *Rhetia*, I should out of my bounds. The
learned *Mark Velser*, and others, have enough remembered it.

323. Constantius' *worthy wife*————

That is *Helen*,[3] wife to *Constantius* or *Constans Chlorus* the
Emperor, and mother to *Constantine* the Great, daughter to
Coile King of *Britain*, where *Constantine* was by her brought
forth.[4] Do not object *Nicephorus Callistus* that erroneously
affirms him born in *Drepanum* of *Bithynia*, or *Jul. Firmicus*[5]
that says at *Tarsus*, upon which testimony (not uncorrupted)
a great Critic[6] hath violently offered to deprive us both of
him and his mother, affirming her a *Bithynian ;* nor take
advantage of *Cedrenus*, that will have *Dacia* his birth-soil.
But our Histories, and, with them, the *Latin* Ecclesiastic
relation (in passages of her Invention of the Cross, and
such like) allowed also by Cardinal *Baronius*, make her
thus a *British* woman. And for great *Constantine's* birth in
this land you shall have authority; against which I wonder.

---

[1] V. Kenulph in Epist. ad Leonem PP. apud G. Malmesb. lib. 1.
de reg. et l. de Pontific. vide Basingstoch. Hist. 9. not. 11. Stowe
Survey of London. pag. 479.
[2] Joann. Carnotens. in Epistol. 272.
[3] *Helen* mother to *Constantine*.   [4] *Constantine* born in *Britain.*
[5] Mathesews. lib. 1. cap. 4.
[6] Lips. de Rom. magnitud. lib. 4. cap. 11. nimiùm lapsus.

how *Lipsius* durst oppose his conceit. In an old Panegyrist,[1] speaking to *Constantine: Liberavit ille* (he means his father) *Britannias servitute, tu etiam nobiles illic oriundo fecisti ;** and another, *O fortunata et nunc omnibus beatior terris Britannia, quæ Constantinum Cæsarem prima vidisti.*† These might persuade that *Firmicus* were corrupted, seeing they lived when they might know as much of this as he. *Nicephorus* and *Cedrenus* are of much later time, and deserve no undoubted credit. But in certain oriental admonitions[2] of State (newly published by *John Meursius* Professor of *Greek* story at *Leyden*) the Emperor *Constantine Porphyrogenetes* advises his son *Romanus*, that he should not take him a wife of alien blood, because all people dissonant from the government and manners of the Empire by a law of *Constantine*, established in S. *Sophie's* Church, were prohibited the height of that glory, excepting only the *Franks*, allowing them this honour ὅτι καὶ αὐτὸς τὴν γένεσιν ἀπὸ τῶν τοιούτων ἔσχε μερῶν,‡ which might make you imagine him born in *Gaul ;* let it not move you, but observe that this *Porphyrogenetes* lived about 700 years since, when it was (and among the *Turks* still is) ordinary with these *Greeks* to call[3] all (especially the Western) *Europeans* by the name of *Franks*,[4] as they did themselves *Romans*. Why then might not we be comprehended, whose name, as *English*, they scarce, as it seems, knew of, calling us *Inclins ;*[5] and indeed the inde-

---

[1] Panegyric. dixerint licet, *Maximiano*, etc.

* He freed *Britain* of Bondage, Thou ennobledst it with thy birth.

† O happy *Britain* that first of all sawest *Constantine*. Panegyric. Facerem. *Constantino*.

[2] Constantin. Porphyrogenet. de administ. imperio. cap. 29. Jo. Levinæum ad Panegyric. 5. haut multùm hic moramur.

‡ Because he was born in those parts.

[3] Histor. Orientales passim et Themata Constantini, cum suprà citato libro.

[4] *Europeans* called *Franks*.

[5] Nicet. Choniat. 2. Isaac. Angel. §. ult. Ἰγκλῖνοι.

finite form of speech, in the author I cite, shews as if he
meant some remote place by the *Franks*, admitting he had
intended only but what we now call *French*. If you can
believe one of our countrymen[1] that lived about *Hen.* II.
he was born in *London ;* others think he was born at *York :*
of that, I determine not.　Of this *Helen,* her religion,
finding the Cross, good deeds in walling *London* and *Colchester* (which in honour of her, they say, bears a Cross
between four Crowns, and for the Invention she is yet celebrated in Holy-rood day in May) and of this *Constantine* her
son, a mighty and religious Emperor (although I know him
taxed for no small faults by Ecclesiastic writers) that in
this air received his first light and life, our *Britons* vaunt
not unjustly : as in that spoken to King *Arthur*.[2]

𝔑ow it worth iended that 𝔖ibile the sage sede biuore
𝔗hat there ssold of Brutaine thre men be ybore
𝔗hat ssolde winne the aumppr of Rome ; of tweye ydo it is
𝔄s of Bely* and Constantin, and thou art the thredde y wis.

For this *Sibylle* who she was, I must take day to tell you.

329.　*Against the* Arian *Sect at* Arles *having ronne.*

In the Second Council[3] at *Arles* in *Provence,* held under
Constantine and *Sylvester,* is subscribed the name of *Restitutus*
Bishop of *London,* the like respectively in other Councils
spoken of by the Author.　It is not unfit to note here that
in later time the use hath been (when and where *Rome's*
Supremacy was acknowledged) to send always to General
Councils, out of every Christian State, some Bishops, Ab-
bots and Priors ; and I find it affirmed by the Clergy under
Hen. II.[4] that, to a General Council, only four Bishops are

---

[1] G. Stephanides de Londino. Basingstoch. Hist. 6. not. 10.
[2] Rob. Glocestrens.　　　* *Belinus.*
[3] 1. Tom. Concil.　　　[4] Roger Hoveden. fol. 332.

to be sent out of *England.* So, by reason of this course
added to State-allowance afterward at home, were those
Canons received into our law ; as of *Bigamy* in the Council
of *Lyons,* interpreted by Parliament under *Ed.* I. ; of *Plu-
ralities* in the Council of *Lateran,* held by *Innocent* III.
reigning our King *John ;* and the law of *Lapse* in Benefices
had so its ground from that Council of *Lateran* in 1179
under *Alexander* the Third, whither, for our part, were
sent *Hugh* Bishop of *Durham, John* Bishop of *Norwich,
Robert* Bishop of *Hereford,* and *Rainold* Bishop of *Bath,* with
divers Abbots, where the Canon[1] was made for presentation
within six months, and title of Lapse, given to the Bishop
in case the Chapter were Patron, from the Bishop to them
if he were Patron ; which, although, in that, it be not law
with us, nor also their difference between a lay[2] and ecclesiastic patron for number of the months, allowing the lay-
man but four,[3] yet shews itself certainly to be the original
of that custom anciently and now used in the Ordinary's
collation. And hither *Henry* of *Bracton*[4] refers it expressly ;
by whom you may amend *John le Briton,*[5] and read *Lateran*
instead of *Lyons* about this same matter. Your conceit,
truly joining these things, cannot but perceive that Canons
and Constitutions, in Pope's Councils, absolutely never
bound us in other form than, fitting them by the square of
English law and policy, our reverend Sages and Baronage
allowed and interpreted[6] them, who in their formal Writs[7]
would mention them as law and custom of the Kingdom,
and not otherwise.

[1] G. Neubrigens. (cujus editionem nuperam et Jo. Picardi annota-
tiones consulas) lib. 3. cap. 3. et Hovedenus habent ipsas, quæ sunt,
Constitutiones.   [2] Extravag. Concess. præbend. c. 2.
[3] 6. Decret. tit. jure. patronat. §. Verum. c. unic.
[4] Lib. 4. tract. 2. cap. 6.
[5] Brittonus emendatus cap. Des exceptions 92.
[6] D. Ed. Coke. lib. de jure Regis ecclesiastic.
[7] Regist. Orig. fol. 42.

357. Eleven thousand maids *sent those our friends again.*

Our common story affirms, that in time of *Gratian* the Emperor, *Conan* King of *Armoric Britain* (which was filled with a Colony of this Isle by this *Conan* and *Maximus,* otherwise *Maximian* that slew *Gratian*) having war with the neighbouring *Gauls,* desired of *Dinoth* Regent of *Cornwall,*[1] or (if you will) of our *Britain* (by nearness of blood, so to establish and continue love in the posterity of both countries) that he might himself match with *Dinoth's* daughter *Ursula,* and with her a competent multitude of Virgins might be sent over to furnish his unwived Batchelors: whereupon were 11,000 of the nobler blood with *Ursula* and 60,000 of meaner rank (elected out of divers parts of the Kingdom) shipped at *London*[2] for satisfaction of this request. In the coast of *Gaul,* they were by tempest dispersed: some ravished by the Ocean; others for chaste denial of their maiden-heads to *Guaine* and *Melga,* Kings of *Huns* and *Picts* (whom *Gratian* had animated against *Maximus,* as usurping title of the *British* Monarchy) were miserably put to the sword in some *German* coast, whither misfortune carried them. But because the Author slips it over with a touch, you shall have it in such old Verse, as I have.[3]

𝕮𝔥𝔦𝔰 𝔪𝔞𝔦𝔡𝔢𝔫𝔰 𝔴𝔢𝔯𝔢 𝔭𝔤𝔞𝔡𝔯𝔢𝔡 𝔞𝔫𝔡 𝔱𝔬 London 𝔠𝔬𝔪𝔢
𝔐𝔞𝔫𝔦 𝔴𝔢𝔯𝔢 𝔤𝔩𝔞𝔡 𝔱𝔥𝔢𝔯𝔬𝔣 𝔞𝔫𝔡 𝔴𝔢𝔩 𝔰𝔬𝔯𝔯𝔦 𝔰𝔬𝔪𝔢
𝕮𝔥𝔞𝔱 𝔥𝔦𝔦[4] 𝔰𝔰𝔬𝔩𝔡 𝔬𝔣 𝔩𝔬𝔫𝔡𝔢 𝔴𝔢𝔫𝔡𝔢 𝔞𝔫𝔡 𝔫𝔢𝔲 𝔢𝔰𝔱 𝔥𝔬𝔯[5] 𝔣𝔯𝔢𝔫𝔡 𝔲𝔰𝔢
𝔄𝔫𝔡 𝔰𝔬𝔪𝔢 𝔱𝔬 𝔩𝔢𝔰𝔢 𝔥𝔬𝔯 𝔪𝔞𝔦𝔡𝔢𝔫𝔥𝔬𝔡 𝔴𝔦𝔲𝔢𝔰 𝔟𝔬𝔯 𝔱𝔬 𝔟𝔢.
𝕿𝔥𝔬 𝔥𝔦𝔦 𝔴𝔢𝔯𝔢 𝔦𝔫 𝔰𝔰𝔦𝔭𝔢𝔰 𝔭𝔡𝔬, 𝔞𝔫𝔡 𝔦𝔫 𝔱𝔥𝔢 𝔰𝔢 𝔟𝔢𝔯 𝔴𝔢𝔯𝔢
𝕾𝔬 𝔤𝔯𝔢𝔱 𝔱𝔢𝔪𝔭𝔢𝔰𝔱 𝔱𝔥𝔢𝔯 𝔠𝔬𝔪𝔢 𝔱𝔥𝔞𝔱 𝔡𝔯𝔬𝔣 𝔥𝔢𝔪 𝔥𝔢𝔯𝔢 𝔞𝔫𝔡 𝔱𝔥𝔢𝔯𝔢.
𝕾𝔬 𝔱𝔥𝔞𝔱 𝔱𝔥𝔢 𝔪𝔢𝔰𝔱𝔢𝔡𝔢𝔩[6] 𝔞𝔡𝔯𝔢𝔦𝔫𝔢𝔡 𝔴𝔢𝔯𝔢 𝔦𝔫 𝔱𝔥𝔢 𝔰𝔢
𝔄𝔫𝔡 𝔱𝔬 𝔬𝔱𝔥𝔢𝔯 𝔩𝔬𝔫𝔡𝔰 𝔰𝔬𝔪𝔢 𝔭𝔡𝔯𝔦𝔲𝔢 𝔱𝔥𝔞𝔱 𝔫𝔢 𝔠𝔬𝔪𝔢 𝔫𝔢𝔲𝔢𝔯 𝔞𝔤𝔢.[7]

[1] See to the Ninth Song.
[2] But see to the Fourteenth Song, of *Coventry.*
[3] Rob. Glocestrens.　　　[4] They.　　　[5] Their.
[6] Most part.　　[7] Again.

𝔄 𝕶ing there was of 𝕳ungry, Guaine was his name,
𝔄nd Melga 𝕽. Picardie[1] that couthe inou of fame,
𝕮he waters bor to Ioki aboute the se hii were
𝔄 companie of this maydens so that hii met there,
𝕮o hor folie hii wolde home nime[2] and hor men also
𝔄c the maydens wold rather die than concenty thereto
𝕮ho wende borth the luther[3] men and the maidens slow
    echone
𝕾o that to the lasse Brutaine there ne come aliue none.

  Some lay all this wickedness absurdly (for time endures
it not) to *Attila's*[4] charge, who reigned King of *Huns* about
450 (above sixty years after *Gratian*) and affirm their suffer-
ing of this (as they call it) martyrdom at *Cologne*, whither,
in at the mouth of *Rhine*, they were carried; others also
particularly tell you that there were four companions to
Ursula, in greatness and honour, their names[5] being *Pyn-
nosa, Cordula, Eleutheria, Florentia*, and that under these
were to every of the 11,000 one President, *Iota, Beniqua,
Clementia, Sapientia, Carpophora, Columba, Benedicta, Odilia,
Celyndris, Sibylla*, and *Lucia* : and that, custom at *Cologne*
hath excluded all other bodies from the place of their
burial. The strange multitude of 71,000 Virgins thus to
be transported, with the difference of time (the most excellent note to examine truth of history by) may make you
doubt of the whole report. I will not justify it, but only
admonish thus, that those our old Stories are in this followed by that great Historian *Baronius*, allowed by *Francis de
Bar, White* of *Basingstoke ;* and before any of them, by that
learned Abbot *Tritemius*, beside the Martyrologies, which
to the honour of the 11,000 have dedicated the 11th day

[1] Of the Picts.   [2] Them take.   [3] Lewd.
[4] Hector. Boet. Hist. Scotic. 7. ex antiquioribus, verùm falsi reis.
[5] Usuard. Martyrolog. 21. Octob.

of our October.   But indeed how they can stand with what
in some copies of *Nennius*[1] we read, I cannot see : it is
there reported, that those *Britons* which went thither with
Maximus (the same man and time with the former) took
them *Gaulish* wives, and cut out their tongues, lest they
should possess their children of *Gaulish* language ; whence
our *Welsh* called them afterward 𝕷𝖊𝖍𝖎𝖙-𝖂𝖑𝖎𝖆𝖎𝖔𝖓,* because
they spake confusedly.   I see[2] that yet there is great affinity
twixt the *British Armoric,* and the *Welsh,* the first (to give
you a taste) saying, 𝕳𝖔𝖓 𝖙𝖆𝖉 𝖕𝖊𝖍𝖚𝖓𝖎𝖎 𝖘𝖔𝖚 𝖊𝖓 𝖊𝖿𝖆𝖔𝖚, the other,
𝕰𝖓 𝖙𝖆𝖉 𝖕𝖗 𝖍𝖎𝖜𝖓 𝖕𝖔𝖜𝖎𝖙 𝖕𝖓 𝖕 𝖓𝖊𝖿𝖔𝖊𝖉𝖉 for *Our Father which art
in heaven;* but I suspect extremely that fabulous tongue-
cutting, and would have you of the two, believe rather the
Virgins, were it not for the exorbitant number, and that,
against infallible credit, our Historians mix with it *Gratian's*
surviving *Maximus*; a kind of fault that makes often the
very truth doubtful.

360. *Than from the* Scythian *poor whence they themselves derive.*

He means the *Saxons,* whose name, after learned men, is
to the Fourth Song derived from a *Scythian* nation.   It
pleases the Muse in this passage to speak of that original,
as mean and unworthy of comparison with the *Troian
British,* drawn out of *Jupiter's* blood by *Venus, Anchises,* and
Æneas; I justify her phrase, for that the *Scythian* was indeed poor, yet voluntarily, not through want, living commonly in field-tents; and (as our *Germans* in *Tacitus*) so
Stoical, as not to care for the future, having provision for
the present, from nature's liberality.   But, if it were worth
examining, you might find the *Scythian* as noble and worthy

---

[1] Sunt enim antiqui codices quibus hoc meritò deest, necnon ut
glossema illud non irreptâsse, sentire sum potis.
* Half-silent.
[2] Paul. Merul. Cosmog. part. 2. lib. 3. cap. 15.

a nation as any read of; and such a one as the *English* and others might be as proud to derive themselves from, as any which do search for their ancestors' glory in *Troian* ashes. If you believe the old report[1] of themselves, then can you not make them less than descended by *Targitaus* from *Jupiter* and *Borysthenes;* if what the *Greeks,* who, as afterward the *Romans,* accounted and styled all barbarous except themselves; then you must draw their pedigree through *Agathyrsus, Gelonus,* and *Scytha,* from *Hercules;* neither of these have, in this kind, their superior. If among them, you desire learning, remember *Zamolxis, Dicencus,* and *Anacharsis* before the rest. For although to some of these other patronymics are given, yet know that anciently (which for the present matter observe seriously) as all, Southward, were call'd *Æthiopians;* all Eastward, *Indians;* all West, *Celts;* so all Northerns were styled *Scythians;* as *Ephorus*[2] is author. I could add the honourable allegories, of those their Golden Yoke, Plough, Hatchet, and Cup sent from heaven, wittily enough delivered by *Goropius,*[3] with other conjectural testimonies of their worth. But I abstain from such digression.

[1] Herodot. Melpom. δ.   [2] Apud Strab. lib. α.
[3] Amazonic. Becceselan. 3.

END OF VOL. I.

BILLING AND SONS, PRINTERS, GUILDFORD, SURREY.